NO ANGEL
BY MARIE GOTT

NO ANGEL

First published 2024

Copyright © 2024 H & G Publications

All rights reserved. No part of this book may be reproduced, stored in a retrieval system, or transmitted, in any form or by any means, electronic, mechanical, photocopying, recording, or otherwise, without the prior permission of the copyright holder, except by a reviewer who may quote brief passages in a review.

First Edition

This book is a work of fiction. This novel's story and main characters are fictitious. References to real people, events, establishments, organisations, or locales are intended only to provide a sense of authenticity and are used fictitiously. All other characters, and all incidents and dialogue, are drawn from the author's imagination and are not to be construed as real.

For my husband, Jordanne.
Your support means everything.

ONE

Too many drinks at the student's union. A bad hangover: head pounding, stomach flipping, a dry mouth. Another occasion of drinking too much and forgetting the night before.

Adelina tried to open her eyes once more. Blurred double vision, that was a new one. Maybe a concussion from falling over. After all, there had been plenty of bruises before.

A need for water. Something, anything, to wash away the iron in her mouth. Turning to the side, trying not to disrupt the contents of her stomach, she intended to find an old glass.

The world churned, never standing still for a moment to view it. A stinging sensation erupted across her scalp. The rest of her body numb, like the start of cramp before it kicks in.

Adelina wasn't at home. Nor was she in a stranger's bed. The space appeared vaguely familiar. A curved decorative roof. A double bed atop of a storage area. A small stove bringing water to a boil. Two girls perched on a built-in seat.

The space, Adelina recognised it as a vardo, a traditional traveller wagon. As a child, she used to play in her cousins' rotting vardo for hours, making stories about adventures and wishing her life could be like that instead.

Delighted to see the woman alive, the youngest girl let out a screech, garnering the attention of her mother. Margaret Young barely believed her eyes. With the state of her head, she thought Adelina would be rendered unconscious for the night. As she gathered the wet rag once more, her teenage daughter, Moira, scoffed; the whole thing was ridiculous.

Adelina's eyes dashed to and fro. Long flowing skirts and plain blouses. Uncut hair running wild. The vardo, the simple belongings. No technology, nothing battery operated.

Margaret crouched beside her, pressing a bony hand to her head. Dried blood mixed with sweat left a sticky residue on her fingertips. Underneath her breath, she muttered about the woman's temperature.

'Has my mum brought me here?' Adelina asked.

'What makes you think that?' Moira laughed.

'I haven't been in one of these since-'

'One of these?' Moira interrupted. 'You're in a vardo, don't kid yourself, you don't know what this is.'

'I do,' Adelina said, wanting to explain herself.

'Don't worry, you're safe now,' Margaret said, disregarding her eldest daughter's attitude. 'We found you a few fields over, beside a road. You were in an awful state. It's good that you're awake.'

'Do you live in Leeds?' Aisling, the youngest child, innocently asked.

'Why do you ask that?'

'We're near Hunslet; Leeds isn't too far away,' Margaret explained. 'As I told you, we found you not far from here.'

The nauseous feeling that grew in Adelina's stomach couldn't be swayed, it lurched up her gullet as she tried to speak.

'I've never been to Leeds. I don't know why I'm here.'

'Like my mum said, we found you an hour ago, on the outskirts of the city. So, you must be a liar after all.'

'Moira,' Margaret hissed, hoping her tone would be enough to make her fall silent. Wringing out the rag, she turned to Adelina, her voice softening. 'Do you not remember what happened? How you managed to get that, on your head?'

Of course, she knew what happened. Adelina went to speak, to set them straight. Yet when she tried to recall her most recent memories, they were all black. Nothing was there, even as she attempted to replay the day. Only her childhood loomed in her mind and the recollections were hazy like they didn't belong to her.

Adelina recalled her birthplace, her home, she had never

known anywhere else. No matter how hard she fought, nothing else came back. A blank space and only darkness to pull from. In her mind's eye, with every try, the black dissolved into her old-terraced home, with the dark red bricks that defined the area.

'I need to go. I need to get back home,' Adelina insisted.

'It's dark outside. There won't be any trains or other forms of transport at this house,' Margaret advised gently. 'I think you should rest here for the night.'

Adelina nodded, feeling comfort in Margaret's motherly approach. Something about the vardo made her feel safe and at home. After all, the Young family had saved her, they weren't going to do her any harm.

But Adelina didn't know the truth. Earlier, when the Youngs discovered her lifeless body, they nearly left her to rot.

Margaret, her children, and her husband, John, were the first of their group to arrive at the new camp. Keen to get settled, they left in search of firewood.

Golden hour. Hedgerows and tumbled down walls broke up rolling fields. Patches of woodland, the occasional flower still blooming from summer. Most life was dying. Plants withered; trees shed their leaves. Everything that once lived crumbled to the boggy ground.

The Youngs' horse pawed at the mud, frustrated with the growing weight. Firewood overflowed from the satchels draped over its back. Still, Moira chucked another branch in its direction.

'How much longer?' Aisling asked, idly picking at a piece of splintering wood.

Irritated by her sister's constant whining, Moira gave Aisling a harsh nudge. A pet lip formed as Aisling flung herself to the ground. Attention seeking, again.

Margaret cradled her belly. They were about to start fighting again. She couldn't take any more stress, not after the last time. That thought alone sent her gasping for air. No one could understand the pressure that her husband placed upon her.

Margaret lurched forwards, hunching over, hands gripping to a tree trunk. It wouldn't happen again, it couldn't. John stormed to her side, dropping logs as she spluttered.

Sulking, Aisling wandered off, not once looking back at her retching mother. It had all happened before. It would end in tears rolling down cheeks, in sore faces and curled fists.

The narrow lane held an odd silence. Curious, Aisling toddled closer to an indistinct shape upon the ground, her steps disturbing stones and dust, blanketing her shoes in grey. A slight dip on the other side of the lane before the hedgerow began. The thing almost hidden by nature itself.

'What's that?' Aisling called out.

Margaret's attention snapped to her daughter, no longer feeling sick in the same manner. The physical sensation had been ripped into a prolonged state of nausea.

Pale skin met dew dropped grass. A rock the only cushion for a young woman's head. An open wound, gooey with congealed blood.

The woman's skirt cut off before it reached her ankles, stopping at mid-calf length. John couldn't see a stocking line upon her leg. A black silk top, that seemed more like a high society ladies night shirt, disappeared into the waistband of the skirt, shimmering in the last remnants of daylight. Flat shoes with white bottoms coated in scuff marks, the material atop of it brighter than any item of clothing he'd seen before. The piercing red fabric covered her ankles, and even stranger, an off-cream cotton tied the material together at the front.

'Is she dead?' Moira asked.

Margaret approached the body, pushing Aisling towards her sister for comfort. Margaret's caring nature overtook any rational thought. Kneeling, she held her hand across the woman's mouth. As a cool raspy breath hit her skin, she declared the woman alive, at least for then.

'It's going to be night soon, we can't leave her, she'll freeze,' Margaret said, hoping John would help, that he would see sense and not think of anything else.

A drop of blood ran down the woman's cheek pooling into the dirt. Margaret was right, she would perish, but the woman was a stranger. To save her, to take her with them, it would be a risk. Their family wasn't safe and to bring someone else into it, when they didn't know their history, could be dangerous.

'"Lead with God and not your thoughts or your heart," your mother used to say,' Margaret reminded them. 'God wouldn't want us to leave her like this.'

'Are you sure?' Moira asked.

Even the black coat that the woman wore was odd. The material was strange, itchy and textured, unlike cotton or wool, something they hadn't come across before.

'What if she's a whore?' Moira said, taking note of the woman's unclothed chest. 'That would explain her head and being left for dead.'

Even Margaret couldn't deny the woman was obscure. Half of her hair was tied up at the top of her head with some form of bunched material. A thin line had been drawn across both her eyelids, flicking out towards her temples.

'If she was a moll, why would they drag her all the way out here instead of dumping her where they found her?' John said to Margaret.

'Exactly,' Moira added.

'Why would someone drag her all the way out here, to the middle of nowhere?'

'The police don't care about women like her. They wouldn't bother to investigate. Besides, she's not one of us. Nothing good can come from a woman who is dressed like that.'

'We should all stop making stories for her,' Margaret said. 'We don't know her. John, think about what your mother would have wanted you to do.'

All Margaret wanted was to put good in the world, hoping to receive it in return.

Another ripple of red. John shrugged off his coat. Only wanting to shut Margaret up, so they could return home without an argument, he picked the limp woman up.

Adelina believed she was in safe hands. Margaret cared for her. She cleaned her wound and consoled her as she winced.

A kooky off-grid family must have saved her. That explained the lack of technology, the recycled cloth that cleaned her head, the simple belongings, even the clothes that the two girls wore.

Adelina wasn't thinking straight; she didn't burden herself with the thought of spending a night in a foreign place. Instead, she concerned herself with her memories and how she'd travelled south of her hometown.

Incapable of remembering, and somewhat naïve, she believed that everything would be ok, a train would arrive the next day and it would take her home. As much as she hated to admit it, she'd been drunk and disorientated before. Utterly reckless as a teenager, she often woke in odd places.

Intent on checking transport departure times, Adelina patted herself down, only to find her pockets empty. Not a single possession. No phone, no money, no cards. It didn't seem right, to be so far from home and with only the clothes that she wore.

'I think I must've been robbed. Maybe that's why I'm injured.'

'And why do you say that?' Moira said.

'Didn't I have a bag, or anything, when you found me?'

'Are you accusing us of being thieves, or what?'

'There wasn't anything else with you,' Margaret said, her tone lighter than ever to make up for her daughter's attitude.

'I don't have my purse or any money. How am I going to get home?' Adelina said, her voice breaking. Panicking, she decided her only option was to contact the police, to inform them of her situation. Like before, her grandmother would have registered her as missing. 'Wait. I don't understand. If I was unresponsive earlier, why didn't you phone an ambulance?'

That would have been the right thing to do. Not pick her up and drag her off to rest in a vardo, in a location she didn't know. Adelina scuffled away from them, hands rising, fearing they'd been the ones to attack her. That they had kidnapped her. They'd never found her.

'And how would we have done that?' Moira laughed mockingly.

'Do you not own a phone?'

'I told you, she's a liar,' Moira said to her mother. 'I knew she didn't know what a vardo was.'

'You must be confused,' Margaret said. 'The nearest telephone box is miles away.'

'Couldn't you have flagged down a car? They would have had a mobile, surely.'

Moira stopped her escapade. The word meant nothing within the context.

Their perplexed faces sent Adelina's breath hitching. Everyone knew what a mobile phone was, no one could escape them. The Youngs spoke English, with mixed up Yorkshire accents. They should have known.

The old fashioned vardo, their plain clothing, their knowledge. Adelina's wound throbbed.

'I don't feel so well,' she said, touching her sweltering head. The gooey sack on her hairline burst, expelling liquid down her face. She did nothing. The blood and puss poured from her body, and she let it spill onto her lap. 'I think something is seriously wrong with me.'

Margaret shifted, suddenly uncomfortable in Adelina's presence. Moira sighed, of course, another excuse.

'I bet you don't even remember the date,' Moira said.

'It's just turned October today,' Aisling said sweetly, oblivious to her mother's growing discomfort.

'And the year is 1919,' Moira added, giggling.

Adelina flopped backward onto the bed, not caring for the feeling of her brain shattering against the swell that surrounded her skull. The stained wood ceiling, just like her cousins. No, it was 2019, not the 20th century. Surely, they were playing a practical joke on her, after they found her legless on a night out.

'Have you forgotten who you are?' Moira taunted.

A tsunami wave of memories hit Adelina; she drowned in

waves of her own recollection. They came in one after another, hurling into her brain. She saw her house once more, five Barnabas Road, Linthorpe, Middlesbrough. The people outside were younger than they should have been. Her mother, her father, her sister, Leonora. The memories came back in the right order, but they were torture as her life played out before her. Another wave. Gold shining behind her, a building in full sunlight, people passing by holding clip boards and stethoscopes, laughing.

'What's your name?' Margaret said.

'Adelina.'

'I've never heard of that before, it's unusual.'

'It sounds made up,' Moira snorted.

'It's Italian,' Adelina said, not giving it much thought, she'd always found herself explaining the origin.

'Your family, they migrated?' Margaret said.

'No, my dad did, when he was a kid.'

'Keep that quiet. People around here don't like strangers, and they don't like people who are different, Ada.'

'What are you two doing inside?' John said, storming into the vardo. 'You should be out there, helping. Go on, get out of my sight.'

John's tone reminded Adelina of her father. Maybe that was why her hands started to vibrate. In a vague attempt to settle down, her palms grasped onto one another. Chipped painted nails and white skin. No bracelets or rings. Not even Leonora's gold-plated signet band. Everything apart from her clothes seemingly lost with time.

'Go easy on her,' Margaret whispered to him. 'I think she's hurt herself badly.'

John's lips twitched almost into a smile. 'Herself,' it was an odd way of putting things. Hopefully, Margaret had succumbed to the idea that Adelina was no good, like she had done something wrong to be inflicted with such an injury. If her opinion had changed, then getting rid of the woman would be easy.

'Did she tell you what happened?'

'She can't remember. I know what you're thinking, but I believe her, look at how bad her head is.'

The wound seeped, barely crusting over. She must've been struck with some force. At the heart of it, John didn't care why the injury had been inflicted. It unsettled him that she couldn't recall who caused it.

'I don't care what you told my wife,' John growled. 'You need to get your memory back. We're struggling as it is, coming up to winter. So, tell me about yourself.'

With John, Adelina no longer felt safe. The growl in his voice elicited a fight or flight response that sent her stagnant, unable to form words.

'I don't have time for silence. I need you to tell me where you live, if I can send you to someone tonight.'

Most of Adelina's memories belonged to a younger girl. Even if she did recall something, everything, and everyone she knew was in Middlesbrough, miles away and within the 21st century, a hundred years in the future. Whether back in time, dreaming or in a coma, she knew nobody.

A seemingly endless pause. Her gaze dropped to the tatty blanket across her legs. Unable to establish a suitable response, she shook her head.

A high pitch whistle ripped through the field. A series of desperate noises to garner everyone's attention.

'Stay here,' John said to Adelina as he sprang into action, rifling through a drawer.

Instead of clambering back onto the bed in submission, her eyes widened, clearly wondering what was happening outside. John couldn't risk her leaving, or even peering through the window. Unable to control his soaring anger, John pounded over to her. With a harsh shove against her chest, she clattered back.

'Don't you dare get up until I tell you,' John snarled. 'If you do, something worse will happen to you than that cut on your head. Do you understand?'

John grasped at Adelina's coat, bunching the material into his fist and drawing her close, within inches of him. Spit coated her face. Her mind still clouded from waking in an unfamiliar place. Registering a small nod, he released her, sending her squirming away.

A clatter on the side of the vardo. Voices flowing from outside. Moira ripped open the door, panting, her words barely escaping.

'They're here — the Clarks. Jack was right after all.'

'Margaret, come on. They need to see us all. They'll think we're hiding something otherwise.'

Instead of wondering who was outside, and why the Youngs were so fearful of them, Adelina thought about John. The menacing way he looked at her. The violence he easily displayed to her. The warning, that something worse would happen.

With the urge to bolt, she edged towards the tiny window. The Youngs weren't her true saviours. No matter what, she needed to flee, get herself to safety.

Outside, the Youngs gathered together, looking in the same direction. Opposite them, an abundance of men, staring them down. Despite the large number of outsiders, there was only a car and two wagons. The Clarks wanted to show their strength, but they must have been sandwiched inside the vehicles like sardines.

With them distracted, Adelina decided to plot an escape. Squinting, she tried to decipher the opposition: how far back they could see into the field, if they would notice her appearance. All at once, her hope became lost.

A singular man glanced in her direction. Even with the distance, she thought he narrowed his eyes at her.

Adelina clattered down, her body coming to a heap atop of the splintering floor. With the remnants of her adrenaline, she scrambled on her hands and knees to the bed. Shuffling back against the wall, she would pretend she'd never moved, that she was too fear struck to do anything.

TWO

As John collected firewood, his nephew, Jack, scouted the nearby town of Hunslet. Menial labour paid pittance, despite the danger of factories. Not many industries were seeking workers. Too many men needed jobs and those at the camp had the wrong last name. Opportunities needed to be created so the Youngs could survive the hard winter.

A grand home with an ajar window. Jack would *borrow* some money from them. They had so much, whilst his family had so little. It didn't seem fair.

Poking his head around a corner, double-checking the path was clear, he caught sight of some familiar men. No longer interested in the posh parlour, he studied his onetime friends.

The rumours were true after all, the Clarks had gone up in the world. Fashionable tailored suits. Silk neckties shone in the dying light. Overcoats billowed, almost scuffing the ground. Their lavish attire exemplified their growing status within society.

Before the Great War, they were nothing. Every year the Youngs camped on Hunslet Moor, and the Clarks would come to visit them. Together, the two families caused mischief, like young boys always do. Their friendship ended after an altercation, which led to them being told to move on and to never return.

Stories of the Clarks new vicious ways travelled fast. Racketeering, robberies and funnelling it all through an opulent club in the city. People all over the country spoke about them. The Youngs should have stayed far away from Leeds, knowing what the Clarks were capable of. Nothing good could come from antagonising them after all the years spent apart.

'They're back, the Youngs, a couple of runners just told me. Back to the field they claim is theirs.'

The last time Jack saw the Clarks he was a kid, he could barely remember their first names. There was, however, no forgetting their striking appearance. Dark hair, almost black, preened beautifully. Light skin, untarnished by the sun's rays. Not pale and sickly like the malnourished workers in the factories, but like lords and ladies, who could linger in the shade all day.

The three brothers stuck together no matter what. Of course, there used to be four, but that was before the war. If anything, the trauma had brought them closer together.

'Can't wait to get my comeuppance with them, I've been waiting years.'

'Take it slow for now.'

The leader, the eldest brother. Frederick Clark had grown up, no longer jovial and laughing. He didn't speak about violence with a smile upon his face like he had in the past. If anything, he seemed worse, hardened somehow.

'We'll turn up unannounced. Don't worry Paul, we won't let them get away with trespassing.'

Jack bounded across fields with the newfound information; he needed to relay the news before time was up. The Youngs were in danger, they had to leave.

Screaming, Jack neared his family. They needed to pack up, immediately. Thomas, John's father, and leader of the camp, was yet to arrive, they needed to backtrack to meet up with him.

Margaret sought the female elders of the group. In a hushed voice, she tried to sway their opinion on a delicate matter. The women weren't siding with her, they struggled enough without another mouth to feed. Margaret had thought of God, but it only made her seem mad, to rescue some random poorly dressed woman.

Whilst the women nattered, John spoke with the men. They clapped their hands in disbelief at his story, enjoying his mistake. When Thomas arrived, he would smack the poor man across his ears for being so dim-witted.

Upon hearing Jack's yelling, Margaret and the women exchanged glances, unsure whether to run or to take his words as a joke. Surely, Thomas wouldn't put them in such peril.

Between puffs of breath, Jack relayed the encounter. As the stand-in leader, John found himself sweating, his pulse quickening. Summoning all his strength, he tried to emulate what he believed his father would do.

'Don't worry, I know the Clarks well,' a weary voice said. 'This day has been coming for a while. We can't run away, we should stay. I know we'll be safe, I'll make sure of it.'

The frail woman clung to her vardo, attempting to steady herself. Age had taken its toll upon her. Silver hair reached in knots down to her waist like she plaited it twenty years ago and never brushed it since. Her eyes glistened against the setting sun, trying to be a beacon of hope in the dimming light.

Esmerelda, the black witch, she meddled in anything dark and unforgiving. People either feared her or ridiculed her. Most of the group ignored her, convinced she had lost her mind years ago.

John had no choice, his family needed to stay, at least for the night. They wouldn't be able to move on in time, the Clarks would only catch up. They would be branded as cowards and, on an open road, revenge would be served far too easily for what Peter Young had done.

After Jack's tales of seeing the Clarks, young lads were put on watch around the camp. Some struggled to believe his story. They put their faith in Thomas; he must've thought the camp was safe to return to, after all he sent the kids up first.

As night fell, the men relaxed, chuckling at Jack's expense. Only he could concoct such an extravagant lie. Another jibe, a round of applause, and then a lone whistle. The laughter ceased; their attention swayed to the field's perimeter.

More high-pitched tones. Vehicles wound down the lane. Parents relayed hasty instructions to their children: be quiet, hide wherever possible. To improve their chances, the adults banded together, facing the direction of the narrow road.

Headlights snaked down the dirt track, illuminating the trees and bushes and then, finally, them. John bounded over, pushing his way through the group. Margaret trailed behind, occasionally casting a glance over her shoulder. Moira's teenage cousins, Saoirse and Mabel, yanked her away from her mother, so she would remain in safety behind the others.

The cars and wagons continued to roar, despite being at a standstill. The light blinded the opposition. Eyes squinted; hands drew over their foreheads. The Clark's display of authority was audacious.

The vehicles stopped turning over. The field flushed with darkness once more. The twilight welcomed the Clarks like an old comrade. Camouflaged, only sound gave out their positions: swishing parting grass, the odd crack of a branch.

A single man emerged from the centre vehicle. It was not him who stepped forwards first, but another. The light greeted him unkindly. A woman beside Margaret gasped audibly. The man's face was riddled with scars, his slicked back hair flopped as he moved.

'Back for some more, after all this time,' he slurred. 'If you don't remember me, I'm Paul Clark. Though I'm sure Thomas never forgot my name.'

Paul had always been a loose cannon. Apparently, he was born into the world bright blue and not breathing. The cord wrapped so tightly around his neck it left a permanent inking upon him. That was why he was mad. Half dead from his first day on earth.

In the night he looked like he'd risen from hell. He'd changed since their last meeting. The weight had dropped from him, his bones protruding. Cheeks gaunt, face withered. It didn't make him less impeding, with sunken skin draped across him and dark glazed over eyes he appeared menacing.

'I know what you're thinking,' Paul continued, his words stumbling over one another. 'Time's been tough on me. Let's just say it wasn't the war that made me look like this. I'm sure you recall the Gray family, well, they decided to mess with us. They ended up worse. My brother George here, he made the shot of his life...'

Baby-faced George Clark didn't look any older, despite being in his twenties and with two kids of his own. It was impossible to tell he'd spent four years at war. Still mischievous looking, with his twinkling blue eyes and light dusting of freckles. Harmless, not like his older brother.

'Where's Thomas anyways?' George said, speaking over Paul. The retelling of the Grays would only put the Youngs on a defensive and he couldn't be bothered with a fight breaking out so quickly.

'Never mind Thomas, where's Freddie?' Paul said, looking over his shoulder. 'Always late to the bloody party.'

Like a demon, who could only emerge once he'd been called upon, the Clark leader moved from the shadows. From the protection of the night came a self-assured man brash with confidence. An ego on his shoulders, as if he knew fine well his importance.

'Was that the one you were supposed to marry?' Saoirse whispered to Moira.

'No, it was the youngest one,' she replied, eyes locked on her feet, not implanted on the brothers like every other person.

'Bloody hell, I can't see a ring,' Mabel murmured. 'Does that mean Freddie's up for grabs?'

'God, I wish I was promised to him.'

'Too bad you're spoken for, unlike me,' Mabel giggled, a little too loudly.

The noise contrasted with the atmosphere the brothers meticulously created. The Youngs and the Clarks alike turned towards the source of the noise. Frederick's stare delved into them, sending them trembling beneath it. They'd done the worst thing, by interrupting the meeting.

With a tut, Frederick turned to John, looking him up and down, wondering where his father was. Thomas wasn't dead, word would've got to him.

'It's a pleasure to see you after all these years,' John said. 'I know things didn't go too well last time, but we were under my uncle's control then. He doesn't travel with us anymore.'

'I've heard,' Frederick said. 'You're not the leader, so why are you speaking for your father?'

'He hasn't arrived yet.'

'Sent you ahead, has he? Despite knowing we would be here, waiting for you.'

'I know what happened before, but you should remember the good times. My father was friends with yours, we all got along. We're not associated with Peter anymore. Your dad would have understood, we've moved on.'

'I'm not so certain of that.'

'Well,' John coughed, 'I can see you've moved up in the world, maybe you've forgotten where you came from. I've started to hear a lot about you. People all over the country know your name now.'

'People keep telling me that. If you know so much about me, why did you decide to come back and camp here?'

'It was my father's choice. I do believe we've given you enough time to forget and forgive. None of us here today have ever caused you trouble. We've done nothing to you.'

'That's the thing, though. None of you tried to stop Peter.'

'We camped here every winter. What Peter did... it was one time. It's in the past. We're not like him,' John said, his voice tinged with exasperation. 'I'm not stupid, Frederick. I know you've taken over half the city. I know you're after revenge, but Peter is long gone. There must be another reason you're here.'

'Why else would I be here?' Frederick asked, suppressing a laugh. Time had made John irrational.

'First, you want payment for something that should be free. You don't own this land,' John said, trying to sound strong, despite feeling like a duckling compared to them. 'Then you want to get your revenge for something we never did.'

'Jesus,' Paul said, clapping his hands. 'At your age, I thought you'd have learnt – nothing's free, not anymore.'

The other gang members sniggered. Frederick remained

silent, resisting the urge to shake his head as Paul reached inside his pocket for yet another dose of liquid. Like the Youngs, Frederick didn't care for his brother's behaviour.

'Let's not get carried away, Paul,' Frederick said. 'Thomas knew our dad after all.'

Fear over laughter. A precedent needed to be set for the Youngs. Paul, like the daft young girls before, lightened the mood. Frederick wanted things to go his way.

'Why don't we wait for my father?' John said. 'I'm sure he'll be here tomorrow.'

John's final card. The only way he could think of to mellow the situation. Unlike him, Thomas would know what to do, he would have a plan.

'Y'know, I think we'd quite like to speak to Thomas again,' Frederick said. 'We've been waiting a long time to get reacquainted.'

'Do you think he'll arrive by tomorrow morning?' Paul smirked.

John could barely manage an audible reply. In his moment of weakness, George and Paul took the opportunity to dish out some snide hints that violence was inevitable. Unlike his brothers, Frederick's attention wandered.

Saoirse and Mabel were still flustered. Moira had never glanced towards them. Margaret looked over her shoulder toward the back of the camp.

Nothing of merit to see. Just an old rickety vardo in her eyeline. The Youngs had owned it for as long as he could remember. Inside, a candle burned, the light distorting in the wind. A shadow formed. Through the stained net curtains, he thought he saw a figure peeking out towards him. With a blink, the silhouette disappeared.

'Is everyone out here?' Frederick said, interrupting the taunts. 'No one's missing, are they?'

'Why?'

'Answer the question.'

A shiver ran down Margaret's spine. Frederick's tone had

shifted; he could snap at any second. Taking a step forward, ready to make his brothers' words come to life, John stuttered.

'Everyone's out here.'

Frederick didn't bother to nod. The only movement was a slight crinkle of his forehead. Revenge no longer consumed his mind; he became obsessed with John's obvious lie. Someone was unaccounted for, sitting inside the vardo, and he needed to know why.

THREE

Going back in time belonged to science fiction. The only reasonable explanation for the situation was being in a coma, the drugs hadn't kicked in yet. Eventually, Adelina would wake up and forget everything.

No. It seemed too realistic to be like a dream. The stale, dusty vardo. The touch of the ratty rag. The crackling bonfire. The blustering wind licking at her somewhat wet hair. The pulsating gash on her head. The way Adelina felt, it couldn't have been make-believe.

With that thought, Adelina succumbed to the idea of existing within another time. The question of why lingered over her. It was odd; she didn't feel homesick or lost and, at the heart of it, she didn't long for her family. Maybe, she felt such a way because she was uncovering her memories.

Regardless of whether she had fallen back in time or not, she didn't understand the issue with her ancestry. Her head hurt too badly to think about world history. The year 1919 meant nothing to her. In history, she had studied three things: Henry the VIII, his six wives, and the World Wars. She believed that none of that helped with her current situation.

While John formulated a plan to deal with the Clarks, Margaret took charge of Adelina. In the morning, once Thomas arrived, John would take her into the city and leave her be. At least, that's what Margaret hoped.

Adelina needed to work; she couldn't be seen as taking advantage of a free stay. To go outside, with the others, she needed more appropriate clothes. Scouring through old trunks, Margaret tried to find something she could give up.

Picking out the most worn clothes, she toyed with the idea of telling Adelina to run. With the Clarks' appearance, John wasn't in the right frame of mind and, at times, he possessed a nasty temperament. If Adelina went into the trees and followed the woodland path, she would eventually reach Hunslet and could escape to the docks.

Margaret never found the courage. Instead, her old hand-me-downs adorned the woman she saved but ultimately put in danger.

The baggiest blouse enveloped Adelina's frame. A thin blend of the cheapest materials made up the dark skirt which nipped at her waist. The tattered, moth-eaten cardigan itched her forearms.

Adelina made her way to the kitchen area of the camp. The bitter taste of burning wood resonated on her tongue. Long grass swayed around her. With every step, the world turned with her.

The shoes pinched as she waded through the boggy ground. She wrapped her modern-day coat around herself. The polyester material hadn't been invented yet, and the duster coat had never been in fashion. The material was thin, it wouldn't shield her from the cold as the temperature dropped.

The camp was a small, secluded field lined with hedgerows and home to at least a dozen vardos. The windy dirt road in the distance was sheltered from full view by trees. People swarmed the space. Tethered horses roamed in tight circles. Children played with sticks and crumbled stones. They jumped between logs and rocks making their own fun.

A gust of wind tore at the open skin on Adelina's head. The wound would need stitches. No doctors, no hospital, no one she could trust to tidy herself up. The medical care wouldn't be to her standard, diseases were rife with their lack of understanding.

Recollection washed over Adelina. God, she'd been so close to it earlier. The golden building was a part of her university campus, she was training to be a nurse. In the grand scheme of things, it meant nothing, it wouldn't help her return home, but it was a start.

The Youngs gawked at Adelina, never hiding their stares as they spoke about her. They questioned her differences. They didn't take people in; strangers weren't allowed to live amongst them. They were wary of outsiders, and rightly so. Being on the other side was jarring for Adelina.

Saoirse and Mabel traipsed towards her, trying to avoid the soggiest parts of the field. Their hair danced around them, cascading down their backs. Catching their eye, Adelina pulled out her scrunchie, the millennium era throwback trend that had not yet existed. With one action, she attempted to fit in. Her hair fell in layers around her face, trailing down to the small of her back.

To protect herself, Adelina wanted to sink into the background, but she couldn't, Margaret had given her a task. Alongside Saoirse and Mabel, she helped prepare the group's evening meal. Endless questions were directed her way, and she tried to dodge them all.

A somewhat still night. The moon occasionally blocked by thin wisps of clouds. The bonfire spit flames into the cool air, lighting the ground. Youngsters sat on logs, eating wild mushroom soup as sparks floated around them.

A low hum of chatter. Adelina perched herself on a sharp stone next to Saoirse. Beside her, she could be mistaken for her older sister. The same tousled dark hair that would mat easily throughout the day. Light eyes that looked almost yellow around the pupil. Dormant freckles that would erupt in summer.

Mabel and Saoirse couldn't eat, their bowls remained full. Their minds were too consumed with the Clarks, just like the elders of the group. Only the kids ate their soup, not realising the importance of what had happened earlier.

For Adelina, the need to supress her hunger was high, the beige water was surprisingly appetising. The feeling needed to be quashed. The Youngs couldn't see her taking anything from them, she couldn't owe them.

Adelina longed to go home. To do so, she needed to find out how she'd got there. If she went back to the beginning, she could move forward. At least, she hoped that would be the case. That night, when the children and adults traipsed off to bed, she would sneak away to the place Margaret had described.

'Your dad's going to murder you both,' Moira said, taking a seat next to Mabel. 'Laughing like that in front of the Clarks; I'm surprised Freddie didn't shoot you there and then.'

'He wouldn't kill a girl, like me, would he?' Mabel said, clutching her bowl, trying to stop the liquid from crashing over the rim as she shook.

'Don't be silly,' Saoirse said. 'It'll only be men, and ones that get in their way, that they kill. We've got nothing to worry about.'

'Well, you haven't heard about the Grays then, have you?' Moira said. 'Apparently Paul's lost his mind. He doesn't care about anything.'

'Shut up Moira. You're only salty because you can't marry into their family. You're scaring Mabel and probably that new lass too.'

'Why do you care about her,' Moira said, glancing to Adelina, who stared off into the distance, barely paying attention to their conversation. 'God, you're oblivious, aren't you?'

'You must've heard of the Clarks,' Mabel said. 'Even when we were at the borders, people spoke about them.'

'I don't know who you mean,' Adelina said meekly, unsure of how to interact with the girls without any knowledge of the situation or the context of the men who had visited.

'The Clarks are a gang from Holbeck. They rule over everyone; rumour has it they're above the law now,' Saoirse said.

'They're just like us in a way,' Mabel added. 'Their mother–'

'No, they're not,' Moira interrupted. 'They're nothing like us.'

Furious that her cousins were taking Adelina under their wing, Moira stormed off, pounding towards her family's vardo.

'She's a bit touchy about the Clarks,' Saoirse said. 'Some people around here see her as damaged. She was promised to George, but something happened a long time ago.'

'We were all kids. We had no idea. Our great-uncle was in charge. We came here every summer,' Mabel said.

'George and Moira used to spend lots of time together. They held hands and played in the fields.'

'They never kissed; Moira swears on that.'

'No one cares about that. Not now.'

'Other families don't deem her fit to be a good wife.'

'In a way, she's cursed.'

With their soup growing cold, the other two girls took their bowls back to the pot. They would eat tomorrow once Thomas arrived. Unlike John, he would make them feel safe, like they could beat the Clarks.

Stars faded as clouds rolled in. Slowly, the Youngs took themselves to bed. As the fire dwindled, Adelina became the only person sat upon nature's bench.

Bitter darkness surrounded her, with no lamp or heat to warm her bones. Bumps coated her skin, a shiver ran down her spine, not from the dropping temperature but from the feeling of being watched.

Adelina scanned the vardos, the field, and well into the distance. Nothing. No silhouette, no candle still burning. The feeling didn't waver. The bumps remained.

Thinking her mind was merely playing tricks, she moved. It was then or never. The chance to sneak away for good, to never see John's dirty snarl again. As she pushed forward, Esmerelda scuttled out of her way, seeking cover in the shadow of her home. Fate played out before her, decisions setting into stone.

A world without light pollution, without streetlamps and backfiring cars. Only the faded moon and the once roaring fire. Her hands tugged at her sleeves, unsure whether to go back. In the midst of the night, doubt crept up. Unsure if she would find her way to the location Margaret described.

Even if she stumbled across the location, there was a possibility she would remain in 1919. Stuck, she would need shelter. In the pitch black, she wasn't sure she would find another path that would lead her away from the Youngs.

A shadow in the distance. Eyes squinting to register the source. An unnerving feeling growing. Adelina tried to pinpoint the outline, hoping it would stand out against the grayscale backdrop of the night. Distracted, she failed to notice the silhouette looming beside her, growing ever closer.

'Freddie thought you were the odd one out. We've been up here all night, watching your camp,' George Clark said, amusement lining his voice. 'Makes him right, you deciding to come all the way out here alone.'

Upon registering the voice, a high-pitch shriek escaped her. Recognising him as one of the men the Youngs feared, she stumbled backwards. Adrenaline surging, thoughts turning, she dodged, expecting him to throw at least a hand towards her. Off balance, the shoddy heels twisted, sending her tumbling to the floor.

'Bloody hell, don't make that noise again,' George whispered. 'They can't hear us.'

He edged closer to her. Towering over her. Her hands sank into the dirt, ready to push herself up. Moira's words about the Clarks and their taste for violence resonated in her mind. As he leaned in, stretching his hand out towards her, she squirmed away, mimicking how she'd acted with John.

'I'm not going to hurt you,' George chuckled, his stance frozen, no longer attempting to come closer, yet his hand still reached out towards her. He remained still, not wanting to alarm her any further. 'Get up, you'll only catch a cold if your clothes get wet.'

Underneath his coat rested a gun; Adelina could see the holster's strap, the bulging outline of the metal. Running away no longer seemed feasible with such a weapon near her. Hands grasping at the damp grass, she prised herself from the ground, not for one second considering taking his hand.

'Fine, have it your way,' he said, a boyish smirk slipping across his face as she struggled.

Wary of George's bizarre friendly manner, Adelina flattened out her skirt, peeling the grass from her, garnering a wink from him. It wasn't flirtatious in a malicious sense. Instead, he reminded her of school, of teachers and authority, of disobeying them. George acted like a mischievous boy with too much energy.

It was like science class at school: boys flirting with her and her becoming inattentive. At times, Adelina had been disruptive, often scolded by teachers, but mostly because she liked the attention. There was an innate longing for someone to notice her, purely because her parents never cared for her.

It wasn't the time or the place for science class games; Adelina understood that. Yet her eyes still trailed across George, settling upon the wedding band on his finger. Recklessly, her mind came out of the repressed memories of school and childhood.

Not caring if he saw or not, Adelina grimaced at his flirtatious attitude. Marriage should be taken seriously, the most important part being monogamy. If someone wanted multiple partners and couldn't commit to a single person, then they should never marry. But that was Adelina's modern opinion.

George noted her expression and how she didn't try to hide it from him. In response, he tucked his left hand into his pocket, causing her to smile. Maybe they were playing science class games after all.

Adelina enjoyed fooling people like him, but that was her twenty-first-century self. She forgot to alter herself, she didn't try to be modest and docile, like she should have.

Instead, the fool became her. Adelina's smile quickly vanished. Earlier, her mind hadn't played tricks on her. There had been someone else in the distance, watching over them. A shadow of a person, lingering. They had distracted her while George snuck up.

Adelina had forgotten all about the silhouette until Frederick coughed beside her, making her jump into George. With a dash of her eyes downwards, she succumbed to the reality that he had watched the entire exchange. He had caught her being a version of herself she wanted to bury.

The air turned thick as he studied her. Blustering hair

tangling in the wind. Chipped nails digging into the cuff of an unusual coat. Darkening skin a top of her head, only deepening as it neared her scalp. He was right, he'd never met her before, he would remember someone who looked like her.

Adelina shuddered, arms finding her chest, wrapping herself up, seeking comfort. The heat escaped to her cheeks, blistering underneath his gaze. Utterly powerless. Before her two members of an old-fashioned street gang, and she was unarmed, a mere girl with a concussion.

Unlike modern-day gangs, George and Frederick were not teenagers or boys. They were smartly dressed men. No logos, no grey, no soft materials in sight. They wore pin-striped suits, finely tailored. Instead of chunky chains and heavy Rolexes, they had delicate gold pocket watches. Their clothes belonged to the upper echelon of society. Unlike their rambunctious modern namesakes, they were stealthy and unfazed. In a way, with their attire and composed nature, they were attractive.

A perfectly curated image to illustrate to their enemies they couldn't be beaten. They had money, which allowed them to obtain power. They could do whatever they wished. Yet, behind their graceful appearance, sewn into the seams of their clothes, were weapons people only discovered too late.

Adelina couldn't read Frederick, his face said nothing, like he wasn't thinking at all. Yet the dark intensity of his lingering stare hinted at something else. She never became flustered, nor did she look away. If anything, he made her freeze, as if time was still moving around her while she was stuck in her mind, wondering what he was thinking.

The off-white dull blouse, stained across the chest, was far too large for her frame. The fraying skirt pulled at the seams, rippling across her legs and digging into her waist. Frederick scrutinised her, and Adelina couldn't help but wonder why he was so observant of her.

'Where were you earlier, when we came to visit?' Frederick asked, waiting for a response that didn't come. 'You were in John and Margaret's vardo, weren't you?'

The colour drained from her. A slight vibration of her hands, she tucked them more into her frame. Mouth agape, trying to find a response. Instead, her tongue turned dry, cracking underneath the whistling wind. What she really wanted wasn't to find a sentence but to wake up in reality.

'I've been watching you all night. The Youngs don't like you. They all move away from you. You're the odd one out.'

All her thoughts were clarified. The Youngs didn't want her there, they saw her as an inconvenience. By lingering around the camp, she was putting herself in danger. Earlier, John had threatened her, she had seen the malicious longing in his eyes. That's why she was trying to escape. The people in front of her, they wouldn't care about that.

'Where were you going to run away to, at this time of the night?' George said.

The words never registered. Everything she thought had come tumbling out. The two brothers stared at her, and she couldn't remember what she'd said.

Amnesia when confronted with devilish men. They sent people running, fearing for their lives. Adelina blurted out everything she thought, as if she didn't care how her opinions might affect their view of her.

A sudden lurch in her stomach. Bending forwards instinctively she wretched. The bile rose up, through her gullet, splattering across the ground and coating George Clark's newly purchased shoes.

They would put an end to her. Everyone was anxious of them, and now the yellow liquid of her insides was bubbling on the shining leather. The gun would come out, resting against the centre of her head, before it would send her teetering backwards for good.

Instead, George flicked the sick off his feet, coating the grass in foam. His hearty chuckle only ceased when Frederick told him to shut up, that he would wake the Youngs if he carried on.

'See, we're not going to hurt you. We just want to know a few things, that's all,' Frederick said.

'I don't know where I am or what I've stumbled into. I was trying to leave, get away from them. John scares me. If he finds out I've been talking to you...'

'He won't know, because you won't tell him.'

'I'm never seeing him again, so of course I won't be telling him.'

'Cats no longer got your tongue, has it?' George said, bemused.

'Look, you're clearly not a Young, and because of that, you're going to do what I say. Their leader is coming tomorrow and you–'

'All the reason not to go back,' Adelina interrupted, glancing towards a patch of woodland, wondering whether to take a chance.

'Do you not get it, who I am?' Frederick said, tugging her arm, yanking her closer.

The grab was more akin to being manhandled. Underneath his touch, her skin throbbed. The aching didn't matter, no one would save her, even if they came across the scene. The only person she could rely upon was herself.

'Stay at the camp, gather information on them for us, and then I'll get you away from them. You know yourself they're petrified of me.'

'I'm no grass,' Adelina said, wondering if the whole thing was some trick, a way to deceive her. Instead, they looked bewildered. 'I don't snitch.'

'You don't have a choice,' Frederick said, letting go of her. 'Either you do as I say, or I'll come after you. I'm sure you've heard the stories about us by now.'

Adelina nodded, finally succumbing to Frederick. Everything about her disposition changed, she became fragile and fearful. There had been a fire within her to fight for what she wanted, what she thought was right. Frederick ripped that from her because he was too possessed with getting revenge.

'Do as he says,' George said as Frederick paced away. 'He's all talk sometimes. Listen out tomorrow and tell us what you hear, then I'll take you to the train station – or wherever you want to go – I don't break promises.'

'That means nothing when all I've heard are bad stories about you.'

Adelina proved him wrong. Not bothering to reply, he shook his head with a smile. Even after everything, she was capable of fighting for herself. Maybe Frederick should have let her escape, because she had the potential to be trouble for them all in the end.

FOUR

Adelina crept inside the vardo, trying not to wake the Youngs. Finding a thin blanket, she laid upon the hard wood. A couple of feet away, Margaret and John shared the suspended double bed, while Moira and Aisling slept underneath in the storage space. Their blissful breaths reminded Adelina of childhood and long summer days.

The flimsy material did nothing to stop Adelina's body from shaking. Adrenaline, nerves, the cold gripped her. The ridges of her spine pressed into the floor. A simple movement caused her to recoil in pain as her vertebrae rolled beneath her.

Pulling up the cotton blanket, Adelina tried to comfort herself, hoping she would slide into sleep and give her mind some peace. Her efforts were futile. Overthinking, she laid wide awake, desperately attempting to answer never-ending questions, longing to find a way home and escape all the people she'd met in the past.

No longer seeking sleep, Adelina spent the night yearning for her real life. At times, she believed she was dead, alive in a new world, reincarnated. But with death, she thought that the world would be dark, her bodyless soul floating through.

At one point, Adelina did drift off to sleep, and when she did, she dreamt. Snippets of memories collided with vivid recollections of her new world. Horses and travels, Leonora and her pony, Frederick Clark, and the bonfire. She relived getting her stitches, Margaret kneeling before her, sewing needle in hand, hastily pulling her skin back together. It didn't seem possible to dream in a coma or in death. Maybe the truth was something else.

There was one dream, a memory, that Adelina was surprised she could ever forget.

In the dull light, the bleak whitewashed walls appeared almost grey. They stretched upwards, towering over the inhabitants, making them feel miniscule, unimportant to the world and the universe. The flickering fluorescent light cast shadows across the room, elongating the outlines of every surface, as if something was creeping towards them.

Closed blinds. A simple room. A single bed and a table. Flowers shrinking before them. It was meant to be peaceful, though it felt like the end.

Disinfectant hung in the air, stinging Adelina's nostrils. Only a hospital could smell so rancid. To her, cleanliness smelled like roses, not putrid chemicals. A wrinkled petal fell onto the bare nightstand. Death was all around her.

Frail and weak, Nova laid in the bed. It took all her strength to keep her eyes from rolling back. Limbs heavy, growing numb. Her body longed for eternal sleep, but there was something she needed to do first.

A couple of minutes earlier, Nova had mustered enough strength to banish the other relatives from the room. They didn't need to hear what she had to say to her granddaughter.

Nova took Adelina's hand in her own, turning the palm upwards. Eyes closed, she traced the lines. They had always been peculiar, hard to read. She had thought they would change as Adelina grew, but they had only become more distinct. The lifeline forked into two, beginning and ending simultaneously. In her final moments, Nova waited for an epiphany.

Unable to fight her emotions, a tear trickled down Adelina's face. The end had come. The last time her grandmother would try to decipher her palms.

Nova mumbled an ambiguous statement about the lifeline. No matter what, Adelina would move forward. The utterance made no sense. Perhaps, a sign of her brain failing in its final moments. Yet, Nova's face crumpled, lines growing deeper. Even in her enfeebled state, she tried to show her confusion.

Adelina's palms were impossible to read. The only hands Nova had ever failed to interpret. They left her dumbfounded with every try.

Folding Adelina's palm into itself, she fought for a final glimpse of understanding, hoping it would come as she succumbed to the end. Holding onto her hand as tight as she could, she prayed. The touch was a mere pinch on Adelina's skin.

Nova's last stance. From the other side, she would do her best to help, to guide Adelina through a world that would become troubled.

The shifting of bodies made Adelina's chest tighten. Realising what was happening, she became stiff. She wanted to flee, to storm out of the vardo, but she worried about what they'd think of her for interrupting.

Trapped on the floor, in a world she didn't understand. Somehow, she owed her saviours because they'd put a roof over her head for a night. Surely, it was human nature not to leave her in danger.

Adelina couldn't stay another hour in such a place. To save herself from the torture, she needed to find answers. In the dying hours of the night, she decided to defy the Clarks. Instead of gathering information for them, she would return to where she was found, in search of a way home.

With only the children still asleep, Adelina made her escape. Venturing out, into the unknown world, sent shivers running through her. The woodland she'd once longed to run into now encased her, shielding her from the camp's view.

Frost-crusted grass crunched beneath her. Toes burning with cold from the weathered shoes. Further into the countryside away from everything she knew. Idly walking, contemplating her existence and the purpose of life itself. A sense of direction only gained from snippets of a conversation with Margaret.

Dust formed a grey coating on her shoes. Adelina meandered down a dirt road, her mind tumbling back to what Nova had said on her death bed.

Suddenly, the wound stung. A jabbing prying feeling at her stitches. She had never been offered a mirror; she hadn't seen Margaret's handywork. Coming to a halt, her fingers touched the gooey hot flesh. No wonder she felt so off.

Flicking her hand, she tried to make the gloop fall to the ground. Shaking vigorously, she tried again. The slime slipped from her, splattering down. Amongst the frost, near her wound's puss, laid pools of congealed blood.

Adelina fell to her knees, stones grazing her skin. The cold blistered her legs, igniting patches of red. A single sob escaped. Her eyes started to fill. Hands dashing across the frost, she scratched it away only to see rocks.

Nothing. Not a trace of what happened, only the aftermath. With the thawing ground, the blood would slip away and then nothing of her arrival would be left. As simple as that, there would be nothing tying her to falling back in time, like nothing had occurred at all.

A wail begged to be let loose, and she almost let it happen. The emotion disintegrated in her throat as a rumble approached.

A roaring wind sent her hair blustering, swirling around her. Skin as pale as the frost-bitten ground. From the road she was barely visible. If anything, she looked like a ghost lingering on from an accident, a mere reminder that something bad had once happened.

The salty water never stopped spilling. A slight wash of relief as the car began to pass.

Almost too late. The figure in the ditch became visible at the last moment. The car skidded to a halt, drawing up a billowing grey cloud.

The car reversed, moving towards her. Her throat itched, as she held back the sobs that clawed at her insides. Scuffing her eyes with the bobbling cuffs of her coat, she tried to compose herself as she rose.

A sleek car, shining alloys, not many had access to such luxury. The small details, the make and model, went over

Adelina's head. No connections were made. Not until she saw the driver's face. No one could forget the harsh stare of Frederick Clark.

His eyes bored into her, face almost wrinkling as he viewed her. A few hours ago, he told her to wait for Thomas' arrival, now she was in the middle of nowhere with barely a layer upon her.

'What are you doing out here? I told you to stay with the Youngs.'

'Please,' Adelina croaked. 'Continue like you never saw me.'

A man feared by so many, and she asked him for a favour. As soon as she said it, her entire being dropped. To ask for such a thing from a stranger was bad enough, let alone him. Frederick could send her whole world crashing in an instant. Yet, she asked regardless, and she couldn't fathom why.

Usually, he read people well. When he pulled up, he expected an apology, not a request to ignore her. Her words made him more inquisitive. He wanted to pry, to find out more, even though he was running late.

'What makes you think I would continue, when you've disobeyed me?'

'You only saw me at the last minute. Can't you forget and move on? I've got away from the Youngs. I'm not going back, not now.'

Out of all the places to run, she chose a lane with no shelter. A normal person would have gone to the city, with its abundance of hiding places and transport connections. Adelina made his head spin; rarely did people have such an effect on him.

'Why do you want to get away from them?'

'There's an entire story, and I don't think you have time to hear it. You're going to visit the Youngs, aren't you? Hoping that Thomas has arrived by now.'

'I asked a question. Answer me.'

'You're right, I'm not a Young. Yesterday you said you didn't care, so what's changed?' Adelina said, half hoping he'd pull the trigger on her, because if you die in a dream, you wake up. To her, it felt like the only way back.

'Don't make me get out of this car. Tell me the entire story, from the start.'

'John's daughter found me here. I was knocked out. I'd been injured somehow.'

Frederick fumbled with his cigarette barrel, waiting on all the pieces to understand her. There had to be a reason for the way she acted, not only towards him but towards his brother.

'I'm not going back,' Adelina said, her eyes meeting Frederick's with fierce determination. 'They took me to their camp, and I don't know why, because John seems to hate me. I don't want to know what Thomas would have done to me, because he certainly wouldn't want me there.'

Thomas Young arrived early, before the sun broke the horizon. In the shadows, he conversed with John about the Clarks. They were due another visit, but that wasn't on his mind; instead he became obsessed with John's story about an odd girl they'd picked up on the roadside.

Thomas slammed his fist into the vardo. John always made things difficult. The wrong decision had been made; he should've sent her packing straight away. Thomas didn't care for Margaret's feelings or her superstitions, he cared about the impact of letting an unknown woman into the camp.

Furious, he stormed towards the old, rickety home, John hot on his tail. Without thinking, he ripped open the door, ready to drag the woman out of camp for good. They couldn't deal with a leech when they had the Clarks breathing down their necks.

After all they'd done, it turned out Adelina left without a thanks. Within half an hour, she had dashed away, seeking shelter elsewhere. In John's mind, she owed him, because everyone viewed him as weak because of his actions.

When one loses something, they retrace their steps. Adelina's location tumbled from John's mouth. Together, father and son, pounded through the forest, hell-bent on catching her, to show her the trouble she'd caused.

'Why were you here?' Frederick asked Adelina.

'I don't know. That's half the reason the Youngs hate me. I'm trying to remember what happened. That's why I came back.'

'You don't know what happened to you,' Frederick repeated.

The rawness of her eyes made sense. The slumped stance, the constant gaze towards the ground, the way she wrapped her thin coat around herself. Adelina was unsure of her reality.

'I'm not a liar,' Adelina snapped, misunderstanding him, thinking he didn't believe her. 'I don't know why I'm here.'

Flashing lights, blurring vision, Adelina's head pounded. She wanted to protect herself and her integrity, but she couldn't concentrate. Hair blustering in the breeze, it felt like someone grabbed at the roots, yanking the strands upwards.

The door slammed, sending shockwaves throughout the vardo. Moira's eyes burst open. Distant voices of her father and grandfather bickering. The stranger's name sat in the air like a curse had been placed upon them.

Still in her nightwear, Moira snuck out of the storage area. Her mother would kill her, but she couldn't help herself. As John and Thomas trudged over the fields, she followed them, trying to be lithe despite the sleep still gripping to her.

Coming out of the woods, Moira understood where they were heading. At the same place they found Adelina, they would get revenge for her lackadaisical attitude. Moira couldn't wait.

What Frederick thought of Adelina mattered more than anything else. He would be the one to decide whether she would survive, whether she could find a way home. Did she really want to risk it all with a bullet?

Stuttering, she attempted to make up another excuse, another reason for him to let her go. Failing to string a sentence together, she looked away from him, unable to withstand his gaze any longer. She tried to find the way her feet sank into the mud more interesting than the thought of what was going on in his mind.

With him, she never knew how to feel. A man like him should have punished her. Instead, he let her speak, he gave her time, unlike the Youngs. If anything, a part of him seemed soft. God, maybe her ability to judge character had been taken away when she lost her memories.

'I'm sorry,' Adelina whispered. 'I don't know what happened. The Youngs scared me. I want to go home, but I need to remember how I got here first.'

There was innocence written across her, and Frederick believed her, she'd forgotten herself. The true innate version of her on display and she beheld an attitude he'd never encountered on a stranger before. A part of him wanted to solve the mystery, if only to satisfy his curiosity about why she acted the way she did.

'You should have done as I said.'

'But I didn't. I couldn't stay there. I had to come up here. Please, don't tell anyone where I am.'

Another request. Another beg for him to do as she asked. It didn't sit right with him; she couldn't have the power – he held that over everyone.

'I don't make promises.'

Of course, he would say such a thing. Adelina sighed, a slight smile forming. She was kidding herself asking for a favour from him.

Despite all she knew about him, and how he would want to dismiss her, she walked off, away from the camp and everything she knew. No one else came before her, not even a man who wanted to rule over everyone.

Dumbfounded, he watched her walk on. Longing for control, the engine rumbled, the car crawled beside her. His voice low against the tires churning up rocks.

'Get in. After dealing with the Youngs, I'll take you to a train station so you can get away.'

'I'm never going to see them again,' she replied. 'Besides, why would I trust you?'

Others would have taken it as a demand. To save face, he

didn't argue. The car screeched off from beside her. A slight sinking sensation settled in his gut, like something bad was going to happen. The feeling didn't bother him because he knew he'd see her again somehow.

Silence. No shoes against the rocks, no birds or movement in the trees. Everything was still. Adelina froze, the exchange playing over in her head. Her body fluctuated between hot and cold, unable to decide how to feel.

Moira skipped towards the lane. Adelina stood like she was suspended in thin air. Something about her set Moira on edge. A stranger in their group felt wrong, especially one unacquainted with themself. It wasn't just that; as she looked at her, the hair on the back of her neck stood up, like she could sense Adelina didn't belong in the world at all.

Moira jumped, stumbling forwards into the wet grass. An unexpected scene unravelled before her. After watching the initial lurch, she turned back. The actions became too much, even if it was for the best.

Adelina faced the winding road, almost expecting to see Frederick's car again. If he returned, he could change his mind and make her pay for the way she spoke. She needed to move, but she didn't know where to. The countryside, with its trees and hills to hide within, but no shelter to sleep. The city, with its maze of buildings, but nowhere to feel safe at night. Or home, to board a train and go back to the place she was born but wouldn't recognise. The one thing she needed was time, time to remember. Forgetting the danger, she stood still.

Not for long. Thomas jumped towards her, sick of her apparent nonchalance. She disobeyed John, she wandered off, not repaying them by helping or picking up any slack. The cheek, to stay in his son's vardo for the night, but to not hang around for his arrival.

As John thundered towards the lane, he noticed the sleek black car beside Adelina. He concluded she was a liar, a decoy, a spy for the Clark's, she'd never forgotten herself.

With Frederick gone, Thomas' hands entwined in Adelina's hair. With one rough grab, he yanked her backwards, her body clattering into his. A single squeal escaped before his rotten hands wrapped around her mouth.

Thomas was sweaty, despite the cold. A musty scent of old putrid tobacco and decaying teeth. Manure and mud bored into every pore.

'Listen here,' Thomas spat. 'I'll let go, and you won't make a sound. If you do, I'll shoot you dead right now.'

Adelina writhed under his grasp. Her instinct was to fight, to get away. She dug her heels into the gravel, trying to steady herself as she thrashed, hoping to unbalance him. Thomas tightened his grip, her hair pinging, a scream piercing his hand. Overpowering her, he wrestled her toward the treeline.

A tumbling wall against her back, the sharp limestone ripping into her skin. Chewing upon a blade of grass, John edged into view. He felt nothing, he stood by watching; it wasn't his place to interrupt.

'It'll get worse,' Thomas grinned, bearing his blackened teeth. 'I can do more before I put an end to you. Or you can listen to me, and I'll make things easier.'

Two against one. And just like her childhood, she was all alone.

'Good girl. You're bound to get me in trouble with Frederick, and I don't like that. So, you're going to answer my questions.'

Hiccupping, Adelina tried to stifle her tears, but no matter how hard she fought, they rolled down her cheeks.

Such a pity; Thomas thought she would be pretty if she wasn't whining so much. He let go of her arm, half expecting her to crumble.

'Why were you talking to Frederick?' Thomas said, waiting for a response that never came. 'God, if you were a man, you'd be dead already.'

Blank eyes, no longer paying attention to his father's words, as if she had no care in the world. John stormed forward, a crack sounded as his fist collided with her.

Adelina came to a heap at Thomas' feet. His heart swelled with pride; finally, John made the right decision. Together, their fingernails dug into her as they dragged her through the field.

They needed to take her far away from the lane so Frederick couldn't find her if he went looking. John ripped open a gate, its springs groaning, before he shoved her through the opening. The trees and crumbling wall would hide her from view.

They left her for dead, like John should have in the first place. Wiping their hands, smearing her blood across their shirts, they sauntered back to camp. The Clark brothers would be waiting for them. Thomas wasn't scared, he had a plan that Frederick wouldn't be able to resist. Once they were lured in, they would put an end to the Clarks for good.

FIVE

Damp grass gnawed at Adelina's legs. Faint memories of John's actions seeped back. Clambering upright, her head pounded. Despite the pain, she needed to move, to get as far away from the Youngs as possible.

Adelina managed only two minutes before she tumbled over, too exhausted to walk any further. In the dim morning light, she nestled against a rock, her eyes flickering shut.

When she awoke several hours later, life buzzed around her. Rays of sun sparkled through the leaves, casting dancing shadows on the ground. Late-blooming wildflowers, the occasional bee, chirping birds. Orange and red across the dirt, with roots protruding covered in dark moss. Somehow, she was still alive.

Adelina scuffled to her feet on nearly broken shoes. One heel was loose; each step wobbled, threatening to twist her ankle into the mud. A different coloured coat, completely covered in dirt, sodden from the morning grass. The skirt hung heavily, dropping to her hips. Matted hair fell in bunches around her frame. The wound oozed, split back open from John's actions.

Unsure of what else to do, she pushed onwards, tripping over branches. Dark clouds bubbled, colliding with soft grey rainclouds. The skyline reminded her of home, of her industrial town. Adelina couldn't stop herself; she felt the city pulling her in.

Charred buildings grew tall around her. Plumes of vapour infiltrated the air. Gloomy and bleak. The depression of the post-war period. Factories a top of houses. Outhouses and rubbish upon the street. Clothes hanging to dry above squalor. Paint peeling, glass shattering, industry booming.

Fumes burnt her throat as smoke tangled into her clothes. Pollution surrounded her, causing an incessant cough to grow. The piercing noise of screeching metal and churning chemicals created a high pitch ringing that whistled through her head.

Adelina didn't understand the city, she couldn't tell the safe and dangerous places apart. Fear of the Youngs following her, finding her, doing God knows what to her, pushed her on.

Green grocers, butchers, and bakeries. The weekly shop commenced. Market stall owners shouted at the top of their lungs, enticing customers with discounted prices. Passers-by frowned at her, questioning her because of her ragged appearance and wide-eyed stare. They pushed past her, knocking into her, not caring for her space. They tutted as they took in her bedraggled locks, the blood that slipped down her cheek.

Overwhelmed, Adelina tore herself away from the bustling crowds. Alone, on a new road, the voices echoed inside her head. The city no longer felt like home.

'Are you lost, or are you down here wanting some fun?'

A slurred predatory growl. The rough man's friends chuckled. They approached her whilst she wasn't looking. Waiting for the opportune moment to say something.

Tatty shirts barely buttoned. Grimy trousers ripped and rotten. They swayed, unable to keep still. Beards matted with liquor and their own bodily fluid. Yellowing eyes raked up and down her body, mouths' filling with saliva.

'Bloody hell, she's not your average moll, she's gorgeous. What are you doing down here?'

Uncut ratty hair. Scaly scalps and dusty white shoulders. Sagging beer bellies, poking out. Discoloured teeth, loose and putrid, some black and ground down into stumps.

'Going to tell us your price love, or do you want me to show you a good time on the house?'

The bustling stalls continued close by. The shouts of the salesmen. The nattering of old women gossiping. No passers-by on the new street. No horses and carts or motor vehicles. Just her and the group of men, who desperately wanted something from her.

'Don't leave just yet, love,' one of them sneered. 'Let us get our fill first.'

Edging backwards with fists forming, she tried to regulate her breathing. An urge to scream, but she knew it would only get lost against the blasts from the factories. There was nothing but her hands to fight with, no weapon in her voice or in her hand.

'What's going on?'

The voice was familiar, almost filled with an edge of laughter.

The drunkards' eyes widened. Their posture shifted. They shrank inside of themselves. Hands fumbled with one another, anxious at the mere sight of the man. A cold shiver ran across Adelina, she was no longer in danger, because a vicious man had come to save her. From the depths of an alley, George Clark came into view.

The men muttered excuses: they meant no harm, it was only a joke. A badly put together defence, trying to escape a beating. George reprimanded them, detailing the gruesome things he would do if they attempted anything similar again.

Adelina found it bizarre how four men could be so intimidated by one lone man, but it wasn't just the Youngs who feared the Clarks.

The men didn't try to warrant their actions again. No one in the right mind would go against George. The whole city had heard of the atrocities the Clarks could commit. The men valued their hands, their tongues. They knew what was best.

They obeyed George's demand to leave, not once looking back at their prey. Scampering into the alley, they attempted to swallow their relief; it could've ended a lot worse.

Adelina should've thanked him, but instead, she found herself gawking, consumed with the power of the Clarks. George protected her with a word and a look. No one they loved would ever need to be afraid.

'Finally ran away then, have you?' George said. 'You look like you fought your way out.'

'Something like that.'

'Not too frightened, after what I interrupted, are you?'

'I'm fine. Thanks for helping.'

'No problem, we look after those who work for us,' George said, winking.

Adelina didn't feel jovial; it wasn't the time nor the place for science class games, not after the men or her morning locked in darkness.

'I don't work for you.'

'Then why did Freddie tell me to bring you to him if I saw you?'

Adelina laughed nervously, thinking he was joking.

'Flirting again, George?' A woman chirped, her lilted accent not native to the area. The twang was like Adelina's, but from somewhere further up north. Not stopping to chat, the woman's heels clipped, her hair bouncing with every step.

'Ida? What are you doing down here?'

'Wouldn't you love to know,' Ida smiled, glancing back at them. 'Be careful, he's spoken for, and word will only get back to her. You don't want to be on the wrong side of Isla Clark.'

Everyone assumed Adelina was no good, and somehow a prostitute. The presumption made her flush with anger. Of course, George was married, she had eyes, she knew what a ring on such a finger meant.

'Don't worry about her. Paul and I don't really like her, she's full of rubbish at times. Let's get you to Freddie, but whatever you do, don't mention seeing her down here, it'll only cause trouble.'

'And what if I don't want to go with you?'

'Are you daft?' George chuckled. 'You don't have a choice. Freddie will come after you, he doesn't let anyone go. The power he possesses now… if you know what's best, you'll choose the safest option and come with me.'

Expecting her to follow, George paced towards the markets. Adelina remained rooted in place, trying to process his words.

After a few metres, he turned back.

'Come on, you're not going to get far running in those heels.'

That statement alone made her want to flee. But, in heart, she knew he was right; she wouldn't be able to get away from them. Given her luck, she would only get herself into further trouble.

'Like I said, we look after the people who work for us. You've got nothing to be worried about.'

'Why should I believe you?'

'Look,' George snapped, his voice deepening, more demanding. If kindness didn't work, then something else might. 'You saw how those men acted around me. You saw how afraid the Youngs are of me. Come with me, or I'll make you forget everything, all over again.'

Frederick had said something when she begged him not to. Nails digging into the palms of her hand, she tried to comprehend what Frederick would gain from telling George about her memory.

Adelina came from a different place. She wanted peace, to ride out the storm, until she found a way home, until she woke up. Unfortunately, peace didn't exist in 1919, men had brought the war back with them.

After France, they returned home with mental conditions that weren't recognised. Some army medics believed shellshock lasted days. No one wanted to believe it could last longer. Symptoms of illness were put down to cowardice. Of course, Adelina knew about the mental health implications of the trenches, but she had never considered how it affected them at home afterward.

History had taught her about warfare, about winning, but never the aftermath. Teachers didn't touch upon the inter-war period, how society changed. Tensions arose that inevitably led to the second world war, but all she remembered was the leader her country fought against. Dates got muddled together, events lost against the context.

Poverty and deprivation also followed the war. Veterans had little job prospects. Factory workers faced pay cuts despite longer hours. They had to make a living somehow. Men like the Clarks learnt to fight back. The creation of gangs that ruled streets, suburbs, and cities was a product of their society.

George's new approach worked; Adelina traipsed after him. It finally sank in – she didn't have freewill anymore. A puppet with a master, but she would look for a way to cut the strings.

'I don't know why Freddie's so hellbent on talking to you. You've probably forgotten everything from the camp, right?'

Not wanting to engage, Adelina shrugged. Remaining silent, she followed him through a maze of terraced streets. Children played with lumps of coal, never stopping for carts or cars, only for George as he passed by. Sometimes, little boys would run up to him, muttering underneath their breath. Occasionally, he would dig into his pockets and toss a coin their way.

'Are you going to tell me what happened to you then? Your heads been bleeding again.'

Masses of people parted for him. They bustled out of a grand Victorian train station, the kind her hometown had, but she was used to it being decrepit, with broken window panes and rusting metal.

They crossed over a bridge and into the heart of the industry. George didn't care for the bangs or fire that reached out towards him. Adelina jumped with every noise. Even a young kid skipping by would send her shaking.

'You're not from a city, I'll tell you that much,' George said, stopping outside a boarded-up warehouse. 'Go through there, someone'll meet you in the main room.'

Factories rose tall around them. Horse excrement filled the delves in the cobbles. Water lapped close by. The canal shielded from view by worn buildings. A snicket to the docks a few doors down. Men continually went in and out.

'Aren't you going in?' Adelina asked, looking towards the chipped warehouse door.

'I've got better things to do than getting distracted in there. I'll wait here for a bit, make sure you don't run away, then I'll be off. Trouble never stops around here.'

'I feel like I'm walking towards the gallows,' Adelina muttered.

'Not going in would be more of a death sentence. Tell him everything, and you never know, he might let you go. Freddie is unpredictable like that.'

The ragged door gave way to a dimly lit hall. Plaster crumbled from the walls. The rotting floor groaned beneath her feet. Everything was dreary, damp, and in need of replacing. Maybe, Adelina wasn't heading for the gallows but descending into the underworld instead.

SIX

Double doors opened to reveal a long, narrow room. Steel support beams disrupted the space. A cold concrete floor met shabby wooden desks. A mist hung over the workers, anonymising them. The smoke infiltrated Adelina's throat, leaving a burning taste sat on her tongue. A man wrote numbers on a chalkboard. Children passed fistfuls of money to women who counted foreign-looking coins.

Grubby strangers had no place in the Clarks' office, where secrecy was paramount. Frustrated by Adelina's unannounced entrance, Etta decided to handle the rude woman herself.

Etta bore a slight resemblance to George, that went over Adelina's head. With pursed lips and impeccable posture, she exuded an air of snootiness. Flawlessly preened and only slightly older than Adelina, she wore brand-new clothes, including a daringly short, mid-calf skirt made of the finest cotton. Delicate gold jewellery adorned her fingers and neck. Perfectly applied blush complimented her dark ring-curled hair. She looked down her nose at Adelina.

'George told me Frederick wanted to see me. He's waiting outside. I'm not in the wrong place, am I?' Adelina asked, her voice wavering slightly.

'And what does Freddie want with you?' Etta replied, her infamous stony expression nearly as intimidating as her younger brothers'.

'I don't know. George found me, he told me to come here.'

Stained clothes, broken heels, dirt coated her skin. Fraying stitches, bruises upon every inch of her, blood still trickling from her hairline. Etta couldn't fathom what Frederick would want with her.

Etta held a somewhat patronising stance. The cold glare made Adelina feel like she wasn't dressed appropriately for the occasion. With her pounding head, she forgot about the filthy clothes and the bird's nest of hair that clumped at her shoulders.

Later, Etta would have words with Frederick. He was supposed to set an example. Women who weren't affiliated with their family were banned from their den. The girl didn't belong, especially not looking like she did.

'When I say this, I mean it,' Etta said sternly. 'Don't tell a soul about what's in here. If you do, I'll tie you up and throw you in the canal myself.'

Impatient, and frankly indifferent, Etta opened the only closed door. Waiting for Adelina to move inside, she tutted; a naïve bewildered look was plastered across her face. For such a girl to be in such a terrible place was wrong.

'I don't know what his business is with you,' Etta said, feeling compelled to warn her. 'But if I were you, I'd get out whilst I still could. Take that advice from his sister.'

Etta slammed the door, leaving them alone. Adelina's focus settled upon him, Frederick Clark. He didn't look up, too consumed with the documents that cluttered his desk.

Despite the frosted window, the office was dim. Bare concrete floors, no carpet to warm the space, no rug to dry her shoes from the puddle she stood in. The tapping from a leak upstairs. A light stream of water ran down the wall, settling within the uneven floor. An abundance of shelves, littered with notepads and dusty books, a home for silverfish and Frederick's secrets.

Workers voices moved inside of the walls. Their smoke seeped underneath the door. In his office, alcohol overpowered the scent of damp and of the chimneys next door. The harsh liquor tainted her, like it could blister her throat at any moment.

A low grumbling cough prised her away from the décor. With the clearing of his throat, he wondered what she thought of his dreary space. Of course, she'd imagined it differently, less chaotic, more put together. The lavish car, the tailored clothes, his authoritative stance, of course she'd expected something grander.

'You look a little rough around the edges,' Frederick said, gesturing to the chair opposite him.

The reason for her appearance didn't need to be spoken about, she would only lose her strength, and cry. Her ragged looks didn't concern him, he merely wanted to learn about the Youngs. Earlier that morning, when he visited camp, Thomas had proposed an interesting offer to let them stay on the land for winter.

'You admitted yourself you aren't a Young. I want to know whether I can trust you first. The Youngs are awful people, aren't they? So why did you...'

Frederick's mind wandered from the questions he had planned. Leaning back in his chair, he studied her, not attempting to conceal what he was doing. Examining her crinkled outfit and discoloured face, he longed to find answers that she even sought.

'Why did I?' Adelina asked, shifting in her seat, hoping that he would continue.

The girls at the camp had been right about his looks. She never should have thought that. Every moment with him should have scared her. Instead, she found herself thinking about his appearance and how he frustrated her. Every situation they met, he tried to control. It started to grate on her.

'I told you to stay at the camp, why did you run away? I said I would get you out, help you. You knew how much the Youngs feared me. After our talk last night, I thought you would have done as I asked.'

'Well, you were wrong,' Adelina said with a shrug. 'When I left, I hoped that I would never see you or the Youngs again.'

'Your head, was that your injury? Why you forgot?'

'Obviously, that's how concussions work.'

'You act recklessly, especially around me. A piece of advice: think before you speak.'

'I guess I'm not thinking straight, with my head...'

'There's more to you than meets the eye, isn't there? No one behaves like this without something bad happening to them in the past.'

Of course, it went without saying; an avalanche of secrets were being kept from everyone, including herself.

'Make me trust you, believe you. Who are you, really?'

'I told you, I can't remember,' Adelina replied. Her rehearsed speech wouldn't work on him, he'd barely believed her the first time. 'I know I'm twenty-three. I was born in Middlesbrough. That's all.'

'You can't remember what you were doing before? Or what caused such an injury? You were left for dead, Ada.'

'I never told you my name... You spoke to the Youngs about me, didn't you?'

'They mentioned you. They saw us on the lane. I had to set them straight, they'd created this ridiculous story to explain your appearance.'

'I told you not to tell anybody about me, about how I can't remember. I know you told George, and you've probably told the Youngs about me too.'

'You *asked* me not to, people don't–'

'Tell you what to do?' Adelina laughed. 'Listen, if you want to know about the Youngs from me, you have to trust me. Simple. I have no idea why I was on the roadside. I've never been here before. I'm not from a city. This is all new to me. Your brother just had to save me from some disgusting men. In a way, this is all your fault.'

'Calm down. Think about what you're saying and to who.'

Adelina leaned back, the cold leather grazing her arms, briefly cooling her temper. With Frederick, she could never win. He wanted to distrust her so badly.

'What do you want to know about the Youngs,' Adelina said.

Always fighting back because that's what she'd learnt to do her entire life. Though in her time she'd never encountered a person like him before.

Adelina expected him to bite back. Instead, he remained

disturbingly calm, his eyes never drifting from her, barely batting. A part of him wanted to deal with her appropriately, like he would any other person, but the other part liked being at odds with her. With trembling hands, she brushed a stray hair from her face.

'There are so many questions because I never trust people, especially strangers,' Frederick said.

'I'm not a stranger, not now, am I?'

'You're a mystery. You don't even know yourself.'

'I'm an open book. There's no need to worry about me. I hadn't heard of you until yesterday. I want no trouble.'

Adelina attempted to end the conversation. Frederick remained unconvinced; not doubting her memory loss but who she was. If she didn't want conflict, then she spoke to him in a peculiar way.

A drop splattered on Adelina's hand. The leak from upstairs following her. Registering the colour of the liquid, she realised it had come from her and not the ceiling.

'Fuck,' Adelina whispered, wiping the blood onto her skirt.

Frederick wanted to chuckle; he'd never heard such language spoken so innocently. A drizzle of blood ran down her, the consequence of uneasy feelings for him.

Frederick only then noticed how terrible the stitches were – jagged and loose, barely holding her skin together. Done by someone who didn't know or didn't care. They would need to be redone.

'Women who play with their hair are usually nervous. Why are you nervous?'

'Why do you think?' Adelina said. Of course, it was him. She was alone with a powerful man who could end her life in an instant without caring about his actions. Frederick was capable of anything. Everything playing out before her could be real and not fiction curated by her mind.

'I think you could be lying to me and you're worried you'll slip up. You've learnt enough about me to fear the consequences.'

'I'm not a liar. I'm apprehensive of you. How could I not be?

Like you said, I've heard all the stories.'

'What do people say about me?'

'You do bad things. You're above the law. You do whatever you want to whoever you want. The Youngs feared you, and I feel like I should too.'

Another splatter. Frederick took out his handkerchief, not wanting her to lose focus. Finally, he was getting somewhere with her.

A commotion from the main room; splutters of words that neither could understand. The shelves shook, the door collided with the rotten wall. Discarded notes fell around Ida's feet.

Frederick leaned over his desk, arm outstretched towards the filthy girl. Ida never saw the handkerchief or the blood. To her, their hands were almost touching, like they were courting, about to go to a dance.

'Am I interrupting?' Ida taunted. 'You're the girl from earlier, the one who was with George.'

'Give us five minutes Ida.'

'It's fine, I'm leaving now,' Adelina interrupted. 'We were clearly getting nowhere anyway.'

With Adelina, Frederick's face changed endlessly, his thoughts and feelings written across him, completely against what he stood for.

'Getting anywhere?' Ida repeated, her distaste for the situation evident.

'We're not finished, Ada,' Frederick called out. 'You can't leave until I'm done with you.'

'Finished with what?' Ida demanded, her tone venomous. She felt like a ghost, like she was barely existing before them.

Adelina attempted a hasty exit, heels clicking awkwardly against the floor. If looks could kill, then Ida's would have crucified her already.

'I never want to see you near him again,' Ida shrieked. 'If you do, you'll regret the day you set foot in these offices.'

Adelina longed to deal with Ida in the only way she knew how. At home, things would've ended differently, but Frederick was watching. Ida was someone to him, she couldn't act out, he already judged her every move.

An unauthentic self. As a kid, she learnt to deal with her problems through fights, not words. In the Clark offices, she kept her eyes down. It wasn't like her to back off, but she found herself scurrying towards the street.

The staff couldn't tear their eyes away. The gossip began immediately. Adelina didn't care, too consumed with anger towards Ida and Frederick.

On the bustling street, Frederick caught up with her, his hands wrapping tightly around her forearm, gripping onto her.

'You can't leave, I need to know about the Youngs,' Frederick said.

'If you need me, why don't you ask politely for me to stay because right now you're holding me hostage, and I don't appreciate that.'

Another demand. Another attempt to show fearlessness. Frederick chuckled.

Adelina's response was dragged from deep within, long-forgotten memories returning to her.

'Let me sort this mess out with Ida. Then I'll come get you, and you can tell me about the Youngs.'

Adelina expected him to be mad. Instead, he gave the impression he'd backed down to her. The grip on her arm loosened. Sensing she wasn't going to run away, he moved back inside, leaving her dumbfounded. If anything, his last words seemed soft, juxtaposed against his fingers digging into her. In the end, he decided to trust her, despite her being an enigma.

The frosty canal edge burned Adelina's legs. The Clark Company Offices loomed behind her as she waited for Frederick to collect her. The way people stared at her on the street had sent her trailing back inside, but she couldn't hack the looks from the other workers either. Restless, she escaped through a rear door into a small yard.

Quiter. Only a few working lads from the building next

door observed her. A stranger, outside the notorious Clark headquarters was a rare sight; they hadn't seen that before.

'I'm not quite sure what he sees in her y'know,' Etta said. 'I never liked her from the beginning. I can sense things in people.'

At first, Adelina jolted at the sound of creeping footsteps, believing Frederick had come to retrieve her. Instead, Etta stood nearby, puffing on a cigarette.

Exhaling the smoke, she blew it upwards into the sky, letting it slowly evaporate. The girl's back to her, staring forwards. The canal before her, lapping gently. The grey hue not too much different to the smog that hung over the city.

'That goes for you too,' Etta continued. 'I observe and I learn, but you're a tricky one to understand. I'm not quite sure if you'll turn out good or bad in the end.'

Adelina wanted to snort, but she thought better of it. If anything, the words reminded her of her grandmother. Even so, she couldn't bring herself to turn around.

'I'm not sure what you're feeling, but you shouldn't let Ida bring you down. She's no one around here.'

The distant slam of a fist against wood. Followed by roaring laughter from the two women who remained at their desks. Frederick had never been so angry with Ida before. Finally, she was getting her comeuppance.

'Now that's not like him. If it were anyone else, I'd pop back in and check on them, but not with her. I'd throw her in there myself in a heartbeat,' Etta said, flicking her cigarette end into the water. 'I can't do that though. For now, she's at least taking his mind away from France.'

'Don't take this the wrong way,' Adelina said, her mind slipping back in time, forgetting who she spoke to. 'If she's your future sister-in-law, don't you think you should be kinder?'

Etta cackled; it was the funniest thing she'd heard for years. God, maybe she would enjoy having the odd girl around.

'They won't get married. Freddie doesn't have it in him. He's too focussed on business.'

Maybe gangsters across the ages had one thing in common:

love for women and short, one-sided relationships.

'So, are you going to tell me why you're here?' Etta asked.

'What if he doesn't want me to tell you?' Adelina replied. After all, she didn't know how the business worked. If history taught her anything, then Etta was most likely a mere worker, with no real say.

'I'd pry it out of him. Besides, you mentioned George, he'd tell me everything he knows about you. That boy can't keep a secret.'

'He doesn't know why I'm here, and I don't think I do either. Trust me, I'd tell you everything about myself, if you wanted. But if I knew why Freddie told me to come here, then I wouldn't tell you. I know better than to spill my guts, especially when someone like him is involved.'

'Loyalty to a man you barely know. That's the type of person we like, but it's rather stupid don't you think?'

'You're right,' Adelina smiled, looking over her shoulder, expecting to see Etta, but she'd already moved inside. Instead, she saw Ida emerging from the room.

Hushed voices drifted towards her. She studied the water, the way it lapped at the sides of the brick walls, the dirt and grime that sat on top. No matter how hard she tried, her attention kept getting pulled away.

The clipping of shoes, the brushing of material moving further away. The feeling of eyes in the back of her head never stopped.

Ida clocked her outside. Ragged clothes, filthy skin, unwashed hair – Adelina was clearly from the camp outside Hunslet. People were whispering about the arrival of a group up there. Adelina was one of them, no one else would sit on the decrepit ground.

Frederick towered over Adelina, trying to gain her attention. The daylight dimmed, and the temperature turned negative. Reluctantly, she drew to her feet, wiping her dusty hands on her skirt. No matter what, she needed to ensure her survival, and in a way, she thought he would ensure it.

'You remind me a lot of the Youngs, and of my family when we were younger,' he said.

Frederick was right; Adelina was like the Youngs and the Clarks. A part of her was too scared to give it away. She kept her ancestry a secret because of all the things people said to her as a kid. The stereotypes and the name-calling made her feel like she was no good from the day she was born.

The spark of his match was the brightest thing in the dull office. With the cigarette lit, he cast it aside. Adelina wanted to shake her head as he inhaled the toxins. As a nurse from the 21st century, she knew better than him.

'Tell me what you know about the Youngs, and I'll find you a place at a guest house where you can sort that concussion of yours.'

'Why do you care so much about them?'

'A piece of advice, stop asking questions, especially to me,' Frederick replied, his tone sharp.

'What if I know nothing about the Youngs?'

'They didn't let anything slip? They're not notoriously tight-lipped.'

Frederick tossed a few notes and coins towards her. Adelina didn't understand the monetary value; to her, it looked like pocket money. To the workers outside, he'd dished out a month's wages.

He waited for her to reach out, expecting her to stretch her delicate fingertips towards the paper. Adelina knew better. The details of the agreement needed to be clear before she accepted.

'I tell you about the Youngs, you give me that, and then we don't owe each other anything. You'll leave me alone.'

There was agreeing, and then there was her way – an analytical acceptance, only on her terms. It only drew him into her, constantly making him engage with her. He wondered when she would stop acting in such a manner.

'Tell me everything.'

'They despised me, all of them, even Margaret in the end, I think. They don't like strangers – who does? From what I heard, only Margaret wanted to save me. Moira would have left me for dead, and John would have too if he was alone. They didn't speak around me. They were careful.

When you arrived, John was petrified. The group wanted Thomas to talk to you, not him. The girls my age didn't know what delayed him. I don't think John knows Thomas' plans. His face showed pure shock when you turned up.

They're terrified of you. They wanted to flee. That's all I know. I was told to stay inside the vardo when you arrived. I was only allowed out that night when you found me.'

'How can you say that – about them leaving you for dead – without showing any emotion?'

'Because I'm questioning if any of this is real at all,' Adelina said, her voice breaking. 'I don't deserve this. I'm a good person at heart.'

'Aren't we all.'

'I mean it; I didn't deserve what John and Thomas did to me this morning.'

The bruises, the cuts, they were a result of the Youngs, and not a fall as she fled them.

'I didn't want to relive it, I didn't want to tell you. The Youngs are awful people, maybe not by your standards but they are by mine. I didn't deserve to be choked, threatened. John knocked me out, clean. I woke up in the forest alone. They left me for dead, like they wished they had in the first place. They're bad, probably just like you, but the difference is you're not scared of them, and they would do anything to not be frightened by you.'

Frederick scraped back his chair. They did all that to Adelina when they thought she was working for him. He couldn't wait any longer, the Youngs needed to be spoken to.

SEVEN

Margaret found Adelina's old clothes fascinating. The top was light and airy, like tracing clouds. The shoes were made from a hard yet sturdy material that still bent easily in her hands. The rubber sole reminded her of car tyres and nothing more. With great wonder, she placed the peculiar clothes into a bag.

An hour earlier, Frederick had arrived at the camp, utterly irrational. One thought consumed him as he bounded over to John and Thomas. The Youngs needed to leave. After a quick beating, he would send them on their way.

In his car, Margaret noticed a figure, an outline of a young woman. Dark hair, bunching up. Hands pulling through knots. Never looking towards the fire nor the bustling crowd, instead she stared at the interior of the vehicle. Sheepish, insecure, like she'd got into trouble.

Margaret wanted reassurance that her family would be safe. As she approached Frederick, she cradled her belly. Her hair fell in loose curls around her hips, and her light eyes observed him. Her brief glance made his voice trail off.

A ghost of his mother before him. In that moment, Margaret looked the double of her. His words, his actions, what he longed to do, were lost as she watched the scene timidly.

Rather than sending them away, Frederick gave her a spiel about Adelina and how he found her in the city. Margaret never thought such a man would become involved with her. Of course, he would take advantage of her injury, that's what people like him did.

The thought of Adelina being forced into some form of whorehouse run by the Clarks made Margaret's lip quiver. The baby, almost ready to be born, kicked out. Wrapping her hands ever tighter around herself, she longed to protect him from the evil of the world.

Seeing his mother instead, Frederick attempted to console Margaret. Speaking delicately, he tried to reassure her that he would do no harm to Adelina. He was simply going to drop her off at Violet's guest house in the city.

Margaret didn't believe him. Instead, she would try to remember Adelina in the same light, not tarnished by the Clarks. In the end, she only regretted picking her up because her life collided with Frederick.

Frederick cared about women and their emotions; a weakness, John and Thomas thought. Though they weren't privy to everything that had occurred in Frederick's life.

The bonfire's flames licked close to him. He stood beside the blaze, like the danger didn't scare him. In a hushed voice, he reprimanded John and Thomas. Taking a girl and dumping her in the forest was bad enough, but beating her beforehand, knowing she was ill, was even worse.

Thomas and John shrank away like scolded kids. And rightly so, Frederick despised men that hit women. He longed to push further. He wanted to see blood pouring from them. Despite them reminding him of Peter, he couldn't make them leave, Margaret needed a safe place. Once the child was born and a few months old, he would send them along.

Esmerelda scuttled across the field, her hair drooping over her frame. A look instilled in her eyes, she had only one man in mind.

Frederick knew the frail black witch lived with the Youngs. As he discussed business, she stared at him, eager to deliver a warning. Esmerelda didn't concern him, but he should have been petrified.

Isla, George's wife, mentioned her when she learnt of the Youngs' arrival. Old tales of how she told fortunes and cast spells. Whether written into a hand or upon cards, Esmerelda read the future. The world of divination embroiled her. Isla warned Frederick about her, knowing how he was entangled in their culture and the dark sinful world.

Smoke clung to every part of Adelina, saturating her hair and the fibres of her clothes. She recoiled at the smell, knowing it would only becoming more pungent with time until it grew stale. She longed to soak her body in water, to scrub her skin clean of the city's grime.

When Frederick eventually returned to the car, Adelina stayed quiet, her attention fixed on the flickering trees. She didn't ask where he was driving, knowing he didn't like to answer her questions. He wanted to control every conversation. Unless he wanted to speak, there would be no input from anyone, always his way and never the other.

'Your name is Italian, *Adelina,* not Ada,' Frederick said, her name rolling off his tongue awkwardly, as if it were far more complicated. 'Margaret asked if that's why I'm bothering myself with you. It wasn't, but now it is.'

'Bothering yourself? Is that what you call this?'

Adelina failed to understand the issue with her name's origin; she thought Italy was on the British side in World War one, Mussolini hadn't come to power yet. There were many things she needed to learn about this new world that couldn't be found in history books.

In parts of London, Italian gangs like the Mancinis and Bianchis ruled the streets. They were enemies to everyone except their own kind. Occasionally, they had partners, but they always stabbed them in the back in the end. To Frederick, anything was possible, and he wondered if she could be affiliated with them somehow.

'I want to believe you, that you genuinely don't remember what happened, but part of me thinks this fits together all too well.'

'Is it possible to hit yourself with a mystery weapon and render yourself unconscious? I don't remember, plain and simple. What if my name is Italian? I couldn't remember where I was born, let alone the year, when I woke up.'

'You're staying in the guest house until you remember every little detail. There's no other option. You don't leave without telling me. If you do, I'll come looking for you. You don't want to be–'

'On the wrong side of you.'

The inner city grew tall around them, bathed in the delicate glow of oil lamps. The car rolled to a halt, its engine continuing to chug beneath them.

Frederick tossed a handful coins into her lap. The shape and weight were unusual. Unsure of their value, she gathered them together, closing her fist around them, trying to hide any emotion from him.

'I've told you everything I know about the Youngs. This is payment, we owe each other nothing now.'

Frederick had never admitted someone was debt-free before. At times, she pushed all his buttons.

'If you remember anything, you come to me. If you see anything unusual, you tell me. If you need anything, you know where I'll be. Use that money to pay for your stay, you're not getting anything else out of me. Remember, no leaving until you tell me everything. I don't want to see you outside unless you're looking to find me.'

Frederick's utterances never settled lightly. Every sentence carried an aura of kindness laced with violence; he would be nice until he wasn't, until she gave him a reason not to be. What Adelina felt bubbling inside her became juxtaposed against the wild west tales she'd heard.

Without saying goodbye, Adelina left. The words of the black witch chimed within his head; he wasn't ready to believe every word that woman said either.

A flurry of new smells overwhelmed Adelina: a faint twinge of dampness, a mustiness drifting from an upstairs room, and the lingering scent of someone's dinner. The lighting was harsh against the night she'd left behind. The entrance was clean, with no peeling wallpaper or concrete floors. It was the nicest place she'd been so far, even with the old smoke of long-burned cigarettes irritating her nose.

The reception bell rang through the building. Delicate scuffling steps carried her way. Violet Smith, slight and ailing, seemed too frail for the nature of her job, but that didn't stop a smile from appearing on her wrinkled face.

'Can I help you, dear?'

Violet's voice was warm, a soft lilt that made Adelina feel at home. Only she and Margaret seemed incapable of inflicting harm.

Hoping that she would be back in her world soon, Adelina asked for a room for one week. The money grew warm in her clammy grasp. The coins needed to be explained, but she didn't know how to respond to inevitable questions. She needed to fade away, it was too easy to put women in asylums.

Frederick had given her at least twenty coins, like he emptied his spare change onto her. No pounds nor pennies like the modern day. Dishing them out onto the counter, she played dumb, trying to elicit help from Violet.

'I'm not the best at counting,' Adelina said. 'I was never any good at in school.'

A scared, timid creature of a girl. Something had happened to her; she appeared out of her depth. Dirty unwashed skin, far too pale. Bruises, cuts, grazes. The clothes, the new with the old, the woman's history was compelling.

For payment, Violet removed a third of the coins and added two as change. Adelina sighed with relief; Frederick had given her far too much. The amount should have been concerning, but the overwhelming relief made it impossible for her to think about anything else.

The floorboards and stairs creaked ominously as Violet led Adelina to her room. The guest house reminded her of a two-star hotel in an old seaside town, with décor that seemed modern to Violet but felt dated to her.

As Violet unlocked the door, a wave of stale air hit Adelina like a slap to the face. The room was small, but after spending a night in the Youngs' vardo, it felt as spacious as a grand hall. In the corner stood a fully plumbed washbasin, and across the hall, an indoor toilet. Frederick Clark, the feared gangster, could have dropped her off anywhere, at the worst and cheapest of guest houses. Maybe, there was a kind streak to him because Violet's was clean and comfortable.

After lighting the fire, Adelina clambered into bed for good. Shadows from the flames danced upon the ceiling, and she got lost within the patterns they created. She tried to occupy her thoughts with the damp and the fire. Still, a single tear rolled down her face; she was alone in a place she didn't understand.

Memories of the world she had once known spilt into her mind: drinking at the pub with friends, studying for exams, screaming at her good-for-nothing mother. As she tried to recall what happened to her, nothing came back. Only her grandma's words rang in her mind: she would have to go backwards to move forwards.

EIGHT

Embers from the long-burned fire crackled. Sunshine blistered through the moth-holed curtains, casting dappled patterns on the floor. The day was well underway. Stall holders shouted their prices. Women gossiped. Children screeched. Cars backfired. Rickety carriages clattered over the cobbles.

Adelina buttoned up the damp blouse, her clothes had never dried after she hand-washed them the previous night. The coins jingled as she hiked up the skirt. She detested the clothes, the way they itched and hung unflatteringly on her frame. With the leftover money, she wanted to purchase a new outfit.

For a moment, her modern way of thinking crept back. The moist cotton made her forget who had given her the money. She should never have thought of it as hers. If anything, it remained Frederick's. Men like him could change their mind and face no consequence. Spending the money would become her issue, not his.

Sometimes, she felt indebted to him. Frederick had placed her in a clean guesthouse in exchange for what she considered useless information. Without him, she would have been stranded. Of course, it made her question him some more, and the evil reputation he had, because, at times, he didn't seem too bad.

Nowhere else to go, even though she remembered her home. The thought of travelling back there intimidated her. The streets would be somewhat familiar, though the society would be inconceivably different. No roof over her head, no money after the journey. In the guesthouse she was safe, and she decided she would obey Frederick, in the vain hope that one morning she'd wake to her real world again.

The bland dining room was eerily quiet, too much so for the abundance of tables. With the choice hers, she sat by the window, watching the outside world pass her by through netted curtains.

Without taking an order, Violet brought breakfast to her: tea and toast. Adelina didn't care for a choice, she was ravenous.

Outside, George and Paul strode by with unshakeable confidence. They possessed an aura of authority; they could do anything to those around them without facing any repercussions.

'James,' Violet said, approaching the only other person seated. 'I almost forgot. There's another painting my husband brought back from his army days in Africa. Would you like to look at it?'

'I would love to. Are you still planning to bring the other to the gallery?'

'Of course, I think I'll have time this after…' Violet words trailed off as her attention shifted to a commotion outside. Paul had pushed over a cart, sending produce rolling across the road. 'They're not like they used to be as wee nippers.'

'Those are the men everyone talks about. They're the Clarks, aren't they?'

'Yes, I wouldn't mess with them. If you see them on the street, it's best to walk the other way.'

'Did you know them as kids?'

'Their grandmother was my chief bridesmaid. When everything happened with their parents, me and my husband looked after them. We never had kids of our own, so we had the space and money. It was better than the parish getting involved.'

So, there was a reason Frederick had dropped her off at Violet's after all. The guest house was special to him. Adelina wondered what Violet knew about her. Frederick could've instructed her to keep an eye on her. Suddenly, her privacy was ripped away.

'What happened to their parents, if you don't mind me asking?' James said. 'People who live so dangerously astound me. It makes me wonder what situations create them.'

'They were orphaned. Their mum went first. When that happened, I told them not to meddle, but their father was never good. I can't put all the blame on them, for the way they are. They didn't have a chance to stay on the straight and narrow, not in Holbeck.

I've told Dorothy to get away once she's old enough. I told her America would be best, she'd find a good husband there. You know yourself James, there's not much good left here, not after the war. I'm surprised a smart man like you hasn't already gone.'

'My family is here. Who's going to care for my mother when she gets older?'

'That's very kind of you. I hope your selflessness pays off.'

'Wait, before you go, I need to ask. You mentioned a girl's name. She doesn't frequent the dance hall or anything, does she? I want to stay clear of the Clarks, that's all. I could only imagine what would happen to a man if he was caught dancing with one of their sisters.'

'She's their niece and too young to go there. At least, I hope she doesn't go, but you never know with Dorothy.'

'They're parents? Christ, what's wrong with the world?'

'Dorothy is Etta's daughter; she's the eldest Clark kid. Only a few years and I hope Dorothy will be out of here. Those uncles of hers are awful, lost their minds they have.'

The upturned cart lay on the ground, its spilt contents trampled by passers-by. George hunched over, laughing. Paul grimaced as he launched a mushroom at a passerby. The owner stared on, slumped shoulders, nose bleeding, waiting for permission to leave. All because he'd dared to look at Paul the wrong way.

With trembling hands, Violet refilled Adelina's milk jug. James turned around, another question forming on his lips. Only then did he notice Adelina. Now, she seemed intriguing, like a girl he might want to meet at a dance hall.

Beautiful light eyes, framed by dark curled lashes that fluttered with each blink. Hair parted rather strangely, covering half of her forehead, as if on purpose. But still, those eyes, and her silky-smooth skin made her quite pretty.

Adelina peeked around inquisitively, eyes constantly darting. The city was new to her, he could tell. In a few days, the twinkle in her eye would be gone.

Adelina didn't mind his observation of her, he seemed polite, and his dashing good looks helped. James was different than the Clarks; he almost appeared regal, with his dark slicked back hair and tailored suit. He must have been ridiculously wealthy to be involved in an art gallery.

'I'm not sure if you heard me earlier,' Violet whispered to Adelina. 'If you did, please don't tell them what I said.'

'Tell who?'

'The Clarks.'

'Why would I tell them what you said?'

'Don't let them get under your skin. I know what they're like; they'll spot you from a mile off. They'll want to take advantage of a girl like you.'

'A girl like me?'

'I can see how nervous you are. It's a big city, too big for a young girl like you to be alone. I don't know how you got here or what's keeping you, but I'm trying to protect us all.'

'I didn't hear anything,' Adelina said, not wanting to discuss her reason for being in the guest house.

Tutting as she walked away, Violet made it apparent that she didn't believe her. Yesterday, Violet had come across as kind and endearing, but she changed once she sensed the lie.

'Don't fret over her, she's nervous herself,' James said. 'If you're worried about the Clarks, stay out of their way and they'll never bother you, I'm sure.'

'I'm fine, just annoyed that people keep assuming things about me. It's growing old rather quickly.'

Adelina scraped out her seat. Suddenly, the guest house made her feel trapped, like she was under a constant watch. With the nagging thoughts of her existence coming back, she needed to get out, into the fresh air.

The cold would calm her down, it always did. By going

outside, she would be disobeying Frederick's orders, but he couldn't expect her to stay locked within the same four walls forever.

'Do you know the city?' James asked, rushing after her.

'No, but I'll find out.'

'It's no place for a young woman, especially one as pretty as you.'

Adelina blushed; she wasn't used to people saying their feelings aloud – it was usually written down over text or the internet. Her generation had lost the ability to communicate their emotions in person.

'Come on,' James said. 'I'll show you around. Five minutes, to familiarise yourself, then you can go on your own if you want.'

'Ok, but only five minutes. Are you hoping the city will scare me and prove you right?'

'I only want to help; I know how dreadful the people can be around here. You're not from a city, are you?'

'No, I'm not.'

The air was bitterly cold, laced with the acrid scent of burning. Explosions echoed from nearby factories. Men screamed commands at each another as if their lives depended on it. With every boom, she jumped, unaccustomed to the roaring of an industrial city in its prime.

A shop window caught her attention; a mannequin wore a beautiful fur coat and headdress, paired with a magnificent fox shawl. A ridiculous price tag was attached, the clothes costing double her stay at the guest house. All Adelina could think about was its warmth, how it would trap heat and ward off the harsh winter.

'I guess there aren't shops like this, where you come from,' James said.

'I swear, Freddie, it weren't me,' a man cried from behind them. 'You've got it all wrong, I've never been near your Dorothy. I'd never do that to you.'

Like James, Adelina turned towards the commotion. A man pleaded for his life. Frederick's stance was wide, his figure menacing. People avoided the scuffle, keeping to themselves.

Frederick held a man by his throat, pinning him against the wall. Violence, in broad daylight, in the middle of a bustling street. No one shouted for the police. No one interfered. They turned a blind eye to the brutality.

'Spit it out then,' Frederick said. 'Tell me who she's been seeing, and I might spare you.'

'I don't know, I promise you, I'm not a liar.'

The man was a waste of time. Frederick yanked his hand back, letting him collapse. Struggling to breathe, he clawed at his neck, the bruising forming already.

People took themselves far away, fearful that Frederick would unleash his wrath on them. All except Adelina, who watched on. They were under his spell, while she was not. The Clarks didn't operate like modern gangs; they ruled the streets openly, they didn't operate in an underworld.

The beaten man curled into a foetal position, a whimper escaping him. He knew what was coming: darkness for a while, followed by an aching headache that would persist for weeks.

Adelina hurried to catch up with James. As they reached the street corner, she peeked back at the scene Frederick had created, to the blood that stained the cobbles. The attack was over, and a new target had been set. Frederick watched her as she turned onto the next street with a man he didn't recognise.

'We've got to go,' Adelina urged, quickening her pace. She couldn't let Frederick catch up; she had disobeyed his orders. 'He saw me.'

'Who?' James asked, struggling to keep up.

'Frederick Clark.'

James' heart nearly stopped; such an innocent-looking girl couldn't possibly be acquainted with him. In retrospect, he should have left her, but he didn't, he continued to follow her.

Flustered, Adelina ducked into a narrow alleyway. James collided with her as the wooden gate closed behind them. Leaning against the wall, her polyester coat clung to the bricks. James tried to hold his breath. Within minutes she turned into everyone else.

There had been a change in Frederick's face that sent her pulse soaring. She didn't know what to say to him: 'Sorry, I was going stir-crazy already. I only needed some fresh air. I went against your wishes, but I couldn't stay cooped up until I remembered everything, because I have most of my memories. I'm just missing one gigantic thing, how I bloody got here.'

For once, her wish was granted. Frederick's figure moved past, far from her hiding place. With him gone and the street empty, she emerged alongside James. Together, they made their way back to Violet's. Perhaps staying inside, battling cabin fever, was better than the perilous world outside.

'I guess you were right in the end,' Adelina admitted. 'I'm not ready to go out by myself.'

'Are you going to tell me how you know Frederick Clark?'

'Maybe another time.'

Lost in thought and seeking a pure, innocent distraction, Adelina stared at the cobbles as she walked. The alleyway behind her childhood home still had them. As a kid she played out there. Football with her sister. Water balloon fights in summer. Snowmen in winter. Knocking over wheelie bins after arguments. Running from the rats. Hiding from mum.

Eyes down, all the way back. Living inside herself. Once inside, she would relax. But life wasn't easy like that.

A pair of leather shoes stopped her in her tracks. Of course, they belonged to him. They refused to move; they sent James stepping backward. They were expensive, worth too much for an industry man.

'You didn't listen to me.'

'I was getting some fresh air, can't ban me from doing that, can you?' Adelina replied defensively, almost aggressively – or at least, that's how Frederick perceived it.

That wasn't her intention. If anything, she was confused with his attempt to control her, it seemed like he wanted to own her. It unsettled her. As a kid, her parents never questioned her as much as he did.

Frederick didn't know whether to believe her. Adelina was a stranger wrapped up in the mystery of her forgotten memory. The Italian name set him on edge. He paired that with her fiery demeanour. She reminded him of Etta and Dorothy, who both caused him far too much trouble. And there she was, having claimed she knew no one in the city, walking beside a toff.

'Who the fuck is this?' Frederick said, looking James up and down.

'James,' Adelina replied.

'James who?'

'I don't fucking know, I only met him half an hour ago at the guest house you dropped me at.'

'Can he not speak for himself?'

'James Payne, I'm staying at Violet's,' he stuttered. 'I've just got a job at the art gallery.' Frederick laughed, his attention shifting to Adelina. 'I'm looking for a house you see, moved up here, from Oxford.'

'How lovely,' Frederick said, cutting him off, not wishing to hear his backstory. 'Do you ever listen Ada?'

'Do you want a "sorry," or a, "I promise not to do it again?"' Adelina said, feeling more like her teenage self than anything else.

'What have I told you about your attitude?'

Frederick took a step closer, knowing from George that Adelina only seemed to respond to one thing. James shifted from foot to foot, torn between wanting to do the gentlemanly thing and protect her, and being too frightened of Frederick to take action.

'I know what you told me. I left the guest house because I felt trapped after finding out you're acquainted with Violet. James told me not to leave by myself. Unlike you, he was worried about my safety, not because he's distrustful of me.'

'Why aren't you afraid of me?'

'I am, I'm just used to fighting back, that's all.'

'If you were afraid, you wouldn't bother to stand up for yourself. Normally, people make themselves quiet, invisible, like

James here.'

'Of course, I'm frightened. How couldn't I be, when that pool of blood over there is because of your temper? I'm bloody petrified deep down inside.'

The words slipped past her lips without thought to the repercussions. Around him, her brain went to mush; she crumbled under his authority, acting in the wrong way entirely.

'Do what you want, go get your fresh air, but don't complain when neither I nor one of my brothers is there to help you, because James sure as shit won't do anything to protect you.'

There were more important matters to attend to than questioning her. With that, he turned away, leaving her alone with her thoughts, her mind completely consumed by him.

While he resumed his task, trying to dissolve a situation, Adelina had nothing to do, but to think. Think about him. Think about his attitude and what seemed like an infatuation with her.

'Christ, I thought you were dead,' James said.

Adelina remained silent, watching Frederick edge into the crowd. Her pulse never settled. She couldn't stop overthinking, wondering why she felt so powerless and deranged in front of him.

'Are you ok?' James asked, taking a hold of Adelina's hand.

'Yeah, just trying to sort my brain out.'

'I think I have just the thing to calm you down,' he said, taking the opportunity to invite her to go to the gallery.

Not quite knowing what else to do, she agreed. After that morning, she didn't want to go back to Violet's, and staying outside alone wasn't an option. The gallery became her best and only choice.

NINE

James observed Picasso-style paintings that Adelina had never understood. He spoke about the lines, shapes, and colours, and what they meant to him. She didn't scrutinise the art, she didn't care what splashes symbolised. Instead, she took in the decadent gallery. High ceilings, marble pillars. The sun shone through the stained glass, spilling blue, green and red upon the floor, creating artwork of its own.

Joining her in admiring the architecture, James smiled dashingly. Usually, he contemplated the art, neglecting the structure of his workplace.

'Violet should be here soon,' James said, taking a seat beside Adelina. 'She's bringing an old piece her husband acquired. My senior is interested in that medium.'

After her interaction with Violet that morning, Adelina wanted to escape her prying eyes. Half the reason she followed James was to avoid her. Instead of escaping the turbulent world of the guest house, it followed her.

'Don't worry, she'll have forgotten everything by now. Violet's memory isn't great; she forgets my name daily. She tries to remember things by writing them down on a tiny pad at the reception desk. I doubt you've made the cut.'

There were more pressing matters, but Frederick couldn't stop thinking about Adelina and James. Something felt off about them.

Bursting into the guest house, he pushed past Rebecca. Violet considered her a helper, but everyone knew the real reason she lived there. Violet liked to appear prim and proper, but she rented a room on the top floor to Rebecca on a long-term basis. Often odd noises and bangs travelled from her room, lasting late into the night.

'Freddie, what the bloody hell are you doing?' Rebecca exclaimed, stumbling up the stairs after him.

'No questions, which room is the young woman's, the one who checked in last night?'

Rebecca shook her head, unwilling to give up a woman to him when he was acting so deranged.

'Answer me. I don't have time for this.'

Erratic. Unhinged. His voice was a growl. Almost snarling, he delved into his pockets, searching for a weapon. The man before her wasn't the Frederick she knew. Believing he was capable of anything, Rebecca cracked, giving out Adelina's room.

Frederick charged across the landing, ignoring Rebecca's cries. Kicking the door, he fractured and splintered the wood, causing it to creak ajar. Violet would never believe her; she had a soft spot for the Clarks. The blame would fall on one of Rebecca's punters.

Frederick's instincts took over. He was incapable of rational thought, hellbent on finding out who Adelina was and what she was up to.

The room was empty. The only sign of life was Margaret's small bag; he wondered what was inside. Fuck it, he didn't care for her privacy. Rifling through the bag, he didn't care if he ripped or broke anything. He found nothing of interest, only a night top, a skirt, and some peculiar shoes that made no sense.

Empty wardrobes. A clutter-free bedside table. Nothing. Determined to find something, he pulled out furniture and lifted the rug. There needed to be evidence of who she was. There must have been a reason for her appearance, but Frederick found nothing.

No secrets. Nothing hidden. Adelina had told the truth. No notebook, no address jotted down. The only possessions were three things inside Margaret's paper bag. No money. No Sunday clothes. With that, he decided to be done; what he feared Adelina was needed to be left behind, or he truly would go mad.

Screaming from upstairs again. Another odd customer for Rebecca, no doubt. Dorothy wouldn't interfere, not again. Last time, she received a slap to her cheek for interrupting. Apparently, some men liked such things. The thought made Dorothy want to vomit.

The scream sounded different this time, not quite right. Curiosity got the better of her. Wiping a tear from her eye, Dorothy snuck to the bottom of the staircase. She wouldn't interrupt, she would merely find out the cause.

Thank God she hadn't made her presence known. Frederick was upstairs; she recognised her uncle's low, predatory growl. He was frenzied. He must have discovered her secret already. Bloody hell, she needed to find Violet, the only person that could help her.

Behind the reception, Dorothy shoved papers aside, searching for the leather-bound diary she'd given Violet for Christmas. Bloody Niamh, some friend she was; if it wasn't for her, she wouldn't be in such a predicament.

Armed with newfound knowledge, Dorothy made a hasty exit from the guest house. Outside, her cheeks turned wet once more. She wished she could talk to Elsie, her best friend from school. She couldn't talk to her family, they never listened, they only ever made decisions for her.

'It's Ada,' James repeated. 'Don't you remember her from this morning?'

'Eee, I almost didn't recognise her; she looks different in this light.'

Not buying the excuse, Adelina approached James while Violet got lost in a painting.

'Aren't you worried that some awful person might get wind of Violet's problem and exploit or steal from her?'

'Do you really think that could happen to a woman who helped raise the Clarks?'

With a clatter, a young girl, not even sixteen, burst into the space. Upon seeing Violet, she burst into tears, overcome with emotion, barely able to stand. To Adelina, the girl appeared as a young, incredibly afraid teenager, but to the world, Dorothy was an adult.

James instinctively came to Dorothy's side, crouching down towards her. In hushed tones, he tried to soothe her, mentioning he had younger sisters and she could speak to him. Offering her his hand, he attempted to lead her towards his office, away from the public setting.

'Will you shut up? I'm not going with you. I can do what I bloody want. My mother's maiden name is Clark, so I suggest you leave me alone.'

The youngest of the family; the weak link, the cause for concern. Frederick had mentioned her earlier, and now here she was, flustered, in Adelina's presence.

Teenagers could become upset for numerous reasons. What seemed minuscule to adults often felt like the end of the world to them. Adelina remembered her own meltdowns at school; no problem felt small when overwhelmed by hormones.

With James no longer interfering, Violet placed a wrinkled hand on the Dorothy's back. Leaving them alone, James moved into the next room, not wanting to upset another Clark. Adelina stayed, staring at the scene wide-eyed.

'Tell James to make us a cup of tea, love,' Violet said. 'Now Dolly, have you fallen out with Isla or Niamh again?'

In Violet's comforting presence, Dorothy began to calm down, with only small sniffles escaping her. Still, she wasn't sure if she could reveal the truth.

'I'll leave you two alone,' Adelina said as she returned with tea made by James.

'Wait, Dorothy might benefit from speaking to someone closer to her age. Niamh–'

Adelina shifted, turning towards James, who was dealing with disgruntled customers. The public couldn't see such a scene; it would only tarnish the gallery's reputation.

As Adelina's hair swished, the sagging stitches in her hairline became visible. Recognition washed over Dorothy. Her stance changed; no longer confrontational, she became inquisitive, not wanting Adelina to leave.

'You're Ada, aren't you?'

The night prior, Dorothy had sneaked into her family's office. Etta tried to control everything she did, she couldn't go to her for anything. Due to the pickle she'd got herself in, Dorothy needed some money, and with no business willing to employ her, the only option was to steal from the safes.

Tiptoeing into the building, she noted the hushed voices of her uncle and mother. They never told her anything, always keeping her in the dark. Pressing her ear against the thin wall, she eavesdropped on their conversation.

'This Ada, she's going to be trouble for you,' Etta laughed. 'I can feel it now.'

Bloody good, Dorothy thought, pulling away from the wall and stuffing coins into her pockets. They would never know she had been there. Once the missing money was discovered, they would blame Paul. Everyone knew he helped himself to the stash, and he was doing it more frequently.

'You know Freddie, don't you?' Dorothy asked.

'I barely know him.'

Adelina could have said more, but Dorothy reminded her of the popular girls at school – the ones who thought they knew best and would do anything to maintain their status.

Dorothy knew Adelina was lying. The woman before her wasn't just anyone – she wasn't just a mystery or even a stranger – she was the girl who had appeared in her cards. Dorothy considered warning her, but she knew telling her wouldn't change anything.

Violet frowned. A clouded memory lingered from earlier in the day. Adelina couldn't be acquainted with Frederick; the connection struck fear in her, and she couldn't understand why.

'Now, can we stop interrupting each other,' Violet said. 'Are you upset because of Isla or Niamh?'

'No, it's worse than that,' Dorothy replied.

'Spit it out then.'

'Promise me you won't be upset, or annoyed, and you won't tell my mum.'

When Dorothy's grandmother died, Violet vowed to protect the entire family. It was her duty to listen, whether it was the worst news or teenage drama. Reluctantly, she promised not to speak a word.

'I'm late. I'm knocked up. I know I am. I didn't know what to do, so I spoke to Niamh, but the rat-faced bitch went to Freddie. Wants to win him over she does. He's gone ballistic. I'm hiding from him. I can't see him, Vi, he's going to kill me. He'll throw me in the canal himself. It's not just my age or that I'm not married. It's whose kid I've got inside of me.'

Violet swallowed, unable to form words. No clattering of heels. No doors banged between the rooms. No murmurs from the outside. Time itself seemed to stop.

As an unmarried fifteen-year-old Dorothy shouldn't have understood such things, let alone have been in such a predicament. Despite how enraged Violet was, Dorothy needed to be shielded from her uncles.

To be pregnant in the modern day at fifteen was terrible, let alone in 1919. Adelina blamed the lack of education; those who didn't learn, ended up in such situations. After all, that was what school used to say. Regardless, teenagers still fell pregnant, even with all the knowledge and contraceptive methods.

Dorothy's main concern was not her age but her marital status. Having grown up in the twenty-first century, Adelina had a different perspective on sex before marriage. In her time, society was more permissive, with people often engaging in casual sex and relying on protection to avoid consequences. At university, her friends created score sheets, awarding points for drunken hook-ups. With preventatives for pregnancy and diseases, the world changed.

'And who's the father?' Violet inquired, her voice tense.

'Harry Allanson.'

'Harry who went to school with George? Harry who knocks

about with Charlie Black?' Violet asked, praying she had misremembered. 'This Harry is going to marry you, right?'

Dorothy shrugged; she didn't know how Harry would react, as she hadn't mustered enough courage to tell him yet.

'Jesus Christ, Dorothy, you should have known better. Look at what happened to your mum,' Violet said. 'We need to go somewhere private. People can't hear this. You know how the rumour mill works.'

'I don't know if I can marry him. Freddie and George despise him; he's one of Charlie's lads for God's sake. Paul would murder him if he had the chance. Harry left France after a week with a bullet wound to his foot. They think he's a coward, but he swears it was enemy fire.'

'Why him, of all people?'

A loud bang ricocheted through the gallery. Scurrying feet and harsh breaths followed. Dorothy sprang up. A male voice shouted her name, moving through the corridors and inspecting each room. With each shout, his voice grew louder and more agitated.

Dorothy hid behind Violet, trying to avoid the inevitable confrontation. Even then, she didn't regret her choice to be with Harry. She was a young girl in love, and ever since she met him, she adored him.

In a way, courting Harry was her way of rebelling, of defying her family. Adelina would smoke in the alleyway behind her home and drink in the park at night, but she lived in a different world, one with fewer restraints.

'It's Paul. How did they know I was here?'

George and Paul Clark bounded through the streets. Earlier that day, Frederick had told them Niamh's news. Bloody Dorothy, always causing trouble – trust her to get knocked up. If anything, George had seen it coming. A few months ago, Isla had warned him that Dorothy was going off the rails. Just like her mother, she wouldn't listen to anyone.

George couldn't wait to get his hands on the bastard who had touched Dorothy. Paul looked forward to the torture; it had been a while, at least a matter of days, since his hands had gotten dirty.

As they passed The Kings Arms, the pub across from the train station, they noticed a familiar face: Harold Wallace, the old troublemaker. He was brilliant at selling their stolen cigarettes. His trick was to hassle the better-natured people, those unfamiliar with the city, as they exited the station. After spouting some bullshit, most would throw some change at him to leave them alone.

'Now then, Harold,' George shouted. 'You seen our Dorothy?'

'As a matter of fact, I have. About half an hour ago, heading up that way, in quite a hurry she was.'

George chucked a pound note at Harold for the information. The brothers changed direction, heading out of their jurisdiction into a part of the city where being a Clark meant they'd be subject to interrogation.

'How much further do you reckon she went?' Paul said, feeling uneasy about being out of their area without protection.

'What business would she have down here?'

'Something doesn't feel right, maybe we should turn back.'

A car crawled beside them. George itched towards his gun. Paul prepared to fight bare fist. They turned, weapons ready.

'Get in,' Frederick demanded. 'Why are you over this way? I thought you were going to Niamh's?'

'Harold Wallace saw Dorothy going down here,' George muttered, his adrenaline refusing to settle as he obeyed his brother's orders. 'Do you know where she is?'

'She's going to see Violet. Who else has she got to talk to? She's pissed off her real family.'

'The guest house ain't this way,' George said.

'Violet is at the gallery. Rebecca showed me Vi's diary.'

'Is that the only business you've had with Rebecca today?' Paul asked, starting to feel relaxed with another man as back up. George stifled his giggle as best as he could; Rebecca was one of the worst working lasses, as stiff as a bloody board at times.

'Bloody hell, I haven't stooped as low as Rebecca, I'm not you,' Frederick said, taking his brothers off guard for a second. 'I was over that way, sorting that Ada out. Doing my head in, she is.'

'Sorting her out?' Paul said, his elbow digging into Frederick's side.

That wasn't what he'd meant. George didn't laugh. It wasn't like Frederick to admit such things. George wondered why he hadn't punished her like he would any other girl who disobeyed his orders.

James edged out of Adelina's view. There was a one-sided conversation before feet scraped across the floor. A crack. A thud. The women's bodies stiffened, bracing themselves for the brothers' wrath.

Adelina began to create her own stories about the Clarks. Feared by all, even their own niece. She should never have accepted money from Frederick. She had been a snitch, a grass. In theory, she had worked for a gang. God, she should have run away and fended for herself.

The three men looked like they'd risen from hell, their black clothes making them appear like demons, looming over the innocent James who struggled to stand.

Paul's crazed eyes darted around the room. He was menacing, likely on something. George smirked, leaning against the wall, knocking a painting askew. James struggled to stand, scrambling like a deer on ice. Blood dripped down his face, soaking his once crisp white shirt. Adelina tried to hide her disdain; they'd injured a man and carried out the attack with so much enthusiasm.

Frederick noticed her face twitch. They were drawn to one another despite everything crumbling around them. She was everywhere he went, in the middle of all his problems.

The nurse inside Adelina emerged. Moving forward, she went to treat the man who'd tried to be a hero. She wanted to scream at the brothers, ask why they'd been so cruel, why they still hovered near him when he would never go near them again.

Frederick became captivated by her actions, as if he'd come for her and not Dorothy. Adelina persuaded James to sit down so she could clean him up. Surrounded by his attackers, he shuffled to a window seat, his legs vibrating and nearly giving way beneath him.

The family needed privacy. Violet led Dorothy towards James' office, George and Paul followed whilst Frederick remained. Adelina didn't take kindly to stares that were unrequited. The Clarks enraged her; they acted like animals, attacking others without any real reason. Growing irritated, her attention drifted to Frederick. When she caught his eye, it wasn't harsh like she expected. The look seemingly softened as she turned.

'Why are you looking at me?' Adelina asked, trying to sound threatening, but her voice came out much sweeter than she intended.

Frederick didn't respond, he left her alone instead. After his scavenger hunt at the guest house, he no longer viewed her as a threat. He tried to believe her memory loss story. If anything, he found himself wanting to protect her from the city.

To feel such a way, towards a relative stranger, was peculiar. Frederick had a ruthless reputation and usually he wouldn't care, but he did with her. Maybe, it was the way John and Thomas attacked her that made him want to care for her. Somehow, she reminded him of Etta.

No, it wasn't that. Frederick knew fine well why he made exceptions for Adelina, though he couldn't bring himself to admit the truth. At least, not yet.

With Frederick gone and her heart rate settling, Adelina took to cleaning James' wound. On closer inspection, it was nothing more than a few scratches – the type a child would get falling over in the playground. James didn't seem tough nor strong. From the way he fell to the floor, it was clear he had never been in a fight before.

'I'd heard stories about them before I came here. I didn't think it could be worse up here than in London, but it is,' James said. 'Were you a nurse, in the war? You come across like that type of person. You put yourself in harm's way to help me.'

James analysed her features, eyes dashing over her. Adelina didn't mind; it gave her time to think, to relay her life story. Her imagination failed her, conjuring nothing. Instead, she shook her head, disagreeing with his statement. She needed to be careful, it would be easy to fail to fit in.

Instead of making small talk as she cleaned his grazes, she continually looked over to his office, wondering what was going on inside. Every now and then a harsh noise sounded that she struggled to place. There was something intriguing about the Clark family. Adelina prayed that by staying to help James she wasn't being naïve and foolish.

TEN

With drawn velvet curtains, stained ornate rugs, and tatty old furniture, James' office was dreary compared to the rest of the gallery. Paul poked at the fire, the only light source, making the flames grow. Frederick leaned against the wall, chain-smoking, his eyes firmly upon his niece. The thick smoky air washed out their figures.

The women sat on the sofa, under the watchful eyes of the men. Violet attempted to console Dorothy, gently rubbing smooth circles on her back. She didn't need comforting; her blood was boiling. Her uncles only cared about their reputations, and she wanted nothing to do with them. Everyone saw her as a Clark, a person tied to them, not as her own being.

'Final warning,' Frederick said. 'Tell me who the father is.'

A stubborn silence. Dorothy folded her arms defiantly.

'Oway,' Paul urged.

'Bloody hell, Paul, do one will you,' Dorothy snapped. 'You couldn't give a toss; you don't care about anybody these days. The only thing you think about is your flask and the vial in your fucking pocket.'

Paul's eyes narrowed. He longed to find a release in violence, but he couldn't bring himself to beat his own niece. At least, not yet.

Dorothy's attempt to destabilise the family wound Frederick up. She didn't appreciate how lucky she was, to not be homeless or in a workhouse like other kids her age.

'Can you all stop swearing. Have some respect,' Violet said. 'Dorothy, your grandmother hated such words. She would've washed your mouth out with soap.'

'She would have done a lot worse to her, given the situation she's gotten herself into,' George said.

'Cut the bullshit. Tell me who the father is,' Frederick said. 'Any of your friends will tell me if I ask.'

Of course, they would. Frederick always got his way. It would be best if the truth came from Dorothy. That way, she could see his face drop. Finally, she could hurt him the way he hurt others.

'Fine, have it your way. The father of my bastard kid is Harry Allanson.'

The brothers were stunned, Harry was the worst kind of man. Frederick stormed to the easel holding an almost-finished painting of a barely dressed woman. With one swift move, he punched through the canvas.

'What are you doing?' Dorothy exclaimed. 'That might have been worth something.'

'Do you think I fucking care? Don't you dare talk to me like that again. And don't think Harry has gotten away with what he's done. I'm going to find him, and I don't need to spell out what I'm going to do.'

Harry the coward. He'd shot himself in the foot to get out of the war when he was called up. They'd grown up together, born only a few doors down from the Clark's family home. As young lads, they played football on the streets. Despite going to school with the Clarks, he hid behind Charlie Black, Frederick's main rival. If Frederick saw Harry now, he might just kill him.

At the heart of it, Frederick only wanted to protect his family. He longed to provide for them, to bring stability and money. That was why he turned to certain illegal dealings because being on the straight and narrow would only keep them in poverty.

Dorothy rebelled with the wrong man. She thought she was in control, but at her age, how could she be? Harry had taken advantage of her, knowing who her uncles were. The sly dog probably slept with her to get one up over them. Harry couldn't have been in love, not with their age difference. If anything, Harry was a bloody pervert.

With no one guarding the door, Dorothy seized the chance to

escape. She didn't know where she was going, but she needed to leave; she couldn't stand the sight of her uncles any longer.

'Violet, go after her. Make sure she doesn't go back to that piece of scum,' Frederick ordered.

Violet dawdled through the gallery, her withered body holding her back. She wasn't going anywhere fast.

Frederick lost control, unable to contain his rage. He shoved a frame, sending it clattering to the floor. Books were swept to the ground. The office became a jumbled mess around him. His brothers watched, unsure whether to intervene or join in.

'Do me a favour,' Frederick said through harsh breaths. 'Go to the guest house, make sure Rebecca's out. Break into all the rooms. Muddle things up. Pay off anyone who sees you. I did something terrible earlier.'

'Why would you want us to do that to Violet?' Paul asked, forgetting his brother's fragile state of mind.

'Because we fucking need to. That girl outside has gotten into my head, running me around in circles. I found her wandering the city with that art freak earlier, so I broke into her room at Violet's, looking for answers. Rebecca saw it all. Like I said, I can't figure out why I bloody did it.'

George chuckled; a woman getting inside of Frederick's mind was a rare occurrence.

'We were never at the guest house, alright? Take my car. After it's done, find Violet and tell her we'll pay for the damages.'

'You best watch yourself brother,' George said, patting Frederick's back. 'Y'know what women are like, look at Effie.'

'Your office is quite a mess, James,' Frederick shouted, ignoring his brother. 'Might want to clean it up before your boss sees.'

Needing to see the damage for himself, James scampered into his room. Adelina wanted to ask why Frederick would trash the office, but she knew better. Words would only get her into all sorts of trouble with him.

'Why did you come here, to the gallery?' Frederick asked as he approached Adelina.

'I didn't want to go back to the guest house,' she replied, hoping the truth would keep her on his good side. 'I know what you're thinking. You told me to be careful. Violet said a few things about your family earlier and asked me not to repeat them. I was defensive, wondering why she'd think I'd go running to you. I wanted to avoid her after that.'

'Yet I found you here with her.'

'If I knew she was coming here, I would have gone to the guest house.'

'Hindsight,' Frederick muttered.

Once the brothers left, Adelina helped James to put his office back together. For what seemed like hours, they spoke idly to one another. James was twenty-five and one of six siblings. Before the war, he studied art history at Oxford. *Posh*, Adelina thought.

After graduating, he enrolled in the army. All his brothers served, and it felt wrong to waffle on about art whilst they fought. He said nothing more about the war. He spoke without opinions, stating nothing but facts. Everything, from the war to his family life, seemed forced, as if he would break down if he delved deeper.

Adelina was equally vague about her own life, and James didn't press. One wrong move and she could end up in a padded cell. Her life couldn't become meaningless. In an asylum or hospital, there would be no way out, no way home, to the future she understood and felt comfortable in, but didn't really miss.

James shared his plans for the future – a simple dream of living in the countryside, far from the city's troubles. As he spoke, a smile swept across him. He was no longer on edge, his fear of the Clarks momentarily forgotten.

Adelina also began to relax. The gallery's peaceful, quiet walls allowed her to breathe. She should have taken the opportunity to contemplate her existence, because the serenity was soon ripped away.

Frederick returned, his heavy, bounding steps eerily familiar. Adelina was taken aback by his appearance. Within the time apart, he'd unravelled. Creased clothes, rips at his waistcoat, blood pouring from a gash on his cheek.

'You need to go,' Frederick said. 'There's been a break-in at the guest house.'

'Did they do that to you?' Adelina asked.

'They? No... No, the thieves didn't do this. I've been to Har–'

'There's been a robbery?' James interrupted.

'Yes. Someone broke in. They stole some things.'

'I need to go. Aren't you coming Ada?'

Part of Adelina wanted to go with James to see for herself what had happened. After all, she didn't want to be alone with Frederick after witnessing his violence twice in one day. However, her kind nature, how she never wanted anyone to be in pain, took over her decision. Adelina's downfall was wanting people to be ok, all the time, and that could never be possible.

'I'll see you later. He's got a nasty cut, I need to check it.'

James' face dropped; he thought she would go with him, not stay with a man that thrived off brutality. Alone and disappointed, he wandered from the gallery.

Blood oozed from Frederick's torn skin. His eye swelled from the impact. The laceration would need stitches, to not get infected.

'I don't suppose you carry a medical kit with you, for times like these?' Adelina said, adopting a gentle bedside manner, hoping to elicit some form of happiness from him. 'I suppose you get yourself in situations like this quite often.'

The robbery didn't concern her; the belongings meant nothing to her. The only thing of value was Frederick's money and that stayed within her pocket. All that mattered was him, that he would be alright like everyone else.

'Are you a nurse?'

'I'm not fully qualified.'

Adelina removed her jacket, needing to apply pressure to the wound. There was nothing else to subdue the bleeding and it needed to be controlled. The liquid leaked down his neck, splattering onto the marble floor.

'You remember something.'

Adelina paused; she vaguely remembered attending university, but the truth escaped her without a second thought. 'Qualified' – she didn't know if it was the right word for the era. God, she gave herself away far too easily to him.

'I somewhat remember,' she said soft and swiftly. 'You need stitches.'

Frederick looked at her with the same stony expression he always wore. But being so close to his eyes, it felt like she could see the cogs turning inside of his mind.

'I can do the stitches,' Adelina offered, wondering if he'd grown quiet because of that. 'If you don't want to go to hospital.'

'No, I'll drive myself. Go back to the guest house, see if your things are still there.'

Adelina obeyed, fearful of the reprimand if she fell out of line. The blood-soaked coat within her hands. An odd tension seemingly growing between them, that she didn't know how to describe.

The guest house was chaotic. Swarms of people searched for missing items. The door to her room hung ajar, cracks splintering through the wood with a clear boot stamped on the white stain. Margaret's bag on the floor, open, contents rifled through.

The jacket slipped from her grasp. The walk back had almost given her hypothermia. Since leaving the gallery, she had clung to it. Frederick's blood marked the polyester, leaving a dark, damp crust. It was unwearable in its current state, and it would remain stained, but she couldn't dispose of it. He'd tainted her possession forever. It would aways remind her of him, and with the weather, she had no choice but to keep it.

The street bustled below. A robbery, in broad daylight, how peculiar. The location was strange too, out of all the hotels and guest houses in the city, a criminal had chosen one linked to the Clarks. Either they were daft or something else was going on.

Eyes burned into her head, snapping her out of her daydream.

George rested against the doorframe, his face settling into a smile. Always jovial, the typical youngest sibling, never taking anything too serious.

'It's terrible what happened,' George said. 'They've made a right mess.'

Unlike him, she didn't find the break in funny.

'Violet's going to have to shut up shop, sort this place out. 'Cos of that, Freddie's asked me to collect you.'

'That doesn't surprise me.'

Adelina's life was up in the air once more. Every night spent in a different place, never getting to know a location for long enough. Following Frederick's orders was the only option, without him she wasn't sure she would survive. The world she found herself in was unlike hers, and every person that meandered down the street started to frighten her. Without Frederick, she had no protection, and she started to long for that from him.

ELEVEN

The familiar Clark offices before them, just as grim as the day before. Rain fell onto Adelina's bare skin. George walked ahead, letting her trail behind. Something told him, that she wasn't going to run away, that she'd learnt her lesson about how harsh Leeds could be.

George didn't understand Frederick's obsession with her, she seemed like anybody else. Loads of girls were just as pretty as Adelina, many of them were also far away from home, like her, but Frederick never acted so irrationally towards them.

Thoughts of women occupied his mind. Neither of his older brothers were married, despite being in their late twenties. Only he had a wife and children. Paul enjoyed the single life, going down to the docks without any hassle, he couldn't tie a girl down if he tried. Frederick was far more complicated.

In some ways, the war affected Frederick the most. Before France, there had been a woman he intended to marry. War got in the way of their union, and when he returned, it was too late.

Effie waited for years for the war to end, but before Frederick returned, she learnt of her family's plans. The lure of Australia, the money the government gave to families to establish farms, it was like a dream for them. She faced a difficult choice: leave and never see Frederick again, or stay in Leeds, alone with no family, hoping that Frederick would return to marry her.

George and Paul were demobilised before Frederick. They left as rambunctious boys, returning as mere shadows of their former selves. And Robert, well, he never returned. That made Effie's choice simple. She moved before Frederick came back from France, never seeing his face again, though carrying the small army photograph with her to the other side of the world.

A year ago, they were still at war. During that time, there had been fleeting romances, but none came close to Effie. If anything, she had broken him.

Ida and Frederick weren't courting; he simply saw her in his spare time. There was hope at first that she might make him forget. If anything, Ida made him think of Effie more; he missed their innocent youthful love.

Adelina moved past George, who stood in a trance. Without needing to be ushered in, she entered the offices. Whenever George remembered the war, he became stuck in the past, reliving the never-fading memories of the trenches. He couldn't deal with business; he needed to take the edge off the day.

The bustling office. Paperwork piled high upon desks. Writing on the chalkboard. Money exchanged brazenly. The same place but with a different atmosphere to the day prior. The workers shifted their gaze to Adelina, gossiping as she trampled towards Frederick's room.

Tapping on the frosted glass, the door creaked open, unveiling him at his desk. Hard at work, as if he ran a proper business and not something illegal. Unlike the day before, he was quick to look up.

'You didn't,' Adelina began, noticing the still leaking wound. Handkerchiefs scorched with blood laid on his desk. He'd never gone to hospital like he said he would.

'Sit down,' Frederick interrupted, pulling a liquor cart towards him. 'How're you feeling?'

'I'm fine, how's your head?' Adelina said. All she cared about was the cut, nothing else.

'How's your memory?' He replied, not wanting to divulge anything about himself. He didn't care for his graze, so why should she.

'Not as good as it should be,' she said honestly.

'But you remember some things, like training to be a nurse.'

'I can't remember how I got here, no matter how hard I try. I recognise nothing. It's like I can't comprehend this world.'

'I assume you want to go back home?'

'Yes, eventually, when I've got money of my own,' she lied, trying to find excuses that would make sense to him.

'If you go back there, to your childhood home, are you certain you still live there? The Youngs found you down here, not up there.'

'You're right,' she admitted.

'You'd need a lot of money if you went back and then realised you moved away years ago. You don't want to put yourself in further danger.'

'I know, that's why I need to wait, and get money of my own.'

Frederick sipped on his drink, mulling over his words. Her life was in peril just sitting before him. She shivered lightly, the coat still across her lap. Against the grand chair, she looked small and lost.

'I can take you to another guest house with the rest of the money I gave you. Or there is another option that might be safer for you in the long run. It'll give you a chance to save up so when you do go north, you'll have a safety net.'

'I'm not sure I want to know the second option.'

Adelina repositioned herself, trying to understand his game. His actions pedantically thought out; he had a reason for every word that moved past his lips.

'I only offer it because there is a part of me that wants to believe every word you say.'

'Are we going over this again?' Adelina sighed, feeling frustrated by his scepticism.

'You're clearly educated. I doubt you were raised like I was, if you've been training to be a nurse.'

'It's wrong to make assumptions, you don't know me. I had...' Adelina nearly told her life story, about how she grew up in the worst ways. To him, it would seem like nothing. The poverty of her childhood wasn't on the same scale as his. 'Yes, I'm educated.'

God knows how she made it to university. At times, she'd taken the mick at school. As a teenager, she often bunked off. At sixteen, she left school with barely any qualifications. It took a harsh event to set her on the right tracks, one that she hadn't remembered yet.

'That's sorted then,' he said. 'You can start tomorrow.'

'I don't understand,' she said, thinking she'd misunderstood him because her childhood had been flashing through her mind. 'Start what? You never told me about the second option.'

'I'm offering you a job, here, at my company. You'll be paid well. Then, when you're ready, you can go home and see if it really is home. If it isn't, you'll have money left over, to tide you through until you find a flat, another job. See, I'm helping you.'

'This isn't a company. It's not a safe place. Why do you even want to help me?'

'We have some legitimate betting stalls at racecourses in York, Ripon, and Thirsk. We own a club in town too.'

'I don't think I can help with any of that. You've made a business out of terrorising people. You're probably washing money through this *legitimate* business. I don't want to work for such morally corrupt people.'

'You'll work here, nowhere else. You'll do admin, paperwork. Nothing morally wrong,' Frederick coughed. 'Then, when we need you, when we're injured, we'll have you. Our own private nurse.'

'You want to use me for my skills? You act like you want to help me, but you only care about yourself. I may be lost, but it's wrong to take advantage of that. I'm a good person. I don't want trouble. I don't want to be involved with you. I don't understand your business, and I don't want to.'

No, she couldn't work for him; she was a lawful person, not violent like him. She wanted to walk out of the office, away from the Clarks forever. As she attempted to leave, he dashed in front of her, blocking her path.

'You won't make it alone out there. Trust me. I helped you with the guest house. Now I'm willing to go further: employ you, give you somewhere to live. You'd be on the streets if it weren't for me. If it weren't for George finding you yesterday, what would you have done? Ask yourself, is giving you a job and a means to go home, taking advantage of you?'

No. Adelina shook her head.

Frederick's words made unsettling sense. Without his offer, she would have nothing. There would be terrible situations, ones she couldn't fight back from. There was never really a choice; her only option was to follow him with the hope he would protect her. Then, one day, hopefully, she would mysteriously return to her previous life. Even as she thought it, she knew it was a pipe dream.

Of course, Frederick wanted to take advantage of her situation; he wanted to use her knowledge. He had plans that unsettled even him. A nurse at his disposal, that would blindly follow him, could make his family great. He needed her, but she needed him too, and she decided to profit from that. In a way, she had some power over him.

'Answer me this, do you want me close because you need me, to help you, or do you still not trust me, and who I say I am?'

'In some ways you're a threat. I can't deny what the black witch said to me.'

'Freddie,' Paul shouted, barging into the office. 'George has gotten into trouble at The Kings Arms, he's with Charlie fucking Black's lads.'

'Bloody hell, what's he done now?'

'Not sure, but y'know what he can be like after a drink.'

'Isla's not heading over there, is she?' Frederick asked, rummaging through drawers, and stuffing his pockets with bullets.

'She doesn't know, her and Lydia have gone to the pictures.'

'Jesus, maybe we're paying them too much,' Frederick muttered.

'You can't go,' Adelina said, sending Paul snorting; a lass trying to tell Frederick what to do was ridiculous. 'I'm serious. Your head, you never got the stitches.'

'Do you think that matters right now?' Paul chuckled.

'Stay here Ada, I won't be long.'

The side of him people spoke of awakened. His eyes blazed,

and his chest rose and fell drastically. A different lower tone to his voice. She'd witnessed it before, but now she decided to wait and help in the aftermath. It was the only option. The Clarks would protect her; no one would dare go near her because she would work for them, a family everyone was terrified of.

'Once I get back, I'll let you see to the scuff then.'

Most people ran away from him, despite any circumstance. No one waited for him to return. He wondered if she would stay and be true to her word. If her reason to wait was naivety or something else entirely.

TWELVE

Charlie black was a rotten no-good gangster and self-declared ladies' man. If a woman ended up in his bed, he paid for the privilege. That's what George said when Charlie's men harassed him at the pub.

If Frederick or Paul had accompanied him, they wouldn't have done anything. They took advantage of George on a rough day. It wasn't often that you got a Clark alone, without any back up.

As the argument started, the landlord, who paid the Clarks for protection, instructed one of their runners to go to the office and inform them of the situation. That information sent Paul and Frederick pounding towards The King's Arms.

George invited Charlie's lads outside, away from the newly decorated pub, so they wouldn't ruin it. After all, he didn't want to refurnish the building when their blood would be draped across the premises like new curtains.

Rain steadily fell, forming puddles in the dips of the cobbles. Oil lamps cast a dim glow across the sodden street. Only George and the other men squared up to one another.

'Now, who am I having first?'

Lawrence stepped forwards, aiming to punch George's cheek. Moving too fast, he slipped on a cobble and stumbled forward. George punched him in the gut, causing him to stagger away, spluttering.

The next one came, but now George was ready for the fight. Gradually, he kept the men at bay. The winner of a race isn't always the fastest. His goal wasn't to knock them all out at one. He would dodge them, let them tire themselves out. Then, he would pick them off.

Paul bounced towards the scene, swigging from his cannister, and swallowing some pills, fresh from the docks. He thrived on the exhilaration that came with an old-fashioned fist fight.

Edward pounced, hands finding the lapels of George's coat. An ear-piercing scream. Edward tugged madly, trying to release his palms from George. Seizing the opportunity, Lawrence rushed to his feet. He never saw Paul approach. With one fist he was out cold. The next man was taken on with great enthusiasm.

Frederick flicked his cigarette at Edward's feet. Gripping his collar, he ripped him backwards. Edward's palms split open, contents falling to the floor. Skin dangled from the fishhooks behind the lapels of George's coat.

'Oh, fucking hell Freddie,' George said. 'Isla's going to kill me.'

Pissed off with Edward's shrieking, Frederick shoved him. Wishing to shut him up for good, Paul slammed his foot down. George applauded his brothers, ready to make a joke.

'Get down,' Joe Black said, leaving the safety of the shadows. He'd watched it all, not coming to the aid of his comrades, but waiting to take the Clarks off guard.

Joe reached for his gun; he would shoot them as they begged for their lives, he would make his uncle proud. Frederick wasn't going to die outside of The King's Arms, of all places. He knew Joe would be waiting, that's what the little bastard did. Frederick pulled his trigger before Joe had a chance to react.

THIRTEEN

The brothers' voices faded. At times, Adelina felt like she could hear distant roars of pain. The industry never ceased to stop, churning and squealing. Surrounded by a constant noise, from the factories to the workers passing by.

Adelina imagined the men as nothing but frenzied beasts. Violent words met with fists and knives. A crack sounded through the air; it didn't sound like a clap from the factory next door, but more akin to something she'd heard in a movie before.

The air grew cooler, the night drew in. With no fire, her skin prickled. The tainted jacket waited for her to reach a tipping point, where she would become coated in him.

Footsteps carried towards the office, sauntering into the main room. Laughter echoed. The books shook against the wooden frames. Fight or flight. Adelina feared the worst. There was only one weapon she knew how to use.

'Did you see his fucking face?' George laughed, trailing his hands across unorganised papers, not caring if they spiralled to the floor. Turning to Paul, he raised his hands, mimicking a gun. Lifting his hand up to cock it, he mouthed *pow,* pretending to shoot him.

Staggering, Paul groaned, falling towards a desk. More papers drifted across the floor, and through the open door to Frederick's office. They didn't care what was written upon them; all they felt was elation and success in winning and living another day.

The revelry made them oblivious. They didn't see Adelina emerge from the office. They paid no attention as she leant against the door frame, bottle in hand. In the end, she didn't need the glass as a weapon. Instead, she kept a hold of the liquor in case they were injured.

They beheld wide smiles, adrenaline still thumping through their bodies. They dealt most of the blows. Their clothes were wrinkled, their hair out of place. Their bruised and bloody knuckles spoke their story.

Paul formed a gun with one hand while gripping his make-belief wound with the other. The motion of his hand titling caused George to stumble. Completely unaware of her presence even though she stood in the doorway, watching their imaginative play. The brothers acted like young kids, not fully-grown adults.

George flailed his limbs, crashing into a filing cabinet. Hands gripped at his stomach, struggling to keep his intestines inside of his body. The overreaction, the simple game, she started to laugh. The brothers tried to convince everyone of their hard ways. Earlier, they appeared so menacing to her. As they engaged in childish play, they looked the opposite.

Noticing Adelina, Paul dropped his hand, his gun. She had stayed whilst they fought, as if she wasn't scared, as if she was one of them. With a sick groan, Goerge formed his hand into a gun, cocking it at Paul. With him no longer engaged in the action, he followed his stare, his body moving towards Adelina.

'Pow,' George said, his hand still raised.

The excitement drained from his voice. Embarrassment crept over him. For some unbeknown reason, Adelina immersed herself in the game; she fell forward, hand gripping at her side. With dramatic moans, she crashed into a desk, flinging the bottle on top. Spinning round, she fired her own gun at George. With the completion, she winked at him. Science class games.

The Clarks' excitement was contagious. The game transported her back to being a kid with family. The Clarks were easy to be around when they were jovial. For that short interaction, she forgot the different century, how she didn't belong in their world.

'Enjoying yourself,' Frederick said, leaning against the wall, observing them. 'Are you?'

Stern words, like he didn't approve of their exchange. Flushing cold, Adelina dropped her hand. She gave herself away, screaming from the rooftops that she didn't belong. A lady wouldn't have acted like that; they might have wanted to partake, but social conventions wouldn't allow them.

But women did act like that, behind closed doors and in front of family, especially in the Clarks' world. George cackled at her sudden change of expression; she wasn't scared of fighting, but words intimidated her.

'Right,' she said, flattening out her skirt, ensuring her modesty once again. 'A cloth or something.'

Before she finished her sentence, Frederick sent a handkerchief flying her way. Like in the gallery, she went straight to her duty.

Adelina doused the material in liquor. She didn't question the alcohol's quality nor its age, she hoped it could easily be replaced. Paul and George weren't overjoyed – they looked after themselves, they didn't need her.

'Ada was training to be a nurse,' Frederick said. 'I've invited her to help us before she returns north.'

They'd never discussed needing outside help. A stranger shouldn't be within their ranks. Frederick often left them in the dark, but recently the frequency of it disgruntled them. At times, he ordered them to do tasks without a care for their lives.

The newfound silence, the questioning look upon Paul's face. Adelina needed them to come around to the idea of her. Without their approval, she would have nothing. Without Frederick and the job, she would be alone and vulnerable in a world she didn't know or understand. He was giving her a chance to remember, a way to solve her situation.

Adelina coaxed George over. The alcohol and rag were her only tools. His knuckles were grazed and bleeding. Despite his hands showing the battle he'd clearly fought, he had no further wounds. Without a thank you, George moved away, leaving her to treat Paul.

Whilst George attempted to make small talk, Paul remained

silent. As she cleaned his injuries, she waited for him to wince or pull away, but he remained stiff as if he felt no pain. A rigid stance, a disposition to not be messed with, he unsettled her. She had no idea the concoction of drugs he took to keep his mind at ease and away from his memories.

Paul and George stuffed their hands into their pockets, as if to erase any trace of their injuries and the last hour of their lives. They waited for an instruction, not knowing what to do with themselves. They soon understood what Frederick wanted; it was written across his face, in his frozen stance. He wanted to be alone when he was examined, but he couldn't say the truth aloud in front of her. Clicking on, they wandered back to The King's Arms, wondering if something more was going on.

Alone, Adelina waited for Frederick to move or to utter a word. He remained against the wall, smoking. He took his time; he could cause anxiety, set people on edge, make them weak with his power. If he had questions, under those circumstances, she would give away the truth.

Adelina noticed a sewing kit atop of a desk – he must've brought it in whilst they played. Falling back into line, she moved towards the kit, bottle of liquor in one hand, the handkerchief stained with his brothers' blood in the other.

Adelina had been in her final year of university; graduation was a matter of months away. The last exams approached, and she worked harder than ever. Stitches were things she'd accomplished many times, though she'd never carried out the procedure with a home sewing needle.

'Would you like to sit?' Adelina asked.

He wanted to be in control of everything, his decision always. After finishing his cigarette, he slunk into the chair. He prepared himself for the procedure, not used to feeling like he did.

Of course, he'd been injured before, he served in the Great War. He wasn't accustomed to being treated in his offices, so close to home, with a woman he knew. He was more familiar with strangers, dreary hospitals, and sodden trenches.

'You should have let me do this earlier.'

Adelina washed his wound, never garnering a response. Frederick didn't want to talk, he wanted to avoid her. Moving close, she dabbed at the cut with a cloth, cleaning his skin, taking her time.

'Usually, I would numb people for this kind of thing.'

Needle and thread within her grasp, she dropped her gaze, wondering if he listened to her at all. His stare drifted off into the distance, trying to think of anything but the war, because she reminded him too much of someone else.

The situation became overwhelming. Frederick reached for the alcohol; it was the thoughts not the pain.

Adelina waited for him to finish. The old-fashioned way of pain relief. No longer could she call upon anaesthetists or hook up invasive forms of medicine. Used to being in control, she felt uneasy letting her patient self-medicate.

The needle dug into his skin, pulling the flesh together once more with black cotton thread. He didn't stir. He didn't flinch. Numb to everything.

Frederick had dealt with far worse, injuries she'd never witnessed. The visions of his comrades dying slowly still fresh in his mind. She'd seen the aftermath of car accidents and stab wounds, but never a gunshot victim; she couldn't comprehend seeing a man hold their own bowels within their hands like he had.

A neat and tidy wound. With some luck, it would heal without a scar. Sitting back, resting on the edge of the desk, her gaze lingered over him. His head was full of thoughts, and she wanted to understand why.

Not knowing what else to do, she cleaned up. Moving behind the chair, coming to the other side of him, he reached out for her.

'Thank you.'

'It's my job now.'

Adelina smiled; she confirmed his offer with four words. It was what she had to do to survive, and she didn't mind because it felt like home to care for them.

Enough was enough, he let her move away. In his head, he

prayed, not to a single God but to any higher power that would listen. He hoped she told the truth about herself and that there would be no revelations.

'You start tomorrow at eight. Isla will be here to help you.'

The list of tasks rapidly growing in his mind weakened. Adelina stopped clearing up, holding on to every one of his words instead.

'You need a place to stay,' Frederick said, coughing, unsure of his thoughts. 'You have a choice. I can take you to another guest house, though they're all far away from here, and they're not as nice as Violet's. They'll eat into your wage too, you'll have barely anything left after. Or, I know of a spare room, a few paces away from where we are.'

The choice caught Adelina off guard. It was impossible to decide, he didn't detail the room at all.

'And where is…'

Adelina changed her mind; the choice couldn't be hers. She wanted to owe him nothing more – he couldn't hold anything over her. She needed to remain smart, one step ahead, just in case things went south.

'I don't want to be any more trouble, whatever is easiest for you.'

'It's best to be closer, in case I need you. As per our agreement.'

'That's understandable.'

'The spare room then.'

'Can I ask, whose house the spare room is in?'

'Mine.'

Too late to change her mind, she'd already signed her fate away to something unknown. God, she should've guessed such a thing would happen with him. So much for being smart.

'Is that still fine?'

'Yes, why wouldn't it be?'

In the end he was right; far too innocent, she didn't understand the implications of choosing the bedroom along the hall from him.

'I don't want to accept anything more from you.'

'It's my old family home. I'm barely there.'

'I'll stay out of your way. Until you need me.'

They both spoke their truth, for once not concealing it from the other.

The night disguised their identities. The coat across her arm, bumps rising ever more. Teeth starting to chatter. Frederick took her to the small, terraced house where all the Clark children used to live.

Something about the road reminded her of home. Red bricks charred from coal. Peeling wooden window frames. Thin houses that opened up like Tardis'. Heavy doors, creaking floorboards. Damp encased into one's nose. Fraying wallpaper, crumbling plaster. No windows on the landing. No pictures nor paintings. It was home, her childhood sealed in a bottle. A sudden sense of belonging overcame her.

Frederick showed her to the bedroom. It was a box room, only large enough for a single bed and a chest. The space was perfect. If it were her childhood, there'd be a bunk bed, pink curtains draped from the walls, broken drawers, grandma's cooking floating upstairs.

'It's…'

'Not much,' Frederick interrupted.

'I was going to say it reminds me of my childhood.'

Adelina took in the space. Dashes of her past were in front of her. She swore she could see Leonora, sitting atop of the bunk bed, smiling down at her.

'You're starting to remember more,' Frederick noted, his eyes staring into her back.

'I am, but my memories are stuck in the past, that's not going to help me now.'

Adelina pulled away from the image of her sister. Turning, she traced her fingers across the dusty drawers. Frederick nodded, barely able to look her in the eye, as he muttered his version of a goodbye.

'I've got to get back to business.'

Adelina sat on the bed, the mattress squeaking. She didn't

quite know how to feel in her new lodging. At times, Frederick seemed kind, and she had to try to remember the violence he was capable of. Maybe the concussion was still affecting her, allowing her to make such terrible decisions. Frederick was dangerous, but when she was alone with him, she forgot everything.

FOURTEEN

Like the rest of the street, Adelina woke up with the bell ringer. In the dark, she rifled through the chest of drawers, hoping to find better-fitting clothes. In the bottom drawer, she discovered forgotten attire.

Dorothy's old wardrobe had grown dusty, the items left behind since her move a couple of months ago. Better skirts and blouses awaited her at Etta's new home across the road. The family's business ventures had gained traction. With their ever-increasing status, Etta had managed to blag her own home. No longer did they wear tatty garments from the cheapest market stall. Dorothy and Etta now purchased everything new, from the poshest of department stores.

Adelina found a plain grey dress, the fabric lightly worn and rather small. She wasn't sure if she was thin enough, but she hadn't eaten properly in days. The constant rumble in her stomach reminded her of that, but she never wanted to ask for anything, not wishing to be a burden.

The dress was a little too small, but it was a hundred times better than Margaret's misshapen clothes. A cardigan littered with moth holes completed the outfit. She still wore the half-broken heels. On payday, she would have to purchase new shoes, ones that didn't pinch her toes or send her stumbling on the cobbles.

Touching her face, she watched the person in the mirror do the same. Adelina barely recognised herself. A swollen, oozing lump hidden in her hairline. The stitches were horrific, they barely held the skin together. The memory of receiving them foggier than ever. They needed to be replaced, they were jagged, they did nothing for her.

Going to a hospital was out of the question; there would be questions about her, her wound, and how poorly the stitches had been done to begin with. Instead, she left for work, trying to put the thought of the stitches to the back of her mind.

Adelina expected the office to be the same as every visit prior: smoke curling up into the room, an array of bustling workers, children bumping into one another, throwing money and slips onto desks before skipping off.

A quiet space greeted her. The remnants of George and Paul's boisterous antics were still evident. Paperwork lay crumpled on the floor, pen pots and organisers were knocked over, and the sewing kit was half-stuffed in a draw.

'What are you doing here again?'

A woman, about her age, glanced her up and down from the back room's doorway. Isla Clark, George's wife. He had never told her what happened the night prior. He had never mentioned Adelina, not even when she'd asked about the odd woman that traipsed into the offices.

Isla was beautiful; porcelain skin stood out against dark eyes and hair. Everything about her appeared wild, from the curls piled a top of her head to the makeup smeared onto her eyelids. Unlike the women outside, she didn't follow the current fashion trends but her own.

'Oh, bloody hell,' Etta said, startling herself as she nearly walked into Isla. 'I almost forgot about her.'

'What's going on?'

'Frederick's hired her, to help,' Etta said, her lips pursing, trying to hold in a smile.

'What?' Isla laughed, thinking Frederick would never do anything so absurd. 'Why would he do that?'

'I don't have a clue really.'

Adelina tried to form words that would explain Frederick's actions, but their gaze upon her made them disintegrate.

'He's told me everything,' Etta said. 'You were training to be a nurse before you knocked your head. You don't have a clue who you are now.'

'I know who I am, I just don't know where I belong. I can't remember if my home is the place I still live.'

It didn't half sound odd, Etta and Isla thought, though they knew better than to question Frederick's decision.

'Just because he wants you to fix his cuts and scrapes, doesn't mean you'll get away scot-free in here,' Etta said, dumping a thick leather-bound book onto a desk. 'You'll be good with numbers then, won't you?'

'Please say yes,' Isla said, picking up the letters the brothers hadn't cared for.

'I normally do the books, but I have far too much on my plate at the moment. Isla hates the accounts, Lydia only messes them up, but you – Freddie said you're quite articulate, like you went to a fee-paying school, not one of the daft ones we went to.'

'You're joking, aren't you?' Adelina said. Her primary school had been one of the worst in England. Most of her time had been spent in the local park or shopping centre rather than school. Only at nineteen, when she enrolled in college for the first time, did her education change.

'Just give it a try,' Isla said, referring to the sums in the heavy bound book. 'It'll do us a favour.'

'Besides, Freddie said I shouldn't involve you in anything bad,' Etta said. 'You do realise where you are, don't you?'

'Did he really say that?' Adelina asked, astounded that he'd listened to her.

'I haven't got all day,' Etta said, opening the book to a page littered with jottings. 'Look at this and tell me straight whether you can do it because you better not make any mistakes.'

With the confirmation that she could do the maths, Etta left for the back room. She walked with authority, as if she owned every brick the building was constructed with. Everything about her was a show – from the way she held herself to the way she pinned her hair.

'Lydia will be here shortly,' Isla said, gathering a bunch of handwritten notes. 'She's in charge of meetings and filing. I'm here to keep the kids in order, make sure they're coughing up the right money, or I'll set George on them.'

'Where are they, the brothers?'

'Out on business. They're never here. We're always stuck inside while they're off galivanting, having their fun.'

Isla's bitter tone took Adelina by surprise; she didn't understand why Isla would long for such a vicious world. But Isla wanted freedom, to not be trapped indoors. At times, she failed to acknowledge the danger of her husband's work.

For Isla, it was like Groundhog Day; she would wake, take care of her children, and then leave them to scuttle off to school. Once they finished, they would go to one of her friends' homes. All the while, she would be inside the dingy offices, barely getting pittance for her work. Other women stayed at home, running the household, ensuring everyone was well-fed and the place tidy. Isla was expected to fulfil all the responsibilities of a wife alongside working for her husband's family.

Isla slumped into her chair; every inch of her body ached. Every day, the offices ended up in the same disordered state. All she knew was work. As the days went by with Frederick breathing down everyone's neck, she felt increasingly worse. Sometimes, she wanted to put her own family first.

'Do you know what this place is?' Isla asked, forgetting that Adelina needed to concentrate on her work.

'Freddie said something about a club and racecourses.'

'So, you don't have a clue where most of the money comes from.'

'I'm not sure if I want to know.'

'Relax, I won't hurt you. You're one of us now, aren't you?' Isla said, peering over, waiting for a reaction but never garnering one. 'Would you really be against helping me after you've finished adding all that up?'

'Why? What are you doing?'

'Separating the slips into categories, but once that door opens and the kids come running in, there'll be even more to do. It's dead simple: a pile for each race, for each ground.'

Betting slips. Isla processed them for the brothers. Adelina realised her work but couldn't grasp the illegality. She didn't know the history; she didn't realise being in the building broke the law.

The kids would take bets from people on the streets. Their men would go around the pubs and clubs shouting odds. Racing was like the lottery; it gave people hope of winning money so they could better their lives.

It was more than that. The Clarks didn't just take bets, they fixed anything they could, from football to boxing. The only form of legal betting was on a racecourse pitch. Only in 1960 did betting shops become legalised.

Without that knowledge, Adelina told Isla she would help her, thinking it would be like working in a high street bookies. She didn't realise the gravity of the situation, how laws were being pushed through parliament to stop people like the Clarks.

'You have nothing to worry about,' Isla said, grinning. 'The kids are faster than the coppers, and even so, most don't care what we do. All of them would turn a blind eye for a bit of cash. Remember that if you're ever in trouble.'

Lydia meandered into the room, her chin lifted and her eyes sharp. Dark curls framed her face, set nearly beneath a stylish cloche hat. The way she carried herself made Adelina think she thought well of herself, like she was better than everyone else. The confirmation came when she looked Adelina up and down, scoffing at her presence.

'Finally got some help,' Isla said to Lydia. 'Maybe he's finally listened to you.'

'Don't kid yourself, Freddie only thinks about himself.'

Lydia's harsh stare made Adelina uncomfortable, as if she didn't belong in the office. Etta didn't seem to care, Isla appeared happy she was there, whilst Lydia continued to grimace, hating her without getting to know her.

Sensing the change in atmosphere, Etta returned to the main office. There would be no time to dwell on Adelina's presence. Unlocking the doors, the day's work officially started.

Gang members made their way in, throwing fistfuls of money and scraps of paper at the women. Adelina continued to add up. Isla tried to keep her desk organised. Every now and then, the room filled with Lydia's low grumbling voice as she took a phone call. Occasionally, Etta would scream at an unruly child who was not taking their role as a runner seriously.

By mid-afternoon, with Adelina's help, the papers were sorted into categories: football, boxing, greyhound racing. With one task completed, Isla brought in a pot of tea. With no fire, the women sat in their coats, rubbing their hands upon the china.

'Just as we bloody sit down,' Etta muttered as the door slammed. She couldn't be bothered with her brothers' hooliganism, not after working all day.

Unlike those outside, they weren't scared of the boys. They didn't move; they continued to sit, tea in their hands. At times, they had the brothers wrapped around their fingers. They didn't bat an eyelid at George's hyper disposition, chuckling about how he'd shot a man.

'Thank fuck the Youngs are on the back foot,' Paul said, gulping liquid from his flask.

'Don't get ahead of yourself,' Frederick said. 'Something's off with them.'

Patterns clung to the sides of Adelina's teacup. Tilting her head, she tried to decipher them, hoping to find a sign she was so desperate for.

'Can you read them?' Isla asked.

'No, my mum used to. As a kid, people would pay her to read them. They would come to the house, but my dad didn't like that.'

'Etta reads them; you should ask her.'

'I don't read tea leaves for people who aren't like us,' Etta said without a second thought.

'But her mum read them, she must have learnt somehow.'

'Are you like us?' Etta asked, her mind wandering. She wouldn't feel so on edge if Adelina said yes.

'Is that why you were with the Youngs?' Isla said, forgetting her previous promise to Etta. As they made tea, they had gossiped about Adelina, and Etta had made her swear not to repeat any of it.

Frederick tried to act like he wasn't eavesdropping, but his mind turned with every word. The Youngs were known liars; they could've had Adelina for weeks. The girl's memory loss could have been their doing. He hated not knowing, so he conjured his own explanations for her appearance.

'I guess I'm sort of like you. My grandma grew up travelling, she told the best stories. As a kid, she frightened me, she told me I have the gift of contact, that I've received smoke signals.'

Isla loved to hear stories about her ancestry and travelling; it reminded her of being a child with no care in the world. Isla missed the tales by the bonfire, being in a different place every week. She only stayed in Leeds because George wouldn't leave.

'My mum read tea, my grandma read hands. Anyone she met, she would examine them first, see if they were worthy. In a way, she judged people through them,' Adelina said, opening her palm as if Nova was there with her.

'My mum taught me how to read hands. I can have a go. I might see the same thing as her,' Isla said.

'Maybe another time,' Adelina said, snapping her hand into a fist to protect the lines from Isla. The deeply engraved nature of her love line, the forked lifeline that began and ended all at the same time – what Nova read had become true. Adelina did go back, and she couldn't let Isla see that.

'It's a load of bullshit,' Paul said. 'Crinkles in your bloody hand, that's all they are. They don't hold the meaning of life.'

Paul took another gulp from his flask, not caring to share with his brothers. George's mouth twitched in amusement at Paul's harsh scepticism. The comment would enrage Isla; she believed in the nonsense too much.

Adelina glanced towards Frederick, wondering what he thought. His face was straight, his gaze lingering over her. The prophecy was coming true. The words of the black witch chimed in his head. It couldn't be right, what she said. Adelina came across as innocent, caring, too good for his world.

The blaring ring of the telephone distracted the room. The Clarks turned to Lydia, waiting for her to put an end to the noise, but she sat still, blatant envy sweeping across her, sending the palms of her hands sweating.

Lydia observed it all. It was subtle, at first – the way Frederick glanced at Adelina. It was the same serious aura he projected with anyone, but Lydia knew better than most. He was fighting against himself. He tried to appear disinterested, but the façade didn't work on her. Frederick had never had to act before.

Lydia answered the phone, muttering to the person on the other end. As she spoke, Tom, Frederick's right-hand man, bounded in.

'You need to go to the Clarendon, now. Timmy from the butchers just saw Charlie Black go in there.'

'More bleeding trouble,' Etta said.

'Best get going Freddie,' Isla giggled. 'Your dearest Ida will be all worked up, yet again.'

George cast a harsh look to his wife; it wasn't the right time for such comments. The appearance of Charlie on their turf meant nothing good.

Frederick sauntered over to Lydia's desk, taking a spare gun from her drawer, not caring for the daggers she sent his way.

'You don't have time; I'll close up the shop,' Tom said. 'You just need to get yourself there, now. God knows what he's doing.'

'I'll follow,' Frederick said to his brothers. 'Get going, I'll meet you there.'

Paul and George followed orders, scampering out onto the street. Again, George left without the leader. To Isla, it symbolised who Frederick was – a man who sent in his brothers first.

'Always them in first, isn't it?' Isla said as Frederick rifled through drawers, searching for something.

'I'll close up, you ladies get yourself home,' Tom said, receiving only stern looks in response. 'Come on, Charlie Black is no joke, you know that.'

'I don't know who he is,' Adelina said. Everyone feared him on the same level as Frederick, and even he seemed to be unsettled when it came to Charlie.

'Charlie is the potential end of us,' Frederick said.

'You're stupid Freddie. You've lost your bloody mind,' Lydia said. 'Isla's told you there's enough money coming in through the club for us to survive. You should pack in the violence. It's not going to end well with Charlie.'

'Shut up, Lydia. Close up the shop, get word out to the runners – you know what to do. Adelina, stay here in case we need you.'

Lydia's lips pressed into a thin line as she looked between Adelina and Frederick. Whilst her and Lydia had jobs to do, Adelina could stay. With a guttural laugh of disbelief, Lydia turned sharply on her heel. She wanted to speak, to scrutinise Adelina, but she had no time, she needed to follow orders. Word had to be spread that the Clarks were closed for business, until the storm blew over.

FIFTEEN

Before the war, the Clark's headquarters were at The Clarendon. With their expansion and Frederick's growing obsession with status, the offices were a new addition.

The Clarendon was like any other pub, with hardwood floors and dark-stained panelling halfway up the walls. Shades of brown concealed the dirt that came in with its punters, mostly factory workers. Every corner was separated into booths, with a few lonely tables scattered around.

Charlie Black sat between two burley men, his slicked-back blonde hair still showing the lines from a fine-tooth comb. His eyes shifted to the barmaid, the one with golden streaks and rosebud lips. Winking, he raked his gaze across Ida's body.

There were complex relationships, endlessly changing, between the racecourse gangs. The Charlton family owned north of the Ouse. The Mancinis fought with the Kings for the south. The Midlands, heading up to Leeds, had Charlie Black, who was undisputed until last year.

The gossip started after the war – whispers about the Clarks, how reckless they could be, how they couldn't control themselves. People told Charlie they would never be anything more than a petty street gang, that they would never bother him. Little scoundrels operating in Holbeck, they would never move out; it wasn't worth the hassle to take over such a shithole.

Charlie should've listened to Harry Allanson. Within weeks, everything changed. Now all he heard about was the Clarks' expansion and their famed leader.

Charlie's downfall was unpredictable; he thought he was untouchable. The Clarks took his territories when he left on business. The men he put in charge weren't loyal to him, but to money. When he set his sights on Birmingham and London, he forgot to keep an eye on his hometown.

After he lost most of his home turf, Charlie spent time in North London, trying to garner allies for his fightback. Despite fleeing, he still held a monopoly on legal betting pitches and racketeering for Beverly and Chester racecourses. After Joe got himself shot – by none other than Frederick – Charlie had to come back. It was time to do something.

David Hunter, the landlord of The Clarendon, paced nervously. A war was brewing, and the pub was in the firing line. One wrong meeting and everything would need replacing. David wasn't one of the Clarks' men; he wanted a good life, free from violence. He wanted to leave the barbarity in France. Unfortunately, in 1919 there were only two choices: be in control or be controlled.

The pub wasn't what George and Paul expected. The place was deserted, no punters in sight. Only Charlie, his people, and the staff. Paul wanted to take care of Charlie there and then, believing it would be easier that way. George didn't want to end things quite yet; he understood the importance of waiting for Frederick.

Seizing the opportunity, Paul pulled his gun from its holster. Laughing, Charlie and his men mirrored him, daring him to pull the trigger. Outnumbered, two guns pointed towards Paul, another directed at George.

'Go on then, pull the trigger,' Charlie sneered. 'Watch how your life'll end seconds after.'

No quite knowing what else to do, George reached for his gun. Flashbacks flickered through his mind. He needed to get out of the situation; no one could be hurt, not in the bloody Clarendon.

Enough of a show. Charlie wanted to end the standoff immediately. His aim veered, the barrel pointing towards Ida instead. She shrank away behind the bar, losing all colour, too panic-stricken to duck. Only one person could save her.

God answered Ida that evening. Frederick sauntered into

the pub. Nothing intimidated him. He lived from day to day, wanting more but not caring he could die at any moment getting it. Death no longer scared him because everything good about him had died in France.

'Charlie,' Frederick said. 'Let's talk business alone, shall we.'

Out of pure curiosity, Charlie agreed. If they could work things out, maybe he would regain his land at some point. It would never be his intention to work alongside the scum, the non-natives. For a while, he would give them the impression he was on their side. Eventually, he would trip them up, stealing everything from them. In the end, they would be nothing but pawns in his game.

The two left the room, entering the small back office together, much to David's dismay. Frederick treated everything like his own and David was getting sick of it. David wanted to be left alone in his endeavours, to run the pub how he wanted. In a way, Frederick was the true landlord – he could do and change anything he wanted.

Flustered, George and Paul kept a firm hold on their weapons. George didn't understand how the chaos had been avoided. Regardless, he was relieved, he didn't want to die, he had everything to live for. Isla had been his reason to come home from war; he needed to care for her and their children.

Paul leaned against the bar, waiting for David to pull him a drink. Paul never thought too much, it only gave way to anxiety and self-scrutiny. The war had damaged him beyond repair; he found normality difficult. The acts he committed to survive plagued him. At times, he questioned why he tried so hard to come home. In a way, maybe it should've been Robert who returned, not him.

David pulled the men a pint each, hoping to subdue the tension. Paul gulped his drink. Facing the liquor shelves, he wondered which spirit would make him inebriated the quickest. George rested backwards onto the bar, eyes firmly planted on the enemy. David stood by, ready to refill drinks, hoping that his family's pub would not be destroyed.

Ida hadn't moved. No one noticed her presence once Charlie lowered his weapon. Her body had seized up in fright; her life had been on the line so quickly. As the barrel pointed towards her, she thought of her family, who were so far away. Her little sister, Eva, flooded her mind. She didn't want to leave her; she'd already lost three older brothers.

While Frederick thought of every moment beyond his near-death experience as extra, Ida felt completely petrified at the thought of being locked in darkness forever. She wanted more from life than she had so far. When Charlie aimed his gun at her, she not only thought of herself and Eva but of Frederick too. There was courting, and then there was falling in love. Ida hadn't meant to fall for him so swiftly, but there she was, in what could have been her final moments, thinking about him.

Ida was still locked in her mind when the leaders returned. Charlie chuntered to himself, a series of warnings evading his lips only to save face. None of what they agreed upon would stay true for long. Even if Charlie kept his side of the promise, Frederick wouldn't.

With Charlie and his men making their way back to their tiny slither of the city they had left, Frederick took a freshly poured pint from David. George and Paul wanted answers, but Frederick kept the agreement to himself. He would never talk freely in front of David or Ida.

'Close up shop,' Frederick said, swallowing the remnants of his drink. 'There'll be no other punters in now, not once word spreads.'

David obeyed, not wishing to disagree with him. George and Paul downed their drinks. They would go their separate ways – George back to Isla, relishing in her warmth in bed; Paul to the docks, looking for a way to spend his night. Frederick would take Ida home, knowing she was in no fit state to go by herself.

They exchanged no conversation as they walked to her lowly flat. Frederick, consumed with plans, wondered how he would overcome the issue of Charlie. Ida became preoccupied with her own feelings, questioning her reason for going to Leeds. If anything, she had only gotten herself into trouble by leaving home. God, her family would be disappointed to know she'd fallen for a man like Frederick.

Ida wanted to forget the night with him; it would never happen. He was lost to his mind, too much so to care for her feelings that night.

Ida managed only two steps up to her room before she collapsed to the ground in tears. The world crashed down around her. She wanted him, no one else, but he would never be hers forever. Realising the gravity of her mistakes, the pain doubled. There's no swaying the heart once its set upon someone.

SIXTEEN

The night prior, Frederick skulked his way past Adelina like he never asked her to stay at the offices. After a few hushed words to Tom, he locked his office door. Lighting a candle, he commenced work immediately. When she returned for her shift the next day, the light was still glowing.

Adelina pressed her ear against the wood, trying to tune in to the other side of the door. All she could hear was the roaring of the industry, the laughter of the women as they worked, and the children's harsh steps across the concrete.

Adelina didn't understand Frederick and his business, the pressure he put on himself to stay awake for so long. She wanted to knock on the door, to ask if he needed help.

'What are you doing?' Lydia asked. 'There's work to be done.'

'Aren't you concerned?' Adelina whispered. 'He went in there last night, and I'm sure he hasn't been out since.'

'That's what he's like,' Isla said. 'Don't worry about him, he can handle himself.'

'When he came back last night, he ignored me. Even Tom said he acted weird.'

'Charlie Black's more important than you,' Lydia said. 'If he fancies it, and we let our guard down, we could all end up dead.'

'All of us?' Adelina questioned, her pitch rising.

'That won't happen,' Isla reassured her. 'Freddie, George, they won't let Charlie come back from the hole he's in.'

'Why did he ask you to stay here, anyways?' Lydia asked.

'In case he came back injured, I think.'

'And what are you going to do?' Lydia replied with a snort.

'Did no one tell you? I was training to be a nurse.'

Isla returned to the paperwork, trying to avoid Lydia. No one mentioned Adelina's past to her, as if they were trying to keep it a secret.

'If you're so important, sleeping in his house, taking care of him, why is he still making you work here, for, I assume, barely anything?' Lydia's voice changed, no longer inquisitive but dropping into a snarl that barely hid her creeping feelings. Something lingered inside of her – events that Adelina couldn't understand, ones that not even Isla knew.

A voice bellowed inside of the offices, a stranger to Lydia but a demon to Adelina. A man she thought would never be inside the building. With a few large strides, he towered over her.

'So, he kept you around then?' Thomas growled, his lips curling up as his tongue ran across them. He couldn't wait to get his revenge on her.

Flanked by George and Paul, John chuckled menacingly. Adelina flushed cold. The Clarks wouldn't protect her forever; soon she would be left without them, and all the things the Youngs threatened her with would come true.

'Go home, Isla. May's fallen over coming home from school; I think she'll want her mum,' George said.

'Let's talk business, leave the women to do their work,' Frederick said, ushering the men inside.

'Come on,' Lydia said with a cough, knowing the two people who entered the offices were the worst kind of men. 'We need to clear this paperwork today, and we're one down now.'

'Why did Isla leave?'

'Do you really need to ask?'

'If she gets to leave, why should we stay?'

'We're the hired help. We're not family. We're not one of them. There's a difference.'

'Right,' Adelina whispered. She had never noticed the difference between her and Isla, and the way they were treated.

'Leave, if you really want. I'm not going to stop you.'

'It's fine. I'm not scared. I can protect myself.'

'Sure, you can.'

Silently, they plodded on with work. The men's voices drifted over to Adelina, sending bile creeping up her throat. Really, she was petrified of them. But surely, the Clarks would protect her. What Lydia said couldn't be that true. George had told her they looked out for their own; by working for them, she was one of them.

'*Has she remembered then?*' Thomas Young sniggered, speaking in broken tidbits of Shelta.

'*What does that matter to you?*' George replied.

'*Got a thing for her, have you? That's strange, I thought that was your wife earlier. The one with the–*'

'*You're just trying to get under my skin because of what happened with your granddaughter, aren't you?*'

'*Nah, I think you've definitely got a thing for her. Probably had her already, haven't ya? How was she? Like a loose old tart, I reckon*'.

'*Definitely a whore of some description,*' John added. '*I bet she wore that silk top for you. Tell me, was she better than your wife? Because truth be told, well-used or not, I'd love to give her a go.*'

John cackled. Noting Adelina's perplexed expression, he winked. Intending to make another remark, he turned to George, his hand rising, about to make some sort of lewd gesture.

Frederick lunged forwards, pushing past the men. In one swift motion, his arms wrapped around Adelina, dragging her away. With the strength only a tortured woman could muster, she thrashed toward John.

'What the fuck do you think you're doing?' John screamed. Gargling up saliva, he spluttered and hacked. The spit spun toward her, splattering on the concrete and soaking her shoes as Frederick held her back.

A millimetre to the right, and it would have caught Frederick too. If that had happened, he wouldn't be holding on to her but finding a weapon to put an end to John. Sensing that a bloodbath was seconds away, George stepped in between them, attempting to escort the Youngs from the building.

With the clipping of heels registering in Frederick's mind,

Adelina wriggled free. Fury found a new focus. With a blistering face and clouding eyes, her hands found Frederick's chest. Harsh shoves into him, trying to get him to back away. The emotions never dissolving, her hands finding him repeatedly.

Frederick remained still, composed, standing like a brick wall. Though his eyes turned deadly, rage simmered within him, and he tried to contain it.

'Are you going to let them talk about me like that?' Another bang against him, she wanted to do worse, but it was him, and she was in front of his family with murderous weapons attached to their hips. A sane person wouldn't have touched him, but she felt the opposite. 'Are you really going to do nothing? George said before you would look out for me, that if I worked for you...'

The tapping came closer. Finally, she realised. Any other time, and she would have been unconscious already for treating him so badly. Throughout, his demeanour had shifted, never focusing on her, but on someone behind her.

Etta's heels scraped across the wood, like she thought about stopping for a moment. Instead of imploding, of shooting the men dead right then, she continued to walk like they weren't in the room.

'Come on, let's get going,' Paul said, being rational for once, guiding the Youngs away.

Etta never stopped walking. Instead of going to the back room, she found herself outside, staring over the canal as factory workers gawked at her. 'Nothing happened. Nothing happened,' she repeated to herself over and over. All the time the grey waves called to her because she could never forget what happened with Peter.

In the dead of the night, at least once a week, she would remember every minute detail: the flecks of the sunlight on the vardo wall, the coarse bedsheets, the scratching of her throat, the burning of her eyes.

Alone with Frederick in his room, Adelina stood, unwilling to sit. Whilst he watched over her, always astonished by her. It wasn't often people caught him off guard, yet somehow, she kept doing that to him.

'I told you what they did to me,' Adelina said. 'Why would you let them say that about me? That's not looking out for me. That's not keeping me safe. By saying nothing, by not putting them in their place, you're only encouraging them. You see that, right? You know how this could end.'

The desk was chaotic, a sea of paperwork crowded the surface. Handwritten notes, laid out like spiderwebs. A glass of alcohol close by, ready to drown any doubts. She waited for him to speak, to fill the air with his deep, gritty voice.

'I should be out there, checking on Etta.'

'Go see her.'

A part of him didn't want to. Adelina appeared worse than Etta, more vulnerable somehow, he didn't want to leave her. He was making excuses. He didn't want to feel like he failed Etta. Seven years had passed and still no repercussions, no retribution. Frederick's biggest regret.

Edging towards the door, his mind became hellbent on finding words to comfort his sister. Behind the wood, he found Etta standing over Lydia, giving out orders as if she hadn't been reminded of her past five minutes prior.

With a harsh click, he locked the image of her away and returned his focus to Adelina, who was wiping her eyes, trying to swallow any remaining emotion. In some ways, she felt like a disgrace. She should have held herself together, to not appear weak in front of him, of all people.

'Forget it,' Adelina said, her lips pulling up slightly in an attempt to smile, to portray herself as strong and unaffected by the Youngs. Hopefully, he would fail to recall how she'd pummelled his chest, how she had treated him.

'No.'

A stern unrelenting stare. Slowly, her mouth returned to its natural state. Instead of her voice quaking, it became her hands as she waited to be reprimanded. In a way, he appeared austere, unsympathetic.

'I let them say those things because I don't allow people to get underneath my skin.'

'Of course, they're going to upset me, saying such awful things.'

'You shouldn't have known what they were saying,' Frederick sighed.

'I don't understand.'

'They weren't speaking English, Ada.'

'My grandma taught me bits of Shelta as a kid. I know enough to understand what they said.'

'Your grandma taught you…' Frederick said, shaking his head slowly, trying to process the new information. 'When you mentioned your grandma read hands, I didn't think to ask. So many people pretend to have gifts and connections now, with all the widows.'

'People pretend to be like us?'

That was unfathomable to Adelina, she had spent her whole life burying that part of herself, so she didn't get picked on.

Frederick's jaw tightened, his fists clenched. He should never have questioned her. God, she was one of them – no one could teach themselves the language. She was never a spy, or anything bad. He should've believed her from the beginning.

SEVENTEEN

Forget truces; Frederick would make the first move. After spending all day cooped up in his office, he finalised the plan for Charlie's downfall. Soon, the entire city would be his.

For once, he decided to relax. The Clarendon was bustling, thick with punters. If he was honest, he was already half-cut from the liquor he'd been swigging all day.

The crowd at the bar parted as he made his appearance known. Without asking, Ida poured him a drink. She flapped her hand, rejecting the money he tried to push over the bar. On the house, as always, David couldn't have it any other way.

Frederick leaned against the counter, sipping neat liquor. The air clouded, heavy with smoke. To Ida, he seemed like a mere apparition.

'A busy day?' Ida asked.

'Why do you care?'

It was unusual; Ida never asked about work, she never uttered a word about his true job. That's the way he liked it. At times, she seemed scared of what he really did. There had been occasions where he spoke to her about business, but only when he'd been too intoxicated for his own good.

Frederick didn't like to burden people with his thoughts. He preferred to keep his secrets close to his chest. Those small words from Ida set a different precedent, making him wonder why she asked.

As Frederick moved towards his brothers, Ida's heart sank. The shouts from the other punters, trying to get her attention, meant nothing when she'd been struck down by him. After Charlie, she became far too scared of losing him.

The brothers became progressively more inebriated. Frederick hadn't been so drunk for a while; he swayed even when he tried to sit still. The world churned around him. He didn't feel ill, he cherished the sensation.

Last orders and kick-out time approached. The time meant nothing to Frederick, he could stay forever if he wanted. But, with every sip, Ida's stare burned into him. She wanted to go home with him. Any other night, and there wouldn't have been a question.

Even with Ida serving him, her eyes constantly upon him, his mind wandered back to the events of the day. He'd been an ignorant fool; the entire time Adelina could speak the same language. He should never have doubted her. Ultimately, every word she said came together perfectly.

Paul and George chuntered about a woman they'd seen earlier. They debated fiercely about whether she was prostitute. Of course, Paul wanted to try her out. Frederick didn't care for their conversation, too infatuated with the thought of Adelina alone in his home.

New to the city, she only knew his family. He wondered what she was doing, whether she was sleeping soundly. He hoped the Youngs hadn't spooked her. That she hadn't taken off into the night like the first time he met her.

As the last orders bell rang, Frederick moved, his drink still three-quarters full. The snow slowed him down, as did the swaying of his body as he tried to pace onwards.

The house was silent. For a moment, he became concerned that he'd woken her, that there'd been nothing to worry about at all. As he stood at the bottom of the stairs, he heard a sharp intake of breath, paired with a bang. Without knocking, he shoved open her door, entering the bedroom.

With the office closed on Sundays, there would be no consequence for Adelina's actions on a Saturday night. Frederick barely returned home; he would never know her plans. Of course, stealing from him was bad, but she had no other option.

After finishing work, she smuggled the sewing box and a bottle of alcohol to her bedroom. The stitches were a state, they needed replacing and she lacked the courage to ask anyone else for help.

Performing the procedure on herself was crazy, but without intervention, the wound would never heal properly, it would only get infected. Each time she thought of replacing them, her stomach churned. The stolen liquor would hopefully stop the sensation. The overproof rum scorched her throat, strong enough to knock someone into a coma. The drink would be her form of pain relief, her Dutch courage.

Minutes then hours ticked by. Adelina remained in the same position, staring at the wound in the mirror. Sterilised instruments laid out, waiting. She gulped down the alcohol, waiting to feel tipsy.

With a slight sway, Adelina took a pair of kitchen scissors to the thread. Cutting away the cotton, she pulled it from her skin, grinding her teeth. Even with the alcohol, she felt every yank, the thread slowly unravelling her.

Another swallow of alcohol. Another burning sensation. She doused herself in the liquid, feeling it reverberate atop of her head. With a harsh intake of breath, she stabbed herself in the head, pulling the needle through her torn skin.

Another gulp. Another breath. The needle moved again. Thumping the floor, holding in a cry, she became petrified that she wouldn't be able to complete the procedure. Eyes watering, she picked up the bottle.

Frederick charged in, eyes wild, searching for the source of the commotion. It wasn't the sight he had envisaged. The needle dangled from her head, tied to the string that laced into her skin. Pale, eyes bloodshot, the alcohol beside her nearly depleted.

'What are you doing?' Frederick asked, a laugh escaping him.

After everything he'd seen at home and in war, nothing could have prepared him for the sight of Adelina trying to stitch herself back together. For a moment, there was no pain, she couldn't help but giggle too.

'You said yourself they needed changing.'

'Not like this.'

The bedroom door banged in the breeze, but neither of them cared. Sinking to the floor beside her, he examined her handiwork. Despite the intoxication, she had done alright.

'I've got this far by myself,' she said, taking another swig of alcohol before offering it to him.

The man who spent most of his time emotionless smiled frantically at her. The stitching of herself, the offer of his own alcohol back after she took a gulp. No longer a shy girl, she evolved before him, revealing her true self.

Adelina returned to the wound. The blistering sensation sent shock waves throughout her. Unable to take the pain, she dropped the needle. Upon seeing his grin, she joined in.

They were different. They had always been serious, never laid back. The pulsating gash didn't change how happy she felt because, for once, Frederick seemed like his jovial brothers. Leaning towards him, she took the bottle back.

The feared gangster, that even she'd been afraid of, laid bare before her. Not only was he drunk, swaying erratically, but laughing like never before. It was a side of himself he'd hidden away since his return from war.

'I need to take breaks; it hurts so fucking much.'

Adelina set the bottle back down at his side. Two more stitches, and she would be done, he was sure. Light curls fell down her back, dangling against him as she moved. Her eyes dashed across him, still too scared to linger.

Frederick felt something inside him that he hadn't in a long time: a desire to move forward, to take her into a kiss, to make her his. The wrong thing to do, but he desperately longed to. Something about the interaction made him feel like a kid, like he did with Effie before the war.

So close to her, he finally realised how similar they were. The same dark hair, with a few caramel streaks here and there. Light eyes, flecks of green, a dash of brown, a ring of gold around the pupil. A dusting of light freckles that would only grow more pronounced in summer.

'I'm sorry for being so drunk, I had to drink to be able to do this.'

The constant apologies that floated from her lips were unique. When intoxicated, she acted so free and innocent. He'd never know a woman be so naked to him, stripped bare of everything. Frederick gave into himself, and she was oblivious.

'What an earth are you to two doing?'

Etta stood in the doorway, furious. The pair had no care for anything; the front door had been left wide open. Only by chance did she notice from her own bedroom window across the road.

The pair ceased to smile, petrified of the growl Etta emitted. Their cheerful nature vanished, and with it, all sense of pain returned to Adelina. Noting the needle free-falling, Etta frowned. They were both as stupid as the other.

With the three of them in the small room, Etta completed the final two stitches. Knitting her skin back together, she scolded them like children who had cut each another's hair.

Without speaking to Etta, Frederick moved from the room. What he felt would be buried deep within him. The skipping of his heart as he admired Adelina had been the wrong emotion. He didn't want innocent love; he didn't want to feel like that again. All he wanted was a girl that could take his mind away from the past, and Ida, at times, was that.

'I'll give you two pieces of advice, like an older sister,' Etta said to Adelina, wanting to give the young girl a helping hand. 'One, never attempt to do such a stupid thing to yourself again, particularly alone, you always have me to call on. Two, stay away from my brother, he's no good, he'll only ruin you.'

'I'm not interest in–'

'It doesn't matter what you feel, not with him.'

Etta closed the door. Resting upon the other side she tried to resist the urge to bound into Frederick's room and slap him across the face. The way he looked at Adelina was something she'd seen before. Such emotions were no good, not for him, nor for Adelina, and definitely not for the business.

EIGHTEEN

Laughing, Adelina bid farewell to Isla. Another day of hard work beneath her belt. Tomorrow would be the same: work, chatting, and going back to darkness.

As she neared Frederick's house, she noticed a familiar figure shuffling by. The same smart suit from the guest house, from the gallery. James was on the wrong side of town for his rank in society.

Adelina called out his name. James' upturned lips fell as he recognised her. Turning his back, he walked away, each step quickening, moving down an alley, further away from Frederick's home and Adelina's safe place.

'It's me,' she said, running after him. 'Ada, from the guest house.'

A mistake, surely. With the different clothes, and healing cut, maybe he didn't recognise her.

Grabbing his arm, James flinched. She only wanted to ask him questions about Violet, the robbery, and what he'd been doing.

'Piss off.'

A harsh push sent her tripping back, caught off guard by his rough reaction.

'I want nothing to do with you.'

Confusion swiftly turned into anger. Easily hot-headed, Adelina never learnt to control her emotions, thanks to her fractured childhood. In the modern day, she'd grown out of her outbursts, but the new environment only harboured her fiery temper.

Fuck him.

Turning away from James, Adelina walked home, trying to

repress the emotions boiling over. From the top of the street, she noted Frederick's car parked outside. At least she could get the encounter off her chest instead of waiting for Isla in the offices.

'I've got to tell you this, you won't believe it,' Adelina said, walking inside the house, imagining Frederick to be alone, studying the newspaper like usual. 'It was bizarre, do you remember…'

The words tumbled from her lips without thinking about the consequence. She needed to share the experience; James looked at her as if she was Frederick.

What she experienced on the street was nothing compared to the scene that unfolded before her. Unfazed, Frederick stood broadly, Etta opposite him, eyes wild, hands holding a shaking gun to his head.

When Frederick heard the door, he thought it was Adelina returning from work. Though the footsteps drew too close to him. By the time he realised it wasn't her, he couldn't do anything to calm Etta down.

'How long have you known?' Etta spluttered, her voice breaking, her eyes burning.

'About what?'

Etta had been about to speak, but Adelina interrupted, yapping about something that didn't matter. Etta didn't want the conversation in front of her, but she wasn't going to back down either. The police, Charlie, anybody could have walked in, and Frederick was going to be hers.

Like always, he remained detached, occasionally blinking. Adelina didn't know whether to stay or leave, whether she was even capable of moving. The Clarks were fighting with one another, a death sentence in one of their hands, yet it seemed like an average evening.

'How long have you known about Dorothy?'

Etta's voice was no longer deep and scratchy but rising like howling wind. The last thing Etta wanted was the same outcome for Dorothy that she had been dealt. She wanted more for her children, but Dorothy and Mark were incapable of understanding the sacrifices she made.

'A few days. I was trying to sort it out myself.'

'It's women's business,' Etta shrieked. 'Not yours.'

A deep gargle turned into a sob as it escaped her. Feelings crushed her, rupturing her stomach in waves of turmoil. The gun wobbled. Adelina stepped forward, intending to comfort her.

No. Etta wasn't going to back down, she would pull herself together. Finger twitching onto the trigger, she forced herself to stand straight.

'Do it,' Frederick said.

That was just like him: distant, cold, uncaring. After the war, he seemed to have no emotion towards anyone or anything. That was the difference between them.

A tear rolled down Etta's cheek. She could never do it, no matter how much she wanted to. In the end, she would hate herself for pulling the trigger, she would despise herself more than the hatred she felt for him in that moment.

'I'm her mother, I should have been the first one to know,' Etta said, deciding that it wouldn't be the end. Etta couldn't let him win the argument. While his brain wouldn't be shattered into pieces across the floor, he wouldn't get his way either. 'George and Paul are idiotic, they probably thought I knew. But you, you sure as shit didn't. You've been too busy galivanting around with every woman in Holbeck to care about your own blood. Think about what people will say about us when they find out about her. You won't like it then, will you?'

'They won't say anything, I'll sort it.'

'I'll make sure of that, not you. And Ada, I suppose you knew as well?'

Speak the truth or create a lie. Adelina's cheeks flamed red, her mouth hung open, unable to form a response.

'Everyone knew but me. Being a woman, you should have told me, you should have known. You're too loyal to him. He hurts everyone in the end, remember that, Ada.'

'I didn't realise,' Adelina said, not wanting to make an enemy out of Etta. 'I can help. I'll do anything, I'll talk to Dorothy, persuade her to do the right thing.'

It would be easy, Dorothy liked Harry – at least that's what she gathered from the gallery. Adelina was mistaken, the right thing wasn't getting the two to marry but convincing Dorothy to do something wrong by legal standards.

Etta had learnt the hard way that marriage because of a child isn't a fairy tale. The best thing for Dorothy was to get rid; she wouldn't be in an unhappy marriage then. There wasn't another option. Single mothers to bastards were looked down upon, and the whole family would be tarnished with the same brush. An abortion was the best chance for a life for Dorothy. Etta pushed past Adelina, urgently needing to speak to her daughter.

'You should have told her,' Adelina said to Frederick, frustrated by his blasé attitude towards someone who was clearly hurting.

'You're not family; you can't tell me what would be best.'

'Etta looks up to you, she relies on you, she's bound to feel betrayed.'

Adelina shrugged; it was the truth. At first, she wanted to jibe at him, just a little, to elicit a response, wanting his emotions to come into force. She hadn't been thinking rationally, to try to do such a thing, to such a person.

'Don't ever tell me how to handle my family again. You don't know half of what's happened to us.'

'I didn't mean it like that,' Adelina said, not wanting to apologise when she didn't mean it. 'Forget I said anything.'

Catatonic, he stared at nothing, his brain forever churning. Adelina was on the wrong side of him, on edge because she'd spoken her mind.

'I forget who I'm with,' Adelina said, wanting to fill the void with something, but it didn't matter, he walked out the house and slammed the door behind himself.

NINETEEN

The same events played out daily. Adelina joined Isla, and together they tidied the room before commencing work. Lydia arrived late, meandering past the mess and slinking into her chair with a sigh. One worker remained missing. After the incident with Frederick, Etta had vanished, too consumed with her daughter's growing problem to work.

Fed up with waiting around for Frederick all day, every day, Adelina decided to drop paperwork off onto his desk. When Lydia and Isla tried to stop her, she told them it would be more efficient, not caring that his office was off-limits. After all, she spent hours in his home, which seemed more personal than a room in a ratty old warehouse.

Sauntering to his desk, she took her time to look at the details she'd missed when in his presence. His worn empty chair, patched together in places. The misted window, a slight crack in the bottom corner. The depleting liquor atop the rusting drinks trolley.

The door crashed behind her. Adelina jumped, squeaking at Frederick's towering figure. The papers flurried to the floor. Always the wrong timing; she needed to listen and learn.

Flustered by his sudden presence, she stuttered an explanation, retrieving the papers. She didn't care for the cuts that grazed her fingertips, too busy thinking about something else, trying to cover her tracks, to make him forget what she'd done.

'I never finished, the other day, when I said something strange happened. Have you heard from James Payne? I saw him on your road. I tried to speak to him, but he ran away from me with this scared look upon his face.'

The change in dynamic was uncomfortable. It sent him reaching for his glass. He asked questions and started conversations, not her or his workers. Instead of scolding her, he replied, believing it would be easier.

'Haven't seen him.'

'*Since when,*' she wanted to ask, but she knew better.

With no reason to stay, Adelina started to leave. Frederick wasn't finished. Thrusting his hand out towards her, he grabbed her arm.

'Don't talk to him again, I don't trust him.'

With his hand gripping her, she paused, thinking about what he'd spluttered. If she understood Frederick the way she thought she did, then he wasn't telling the truth.

'Wait, are you… No, you said something to him, didn't you? I know what you're like. Don't try to lie.'

'I didn't say anything.'

'Then what did you tell your brothers to say?'

A snort wanted to escape him. Adelina was far too analytical for his world. No other person drew conclusions as fast as her. But Frederick placed her on a pedestal because he didn't want to believe he could be easy to read.

'George told him to stay away from you.'

His clasp loosened. She didn't care, she wasn't going anywhere.

'That can't be all he said, James was petrified of me.'

'I don't like him. I'm wary of him. I saw the way he looked at you,' Frederick said, pulling his hand away from her and placing it on a glass instead. 'At the time, I didn't trust you either. I needed to deal with it.'

'What did George tell him? I need to know.'

'To stay away from you. That you have a reputation for being down the docks at night. Got yourself into a bit of trouble, and if he knows what's best for himself, and doesn't want cutting up, then he won't speak to you again.'

'You threatened him?' Adelina laughed; it was ridiculous. 'You told him that I sell myself?'

'Look, I'm not sure how the world works where you've come from, but I've got to deal with stuff around here. No point in getting hurt, you're still alive. You don't know who James really is. There's something about him; he's no good, alright?'

'It's all about you, all the bloody time,' Adelina said, outrage sweeping over her. Being within his presence infuriated her. 'What the fuck would James do that would be so bad? He's a resident at an art gallery, not some wannabe gangster king like you. You should've left me alone if you didn't trust me or him. God, Freddie, a rumour could start with comments like that. It's no wonder people look at me like–'

'It's because you're a new face, not because–'

'Sure.'

Without thinking, Adelina left, moving towards the art gallery and away from Frederick and the familiar streets of Holbeck. With every step she grew closer to Charlie's territory.

At the heart of it, Adelina didn't care for James or his opinion of her. She cared more for her integrity. Other people needed to know the truth – that she didn't go down the docks at night.

The gallery appeared quieter than before, with only a few people browsing the artwork. Adelina rushed to James' room, moving past a still-splintered door.

The gallery's patrons questioned her presence, wondering why security hadn't intervened. Such a rumour would, unfortunately, fit her well. All because of the way she dressed, the bruising on her head, the area she lived, and the people she worked for.

'What are you doing here?' James said, shuffling away from Adelina.

A trap, constructed by Frederick, surely. She had no business there. He waited for another dreg of society to bound into his office.

'I'm not what Frederick said. They're compulsive liars who try to control the world only to benefit themselves.'

Adelina pulled at her thin cardigan. Even after washing her

coat, she couldn't wear it. A chill clung to her body, her fingertips turning to ice despite the fire burning inside of her.

Of course, Frederick orchestrated the lie, and James had suspected that immediately. In the moment, he feared a Clark would bound in behind her. He couldn't find a word to speak to her, let alone the truth.

Adelina called out Frederick's lies, and with James stuttering away, she concluded he didn't believe her. Nothing she said could change that. When she approached the gallery, she thought she would be relieved after speaking to him, but as she left, she only felt furious. She relied on Frederick to protect her, and he conjured stories behind her back that could ruin her name instead.

'Who's that?' Lawrence said, looking towards a young woman he vaguely recognised.

Cookridge Street, the gang's local spot to hang out. The public baths on one side, the gallery on the other. There, they often picked on unsuspecting victims. They would steal their money, their cigarettes, before giggling towards the nearest pub.

'Who are you on about?' Edward said.

'That one, there, I've seen her before.'

'I don't recognise her.'

'I'm sure I know her; I think she was here the other day.'

The two men gawked at the woman without a coat, following her path as she walked towards the square.

'There's an abundance of girls, and you're interested in that one?' Charlie sneered, sending the men jumping. The tram he rode for free screeched off from beside him. 'Look at her, she's probably some moll.'

'Wait, I do know her,' Edward said. 'She was here when all the Clarks were, the other week.'

'What?' Charlie growled. 'The Clarks were here? On our land?'

'All of them, we couldn't do nowt,' Edward stuttered. 'You weren't here and–'

'I know why I remember her,' Lawrence said. 'She left with

Freddie, didn't she? That's her, I'm sure.'

'Well, what's she doing back here if she knows the Clarks?' Charlie said.

For a while Adelina walked aimlessly. Frederick was meant to keep her safe, but at times he seemed to create negative situations for her. She longed to go back to the place the Youngs found her, so she could hit herself over the head and pray she would return home.

In her heart, she knew that wouldn't work. With nowhere else to go, she headed towards the warmth of the offices. There she would at least find comfort in Isla, who would try to understand why she felt so emotional.

Passing by The Clarendon, steps thumped towards her, edging closer. Expecting one of the boys, she turned. The person gripped her, stopping her from moving. Nails dug into her, scratching her skin, drawing blood to the surface.

'Where the bloody hell have you been?' Lydia snapped. 'Freddie is out looking for you, we all are.'

'I thought we'd never find you,' Isla panted, finally catching up.

'I'm not sure why Freddie's so fucking worried,' Lydia said. 'Because here you are without a care.'

Adelina's anger never subdued, it simply laid dormant at the same height, but with Lydia, it rose once more. She bit the inside of her cheeks, trying to hold on to the choice words that sat upon her tongue.

'Are you going to say anything, perhaps an apology, or are you just ignorant tart?'

Lydia waited for a response, eager to bite back. Adelina needed to be put in her place. The words were met with silence, despite the workmen grinding to a halt around them.

'Bloody hell, have you forgotten how to speak as well?'

'Calm down,' Isla said, placing a hand on Lydia, trying to cool her temper.

A little kid, one of the gang's runners, sprinted off. David peered out of the pub window, observing the scene, wondering what was happening.

Charlie paced back and forth, wanting to beat his men for being so pathetic. They let their enemies swan into their territory unquestioned. They would think they could do anything. No wonder their district was shrinking.

'How do I make this clear?' Charlie barked. 'The next time Frederick Clark steps foot in–'

'Charlie,' Edward said, far too excitedly. 'He's there. Freddie. He's back.'

'What do we do?' Lawrence asked, squinting as he tried to find their rival among the people.

Bloody hell, the Clarks thought they owned him already. They blatantly disregarded his postcode. As Charlie reached for his revolver, the cold sparking up his hand, he had a change of heart.

The girl from earlier flashed into his mind, the one his men recognised. Only five minutes ago she left, looking lost and frustrated. Surely, that was no coincidence.

'Wait and see what happens,' Charlie ordered. 'I want to know who that lass was from before. I have a feeling that she's nothing but trouble for our friend over there. If I'm right, maybe we can make Freddie's life as miserable as possible before we put an end to him.'

'What's happening?' Ida asked, joining David at the window. Recognising Adelina, she grimaced. The woman was hanging around like a bad smell.

'I have no idea. Even women are fighting on the streets now. What kind of world do we live in?'

'Frederick Clark's,' Ida replied, never looking away from the evolving scene.

With nothing nice to say, Adelina remained silent. Instead of speaking her truth, she turned her back on Lydia, deciding to go back to her room.

'Jesus, you're so stuck up, thinking you're better than everyone else. I know you don't have a clue what you're doing. I don't know how you swindled your job, how you managed to make Freddie so infatuated with you, but you've got it all coming. He'll only drop you like he does every other girl. He might treat you like a little princess who doesn't belong in this world, but he'll change. I'll never treat you like everyone else does to appease him. You're not special.'

Adelina stopped; she couldn't keep her words in, not when her blood was starting to boil. Isla shifted forward, uncertain where the situation was heading.

'I don't understand,' Ida whispered. 'I told her to stay away from Frederick, but Lydia seems to think there's something going on between them.'

'Shush,' David hissed. 'I'm trying to listen. Besides, you've brought this on yourself; I told you to stay away from him.'

Ida's jaw trembled, her mouth flooded with saliva as she tried to swallow the tears away.

'Fine,' Adelina said. 'So be it. Here's the truth. Freddie's a twat, spinning rumours that I'm a whore. I don't think he's infatuated with me, if he was, would he make up such things? All you do is treat me like an idiot. I'm a nurse, and that's why he needs me. So shut your mouth and get back to minding your own business.'

Stuck in the middle, Isla couldn't believe the unravelling of the women. A part of Adelina willed herself to walk away, and eventually, she gave in, pulling away from Lydia's harsh stare.

The last thing Adelina expected happened. Without a warning, Lydia came at her. In such a year, she hadn't thought a woman would be violent towards her. She'd been too busy thinking about the men, how they could hurt her, neglecting to think about the women and how they were just as tough as men in the Clark's world.

Whatever movement Adelina managed, it came too late, she found herself stumbling back from a blow to her face. Isla screamed, scrambling to move between them. Adelina, in a torturous fury, forgot where she was.

Lydia's nose crunched. A shriek pierced the air. A crimson river began. Her hands fumbled across her skin. The liquid oozed down her. Adelina continued to stand over her, fists balled, waiting to react again.

Adelina's harsh breaths fell across the street. Even some of the male onlookers took a step backward. With the adrenaline, she didn't recognise her own injuries. If anything, she was ready for more, hands still crumpled, body standing tall.

Lydia clutched her face; she never thought Adelina would be capable of such a blow. With her education and fancy language, Lydia thought she wouldn't know how to fight.

'Jesus,' Paul said, sauntering towards the crowd, clapping. 'You never told us you could fight.'

'Why would she?' Isla said, not knowing who to help first.

'Where did you learn how to do that?' George asked.

'Bloody hell, does it matter?' Paul sniggered, leaning against the wall, relishing in the aftermath. 'I think we should round up all these onlookers and get them to pay us a shilling each for the entertainment.'

Even in their world, it wasn't the norm for two women to fight. Without making threats, the men started to dish out money, chucking coins towards Paul. Finally, Isla got her taste of freedom.

The excitement unsettled Adelina, only heightening her anger. Violence shouldn't be perceived in such a manner. At school, she was used to being told off, receiving detentions and exclusions. Their reaction did nothing to calm her. Before she argued with anyone else, she attempted to make another brash exit.

Ready to sprint away, she turned, crashing into a body. The joking ceased. Men scurried away. Punters withdrew from the pub's windows, acting like they'd never watched. All because of the unsettling look upon Frederick's face.

He found Adelina's rage easy to read – displacement and

negative feelings that had erupted within her for years. Almost at boiling point, she would do anything to anyone if they deserved it in her mind. He knew all too well the look that glistened in her eye.

'Wait over there,' Frederick demanded, pointing towards The Clarendon. 'Isla, make sure Lydia gets home ok.'

Lydia let out a sharp, abrupt laugh. Frederick proved her point: the woman who lost her mind would wait for him to see to her, while she would continue to bleed with only the help of Isla, who didn't really care for her.

'There's a surprise, Freddie's little princess doing what he says. Maybe you are a whore, but just for him.'

As she dealt the blow of words, Lydia moved her hand away. The blood entered her mouth, staining her teeth. She didn't care, she spat it back out towards Adelina. The smuggest of looks upon her thin lips, knowing that Adelina had to fight every cell in her body, to not do or say another thing.

'Take Lydia home, Isla. We'll talk about this tomorrow.'

'Let me go,' Lydia said, snatching her arm away from Isla. 'I can take care of myself, I always have.'

Sighing, Frederick looked towards Adelina, checking up on her anger. The place she once stood was deserted. His eyes dashed around, unable to find any trace of her.

'Down the alley,' George said, patting his brother's back. 'I bet she's down by the canal, worried about what you're going to say to her.'

Adelina needed to cool herself down, she couldn't stand Lydia's smug face any longer. Her mind kept tumbling back to school, to everything she'd tried to forget.

Grey water lapped at the crumbling canal walls. Machinery from the tower works grinded. Trains shrieked as they slammed on their breaks. Men guffawed as they passed on barges. Overwhelming noise floated around her, yet she was at a standstill.

Not caring for the dirt, she took a seat on the edge of the canal, legs dangling over. The Clarendon behind her, towering over her. The storage space windows looked out to her. A bedraggled cardigan on her frame, she melted into the dreary landscape.

Ida glared out of a cracked window, wondering why Adelina hung around. With a scowl, she felt herself about to yell, about to storm out towards the woman, to tell her to stay away indefinitely.

On David's call, Ida's face flattened once more. Trying to remain unflustered, she left the store with the bottle he'd told her to retrieve.

'Let me look at your face,' Frederick said, emerging from the cut, never startling her because his presence came with an all-consuming aura.

Adelina didn't want to turn around, she wanted to get lost instead, to find peace with herself. Her emotions jumped all over, never settling on a feeling. She wished she could be like other people – in control of themselves – but she'd always struggled.

'Do you want to tell me what happened?' Frederick asked, though his voice faded away against the machines and the barge that floated by. 'When I was a kid, I used to come here too. I would try to forget as I stared at that murky water, but all I would see was a reflection that I didn't recognise.'

Without thinking, he found himself talking. Why he said such a thing, he didn't know. If Adelina wanted to be alone, he should have granted her wish. Yet he couldn't help but wait for her to speak, to open herself up to him.

'I fought a lot as a kid,' Adelina whispered, hoping the wind would blow her voice away. 'I didn't know how to deal with my feelings. Children can be nasty. Instead of biting back through words, I lashed out.'

'You sound like Etta.'

'I'm not sure, she seems so tough now, yet here I am, trying to calm myself down.'

'You were calm enough to take yourself away, I didn't have to pry you away from Lydia.'

'Only because you were there. The fear of you trumps my innate disposition.'

'Maybe you haven't made me happy, but I bet Paul's pleased, from the money he garnered. Silver linings and all. Just don't let him scout you for a fighting opportunity.'

Adelina half-heartedly laughed. A joke, but she didn't really feel like reacting. Too busy thinking about herself, she failed to recognise how different he acted, a version of himself she hadn't met while sober before.

'Come on, let me look at your face.'

Nothing. No attempt to move. Not even a quick glance over her shoulder. All her attention was focussed on the water, not even lifting her gaze as a boat floated by.

'You said you were scared of me. If you were, shouldn't you do as I ask?'

A slight smile; he had a way with words, spinning sentences to get his own way. She couldn't let him have that, she wanted to be in control of her own destiny regardless.

'What happened to you, for you to be so stubborn, for you to be so full of all these emotions?'

'I can't remember, you know that.'

'That's a lie, isn't it?' Frederick said, taking a seat on the canal's edge, feet overhanging, nearly in the water, the distance between them great. 'You remembered about training to be a nurse.'

'This is different.'

'Because you don't want to remember?' Frederck said, briefly looking towards her, waiting for a reaction to slip across her. Only a silent swallow. 'I can barely remember being a kid. What I do recall, I don't like. I used to sit out here, with my dad in the pub, listening to the fights he would start. I would wait for him to get chucked out, make sure he didn't fall in the canal.'

Adelina glanced towards him, wanting to see the emotion written across him. A stony expression as always. Eyes on the waves as they crashed into the wall, his mind locked in another time, falling back to experience things he despised to remember.

'In the end, I got fed up. I let him fall in once. He stumbled out and walked straight past me. He screamed bloody murder. I thought I was a goner,' Frederick said, his lips turning upwards, albeit slightly. 'It's funny looking back at that. I was petrified of my dad.'

'I was too. I used to hide in the cupboard underneath the stairs.'

'Could you not think of a better place than that?' Frederick chuckled, before they turned silent against the industry once more. 'I don't usually talk about my past.'

'So, why are you?' Adelina said, turning to him.

'Because you remind me of someone.'

'Etta, you said before,' Adelina said, not realising that he now meant someone else entirely. Turning to her, eyes settling upon her, his mouth parted.

'Freddie,' Ida called from The Clarendon's back door. 'Can you help me change this barrel? David's busy serving, a shift at the tower works has just ended.'

'I'll be two minutes. Wait here, Ada.'

Grumbling, he wiped the dirt from his once pristine clothes. Underneath his breath, he muttered about David and how badly he ran the pub.

The cellar was dimly lit. Old stagnant water, mould growing up the walls. Cluttered pallets and boxes. The old lingering scent of ale in the air. A scrape of the barrel. The ever-watching stare of Ida. A hiss as he tapped the beer. Her voice floated to him, but he was already climbing the stairs, rising into the light once more.

'Why were you talking to her?' Ida called.

'Don't act like you and David didn't watch out of the window.'

'I'm not. I just don't understand why you're talking to her.'

'Ida, don't worry yourself with business that has nothing to do with you.'

Coming to ground level once more, he snuck a glance out of the window, trying his hardest to avoid Ida's longing gaze. An empty canal before him. No figure upon the ledge. Nothing of her remained.

'Where are you going?' Ida asked, stumbling after Frederick as he burst through the storage door.

'I need to find her.'

'Why?' Ida said, almost screaming, but he never bothered to respond, leaving her to stare at his fading figure, feeling smaller than ever.

TWENTY

All Adelina wanted was her bed, to let sleep take her away and then, hopefully, when she woke, she'd be more stable. The emotions and memories that swarmed her body made her feel like an overflowing jar, fury spilling over the rim.

Unlocking the door, she paced into the living room. The ambiance was different than usual. When she returned from work with no car outside, it would be silent inside with no crackling fire. Noise would seep in instead: people milling about, children playing, women gossiping, the couple next door fighting.

The opposite met her. No light chatter, no arguments. The spluttering of a freshly lit fire. Cigarette smoke hung in the air, scratching at her nose. The weighted aura of him.

'What are you doing here?' Adelina asked, still in the doorway.

'I live here, this is my house.'

'But you're barely here, you're always out. Your car isn't outs–'

'I wanted to look at your face. You left before I had a chance.'

'Now you know what it's like to be me.'

'Just sit down, Ada.'

Just like him, she wanted everything to go her way. She longed to be in control and not pandered to. What happened with Lydia was a mistake, she wanted it to be forgotten.

'How did you know I would come back here?'

'I wasn't going to scout the city for you again. I was going to wait for you to come to me. I know you don't want to be out there, alone, without my family's protection.'

'I don't understand. How did you get here before me?'

'I have a car,' he said monotonously, growing sick of her not listening to him.

'It's not outside. Maybe some kids have pinched it...'

'Really?'

'Yeah, it's not the–'

'No one would steal my car, Ada. It's in the alley, away from you...'

'Shouldn't you have driven past me?' Adelina asked, edging towards the staircase, wanting to make a run for her room, to lock the door on him like she'd done as a kid with her parents.

'Sit down, Ada.'

'Why?' Adelina said, coming in line with the first step, her head snapping to him as she spoke.

The mantelpiece mirror displayed the reason. Blood seeped down her head, drying in splatters. Hair clung to the liquid in places. The whole time she hadn't noticed the degree to which she'd bled, too consumed with her mind and the bubbling anger.

'God, Lydia did this to me.'

'Someone needs to check you over,' Frederick said, his voice growing lower, needing her to listen to him, to stop going against him.

'I can do that myself,' Adelina said, drifting to the mirror, moving past him without a glance in his direction.

'You can admit you need help sometimes,' he said, watching her intently. 'I even do.'

'You rarely admit that,' she said without thinking, a flutter of her eyes towards him before she lied. 'It's only a scratch.'

'Is it? Or am I going to find you trying to stitch yourself back together again?'

'Why can't you let me leave? I'll be fine.'

In her room, she would clean the knocked stitches herself with the witch hazel she bought at the market. She didn't need him to help her, she had herself, and at home, after fights, she had always been good enough.

'Would you let me leave?' Frederick said, watching as she paused. 'I don't think you would.'

'I'm nothing special, Freddie. I look after you because George said you would keep me safe. You put a roof over my head. You've given me a chance to remember myself. What have I done for you? Given you a couple stitches in your office and cleaned your brothers' hands. I'm more of a burden on you than anything. So, why an earth do you care about my head?'

'I want to look after you because you remind me of someone. It's all been because of that. The house, the job, all because you're like someone else.'

'I know, I remind you of Etta. You told me at the canal.'

'No, someone else.'

'Who?' Adelina asked, curiosity taking over. Waiting for an answer, she sank into the leather chair. The material cold against her, tearing into the cotton clothes that felt so thin against her.

'You'll never have heard of her,' Frederick said, edging towards her. 'It doesn't matter.'

'Did you say that because you knew it would make me sit down?'

'Maybe. It's not a lie though, you do remind me of someone. You're like her reincarnated.'

'So, she's not here anymore?'

'I guess you could say that.'

Adelina wanted to ask more but she thought better of it. Instead, she gave in, letting him get his way. After all, he'd tried far too hard, and she knew he would never give up.

Adelina shivered; she told herself it was the screeching of the stool as he dragged it to the side of her. It wasn't because of him and the way he was looking at her. No, she didn't feel anything when he looked at her with sympathetic eyes. He saw her as someone else, not herself.

Frederick pulled out a clean handkerchief, pouring some liquor onto it, mimicking the actions she'd done before. As he moved the cloth delicately over her, she wished to repress the sensation that he, somehow, cared for her. Seeking to distract herself, she watched her blood stain his belonging for a change.

'I can't believe Lydia did this to me.'

Glancing up, she wanted to know his thoughts, if any

emotions were running through his mind for once. He was too close, his breath hot against her skin. Nothing was written across him, only concentration as he continued to dab.

For the first time, she observed him in a way she took him all in. From the light bristle roots to the side of his hair, to the longer strands atop his head. Emerald eyes, almost appearing black in the dim light. Lips parted slightly, continuing on.

'You don't suit this,' he said, and somehow, he appeared disappointed in her, like she shouldn't have allowed herself to be hit and become frustrated with Lydia. 'I know what you said earlier, but you need to be careful, especially around here.'

'You made me so angry, with what you said about me, then she started. I can't control myself sometimes, no matter how hard I try,' Adelina whispered.

Never did he stop caring for her. Cleaning her up. Checking the stitches that had been knocked. Making sure the bruising wasn't anything to be concerned about.

There was something about him; Adelina realised that. The stories she heard guided her, she never wanted to get on the wrong side of him. Yet despite all the anger that resided within her, she fell for his gaze. He made her forget everything. The tales were in her mind, but he was forever changing, a mesh of people.

'How can you be like this, helping me, being so kind, when not too long ago you made up such awful things about me?'

'Because I try too hard to ensure a good life for my family.'

'And saying that about me was going to make you go up in the world, was it?'

'I realise now there was no point in saying that.'

'That's as close as I'm getting to an apology, isn't it?'

'Why do you want one so badly?'

'I'm not sure, isn't it the right thing to do?'

Just like the night in her room, Frederick's gaze took over. He gave into himself, his willpower no more. All he needed was a few moments with her to stop him from thinking rationally.

'I'm sure it's fine now,' Adelina said, hoping that he would move away and stop looking at her like she was someone else.

Without the alcohol, she became aware of what he thought; his eyes pulling away from her graze, to her eyes, and then to her lips.

'Who was she, who I remind you of?'

'Why do you want to know?'

Frederick had spread lies, he'd said unsavoury things, but regardless of that, he'd taken her in. In a way, he cared for her. He appeared soft, she forgot who he was. The sparkling feelings that erupted within her began to make sense.

Like they were caught in time, her brain raced against his slow movements, unable to stop what was coming. With a smooth yet calm sense of vigour, he took hold of her neck. There was time to say something, to move away, but she stayed still, letting him close the distance between them.

With a jolt, she pulled away. His motions hitting her with an abrupt intensity.

'I'm not the girl you were in love with.'

Frederick knew that, in a way, she was similar to Effie, the spitting image, but her personality was ever so different. The way they argued, the wit she beheld, the power she fought for. Almost like Adelina was a version of Effie to suit the post-war him.

No, he shouldn't have thought that. There was Ida and Adelina's peculiar situation. They lived together, worked together, and argued all the time. God, he acted irrationally.

'Fuck,' Frederick said, backing away. 'I shouldn't have done that.'

'I never wanted to cause any trouble.'

'Trust me, you are trouble.'

'No, I'm not,' Adelina said, becoming defensive of herself, frustration bubbling back.

'Forget that happened, ok?'

'You know how bad my memory is.'

Trying to avoid being close to him, she walked the longest way to the staircase. Her cheeks blushed a brighter shade of pink by the second until she turned a blistering red.

'I'm going upstairs, to my room, to be alone,' Adelina stuttered, not quite knowing how to act around him anymore. 'Thanks for looking after me.'

Frederick continued to stare at where she once sat. An unlit cigarette in his hand, the matchbox so close but his thoughts took him far away. The words of the black witch rang out inside of him. The more time he spent with Adelina, the more he moved into hot water.

TWENTY-ONE

The dark room greeted Adelina as if she was within the devil's lair. No outline of the bed nor the chest, all matter melted into a pool of darkness. Her eyes were heavy, wanting to lay back down to rest, but there'd been a noise, something loud within the house.

For all she knew, she could have been in the old, terraced house alone without any protection. An intruder caused the noise, surely. Her rational brain told her to remain inside the bed, unsure if she would be able to fight without any weapons when they would possess guns and knives.

White splodges, almost turning grey as they dashed around, infiltrated her vision. She tried to see anything, hear something once more. A gale outside, the wind rustling discarded wrappers, knocking coals from their piles. The house was quiet; the bed didn't creak, the doors didn't sway in the breeze.

Peeking behind the net curtain, she looked to the street. Lamps burnt low against the slim moon. The pavement was engulfed in a smatter of snow. No soul upon the road, an empty lane and sleeping houses.

The noise happened again; an odd sound that drifted through her door. Only then did the smell float towards her – a deep burning scent that reminded her of chemicals and nothing good in the world.

Needing to find the source, she pulled back the bedsheet. Dorothy's old cotton nightgown clung to her body. The air prickled at her skin, yet she didn't feel its chill. When the floor greeted her, she never felt cold spikes tingle up her legs, she felt nothing, inquiry took over her senses.

With another clatter, she realised the noise never came from below her feet from a robber or from the living room rug getting caught on fire. The enemy resided inside, lingering across the hall, waiting for her.

Candlelight spilt out from underneath his closed door. It flickered in the breeze, casting shapes across the floors and walls. Shadows drew out across her. Smoke found its way through the gap. The air turned heavy, gripping at her neck, constricting her chest.

Light shallow breaths – at least that's what she thought when she placed an ear against the wood. The burning of something resonated with her more. A cackle of a fire that didn't belong within a chimney breast.

A simple answer to her question. How foolish to think of anything else. The scent, the noise, she hadn't realised drugs were abundant in the olden times.

The aroma didn't belong to marijuana, the drug of her age. What met her in the doorway was something different, far more powerful. The substance was a mystery to her. The narcotic, although prevalent in his time, was not common in hers, there were nicer ways of getting high.

Frederick didn't long for euphoria. He didn't want elation, he wanted to escape. Adelina failed to understand, not having lived through the same historical events as him.

The harsh chemical taste. The burning, crackling. The dancing light. The whipping of air underneath the door. The cold that smacked her over and over.

In the modern day, innocence didn't truly exist. A sheltered upbringing only led towards the unknown. The Clarks often thought of her as innocent, not realising the kinds of things she'd experienced.

Education on drugs started in primary school. At age ten, a teacher gave out a narcotic guide from 'Talk to Frank.' An encyclopaedia of substances with explanations and warnings, trying to get people to seek help.

At a friend's house, she watched *Pineapple Express,* and the thought of a fun time followed her home. After the film, she dabbled, rolling up dark green balls in paper, eating hallucinogenics with packets of crisps at the bar with a pint in hand. Like half the people in her town, she took illegal substances, but nothing to the degree in front of her.

Adelina wanted to distance herself from him. The actions of the day before were not something she wanted in her new life. She longed to fit in, not stand out. Frederick had helped her, but he'd also opened her up to so much more. Those thoughts faded as she sought to save him, she couldn't leave him in danger.

Shallow, faint breaths against a harsh crack. Flames grew, lapping at a discarded towel, moving closer to her and to the man they wanted to consume. With one swoop she dropped the contents of his glass to the floor. The fire erupted, spurting upwards towards the ceiling, engulfing even more.

Adelina left; she could do nothing else with his possessions. He never harboured anything good. Floorboards caught at her feet, casting splinters into her bare toes. She ran for the bucket of water she'd intended to heat in the morning. Emptying the contents, she extinguished the fire, flooding his room.

Sopping wooden floor. Melted fibres on his beautifully tailored coat. The silk lining slipped to the floor, trailing into the puddles. The remnants of the rug in small dusty piles. Breath heavy in her chest, the adrenaline refused to settle. All the panic to save him, yet he did it to himself.

Moving towards him, the floorboards welcomed her knees with a warm touch, as if she were meant to be beside him. The smoke settled into her hair. The chemicals tainted her tongue.

The man she feared lay weak before her, locked in a slumber, oblivious to what had happened and the peril he put them both in. It should have made her angry, but his soft breaths only made her feel sympathy.

'What would you have done, if I wasn't here?'

Adelina wanted to comfort him, speaking softly as if he could hear, so he would know she was there to take care of him. With a single hand, she brushed his hair; fingers styling his locks, so he became the man she knew, not the unstable person before her.

Watching his chest rise and fall, she prayed, hoping that he would be ok. She shook her head. She only ever prayed in the harshest of moments, because only then did she want to believe in something greater than herself.

Frederick would never speak of the night with her; he cared about appearances because his business relied on it. The others would dance around her questions, whether it be his siblings or Isla. Adelina wanted to understand, but she'd missed out on a whole world, a history she did not know and a war she couldn't fathom.

Adelina hated to admit it, but she started to believe that she was trapped within the new world indefinitely. She needed someone to talk to, someone who could help her understand the place she'd found herself.

Only one person would talk to her about the Clarks. Adelina wondered if she would get a truthful answer from Violet. After all, she only wanted the Clark's history. Knowing their past, she hoped she could help Frederick in the present.

TWENTY-TWO

Frederick gripped a crystal glass, almost crushing it. Unable to bring the liquor to his lips, it grew warm in his hand.

'Unlock the bloody door,' Paul demanded, fists banging on the locked office door. 'Stop ignoring us.'

'Oway, we're not leaving,' George said, shaking the handle, hoping something would give. 'We've got all the time in the fucking world, without you bossing us about.'

They would never quit. The three brothers would be together until the end. They would never leave one behind. Not after Robert. Not after the war. Enough was enough, Frederick rose. No matter what he did, the war always called after him.

Grinding his teeth, he pounded towards them. With the door unlocked, it swung open. Paul fell inside, his body moving with the wood he'd been leaning against.

'What do you want?' Frederick asked, shrugging on a scabby coat; the tweed was falling apart at the cuffs, slashes littered the torso, old bloodstains upon its arms.

The day prior, he was his usual ruthless self; now, before them, he appeared broken, as if he had just stepped off the train from France.

Last year, when he arrived back, all sense of himself had slipped away. In the trenches, he got used to fighting, to living day to day. Then, as a clock struck eleven, he was told to revert back, to become a person he'd long forgotten.

With Effie long gone, no one could pull the old him out. The city of his youth became his new battleground. The things he did to gain territory scared everyone; they couldn't see him dissolve back into madness again.

Isla, seated at her desk, attempted to resume her work, eyes sinking to the paperwork, but Frederick hadn't moved, and her husband glanced towards Paul confused. Lydia half-smiled, unsure how to take the change in Frederick. At the sight of her, his stomach dropped. Her eyes were as dark as coal, skin tarnished with purple smears. Porcelain no more, she had turned dull, enveloped in a grey hue.

Acting as if she'd never been away, like she hadn't been missing for days, Etta trotted into the office. Hair pinned back, makeup delicately applied, a new dress from the most expensive store upon her frame. Raising an eyebrow at Frederick, she tutted. As much as it displeased him, she could always tell whenever he was in trouble.

Fredericks nightly escapades had caught up with him. Unkempt hair, raw bloodshot eyes, tatty clothes – he looked like he belonged to the streets. He was falling in too deep, and Etta couldn't find the right words to confront him.

'Do I need to remind you, of your meeting with the Youngs?' Etta asked, trying to illicit a reaction, but somehow, his poker face remained. It was the one thing he continued to be capable of, even when he lost all his common sense.

The Youngs were the last thing on his mind, but he needed to go. The Clarks had to keep them sweet while they dealt with Charlie. For now, they had far bigger fish to fry.

'Are you sure you're ok with them staying?' George asked Etta, his voice low, not wanting to draw attention to his words but needing to ask for his own sake. If Etta wasn't happy, then he wouldn't comply with Frederick, for once he would go against him.

'Why wouldn't I be?' She said instantly, her voice cracking slightly. With a small smile, she made her way to the back room.

The guest house stood silent, light spilling out from the panel above the front door. Drawn curtains in every window. Despite continuous banging, there was no sign of life. The wood grazed Adelina's knuckles. With each slam, she impacted more force until her hands turned red and sore.

'Violet,' Adelina shouted, looking up, hoping to catch some movement from the floors above. 'I need to speak to you.'

'Haven't seen her for a while,' a shopkeeper said from across the road. 'Think she's moved out for the renovations. They'll be beginning soon.'

That didn't seem right. Etta told her that Violet didn't want to leave her beloved home and business. Her late husband had passed in their room, and she couldn't stomach the thought of being away even for a night.

Adelina tried the door again. A peculiar, unsettling feeling ruptured inside of her. In an ideal world, she would have contacted the brothers, but she didn't know the office telephone number. She forgot that operators existed, that she could've asked them to patch her through.

The back alleyway's gates were unlocked and open. The cut void of people. From the path, Adelina could see the kitchen door of the guest house cracked ajar. Snow infiltrated the room, soft flakes settling on the tile floor. The pure white dissolved into the darkness of the property.

'Violet?' Adelina questioned as she pushed through the door. Her steps crunched, leaving a trail in the snow behind her.

A buzzing silence irritated her ears. Shivers ran across her body. Folding her arms across her chest, she tried to get some warmth back, but cold festered deep within her.

'Violet,' Adelina said half-heartedly.

The silence grew, becoming stronger. An ungodly scent emanated from the living room. Stale air drifted towards her as if carried by a breeze. An unfamiliar scent, yet instantly recognisable.

Shaking, she thrust open the living room door, fearing that another second would sap her remaining strength.

A single sharp shriek escaped her. The scene was far worse than she could ever have imagined.

Adelina retreated. A surge of wind came from nowhere, as if God himself had changed his mind, deciding she shouldn't have been the one to discover Violet. The gust came from every angle, conflicting upon one point.

With a thump, the door sealed her away and silence resumed.

Frederick fell under Esmerelda's spell; he couldn't help but follow her into the vardo. Preoccupied by her warnings, he didn't speak to his brothers as they returned to the offices. Lost within her words, he only snapped out of it when he saw Adelina.

What she did the night prior was obvious. Since the incident, he had sought to avoid her, intending to continue the charade. He didn't want to accept what he did to get peace. If anything, the habit made him weak.

A weighted ambiance hung in the air. Across Adelina's shoulders rested Etta's newly purchased fur shawl. Shivering, she spilled alcohol over the edge of a rocks glass, splattering onto her desk. Another person broken down by him. His nightly activities had changed her for the worse.

The offices weren't busy. It was only him, Adelina, and Isla. Vacant despite the hour. An abundance of paperwork and neither of them worked. No men deposited money. No kids came in with betting slips.

Isla squeezed Adelina's hand, seeking to reassure her before she left. Questions from Frederick would be too much; Adelina couldn't relay the horrors again – it would cause too much pain. So, Isla beckoned him into his office.

For the first time, Frederick heard the way the building reacted to him. The boisterous workplace was silent, only his breaths and the light scratch of his feet as he moved. The outside world louder than him, than what his workforce created.

'Ada visited Violet today,' Isla whispered, pushing the door to. 'She didn't answer, so Ada went around the back. The kitchen door was open...'

Isla didn't know how to say it. Pulling her cardigan closer, eyes flickering to the floor, she looked like a lost young girl, not the wild, strong woman he knew.

'Violet's been murdered.'

George and Paul's rambunctious voices pierced the office. They galivanted through the building, displaying their usual theatrics. Rehashing their visit, they detailed how the Youngs stared at them, relishing in the anxiety they caused.

As silently as possible, Frederick made his presence known. With a single stern expression, he commanded their attention. Paul muttered under his breath, questioning Frederick's change in demeanour.

A pang of jealousy met a surge of anger as George found his wife alone with Frederick. Isla didn't seem like herself, eyes heavy with dismay, skin stained from spilt tears. Without wasting time, Frederick relayed the story.

'That can't be right,' Paul said, his hands reaching the back of his head. 'Violet would never hurt anyone. Why would someone do that?'

'Only a monster would murder an old, defenceless lady,' George said.

Paul turned erratic, pacing the room. Recently, he couldn't deal with anything. One small thing and he could no longer think rationally. Violet's death wasn't miniscule, it was mourning on a large scale.

Frederick needed Paul to calm down, he couldn't have Adelina overhearing them. With choice words, about what they'd do to the culprit, he tried to simmer his brother's emotions.

'I never thought death could be so bad,' Adelina said as she entered, startling the office's occupants. 'She was barely recognisable.'

Almost an apparition. Glazed over eyes. Stuck within her memory, unable to move past the vision of Violet. A shell of a person, crumbling before them. She stared at nothing, yet seemed to pierce every one of their souls.

'It happened some time ago – the smell, the way she looked...'

They gawked at her, mouths hanging open. They didn't believe her. Somehow, they thought she'd mistaken the body, the pile of decaying flesh on the floor.

'It was her – it wore her clothes.'

No one comforted her, too possessed by their own thoughts. George stormed past her. Growing up, Violet had been like a mother. In a fit of rage, he barged into Lydia's desk, sending her belongings clattering down. He didn't care for the broken typewriter or the chipped floor. His once baby blue eyes had shifted to a dark grey. No longer did he appear innocent and childish, but a man capable of anything.

'We need to find the bastard who did this,' George spat. 'I'm going to slit their fucking throat. I'd put money on it being Charlie Black.'

Trying to remain composed, Etta sauntered inside. George wiped his lips, smearing his spit across his coat. Paul wished the contents of his hip flask hadn't been swallowed. Frederick moved to meet Etta, trampling over documents.

'You best be going then,' Etta said to Frederick. Only he could find the scoundrel and put an end to them. Frederick would take the burden of inflicting the same torture upon them. The other family members didn't have to sacrifice that part of themselves.

The dreaded buzzing silence returned. The world changed so drastically around Adelina, and she could do nothing to stop it. Dynamics between the family constantly shifted, and she was incapable of keeping up.

Life before had been wrapped in cotton wool. At university, Adelina found peace and calm. With her vocation, she paved a way out of her childhood constraints. But the wool unravelled as she went back, leaving her wary with no guidelines on life. No do-overs, no safety ropes to help her avoid danger. No escape.

In that moment, she knew the feeling of pure happiness would be forever unattainable for her. Darkness would be all she could feel for the foreseeable future.

TWENTY-THREE

With Violet's death, Frederick became distant, barely spending time with others. Isla and Adelina grew closer, struggling with the brothers' newfound angst. They didn't want to go home at night, often staying in the offices until late, chatting and drinking tea. With Isla, Adelina described her childhood, missing out technology. Isla seemed to understand her, and with her, she felt a belonging.

The runners continued their errands, taking advantage of the regular clientele. The offices remained busy. The women pushed on. The brothers hardly came by, and when they did, it was mayhem.

The women no longer felt safe outside. The streets were cluttered with burly men, looking for trouble, eager to solve a crime with their own hands. The community mourned the death of an innocent widower, and they wanted their revenge.

Of course, the police were involved. With little evidence and no crime scene unit, they relied on hearsay. The day Adelina discovered Violet, Frederick went to the guest house to speak to the police. Sergeant McCormick, after all, was on their payroll.

Etta never returned to work, too consumed with creating her own timescale of the murder at her home. George and Paul sought to do anything they could. Frederick never slept; the drugs kept him awake. He couldn't rest until he found out the truth.

Isla remained silent on Violet's death; she never spoke to her husband about the matter. While she wanted reassurance that the killer wouldn't come after her or the other women, George became cold, unable to talk about anything. He was in pieces over Violet because he'd only ever known her. The memories of his mother had long faded.

Unacquainted with Violet, Lydia plodded on. At work, she did her best to help Adelina; it wasn't a sight anyone should find. Dorothy locked herself away, unable to cope. The one woman she trusted was gone, and Harry had done a runner. People told her that he didn't want to be tied down, while she lived in hope that he would return, at least to comfort her at Violet's funeral.

Adelina struggled. The lethargic feeling didn't deplete with sleep. At night, she tossed and turned, waking with sweat dripping from her. Every time she closed her eyes, she saw Violet. Not the same lady she first laid her eyes upon, but the lifeless, cold bones that greeted her last. Sunken face, drying skin that clung to her, all depleting into a mess of her insides.

A sharp arctic wind blew as people gathered outside the church. They wore their best clothes, ready to pay their respects. Numb, Adelina didn't dust the snow from her shoulders, she let it penetrate the cotton of her new coat.

The Clarks sat in the first pew. Not wanting to intrude, she took a seat towards the back. Those who shared fond memories of Violet deserved to be further forward.

James Payne took the final seat behind Adelina. The remaining mourners stood at the back of the church. Ida sat beside Frederick, her blonde hair rustling in the breeze. With delicate movements, she rubbed her thumb on his thigh. He didn't need affection or reassurance, but he let her do it, not wanting to upset her.

The service began. A celebration of life and mourning of death. Handkerchiefs withdrew from pockets, eyes wiped as people tried to stifle their cries. Adelina remained detached. Every night since finding Violet, the emotions had been too much. In that moment, she felt no more, all dried up.

As people began to leave, Adelina's attention drifted towards Frederick, wondering if, for once, she would see sadness or any form of emotion. Instead, she found Ida scowling at her.

Scurrying away from her gaze, Adelina looked to the front of the church. The vicar, the mourners, all overlooked by the coffin, and only she knew the state of what lurked inside. The memory itched at her eyes, clawing at her throat.

Blinking away a tear, her body flushed cold. Frederick's eyes delved into hers – the first time they'd observed one another in days.

There were many things he wanted to say; he sought to build up courage, creating a script inside his head. Above all else, she needed to be comforted. Completely alone with her experience, with no one to confide in. Wanting to console her, like he should have from the beginning, he moved towards her.

Ida couldn't have that, not in such a public setting. Like with Adelina, Frederick was Ida's protector. There would be complications if she couldn't have him. Sensing she was losing, she reached out to him.

Ever the actress, Ida's eyes filled with salty water, almost spilling over the rim. Frederick couldn't leave her; she would only make a scene. Staying beside her wasn't a form of sympathy, even if it could be mistaken for it.

One arm found its way around Ida's back. The touch of his skin against hers did nothing for either of them. Detached and austere. It couldn't be a simple separation for them – he only kept people close in case he needed them.

The Clarendon was bustling. Punters filled the bar, every seat taken. They celebrated Violet's life in the traditional manner.

The Clark family sauntered in, sending mourners scuffling out their way. The women parted from the men, moving to the largest corner booth. With one look, the male occupants scampered away.

Etta restyled her hair, brushing a piece behind her ear. Dorothy sunk into a chair, arms folded tightly. Isla and Lydia giggled, feeling powerful for a little while. Ida wanted to roll her eyes, they acted like schoolgirls.

Paul leaned over the bar, searching for David. Impatiently tapping his hand, he begged for a bartender to come. George eyed up a young woman, her back to him, her long hair braided. Women weren't allowed in pubs without a male accompanying them.

Adelina had only been alone for a minute. When she arrived, James came to her side, uttering an apology for the way he behaved before. Without missing a beat, he asked her about the rumour: people had been talking about her, saying she'd found Violet. Everyone now knew her name and who she was affiliated with.

Feeling sorry for Adelina – after all it must've been quite a horrific sight – James offered to buy her a drink. When she accepted, he placed the order and left to relieve himself, intending to speak to her more afterward.

A barely touched glass of white rum on the bar. The drink Adelina enjoyed at home left an odd taste upon her tongue. Cheap quality, a lack of sweet bubbles to accompany the burn. The alcohol only put the world into perspective, showing how everything was vastly different, and she found it so hard to get used to.

A stern cough. A shiver ran through her, concluding who lingered behind her. Not wanting to anger him by not acknowledging his presence, she turned to him.

'Are you ok? You looked upset earlier,' Frederick said, his tone lighter than she was used to.

'I'm fine,' Adelina lied, wishing she could talk to someone about her experience, that she would feel safe and comfortable with them. But she couldn't do that, no one spoke about their feelings, they hid them away instead.

James returned from the bathroom, his face dropping as he observed Frederick towering over her. Frederick clearly wanted to say more to her, but he dreaded her response, concerned that she would bring up the night in his room. Even if he wanted to speak, to tell her his mulled over thoughts, Isla ripped the chance from him.

Noticing Adelina, Isla dashed to her side. When she married George, she struggled to fit in with her husband's family.

Growing up, her life was chaotic, full of travels. In a way, with marriage, her world turned bleak. The only person that supressed Isla's urge to run away was Adelina. They seemed to understand each other, both longing for a place that only existed within their memories.

Isla wanted a true friend at the table. Together, they didn't take the world seriously, unlike Dorothy or Etta. Lydia couldn't relate to them, neither could Ida, but Isla didn't care for her. Ida seemed to dislike everyone except Frederick, who she was far too besotted with.

For a mother and a wife, Etta thought Isla was a little too wild. With marriage, she should've settled down. George was always out, working or drinking, and Isla never understood why she should be so different to him. Bored and frustrated, she hosted weekly gatherings at her house. Etta begged George to set her straight before she turned into a loose cannon.

No matter what, Isla got what she wanted. Rum danced inside of the glass as she dragged Adelina to their table. With Frederick behind her, Adelina smiled, giving in to a happier emotion.

Adelina sat beside Isla, the rest of the women forming the back of an arc. Etta and Dorothy in the middle, Ida opposite, sending an icy glare her way. Lydia had excused herself, wishing to powder her bruised face some more.

The men brought over buckets, bottles, and glasses. They came with strict orders to celebrate Violet's life in their own way.

James took a seat at the bar, glass of cordial in hand. With his back to the bartenders, he watched over the Clarks.

Paul shuffled into the table, taking a seat beside Ida, whose body stiffened. He gave the seating arrangement little thought, too consumed with the need to quench his thirst. Because of him, the couples didn't sit together.

'White rum, just for you. No one else here prefers it.' Frederick said, leaning into Adelina. As he set the bottle down, she looked forward, trying to compose herself.

For Ida's sake, Adelina tried to stop herself from smiling, though her muscles twitched as she registered his warm voice on her skin. Intending to thank him, she glanced towards him, but he was done, already moving away from her.

It couldn't be as simple as that. Frederick should have known better.

Their behaviour angered Ida. She was no longer just jealous of the way he looked at Adelina, but also envious of how the family acted around her. Isla had taken Adelina under her wing, while they never welcomed Ida or gave her a chance to prove her worth. It was degrading to learn Adelina's story from Tom – Frederick should have told her, she was courting him after all.

The Clarks accepted Adelina, a stranger they found in the hands of a scummy family. By all accounts, they rescued her without any money, plucking her from a curb looking like a cheap whore. The tip of the iceberg came when Frederick took the last remaining seat, between George and Adelina.

'Why are you always hanging around like a bad smell?' Ida said.

The passion turned her ugly. The conversation around them fell silent. Adelina swallowed, not wanting to fight like she had with Lydia but finding her adrenaline soaring regardless.

'Isla invited me, I wouldn't intrude without an invitation.'

Ida didn't care, she wanted her to leave. Speaking over the top of Adelina, her voice screeched. Paul winced as the decibels increased alongside her pitch.

Adelina's body, hot with anger, flushed cold. There wouldn't be another instance of her losing her temper. Ida was unaware of what occurred underneath the table cover. Frederick rested a hand upon Adelina's thigh, telling her to relax, to not bite back, that Ida wasn't worth it.

To touch her there, in such a place, was wrong. He shouldn't have done it, but he couldn't help himself. He chose a side, hoping Adelina wouldn't slap him later.

'Leave. You shouldn't be here,' Ida said. 'This table is for family and their partners. You're neither of those things.'

'Shut up,' Isla said. 'Ada is family, she's like my sister. I'd rather her here than you.'

Etta sipped on her drink, enjoying the evening's entertainment. Ida chose the wrong time and place for a disagreement; she would only get it in the neck later from Frederick for being so disrespectful.

Paul relished in the dispute, knocking back his glass. George encouraged his wife, clapping his hands, forgetting the event he attended. He loved Isla speaking her mind, even if she had no control over it sometimes.

Seething, Ida's nostrils flared. The fury grew as Frederick continued to do nothing. If either of the women were closer, Ida would have slapped them, taught them a lesson.

Frederick wanted no part in the argument, they were at a wake. Not wanting Adelina to escalate the quarrel into a fight, his touch lingered upon her thigh, giving her support, choosing a side indefinitely, one that they would only know.

For Ida, he chose a side by saying nothing. All the Clarks were against her, backing a woman they barely knew instead. With one foul movement, Ida left the table, shoving her way through the crowd.

James scraped back his stool, following her. Like the other punters, he witnessed the entire situation, and unlike the Clarks, he couldn't leave a lady to walk home alone.

In one mouthful, Isla finished her gin, relishing in the cheer of her in-laws. Adelina smiled, appreciating her fire, her will to protect her family and friends. Even Frederick chuckled, the thought of Ida falling to the back of his mind.

The group grew increasingly intoxicated. David kept the Clarks well supplied as the night continued. James returned to the bar, cordial in hand. Slowly, Adelina drank the bottle of rum, unaware of its reputation. Lady's drank gin, navy men drank rum.

The liquor started to talk. Adelina became confident, forgetting her experiences. It wasn't a good sign, but she didn't realise. At home, she loved to drink, the sensation made her elated. Since she was a teenager, she lived for the weekends –

everyone in her town did.

Slurred speech. Unintelligible chatter to anyone sober. James observed the dynamics of the group; the way they moved around each other, sitting next to different people with every drink. Two people remained side by side, drawn together by fate and alcohol.

George and Isla burst into hysterics. The most intoxicated by far, but it wasn't a negative. They relished the sensation, the swirling movement of the room. They forgot the past five years. They felt alive once more.

'I never said thank you,' Frederick said, gaining Adelina's attention. 'For the other night.'

'There's no need to say thank you. We don't have to talk about it.'

Frederick expected questions, a conversation. Instead, he found himself nodding, appreciating her response. Why he brought it up, he didn't know. At times, he found her easy to talk to, like he could say anything to her. Ultimately, he mistook her for someone else.

Eyes drifting across her, he found a different person. Adelina sat crossed legs, feet pointing in his direction. Somehow, the clothes she wore were styled different, in a way he wasn't used to.

There were people watching, Adelina was aware of them. Avoiding Frederick's gaze, she looked to her fingernails, her glass, the table – anywhere but him. She knew what he was thinking, everything reminded her of that night in his living room.

'Why did you go to Violet's?' Frederick asked. His glass was depleted, his own bottle of whiskey almost gone.

The alcohol set in. Her gums numb against her tongue, teeth clattering as she spoke. The straight rum had done wonders.

'I thought you would have guessed,' Adelina said, words spilling out of her like she was talking to an old friend. 'I wanted to understand you, your actions, the way you behave.'

'Why?'

'I can't comprehend this world. It's like I've lived a different life to you.'

'You have. You never went to war.'

'Mhm,' Adelina mumbled, taking another sip. 'I can't imagine what that was like.'

'You don't want to.'

Paul dashed cocaine across the table. The powder spilt out; he didn't care for its monetary value. With the line placed upon the somewhat sticky surface, he passed the vial to George. It was everyone's.

Paul snorted the substance. Eyes growing wide, he straightened his jacket before he moved to the bar. Earlier, he had noticed someone he wanted to go home with. The white powder was a new form of Dutch courage.

George and Isla giggled as they completed their lines. Desires building higher within them, they couldn't wait any longer. They drew to their feet, galivanting towards the exit.

The small purple vessel was passed to Adelina. Without taking another look, she handed it to Frederick like a grenade that could be ignited at any moment. The others were oblivious to her decline, yet his eyes grew narrow at her; she said no to snow but would drink rum all night, something that would change a person's emotions more.

'I've never done it,' Adelina said. 'Actually, I'm scared of it.'

Laughing off her statement, Frederick placed the vial into his pocket. He didn't need the powder; he preferred other things, and the girl in front him understood that all too well.

Repositioning herself, Adelina's leg brushed against his. A mere touch meant nothing to her; people knocked into one another all the time in the modern day. Instead of acknowledging it, Adelina took another sip, and with each swallow, the burning faded.

'Freddie,' Adelina said, placing a hand upon his leg, trying to gain his attention. There were things she wanted to understand, and, in her state, she couldn't help but ask. 'What did you do in the war?'

An air of innocence ran through her, despite so many things pointing otherwise; she drank like a navy man, rested her hand upon him as if they were courting and alone. With a few drinks, she lost who she ought to be in 1919.

'Many things. For a while I was in the fourth army. That was when...'

Frederick's thick voice sent her mind unravelling. She shouldn't have asked, but he intrigued her. The mere name of the fourth army meant nothing to her, she brought herself to nod, to say nothing in return.

Little did she know that it didn't matter what she said or did. Frederick became preoccupied, wanting nothing more than to tuck a stray hair behind her ear. All because of the similarity between her and Effie.

Even with her talking of the war, she made him become the person he was before. Frederick's body turned into her, their legs touching ever more. She didn't flinch, she didn't try to move at all.

'Usually, I don't talk about the war.'

Adelina's brain turned up little once more. A few years prior, there had been a remembrance for the Battle of the Somme. Something about a machine gun, something horrific. It settled within her that what Frederick saw in France would have been far worse that Violet's body.

Frederick thought he knew who was around them, but he grew lost with her. Etta gulped her drink, slamming it on the table as she finished.

'It's late,' Frederick said, pulling away from Adelina, suddenly realising how close they'd become. 'We should go.'

Taking her hand from his leg, she turned away from him entirely. Trying to compose herself, she pulled at the length of her skirt. Stupid, again, losing all sense of herself and the year.

Pushing the chair out, the world spun around her, sending her stumbling. A quick glance to the bottle and Adelina understood why – only a quarter of rum remained. Under the watchful eye of James, Frederick placed a hand against her back, ensuring she kept her balance.

'I'm scared of my hangover,' Adelina said, tripping over debris that littered the road.

'You shouldn't be fearing that just yet. You should be worried about hurting yourself.'

As Frederick unlocked the door, Adelina steadied herself against the wall. Like a gentleman, he let her enter first, hand out ready to grab her in case she slipped.

'You're a good man y'know. You care when you don't have to.'

With little control over her body, she fell towards her bed. The alcohol took its toll on her, every response and movement muted. With simple motions, she discarded her coat and cardigan, not thinking about how it appeared to the man in her doorway.

Clambering into the bed, springs erupted beneath her. The blanket hiked up around her chest, she looked towards him. In his heart, he realised it wasn't right, what he felt about her, how he compared her to a woman who had long gone. No matter what, Adelina, like Effie, was too innocent to be tarnished by him and his world.

'If you think I'm a good man, you don't know me at all.'

'I know who you are and how you treat me. There is good and bad within everyone. You choose one more than the other when it comes to me. At least for now.'

Frederick leaned against her closed door, his head igniting with thoughts. The black witch's vision was coming true, and Adelina could feel it too.

TWENTY-FOUR

The vibrant silk dress caught in the light, highlighting Adelina's figure. The material swayed at her calves as she walked, making her glisten. Etta said the garment was the epitome of fashion. Adelina felt awkward, not used to such an extravagant display. To her, such a gown belonged to someone attending a ball, not the races.

All the women were dressed in a similar manner. Etta wore a delicate lace number, Isla a tiered tasselled dress, Lydia sported a rather garish floral print. They had spent all morning getting ready. Isla became bouncier by the minute, the adventure she longed for becoming a reality.

George didn't want her to go. The races weren't safe places. London gangs were pushing north for pitch space, and the Charltons were pushing south. Every bad man and their dog wanted a patch of land for themselves.

Frederick assured George everything would be fine, like always, he had a plan. By the end of the day, Charlie Black would be left with little power. And if anything did go wrong, they would have Adelina to assist them. It would be an easy day out, Frederick said.

Oblivious to the men's schemes, Isla, Lydia, and Adelina took turns pinning up one another's hair. Pearls from the latest robbery adorned their locks. Dark, chunky eyelashes were coated in the latest mascara. They bit their lips, making the blood rush to the surface, giving them a rouge colour.

Once they arrived, in the back of the men's wagons, Adelina's fear of being overdressed dissolved; the other women's clothes were astounding, so much wealth was displayed on every person. Decadence to a high degree; she'd never witnessed anything like it. The line between rich and poor distorted far more than she'd seen before.

With every step, the four women garnered looks. They seemed more well-to-do than they were, with their glitzy stolen jewellery. 'If we behave adequately, no one will know we're different to them,' Etta whispered as they walked through the crowds.

Punters at the bookmaker stalls were shouting and balling, betting slips stuffed into pockets. Money waved in people's faces. Elegant attire, fascinators, and top hats. Classical music flowing from the ballroom. The light chatter of women enjoying high tea. There was a charm to it, unlike the modern day. As Adelina past the throngs of people, she wondered if it was all a figment of her imagination.

Laughter seeped from the main hall. Clinking glasses and saxophones filled the air. A large internal balcony looked down on a dancefloor, where a crystal chandelier hung between the floors, casting delicate beams of light across the room.

It was a moving masterpiece. Musicians played upbeat songs on cellos, pianos, and trumpets. Champagne swirled in people's hands as they engaged in lively conversation. Couples glided on the dancefloor, partaking in dances Adelina had only seen on television before.

Etta led the women to a table reserved in her maiden name. Around them, people gathered at large circular tables draped with white linen. Wine buckets sat on ice, open bottles of liquor nearby. Waiters weaved through the crowd, balancing silver trays filled with flutes of champagne. When asked, Adelina accepted a glass, having never tried such an expensive bubbly drink.

'That tastes disgusting,' Lydia grimaced.

'Shush,' Isla said, looking around, hoping that no one heard. She didn't want people to question her, for once, she wanted to belong somewhere.

'Maybe one day we'll be drinking this with every meal,' Etta said.

'That's wishful thinking,' Lydia replied.

'I'm not sure. Who would have thought this would be us a year ago.'

'We're going up in the world Lydia,' Isla said, tipping back the glass.

The upper classes would never view them as equals, and unlike Etta and Isla, Lydia could be left behind. Growing irritated with the topic of conversation, Lydia turned to Adelina.

'I'm surprised Freddie's not here, persuading you to dance.'

'Where are the boys anyway?' Isla said, scanning the crowded room and recognising no one. Adelina's head snapped to Etta, questioning her. 'Shouldn't they be here by now?'

That morning, in Etta's bedroom, Adelina fought for space as she fastened her shoes. Lydia and Isla crowded around the mirror, picking at their appearance, adding more blush, moving a pin here and there, adding yet another pearl to their hair.

'Ada,' Etta called from the living room. 'Will you come here for a moment.'

Delicately and slowly, Adelina made her way down the stairs. The new shoes she borrowed from Etta fit her awfully. Unfortunately, they were the only ones that matched her dress. They made her walk more of a teeter, undoing the refined appearance of her clothes and makeup.

Downstairs, George gathered Etta, Paul, Tom, and some other men, around a table. Adelina didn't recognise most of the faces; she'd barely left the sheltered offices or the place she'd started to call home, wanting to avoid the harsh world as much as possible. Not knowing the plan, she looked for Frederick, unaware that he was far away, dealing with legal business while he left his siblings in charge of the illegitimate kind.

Until that point, as George rolled out a scrap of paper, Adelina was in the dark about the Clark's plans. It wasn't going to be an easy day of entertainment; it was going to be treacherous. In hushed voices, so as not to disturb Lydia and Isla, he detailed the plan.

A part of Adelina wanted to turn a blind eye to the scheme, not wanting to realise the gritty reality of their world. She didn't want to see how vicious they could be. In some ways, she liked being in the dark, with that side of them hidden from her.

'So, it's not a day out then?' Adelina whispered to Etta.

'Did you ever think it would be? Come on, you're smarter than that.'

'What about Isla? She doesn't have a clue. She's been talking non-stop about dancing with George. They're not going to see each other, are they? This isn't fair on her.'

'Life isn't fair,' Etta snapped. 'I do commend your loyalty towards her, but if she doesn't go, it would only seem like we are planning something.'

'Planning something for who?' Adelina asked, gaining no response. 'If Freddie wanted it to be genuine, why isn't Ida going?' Nothing, again. Growing frustrated, she continued. 'Why invite me down here? Why do I have to know?'

'Charlie owns most of the pitches at Beverley, if we take over those, then he won't have any left around here. We have the chance to take his power away,' Etta explained. 'No one trusts him in this city, not anymore. Without the races, he'll be left with nothing. If today goes well, we win, effectively.'

'But there's a chance it'll go bad.'

'Like anything we do.'

'So, you want me to know the plan in case anyone becomes injured,' Adelina said, glancing at the men, observing their wide stances as they listened intently to George. 'What's the likelihood of it going wrong?'

A clatter from upstairs sent even the men jumping. Isla shrieked, muffled shouts back and forth between her and Lydia. Sighing, Etta moved towards the commotion.

'If that's my mother's vase, I'm going to kill them both.'

With the plan outlined, Paul sauntered towards the door. Before they left, he needed a few pints in his system. Passing by Adelina, he pressed a gun into her body, winking at her as she took it hastily from him.

The power to end someone's life rested within her hands, and she was too petrified to say she didn't know how to use it. Without thinking about the danger, she shoved it into her bag, praying that no one would disturb her.

The other men drifted off, collecting their weapons from outside before making their way to the pub and then the vehicles. George lingered behind, waiting for them to leave before he turned to Adelina.

On any other occasion, he would've commented on her, telling her she scrubbed up well. With the makeup, the hair, and the dress, she looked like a film star. But he wasn't concerned with her appearance; rather, he was worried about her reaction to Paul.

'I saw the way you looked at the gun. You've never used one.'

George forgot the Clark women were outliers, that average women didn't know how to shoot. For Adelina, guns were restricted things that she never thought about. Not a single acquaintance held a gun licence; after Dunblane, they were hard to obtain, and rightly so. In her time, there wasn't a need for the public to arm themselves.

George couldn't leave her without any form of defence. He held out a weapon that didn't need a lesson to be used correctly. The blade was four inches long, the handle bound with leather, his initials embedded into it. Nodding, he persuaded Adelina to take it.

In the past, when she needed to defend herself, she had her fists. When she got picked on in the schoolyard or jumped in the alleyway behind her house, they'd been enough. Now, she had two deadly weapons in her purse.

'Why did you tell me about the plan?'

'Freddie's orders.'

Do you ever go against him? Adelina wanted to ask, but instead she found herself questioning something else.

'Where's Freddie?'

'I bet you know where Freddie is,' Lydia scoffed.

Glancing at her watch, Etta stood up. Underneath her breath, she muttered something about going to the bathroom. Adelina didn't believe her. Isla and Lydia were too obsessed with the boys to notice Etta's movements. When she reached the entryway, she didn't head towards the bathroom but back outside, towards the stalls.

'You know where he is, don't you?' Isla said in disbelief. A certain anxious look was plastered across Adelina's face. 'Tell me, where is George? I need to know.'

'We deserve to know why we're here alone, why they never followed us in here,' Lydia said. 'Bloody hell, are we bait for something?'

'Calm down, they would never put us in harm's way,' Adelina said. 'I don't know what Charlie looks like, he can't hear us talking about this.'

'Jesus, we are in danger,' Lydia said. 'They're planning on betraying him here, of all places, aren't they?'

'I thought this was a day out, that we would have fun. Business can never wait; it's consuming every moment. I'm always a second thought,' Isla said.

'They're not going to kill him, are they, Ada?'

'This doesn't feel right. They can't do that, not here; everyone'll come after us. I can't believe you didn't tell me.'

'What's the plan. We need to know; we have to prepare ourselves.'

'You're supposed to be my friend. I thought we told each other everything.'

'Etta, George, they told me not to say anything,' Adelina stuttered. 'They only told me this morning.'

'I should come first. They're family, they have each other's backs. We're meant to stick together because we have no one but each other,' Isla said.

'I thought George would know what's best for you. I barely paid attention to what he said about the plan. I just know something's happening.'

'Oh, shut up, Ada,' Lydia said. 'You only want to keep Freddie on your good side.'

'I haven't seen him all day. George told everyone the plan, not him.'

'Sounds like Freddie, putting his brothers in the worst situation instead of himself,' Isla said. 'I should never have come here.'

'Isla, I'm sorry,' Adelina said, her voice shaking, her heart sinking as Isla scraped her chair back, trying to stifle the tears that were creeping up. With an innate part of Isla still wanting to fit in, she raced to the bathroom with her head down, Lydia dashing after her.

'Why are you asking about Freddie?' George smirked. The yelling from Etta's room was only growing louder. 'Was Ida right to be worried about you after all?'

'Shut up. I just want to know how things work around here, that's all. I wanted to know why Freddie's by himself, why he's left you in charge.'

'Do you not think I'm capable?' George laughed.

'No, that's not what I meant, I..'

'Look, I know what Isla says, about Freddie pushing me in first, but she's wrong. I'm not like him. I don't want to be a grand person with a target on my back. I want to make money and get out. I'm too impatient to do it the proper way. Besides, everything Freddie tries to do the right way goes wrong in the end.'

'You don't mind doing the dirty work?'

'I grew up doing this, if anything, what Freddie's doing feels wrong.'

'Do you mean with the club?'

'You've got a lot to learn,' George smiled. 'We started all this by protecting pubs. Our mates would cause the trouble, then we'd come in and promise the landlords we'd sort it. We did, and word spread. We protected people. We would lift a few goods here and there. Now, Freddie's got all these extravagant ideas.'

'Is that what he's doing now, seeing out those grandiose plans of his?'

'Something like that, but I'm not going to tell you, because you seem to want to know too badly.'

'I'd say he'd tell me, but we don't talk too much.'

'Sure. Do me a favour, don't tell Isla about this conversation, or I'll be telling Ida about you and Freddie.'

'You won't have to spout those lies, because I can keep secrets.'

As Isla wept in the bathroom, Adelina stayed put at the table, hoping their friendship could be mended, despite her adherence to the men.

'You're a pretty young woman,' a middle-aged man purred from behind her. 'How did you get in here unaccompanied?'

Adelina faced him, fighting her need to grimace. A smug look crossed his crusty lips. Disgustingly slicked-back hair. An aura about him that made her want to move away, but out of politeness, she returned a weak smile.

'I'm not alone.'

'I don't see anybody at your table.'

'My friends will be back at any moment.'

Peeking towards the bathrooms, she scanned faces, praying she would see one of the women, or at least George or Tom. Instead, she found no one.

'I'll wait with you, until they arrive back,' he said, shuffling into her vision once more. 'Now for introductions, I'm Charlie, I'm a businessman, I–'

'Ada.'

'What brings you here?' He asked, trying to remain flirtatious despite the irritation. 'Did someone invite you? What's their–'

'Yes, they brought me here.'

The nauseous sensation wasn't quashed with the sipping of bubbles, they only tickled her throat as she gulped the champagne.

'Charlie? As in…' Adelina said, the name finally clicking. She'd been so focussed on trying to act uninterested that she hadn't given a second thought to the name.

'So, you've heard of me. Is it you first time, at the races?'

'Excuse me,' Adelina said, trying to act like she recognised someone, hoping he would leave her alone.

'Wait,' Charlie said, snaking an arm around Adelina's waist. 'I'll show you a good time. I'm highly thought of around here.'

'I came here with someone, now excuse me.'

Adelina pushed past him, throwing herself into the crowded dancefloor. The Clarks were there to end him, and he'd swanned up to her oblivious. With that thought, her stomach lurched, sending her towards the bathrooms.

Spilt alcohol formed pools in sections. The beautiful, tiled floor sticky. Old cigarettes were discarded without a thought. A sea of dancing revellers. In the distance, the door she longed for.

'Ada?'

Frederick questioned her at first, not quite recognising her so done up. He wondered why she was alone, and not in the safe vicinity of the seating area with Lydia and Isla. With a minute to spare, he was heading there to check on the women.

'Freddie?' Adelina said, pounding over to him. 'I'm sure Charlie Black is back there, he's just–'

'Of course, he's here, it's his racecourse.'

'No, he approached me. God, he makes me want to be sick, he's repulsive.'

'It's fine, calm down,' Frederick said, his arm finding her waist, bringing her into him. 'Charlie thinks well of himself, probably wanted to ask you for a dance. After all, Etta chose the perfect dress for you.'

'Now's not the time for compliments,' she said, nudging away from him. 'He freaked me out. I was alone too.'

'Why weren't you with Isla?'

'It's a long story. I'm sure he preyed on me as soon as they left.'

'Well, if he's still hanging around, watching you, he'll see I'm with you. Forget about him.'

'Just like that?'

'Just like that,' he repeated, gazing down at her. 'Would you like to know what would make him back off forever?'

'What?' Adelina said, rolling her eyes.

'If we dance together, like all these other people, he would never bother you again.'

'Is this for you, or for me?' She said, annoyed with him but trying to stop herself from smiling at the same time. 'I'm not a possession, some trophy to win.'

'Is that a no?'

Adelina sighed, her lips settling into a smile. It wasn't a firm denial, but she wasn't sure she wanted to say yes either. Frederick took his chance, a hand trailing down her body, taking a hold of her hand.

'Come on, one dance. It'll take your mind off him.'

With a look towards her, he observed how he affected her. Flushed pink cheeks, matching rose-stained lips. Of course, Charlie had taken a liking to her.

'What are you doing?' She asked, the gap between them closing.

'What do you think I'm doing?' He retorted with a boyish smirk.

Without hesitating, he guided her, placing her hand on his shoulder and taking her other hand into his. She didn't fight the movement, a part of her wanted it, despite knowing how wrong it was.

'I've never danced like this,' Adelina said, feeling rather stiff.

'I can tell,' Frederick chuckled. 'Relax.'

'I can't because you're in front of me. You're the reason I'm here. You're the reason I've argued with Isla, why Charlie had the opportunity to speak to me.'

'You always have to fight back, don't you?'

Lawrence puffed on his cigarette, eyes never leaving the couple on the dancefloor. All Charlie's men scrutinised the woman. They were in agreement; it was the same one from their territory.

Edward checked his watch, the first race would start shortly and so far, there'd been no trouble. Charlie could well be clawing his power back. Whatever he agreed with Frederick seemed to be working.

'I'll go check on the bookies, make sure everything's in order before we start,' Edward said.

Charlie paid no attention, too fixated on Adelina. Frederick Clark had gotten a new lass, and he wanted to know if she would speak to him, if she would give up his secrets for a bit of cash.

At first, Frederick and Adelina swayed awkwardly, limbs out of time to the music. With practice, they began to flow together, moving around the dancefloor elegantly, unaware of anyone else.

'I didn't think I'd see you today. I thought you would be too busy with business to do things like this.'

'What do you mean?' Frederick asked. 'Did you want me to ask you to dance? Were you disappointed you wouldn't get the chance?'

'No. I thought you came here to work. I assumed my invitation was to suit your plan. I guess, I don't understand why we're doing this.'

'I can deal with business later,' he said, brushing her off, but she didn't get the message.

'I don't want to get in the way.'

'You are, but I don't mind.'

Isla emerged from the bathroom, dabbing her face, trying to take away any evidence of her crying. Lydia expected to see Adelina slumped forward on the table, waiting for them. Instead, she saw her on the dancefloor. Of course, she never expected anything more from her.

'I don't have time for this,' Isla said. 'I'm going to find George. I'm stopping this, it's too dangerous.'

Too focussed on the scene, Lydia never questioned the safety of them splitting up. The plan was disintegrating, and everyone was blissfully ignorant, all of them living for themselves.

'Red suits you,' Frederick whispered, his lips almost pressed against Adelina's ear.

He couldn't help himself; she looked beautiful. On the dancefloor, he became besotted with her, just like with Effie before. All his feelings were washed away with the mention of a single name.

'If you wanted to dance, shouldn't you have brought Ida?' Adelina said, grinding to a halt. 'This isn't right, you're meant to be with her. You shouldn't say things like that either. You need to remember that I'm my own person, not a girl you lost a long time ago.'

'I'm no angel, Adelina.'

'What's that supposed to mean?'

'Ida and me,' Frederick said. He paused, mulling over his words, trying to find the right thing to say to Adelina.

The music fell silent. Immediately, he dropped his hands from her. People left the ballroom in droves, flooding through the doors. The band prepared for the national anthem. With time ticking on, he needed to leave.

'Follow me,' Frederick said, catching a glimpse of a staring Charlie, still seated at the women's table. 'I don't want to leave you alone with him. Go through that door, once you reach the bench seating, wait for me. Tom should be there.'

'Can't I go with you?'

Adelina felt a knot tighten in her stomach. The change in Frederick that came with the silence unsettled her. She clung to his presence, certain that he would protect her above anything else.

'No, you won't be safe with me.'

'I can fight. You've seen me before; I can handle myself. I'm not sure I want to be alone.'

'Trust me, go through there and wait for me. You don't know what you'd be getting into going out there.'

TWENTY-FIVE

A bland corridor, poorly lit and void of any decoration. It reminded Adelina of the narrow hospital hallways underground, those close to the mortuary.

After the dance, her mind flurried with thoughts. Frederick and Ida obsessively living within her. Their relationship was odd; they never seemed to spend time together, and Ida never seemed to be pleasant in anyone's company.

As the music blared and people swirled around them, Frederick was going to say something about Ida. The chance to understand them was ripped from her, and she would never find out what he thought in that moment because, for once, his guard was down.

The thoughts were ripped from her with one foul push. Locked away in her brain, she hadn't heard the door nor the creeping steps. Adelina lurched forward, trying to regain her balance. Tripping on the hem of her dress, she clattered to the concrete.

They were fine, Frederick and Ida, before Adelina appeared. The drift started the night he left early from The Clarendon. Ida never asked questions before then, but she became too inquisitive, prying into his business.

When they began their courtship, he thought Ida could pull him out of the abyss, but she could only take his mind away from the trenches for a few moments. Ida was a mere bandage upon his skin when he needed stitches.

The more he grew away from Ida, the more Adelina reminded him of Effie, the woman who could fix him indefinitely. Effie was what he fought for, not for the king or country; he served so they would live freely as they grew old together.

Just like Effie, Adelina could leave without a letter or a word. All hope would be lost once more. If anything, Ida was scared he'd do that to her, and he wasn't ready to give up that sort of loyalty.

In a way, breaking things off made him nervous. Such a thing could send him spiralling back down, to how he arrived home. The army had spit him back into society with nothing when he'd been accustomed to violence. He'd fought for four years, living for the hope of something he didn't return to.

Lydia was the last person he wanted to see after he scrutinised his life. Despite him grimacing, she still pushed forward toward him. Stern, arms folded, she acted like a wife rather than someone who worked for him. Charlie, the Youngs, they were right; he was too soft with women.

'If today was all about business, why did you find time for her?'

'Bloody hell,' Frederick sighed. 'Why do I have to explain myself to you?'

'Because you've dragged me unwillingly into a war.'

'Shut up, Charlie's around.'

'I don't care,' Lydia said, her voice rising against his. 'If I knew your plans I would have stayed at home.'

'To the flat I helped you get?'

Every time Lydia stuck up for herself, she got the same response. She despised feeling like she owed him everything, like without him she would have been nothing. Frederick was chuntering on, talking about the past.

'Leave, forget you saw me,' Lydia said, cutting him off, unable to listen to his spiel any longer.

'Wait,' he said, grabbing a hold of her. 'You watched us. You saw Ada go through that door. I don't want either of you to be alone. Follow her, make sure you're both ok. Charlie's lurking about, and this can all go south too quickly.' Waiting for a reply, he prayed that she would agree. 'Please, Lydia.' With a bang sounding outside, he sighed, frustrated that she'd made him late.

An insipid derelict office, barely large enough for two people. Daylight blocked by a rancid sheet of cardboard. Mould upon the walls.

The man's hand wormed out of Adelina's hair. Collapsing, the red silk dress became stained with grey. Small bunches of fabric bobbled together, ripping lines into the material. Lifting her dusty hands from the uneven ground, small pebbles dislodged from her skin.

Standing, she slipped on strewn newspapers and old betting slips. Trying to grasp onto anything, her hands scratched against a worn desk and tatty chair.

Blocking the doorway, the man cackled, finding enjoyment in her struggle to stand. His grizzly voice, expensive suit, and sickly hair made Adelina back into the wall, her heels giving way beneath her.

'You really are wonderful,' Charlie said, taking a step closer. 'A beautiful specimen. It's a shame you didn't let me get my way the first time.'

The distant bang of a race starting. Crowds cheering for their winner. Jubilations as they became victorious. Shattering glasses as they lost. Doubt seeping into them, believing every race had an outcome before the horse set off.

Adelina found herself numb, unable to bite back. Hands flat against her sides, face straight, eyes glazed over.

'I can't serve you, there are rules. When your husband arrives, I'll pour your drinks,' the bartender said.

They would be waiting quite some time; the first race had just begun. No one was inside, everyone was on the forecourt watching the horses, hoping theirs would win. Usually, the bartender would sneak a drink for himself with no one watching over him. Instead, a woman leaned against the bar as if she expected to be served.

'I can wait,' Etta said, trying her hardest to be polite, even though she never asked for a drink. God, she wanted to laugh; her husband was long gone, he certainly wouldn't be coming to buy her a gin.

A series of cracks rang out. Jumping backward, the bartender slammed into the shelves behind, sending the alcohol wobbling. With the commotion, police officers ran through the building, making their way towards the pitch.

'I've read about racecourse gangs in the paper,' he stuttered. 'We're done for if we don't leave right now.'

Journalists were having a field day with the events at racecourses. They loved to sensationalise. The bartender fled the scene, not wanting to get caught up in the fighting. Taking the matches from her pocket, Etta made her way behind the bar; she was going to give the papers something to write home about.

'I only wanted to talk to you, show you around, have a dance, and then maybe some fun,' Charlie said. 'I wanted you to tell me who you are. Why don't we dance as you start from the beginning?'

Pushing himself against Adelina, he crushed her into the wall. He couldn't deny himself of her, not with the way the silk clung to her figure.

Digging his jagged nails into her skin, he ripped her away from the bricks. In the centre of the room, his hands came to her waist. For a moment, he became pleased. In the past, he didn't mind a scared woman. Sometimes, the way they acted only made the lead-up more exciting.

No, he didn't want that, not with her. First, he wanted a reason for why she'd been sighted on his land twice. Then, she would tell him why Frederick was visiting his part of town, disregarding their truce. After all, with them dancing together so closely, laughing and smiling, they clearly knew one another well.

With a broad grin and blood streaming down his neck, George headed toward the ballroom. Clattering around, stuffing notes into his pockets, he bumped into Tom.

'I think we've done it,' Tom said in disbelief. 'I didn't think we would, but we have, ain't we?'

'The days not over yet,' George said in a jubilant tone, contradicting his message. 'Can't relax just yet.'

'There's no coming back from this for Charlie. I burnt up the biggest stall down there. A little trouble from his lads, as expected, but I sorted it. Beverly is ours now, isn't it?'

Blasts from further down the pitch. A fightback ensuing. It didn't matter what Charlie or his men did, the legality of his business had dissolved within minutes. The racketeering side was also in ruins – bookmakers would never trust his protection again.

'Can only be him making that commotion,' Tom said. 'I knew he'd go ballistic. I told Freddie he'd shoot everyone in sight. He's like a bloody baby, spitting his dummy out.'

Police thundered down the forecourt, tackling every man they caught sight of. Streaming from the buildings in their droves, innocent bystanders became trapped in the carnage. The coppers didn't care – every person would be stopped, every potential perpetrator would be taken to the station. Anyone caught red handed would be beaten and sentenced to prison.

'Bloody hell, where have all the coppers come from?' Tom said.

'Round everyone up, we need to leave. This doesn't look good.'

Of course, Charlie wanted more than Frederick's secrets. Once she spilt them, he would treat her to his prowess; what better way to get revenge on the Clarks than to seduce one of their lasses. Charlie would fill Frederick's shoes and rub it in his face – the ultimate retaliation.

In the ballroom, he'd become obsessed with her; he wanted to dance with her, be alone with her. Charlie always wanted what he couldn't have. Narcistic and cocky, he believed he was better than Frederick. After all, he'd owned half the country at one point.

Charlie wanted the Adelina from the ballroom, not a woman

suspended in the air like a lifeless soul. Forcing her hands to touch his chest, he moved her like Frederick did. She couldn't keep her arms up; they sank back down to her side with no control.

Charlie stunned her into criticising the fabrication of the world. Frozen in time, she questioned if any of it was real. As he touched her, she felt nothing – the sensation akin to being in a dream.

One last place to check for Paul, then George needed to leave. The thunderous noise of the police surrounded him. Staring into the desolate space of the bathroom, he waited to hear something, see someone.

A shadow flickered. George edged forwards, gun in hand. With the crunch of a shattering bottle beneath his feet, a wide-eyed figure turned to him, oblivious of the danger.

Stumbling forward, Paul renegotiated his trousers. Coughing, he flattened out his hair, slicking back the messy strands. With a straight face, he nodded at George.

'Take a girl for a quick spin, did you?' George chuckled.

Off guard, George lowered his weapon. No giggling, no voice, no taps of heels, no woman in sight. Only a slumped man, resting against damp tiles. Dark bruising upon his eyes. Blood smeared across his knuckles.

George didn't understand. Glancing at Paul, he noted the scratches upon his neck, the dark puffing surrounding his eyes, the swelling of his fists.

'One of Charlie's men,' Paul slurred. 'Got me in the knackers, but I think I put an end to him.'

The effects of something from the docks were written upon him. Drawn-out words, tumbling into one another. Stammering between the clauses. The twitching of his body as he tried to point to Edward.

'We've got to go,' George murmured, unsure of the situation he'd discovered. With burning overpowering his every sense, he left, hoping that his brother would follow. 'The coppers are outside, rounding everyone up. If you know what's good for you, you'll come.'

'I've been watching you for some time,' Charlie said, his body swaying, forcing her to mimic him. 'I'm better than Frederick y'know. I've got more money, more power in London – that means more than all this playground stuff up north. You should trade sides.'

The words meant nothing to Adelina, she barely registered them, too busy trying to wake herself up, to be back at five Barnabas Road. No matter how much she forced her eyes shut, trying to jolt herself awake, it didn't work.

'I saw you the other day, on my side of the city,' Charlie growled, hand entwining into her hair. 'Tell me what you were doing there. Why Frederick turned up after you.'

The pain never registered. The numbing sensation didn't ripple into a burn. Pieces of snapped hair within his hands. The tightening grip and nothing, like she wasn't within the world at all.

'Tell me, or I'll make you talk.'

Chaos. Women sobbed, mascara running down their faces. They clutched their purses tightly, huddling together, trying to find comfort in one another.

Men pummelled each other with batons and pieces of metal. Gun shots sounded like rainfall. Smoke erupted from inside. People trampled across the pitch, over the grass, trying to find a way out without coming to harm.

The newspaper headlines would be carnage. The fallout of the event would shadow every race for months. The true beginning of the racecourse wars. The fight for power between gangs. No longer just a London thing – the violence had spread across the country.

Police lashed out, dragging men away. They beat anyone who dared to move. Guilty until proven innocent.

Isla screamed for George, turning in circles. A police officer barged past her, sending her tripping. Behind her, a screech. A young man thrashed on the ground, held down by five coppers. Still putting up a fight, they hit him with their weapons, hoping to silence him.

Isla looked towards the man, her face falling as she recognised him. Harry Allanson screamed for help before the world around him went black.

With no response, Charlie's hand moved downward, grabbing a hold of Adelina's flesh. Exasperated that she showed no emotion, he rolled up her dress.

'You're a quiet one, aren't you?'

The silk slinked above her knee, exposing the band of her stockings. The air bit at her unclothed skin. Her eyes screwed shut as he slammed her head on the desk. The clutch bag she had discarded so long ago rattled.

'I wonder what'll make your voice come back.'

No longer trapped. Suddenly, she felt everything. Grit on his fingertips. Coarse bubbles on his palms. Scratchy clothes against her. She saw everything. The darkness of the room, all matter shades of grey, except her, who was a piercing red.

Squirming away, she grappled for her bag. Her body flailed like a fish out of water. With a kick of her leg, she sent him backwards.

With a sour face, Lydia navigated through the remaining stragglers on the dancefloor. Adelina was on her own, she'd chosen the side of the men over that of the women, it was time for her to learn a lesson.

Lydia traipsed towards the table, searching for Etta and Isla. Cheers from the revellers flooded inside: euphoria and triumph. In a way, Lydia felt lost, unimportant to the world, like she could disappear, and no one would ever care.

The men had planned something horrible, deep down, she could feel the despair, the torture. The only thing that mattered was her survival, and she wasn't sure why. Life to her was merely living, she barely enjoyed anything. She longed for something she would never have, and she would have to live with that pain forever.

A man she vaguely recognised sat at her table, one that sent her stomach sinking. Lawrence remembered Lydia looking different. Longer hair, matted in parts, even paler skin, without a flush upon her cheeks, a few hints of purple in patches across her body. How she'd managed to get herself out of the mess she was in, he didn't know. He'd heard the rumours, but he didn't think Frederick Clark would be so stupid.

'Are you still looking for your first customer of the day?' Lawrence asked.

'I think you're mistaken.'

'Come on, surely you haven't packed it all in,' he said, sliding a couple of coins across the table. 'People don't get away from that life for good, it's the kind that calls back to you.'

'I don't know who you are.'

'Had too many to remember, have you?'

'You're at my table,' Lydia said, her voice cracking. 'You should leave.'

'Nah, I'm staying here. I'm waiting for Charlie, he owns this place. I can do anything I want, and that includes to whoever I want.'

'Shouldn't you be out there, keeping order?'

As a gun discharged outside, a rash of bumps infested her arms. Lawrence wasn't a good man, but the noise outside struck more fear into her. Another clap, and then again, until it sounded like France.

'Fuck, I need to get Charlie,' Lawrence said, pushing past her, moving towards the corridor Frederick had urged her to go down.

'I don't know where your side of the city is,' Adelina hissed. 'Leave me alone. Freddie'll murder you for this, I know he will.'

'Why, are you actually his new lass?' Charlie cackled. 'You're not getting out of here free, not now. You pushed me into that wall, you owe me something.'

'I don't. You're a dead man either way.'

Screams, balling shouts. Thumping feet. Blistering noise swirling. Then the smoke. Chemicals burning, the roaring of a fire. Blaring sirens.

'What's happening? You know something. Frederick planned something for today, didn't he?'

Sauntering towards her, he spat at her feet. It was too late to save whatever was happening outside, so he might as well settle upon her instead. Charlie's body pressed against hers, his snide face inches away.

No longer caught in time but living in the present, George's blade made its way deep within him. The world turned to a blur. Adelina yanked the knife out, feeling more than ever.

At first, Charlie didn't realise. A cold numb feeling crept across him. Before he could move, she ploughed the blade back into him. Damp, soaking cotton clung to him. The blood seeped from him, staining through his clothes.

It wasn't over, it would never be for Adelina. Intending to pull the knife out, her hand slipped on the leather handle.

The pain hit Charlie all at once. Thrashing and spluttering, he wormed away, hands trying to find the article still within him.

With a misted mind and needing to feel revenge for what he almost did to her, Adelina ran towards him, shoving him against the wall. The knife he desperately tried to release pressed ever deeper within him.

A shriek from the doorway. Pleas for Adelina to stop. Not once did Charlie utter such words. Too busy calling her all the names underneath the sun. Incapable of settling, she struggled with him, wanting to end it all for him.

'Ada, stop it,' Lydia screamed, her arms wrapping around Adelina. 'We've got to go, you can't do this. It'll haunt you forever, come on.'

There was no sense within her, only a need for revenge, to punish him for what he wanted to do, for what he could have easily done. Scuffling with Charlie, she tried to push Lydia from her. The blood coated her, smearing across Lydia.

'You fucking whore,' Charlie said, hands worming inside of his pockets, trying to reach his weapon.

'Ada, come on, he'll kill us both. His men'll be coming, we've got to go.'

'Leave me alone,' Adelina cried. 'I want to kill him.'

Saying the words aloud, so viciously, made her body flush cold. Lydia won, pulling her away. With Adelina's hand falling from him, he tumbled to the floor.

Hands digging into Adelina, Lydia dragged her towards the dance hall, scampering towards freedom like the other women who flocked inside. Police swarmed the building, the grounds outside. Avoiding Lawrence, who laid knocked out cold, they halted.

'Face me,' Lydia said, her voice shaking. Trembling hands wiped Adelina's skin, trying to smear the blood away. 'You're ok, you're safe.' There was too much, she only turned her skin pink and raw. 'Don't look at me like that, Ada. Don't go inside your head. You need to stay with me because we might need to run again, ok?'

'Where the fuck have you been?' Isla shouted through deep breaths.

'Fuck,' Lydia said as police poured inside. 'We need to go, now.'

Lydia reached for Adelina, intending to yank her away. Facing Isla, an apology floated from Adelina's lips for the pain she caused her earlier.

'Bloody hell,' Isla said. 'What happened to you?' With only a blank stare in return, Isla turned to Lydia. 'Shit, you've got it all over you too.'

Masqueraded against the floral print were patches of blood. Across her arms, her chest, were light streaks of red.

'We've got to go, no one can see us like this,' Lydia pleaded, her voice growing ever higher, tugging on Adelina, trying to get them to safety, not wanting to leave her behind again. 'They'll put us in the nick, come on.'

'Why are you three waiting around,' Etta said. 'Why didn't you stay at the bleeding table?'

In the end, something had gone terribly wrong with the plan.

The men gathered in the car park, cuts and bruises adorning their faces. Adrenaline burned, they finalised their plans, they'd destroyed so many. Their business was ever expanding. Within minutes, they had taken the racecourse from Charlie. He was worthless now, his biggest success had disappeared.

George spewed nonsense about his endeavours, but his words trailed off. Paul nudged him, trying to gain his attention. The tapping in the distance turned into harsh, flowing breaths and stifled tears.

Isla collapsed into George, part of her had thought he'd be getting carted away. Not only was he a free man, but relatively uninjured.

'We've got to leave, now,' Etta said, storming to one of the two wagons. 'There'll be coming for us if we hang around any longer. They're taking people left, right, and centre.'

'What happened to Ada?' George asked, pulling away from Isla, his attention shifting to Adelina's dishevelled appearance.

Once pinned-back hair fell around her shoulders. Mascara rippled down her face, trailing to her neck in streaks. Blood soaked her hands, splattering to the ground from her fingertips.

'There's no time for questions,' Etta said. 'We can all talk later at home. We need to leave.'

'Etta,' Isla whispered, not understanding why she was being so harsh when something terrible had clearly happened.

'Get in, or I'll leave without you. I'm serious, Isla. We'll all end up in bloody prison if we don't go now.'

Not wanting to be surrounded by so many people, most of whom were unknown to her, Adelina stayed put. George didn't want to leave her, there was too much blood on her, and it belonged to someone else.

Tom grew jittery, trying to keep his attention on Paul and the coppers. Paul itched himself with shaking hands, staring around, almost wondering who the women were. The police started to peer towards them, while cars raced around, screeching as they tried to leave.

Etta pushed Isla towards a waggon. With a hiss, she told her to get in front, and to act innocent. George reached out towards Adelina, wanting to lead her in the same direction.

'Don't touch me,' Adelina snapped, pulling herself away.

'We don't have time for this, Ada,' Etta said, her voice lower, more concerned than before.

'Where the fuck is Freddie?' Tom said, noting two policemen wandering over.

'Whose blood is it?' George asked, his mind racing to his brother with Frederick's name hanging in the air.

'Charlie, he... I didn't have a choice, I had to get away.'

'Shit,' George replied, his hands finding the back of his head. 'Where is it, you've got it, haven't you? My knife, right?'

Adelina's head shook. A lurch in her stomach as something other than words crept up her gullet. Memories flooded back. Hunched over, she remembered the monster she became.

'You need to leave,' Tom said to George. 'I'll wait here for Freddie; you lot go on.'

'I don't understand,' Etta said.

'If Charlie's dead in there, y'know who they're going to pin it on,' Tom said, flapping his hands, trying to convince them to leave.

'There's a knife in there with my bloody initials on it,' George said, darting away and throwing himself into the back of a wagon.

The vehicle raced off. Only one wagon remained, waiting for Etta, for Paul, for Adelina to move inside. All the while, Frederick's car stared them down.

Thinking he needed to save his brother, Paul staggered forward, heading for the building. Tom burrowed his hands into his pockets, pacing, waiting for the police to move in.

'I'm going,' Etta said. 'Ada, come on, let Tom wait.'

'You're going to leave without your brother?'

'They're going to swarm us, come on.'

'I'll wait with Tom.'

To leave Adelina was a death sentence, but under the watchful eye of the law, she couldn't haul her into the wagon kicking and screaming.

'It's your funeral,' Etta said, giving her one last chance to follow, though Adelina remained beside Frederick's car.

Etta knew all too well the reason Adelina stayed; a certain look beheld her. Not love nor loyalty, but a desire to be distant, to be alone as much as possible, to ensure she could put someone in their place if needed.

With pursed lips trembling slightly, Etta realised she shouldn't have been so harsh. After all, she acted the same way after Peter, but unlike Adelina, she never got away.

As Etta gained Paul's attention, Tom took a cannister from his pocket and handed it to Adelina. She didn't stir, she didn't try to reach for it.

'I don't want a drink.'

'It's not for that. Hold out your hands,' he said, not once touching her.

Her palms quaked as he dashed the liquor over her. The brown substance washed away the blood. The two police officers were upon them, a few feet away from the still stationary wagon.

'Ada!' Frederick shouted, sprinting past the police, causing all parties to jump. 'I've been trying to find you.'

Relief flooded him; he had been so concerned when she never arrived at the seating area. Noting her hands, his expression turned from light to grave. The last time he had seen her, she was flushing pink from him, now she was pale, with crimson dripping from her.

Adelina was torn. She wanted to run towards him for comfort, to hold on to him because from that point onwards he would be there to protect her, but a part of her held him to blame. Frederick had brought her there, wound Charlie up with his display, and left her alone without a second thought, knowing Charlie was lurking at her table.

TWENTY-SIX

Noises that weren't truly there. They hit off the walls and trapped Frederick within the room. The image of the silk dress followed him everywhere as he tried to sleep. The words he had said... *you look good in red.* They tormented him.

Guilt set in. Frederick had left Adelina, knowing Charlie had spoken to her. Negative thoughts crossed his mind, and he asked Lydia, of all people, not to leave her alone. While business consumed him, someone he cared for was left vulnerable.

Frederick's mind imprisoned him. The black witch's words echoed from the walls. Over and over. Fortunes only meant for him. A fate he wanted to change. But he realised that what was written in the stars, what was etched into his skin, could not be changed. Confined within the boundaries of time, he could do nothing. He would have to succumb to the hand he was dealt.

Beads of sweat flung from Frederick's naked body. Sinking his face into his hands, he found salty liquid across his cheeks.

The walls, the way they spoke to him, it wasn't a nightmare, he knew what they were like. Ever since the war, he'd suffered night terrors. Reliving the mud-infested trenches, his best friend slowly dying beside him.

In his dreams, Bobby would cry out for help, begging Frederick to save him, to do something. As dawn approached, Bobby would plead with him, telling him to care for his sisters, his mother. Before Frederick's eyes flew open with the knocker-upper, Bobby would talk to God instead, praying that all would be forgiven, that he would find his way into heaven.

That night, with the chants, something seemed different.

Usually, his dreams weren't figments of his imagination but relivings of the harshest points in his life. As he laid awake, he waited for the voices to sing again, for destiny to be solidified.

Frederick reached for his watch; it was too early. Leaning back on the bed, the damp sheets itched his skin. The dreary ceiling was his safe place, a space his nightmares usually drowned out. But that night, his mind was full, hijacked by thoughts of Adelina.

For a moment, he contemplated seeing Ida, to try to find comfort in her. At such an hour, she would only question his appearance. If she discovered the true reason for his visit, she would be furious that he possessed emotions for someone other than her.

Frederick needed to banish the thoughts of Adelina. Pulling on his clothes, he downed his drink. George wouldn't be able to help, he never understood him. Paul was useless. Etta, well, she would only slap him silly. With no one to turn to, he left for the offices.

'Any word on Charlie?' Paul said, bounding into Frederick's unlocked office, finding him slumped over his desk, a large glass of alcohol in hand.

'How's Ada?' George asked, dragging a chair across the floor, hoping to irritate Frederick, to wake him out of his stupor. 'I noticed she's not at work.'

'We're moving to plan b,' Frederick said, hating himself more by the minute. He didn't want empathy; he wanted people to not treat him differently. He needed to be seen as threatening all the time.

The office buzzed. Children chattered. Money rustled. Men dropped off betting slips. Lydia and Isla remained silent, somehow holding themselves to blame. After all, they'd left Adelina alone at the table, despite knowing women should always stick together.

'Did she tell you what happened?' Etta said.

She did, though she didn't need to. The look, the glazed stare reminded him of Etta, of Peter, of why he hated the Youngs so much.

After the races, they spent ten minutes on the road in silence, trying to outpace the police that chased after them. Eventually, he found a narrow, enclosed track with trees overhanging the car. There, he turned off the engine. Glancing towards her, he wanted to wipe the lingering blood from her.

Adelina looked off into the distance. Branches swayed gently. For once, sunshine rained down upon them. Light beams burst through the patches of greenery, sending the bonnet twinkling. Occasionally, with a whip of wind, the foliage would bluster too far, blinding her with the light.

The scent of flowers, of pollen, hung in the air. Warm heat spread across her. A need to cool down. An overwhelming urge to speak to him, to open up, but that wasn't like her, and that sent her emotions boiling over. She didn't want the event to change her, but she gave in, telling Frederick about how she lost her mind.

'She told me everything,' Frederick admitted to his siblings. 'The rumours are true, he nearly–'

'Nearly?' Etta scoffed. 'Don't give me that. Nearly makes no difference. It means nothing.'

'Do you not think I understand that? What do you think plan b means? That I'm going to befriend him? Plan b means I'm going to slit his fucking throat, if he's not already dead.'

'We'll have to make a plan for Charlie later,' George said. 'We've got other business to deal with. Has Tom told you yet?'

'Business with the Youngs?' Etta asked.

'Yes,' Frederick coughed, unsure of how she would take it with Charlie's actions lingering in the air.

'Will it be solely business for you, or will you be talking to the Esmerelda again?'

'Business, like always.'

'I warned you not to meddle in dark magic.'

'And I'm not. I never have. And Etta, I want you to know, the Youngs will be gone soon. Regardless of our agreement right now, if I ever see Peter again, plan b will be on his cards as well.'

Tea leaves settled in the bottom of the cup. Etta turned the china, trying to decipher a shape.

Adelina's grey skin melted into the bed. A tatty cardigan pulled tightly across her frame. Anxiously, she waited for Etta to speak. Finally, an opportunity to find out the future, to see if she was really stuck in 1919.

In a way, Adelina felt like she belonged in the 20th century. Growing up, she never felt a true connection to home. Nova thought it was her travelling blood that made her want to be free amongst the countryside. The night prior, Adelina realised Nova was wrong.

Since she could remember, when upset or sad, she would cry and speak to herself over and over: 'I just want to go home.' But she would always be home, within her room, her own bed, at five Barnabas Road. When she wept after the races, remembering Charlie's touch, she never said those words. Instead, she cried as quietly as possible, fighting the urge to go into the room across the hall and seek comfort from the person who would get revenge for her.

'These leaves are quite intriguing. In the middle is the Aquarius symbol, which can mean travel but also unity. In the northern quarter is the Venus symbol, indicating romance or even love. This here is either a cross or a plus. That's difficult when putting it against Venus. A cross means a warning, whilst the plus indicates an addition.'

Adelina wasn't trouble; there was a slim chance she could save Frederick from despair, but she would only become hurt in the process. Etta wasn't the type of woman to sacrifice another for the person she loved.

Adelina nodded, muttering a thank you. The vague leaves didn't fill her with hope, nor did they help her. They left her more confused and vulnerable than ever.

'What should I do?' Adelina asked.

'Frederick will break your heart, harder than you ever thought was possible.'

'I wasn't referring to him... I was asking what I should do, whether I should stay here or try to go back north.'

'I'm telling you what you need to hear. I see the way he looks at you, Ada. You don't have to lie to me about him. I'm not going to reprimand you if something is happening between you.'

'Nothing is happening. There is no romance. Though, in a way, you are right. Freddie could break my heart right now if he wanted, only because I've found an odd attachment to this place. It's strange, this is the only place I've ever felt comfortable, loved, and like I fit in. It's what home is meant to feel like, if you know what I mean. I don't even know if I have a choice to go back to where I'm from.'

'You still can't remember?'

'Vague memories of the past. I still don't know what happened to me, how I got to where the Youngs found me.'

'You come from another world, not a dangerous one like ours. I don't know why you would want this, so I believe everything you say. You really don't know what happened or where you're from. There is romance in your leaves though. There could be an addition, and I'm telling you not to let that happen with my brother.

Take that reading as a warning, Ada. Stay away from him. If you do that, I'll look after you like one of my own. I'll protect you. Once you remember what happened, I'll take you back to where you come from, because you need to realise this life isn't good, and you deserve better. I don't think you know half of it because you shouldn't want this.'

The front door caught in the raging blizzard. Muffled grunts. Stomps as Frederick kicked the snow off his boots. As he made his way inside, Etta made a proposal, wanting to save the young girl in front of her.

'I think you should get away from him. Come live with me instead. I have a spare room. I keep a tidy home; I'm always cooking for Dorothy. I can keep you just as safe as him.'

'Are you really that scared of what you read?'

'Like I said, you don't know the half of it.'

'I'll take the warning. I'll go with you.'

The stairs creaked, and for a moment Frederick thought it was Adelina coming to see him. Disappointed to find Etta, he prodded the fire, making it roar.

Etta clasped onto the teacup, knowing she could never hold her tongue against him. With Frederick, she became a different person, full of venom and fighting for power.

'The black witch said?' Etta asked.

'She wasn't there.'

'Don't lie. I know you can't help yourself, that every time you visit, you speak with Esmerelda. I've told you to stay away, that black magic will only tear this family apart. I hope she's at least told you to sort yourself out.

If you haven't listened to her, listen to me. Freddie, you need to forget your past, the war, and everything that happened with Effie. You've done well for yourself. You're in a good position. You're old enough to settle down now. Choose a woman, marry her, stay faithful to her. It's not hard. That's what you should be doing, not whatever this is.'

Etta gestured to the teacup. For her, marriage wasn't difficult; people just needed to grit their teeth and bare it at times.

Frederick took a seat, waiting for Etta's lecture to finish. A long time ago, he had longed to get married. That was before his heart and mind got lost in the trenches. Everything and everyone changed, even him, and now he wasn't sure if he was capable of marrying, because at one time, he wanted to for love, and he wasn't sure if he'd feel that way again.

'That's Ada's leaves. I see you in them. I see a warning sign too.'

'She's not stupid; she knows what we do. I've told her what I am.'

'You should leave her alone. Without us, she could have a good life. Smart, pretty, educated. She's better than us, better than this. I see the way you look at her, but Freddie, you've got Ida. It's never good to–'

'You hate Ida, don't kid yourself.'

'Being with her is better than what's in that cup.'

Frederick examined the tea for himself, finding nothing but mounds of leaves. No symbols, no warning signs stood out to him. Despite that, it wasn't ground-breaking, that he would be seen as no good.

Frederick and Etta's relationship could be strained. The war, if anything, had brought them closer together. Their parents died young, separately over time. As orphans, they grew up on the city streets, looked after by distant relatives and their parents' old friends.

As a young kid, Etta adopted a motherly approach, far too much so for Frederick's liking. It conflicted with him trying to be a fatherly figure to his siblings because even when their dad was alive, he was a burden.

The embodiment of their parents went wrong. Etta scolded her brothers for their violent actions, wanting them to be the opposite of their father, though she went off the rails herself. At fourteen, she gave birth to her son, Mark. The person she tried to personify since eight years old was suddenly the person she became.

The fire crackled, emitting orange shades across the room, lighting the coffee table and Esmerelda's gift atop of it. The colour drained from Etta's face as if the devil himself had appeared. Her hands drifted across the engraved box, sensing something lurking within.

'You shouldn't have brought that inside of this house. Nothing good can come from that.'

'I looked inside; they were only tarot.'

Etta snorted; at times, Frederick knew nothing about their culture. He should never have touched such a rotten thing.

Listening in, Adelina opened her door. Tarot – that's what she needed, what she longed for. The cards would show her what to do. They would know best. At the top of the stairs, she clasped her hand over her mouth as Etta dropped the box into the fire.

Flames shot from the fireplace, lapping at the rug. Adelina ran to the living room as ash and debris rained down. The inferno called to her. The cards – she wanted to rescue them. All she'd dreamt for since the Young camp, and Etta had disposed of them.

Her hand reached out towards the fire. She was consumed, as if no one else was in the room. Her thoughts twisted and turned, her mind possessed by the black witch. Words spouted to her, the same kind she'd heard in her dreams.

A gift for Adelina, melting into the flames. Frederick reached out to her, intending to hold her back, not understanding what she was doing. With a single touch, a harsh wind whistled down the chimney. A chill engulfed the house, and the fire settled into a dull dwindle.

With a final splutter of the flames, a card was discarded from the fireplace. Scratched paper, burnt around the edges, but the name and illustration still readable.

The Devil.

The card was singed, but the horns of the beast remained. At the devil's feet, a man and a woman stood, naked and chained to their master. In tarot, the devil signifies a toxic relationship in a person's life, whether it be another human, substance, or even a memory. The couple represents desire and shamelessness, pointing towards recklessness within a relationship.

Another warning dealt. Etta didn't want Adelina to step foot inside Frederick's house again, not after the gift for her was reduced to small shreds in the chimney breast.

TWENTY-SEVEN

Living at Etta's was like being with an overbearing mother. Every morning she persuaded Adelina to have breakfast – at least jam on bread with a cup of tea. Afterward, she would coax her into restyling her hair, trying to make her adhere to the current fashion. Not once did she mention Frederick; their conversations focused on other people's gossip. The man down the street was having an affair, a woman from the bakers was pregnant with her seventh, the greengrocers was verging on bankruptcy.

They were together from breakfast until they arrived at the office. Inside, they swiftly separated, both having jobs to complete. One morning, as they chatted away about what needed to be done, they found the brothers impatiently waiting for them.

Time hadn't changed Adelina's feelings towards Frederick. Every time she saw him, he reminded her of the devil, of the card that spluttered from the fireplace.

The witch's gift came to the forefront of every thought. Adelina wondered what its appearance meant for her. No longer did she question her arrival in the new world. Distracted, she felt far away from the races and even Violet's death, separated from the unfolding affairs of the morning.

Frederick paced, his stoicism slipping. A more intense aura surrounded him – teeth grinding, fists crunched shut. It wasn't like him to be in such turmoil. George slumped against a steel pillar, chain-smoking, paying no attention to the new arrivals. Paul gulped from his flask, despite the early hour. Isla leaned against her desk, questioning her husband's downcast attitude.

Lydia waited, thinking she would be told to leave as the family conducted a meeting.

Once a week, sometimes more, the Clarks talked alone. Occasionally, Isla would be involved, other times she found herself locked out in the cold alongside Lydia and Adelina. In the rear yard, they would bitch about not being let inside, garnering stares from men floating by on barges.

That morning, Isla made tea that would only grow cold. Lydia twiddled her thumbs. Etta scraped a chair out. The brothers remained silent, their insides burning.

The women waited for Frederick to speak, to clarify why they were gathered in secret. But he didn't do what people wanted or expected. He drank some alcohol. He lit a cigarette. Through simple actions, he attempted to remain collected, putting on a show, acting like he was in control when he certainly wasn't.

Frederick couldn't put it off any longer. Locking the office door, he sealed all the women inside. Adelina didn't understand why. None of their business, whether illegal or legitimate, mattered. Her only purpose was to care for them, never to listen or do anything serious.

Finally, Lydia got the recognition she longed for. Ida wasn't there, and she could stay. Since before the war, Lydia had been on the Clarks' side, living for them and no one else. When the police came knocking, she protected them. Lydia wanted to be one of them.

After the card, Adelina wanted to distance herself from Frederick's business; she didn't want to know anything more. At times, she considered leaving altogether, only staying because she had found friends in Etta and Isla.

'This isn't my business; I should go,' Adelina said to Etta, a little too loudly. 'I want to remain unaware of the bigger picture.'

'I trust you, Ada,' Frederick said, his voice cutting through the room. 'You need to be here.'

Lydia scoffed; the pair together was the devil's work. Noting the noise, and Lydia's distain, Frederick pulled away from Adelina's gaze.

'Paul found David dead earlier – murdered,' Frederick began. 'There's someone killing the people we grew up with. The people who know us best. You're all here because I trust you. Anyone that is missing, could be the culprit.'

'Even Ida?' Lydia mocked.

'Even Ida.'

At the mere mention of her, Adelina twitched. She'd been lying to herself. The reason she stayed, wasn't just because of Etta and Isla. It was Frederick too. Maybe, if Ida were out the picture, then what happened between Frederick and her wouldn't be the devil's business.

No. Being involved with Frederick in that way wouldn't be a rite of passage to God either. Adelina neglected to think of the tea leaves and the warning that Etta gave her. Somehow, she always thought of Frederick as a kind of childish crush, one that wouldn't go anywhere, so it didn't matter. After the tea, she should have squashed that feeling down until it was nothing. But only the card solidified in her memory, like she was already chained and at the mercy of the beast.

'I don't think these deaths are the work of a lone woman,' Etta said. 'David was a big lad, Ida… she's a small girl in comparison.'

'I'm not saying Ida's killed him. For all we know, many people could be involved in this. We all know how many people we've angered. Our greatest enemy right now is Charlie. I got word that he's alive, messed up, but still kicking. Don't forget we shot his nephew, Joe, as well.'

'We?' Paul repeated.

'Don't you mean you shot his nephew,' George said.

'Don't pick apart my words. This is important. There are many people who could be behind this. We need to find out what the southerners know about Charlie, whether he's managed to get word out that we've stabbed him in the back.'

'Literally, as well as physically,' George chuckled.

'The Italians in London are in issue; they own the racecourses in the south and are pushing north. We've got the Charltons in Newcastle too. Don't forget the Youngs – Thomas might want revenge, you never know.'

'Half the bloody country then?' Etta said.

'We're fucking surrounded,' Isla spat.

'I told you to wait it out with Charlie. This is all your fault, Freddie, constantly wanting more,' Etta said. 'Who's going to be next? Shall we place some bets? You've already put Adelina in danger at the fucking races.'

'What if it's me next,' Isla said. 'Are you going to tell George you don't know? What if it's one of your brothers next, Freddie, because they were in the wrong place at the wrong bloody time like Violet and David.'

'I don't have a mystical ball, Isla,' Frederick said. 'I have no way to see into the fucking future.'

'What's wrong with the old ways,' Etta said. 'What we used to do, we got by then. We don't need the whole of the city, do we?'

'I want more to life than scrimping every penny, don't you? I know you're enjoying your new house and those fancy clothes you're always buying yourself. What about Dorothy? With little money, what are you going to do there?

Did I know this was going to happen, with Violet, with David? Do you see me reading tea leaves? Or listening to fucking make-believe like Isla?'

'None of us know what's going to happen,' Adelina said, seeking to defend her friends but forgetting who she started to argue with. 'We need to work with the facts. What's happened isn't random, it's calculated. They knew who to target. David was easy, he was always alone at night. You told me yourself he forgets to lock the front doors half the time. Violet was vulnerable, frail and weak, all alone in that massive building.

The question is, why did they die? Why would someone murder two family friends? What were they hoping to achieve? Surely, you can answer that, Freddie.'

'This is a waste of my time,' Lydia said, clashing her typewriter keys and resuming work.

'I need a fucking drink,' Paul announced, sauntering out with George following closely behind.

'I'll go to the station,' Etta said. 'Try to find that Sergeant.'

The meeting ended abruptly. The siblings disbanded, leaving the women to plod on with work. The news and the cracks that formed couldn't stop them from opening the shop. They needed to continue, for the sake of their livelihoods.

A battered oil lamp cast a dull glow on Adelina's desk. The never-ending clashes from the buildings next door. The grinding of metal. Loud bangs met with shrieks, sending shivers running up her spine. The day was ending, and without a clock or owning a watch, she didn't realise the time.

Too involved with work, she didn't notice the movement of people around her. Despite recognising the night drawing in, she didn't want to leave. In the offices, she felt safe. She could set her mind on the paperwork, and it wouldn't wander away, bringing up repressed memories.

In the end, Etta would come to retrieve her, she would drag her back home. At least, that's what she thought, with Etta being a motherly figure and all.

Etta, however, was preoccupied by David's death. She took the investigation into her own hands. After finding no trace of Sergeant McCormick in the usual places, she stormed to his house. Breaking in through a back door, she snuck up on him as he napped on the sofa.

With a knife digging into his stomach, slowly unleashing blood, she gathered as much information as she could. No one would believe him, that a woman overpowered him. Being frightened of a lady was embarrassing.

The Sergeant feared for his life, thinking the blade would delve deeper into him, eventually rupturing insides. When met with the Clarks, he always found himself on the verge of death. That's why he accepted their money every week, in the hope that he would stay alive to see his family grow up. With the promise that his wife and children wouldn't come to harm, he turned a blind eye to missing people and blood on the streets.

Pitter-patters of rain hit the office window. Snow seeped away into streams. With a piece of paper in hand, Adelina made her way to Frederick's room, noticing the door slightly ajar.

Groaning, the wood gave way to an empty space. Lashings of rain against the misted window. Vaguely lit from the streetlamp outside. A finished bottle of liquor on his desk. Coat still perched on the back of his chair.

The family was tearing apart at the seams, and he still attended to his business, putting money before blood. Placing the document down, she knew he would sign it instantly, no matter what possessed his mind.

Whenever she found herself in his office, the desk had been full, littered with items. Bar the bottle and her piece of paper, the desk was empty. Adelina couldn't remember him leaving, even though he must've moved past her.

After her outburst at the meeting, no one spoke to her. After the races, people changed the way they acted around her, like somehow, she'd become delicate and broken because of Charlie. That one experience didn't define her, it wouldn't set her life on a different path.

With a tap on the document, she decided to leave, to go back to Etta's and sit in the dark. Headlights radiated through the window. The beam entered the room in a different manner. Something shone on the lapel of his coat. Like a guiding light, her hands fell to the tweed. Pulling at the lapels, cold, glowing metal bit her skin.

Speckles of red drew from her, but she still searched the coat. Several fishhooks were sewn into the lapels. How had she not noticed before? Adelina had been blind to the people in front of her.

The metal prodded and etched her skin. Nothing could snap her from the daze. Adelina thought about its purpose – a defence if someone grabbed the wearer with ill intent. The hooks were only aggressive to the confrontational. But the torture… the pain they could inflict was sickening.

Blood dripped across the coat, splattering onto the chair, staining the floor. Adelina didn't worry about the mess she created; her thoughts became her main priority, even when the door creaked.

His words made no sense. They evaporated into the air. She couldn't remove herself from the medieval nature of the coat. It would be used against unknowing souls. She questioned whether it was right to cause such pain when the person didn't realise the danger.

Frederick's hand came into her vision. In a trance, she held onto the material, gripping the lapel, the hook scratching her. That was until he rested a hand on her shoulder.

The devil before her; he appeared as an angel, luring her into a false sense of security. Cold skin ran over her. The blood transferred to him, staining his fingertips.

Guilt from touching the hooks. Embarrassment at being caught. Hurt at being left in the dark. A tingle from where he held her. Emotions swarmed her body. All because of him. Frederick made her feel alive, like she was living in the present and not dead in a made-up world.

Even without the coat, he held her hand, examining the cuts that grazed her skin. The engraving of his weapon upon her, the naivety of her, washed over him. The way she acted contradicted the way she spoke, a mismatch of a woman, like she'd never lived.

Jagged wounds. A million paper cuts upon her. Lacking the energy or the desire to pull away, she let him hold her. Eyes trailing across their hands, looking at the way they meshed together. When her gaze drifted up, she realised he'd been observing her, completely captivated by her.

It was wrong; they would only hurt each other. Alone in the building, no disruptions, nothing to stop them. The cards had been dealt. The future written out for them. The question to them, was whether it was worthwhile fighting against something when they could go with fate itself.

Before Adelina stood a broken man, his mind still in France. Tied to the devil of war. Self-medicating to banish his thoughts, it only made him ruthless, an evil man to his enemies. Adelina was the devil's advocate, dutifully following him, always beside him. She would never speak against him. She didn't condone the violence, she never saw it with her own eyes – so can one believe in something, when they don't see it for themselves? There are ways of pushing back against everything.

They didn't speak; they understood each other's thoughts already. When they touched, their minds entwined into one. They stared at one another, forgetting warnings, acting upon feelings.

With a sense of vigour, he crashed into her, taking her into a kiss. More of a want than the time prior. A need that had been festering within him for weeks. Uncontrollable, like there was no time, like they would soon wake from their daydream to the harsh reality of what they were doing.

Frederick pushed her against the desk, not wanting her to leave, but she would never do that, he made her forget the world and all that had happened. They didn't notice the paper crumpling beneath them, the blood transferring across them, not even the shattering of the bottle. They lost themselves and time itself.

TWENTY-EIGHT

For once, it was Adelina who could not sleep. The night air nipped at her bare chest, only Frederick's coat over the top of her old nightdress. Opposite her, Etta's home was all in darkness, her room waiting for her. How she would explain herself, she didn't know. Of course, Etta would notice she hadn't gone home.

The house was claustrophobic, the dreary walls made her overthink. The street was deserted, engulfed in a fading orange hue from the gas lamps. The junction was covered in fog, only the houses two doors down were visible. Even outside, she continued to fret, her rash decisions taking a hold of her.

The tweed material caught against the wall, leaving small spirals of unwoven fabric as she sunk downwards. The cobbles didn't feel cold against her, they only gave her a spark of life, a sensation that she still breathed.

Two things sent jolts of electricity through her body: the brisk weather against her bare skin and Frederick when he glanced at her like a lost love. They were the only things that made her feel alive, like her heart still beat and she hadn't died before she arrived in 1919.

There was more to him than just feeling present. Emotions bundled despite knowing he didn't want her, but someone else. Adelina never asked who he longed for or what happened to her. Isla would have told her, but she never brought herself to ask.

The consequence of her actions wreaked havoc on her conscience. The living room reminded her of the cards she'd been dealt, how they were tied to the devil. His office reminded her of death, of fights, of Ida. In Frederick's room, there were her things too: an old nightgown, a stained photograph of them, a brush with her hair still in the bristles.

Prickling on her arm, not from the temperature but from being watched. David's death still fresh, yet instead of moving, she waited to see the outline of a figure. If anything, it gave her hope, closure, that she would finally find out the truth of what happened to her.

Slowly, the person uncovered themselves. A dashingly dressed man who she remembered so well. Soft eyes filled with wonder as he recognised her.

'Do you always sit outside at this time of night?' James said, approaching her.

'It's the first time.'

James slumped against Frederick's house alongside her. They viewed the street, not each other. A leaf continued to travel from afar. Uneven cobbles dipped across the road, waiting for rain to fill them up. Hot blazing chemicals itched at their throat.

The spark of a match. A cigarette dangled from his mouth, the silver case on his outstretched legs next to hers. With the intake of breath, the world became dull once more. Casting the match away, the flame extinguished. Smoke hovered around them.

'Would you like one?'

As a rebellious teenager, giving in to peer pressure, she had smoked a few times, though not enough to become addicted. The fear of cancer, from the adverts and lessons at school, stuck with her. The Clarks didn't know about that, and they encased her in their fumes daily. Giving in, she nodded, she had no hope of life, so she might as well enjoy herself.

Like liquor but harsher. The taste rested upon her tongue. Adelina waited for the buzz, for the psychoactive qualities she'd been more used to. They never came. The end burned away in her hand.

'You'll catch a cold,' James said, trying to not look at her unclothed chest. Noting the undone coat, he wondered if that one also had fishhooks embedded underneath the lapels.

'I'll be fine.'

'I see the way Frederick looks at you and the way you look at him too.'

Adelina paused, waiting for his words to drift away with the smoke; she had nothing to say to him about Frederick.

'Correct me if I'm wrong,' he said, stubbing out his cigarette. 'I think you like him.'

'He's been kind to me,' she said, not wanting to disclose the truth. What she'd done was a sin, and she feared the consequence, even though she didn't truly believe in God, Heaven and Hell. 'Frederick has Ida.'

'I'm not sure, the world is an ever-changing place.'

Too busy filling with anger, at what she'd allowed herself to do, she didn't acknowledge his goodbye. There was a war inside her. The modern-day girl who would've hated to be *that* woman.

Within the shadows of the night, Adelina didn't see her lurking. The woman who dealt her cards scrutinised her. Through the mist, she could see her, the amber glow highlighting her face, the beauty of another time. Sinful lust inscribed upon her. Power running through her veins. Destiny almost written out for her.

'*Listen to me, sinful one,*' Esmerelda said from the shadows.

Like a curtain parting, the woman unveiled herself from the sheath of the mist. Hair dangled around her wrinkled face. Eyes black with divination. The chants she spoke escaped from her charcoal mouth and swollen tongue. The voice was almost hers, slightly distorted, a low scratchy growl.

'*The lines written into your palms tell you your fate. Tea leaves that read the future can ever change. Each chain of events withholds a different outcome. Tread lightly. The card has been dealt. The chains are weak, though the ties are etched into both of you.*'

Crimson leaked from the woman's obsidian eyes. Dripping down her cheeks, she paid no attention to the stream. Lucid skin, hanging over her like she was dead.

'*Every choice is yours to make. There are many different paths to take. Each sin takes you further away. He will beg for you to stay. Be safe, for outcomes can be harsh.*'

Within the grey night, the black witch became lost again.

Running towards her, into the thick haze, Adelina disappeared into its depths. With every step, she saw less of the world. Everything was the same – a dull murkiness hung in the air.

Adelina slammed the front door, not knowing how she made it back. Falling to the staircase, the world spun. An overwhelming nausea devoured her. The fog within her, spluttering from her mouth. Hands touching her cheeks came away with fresh blood.

Leaves fell towards her feet, burnt oranges and reds. Forks of foliage stood out against the damp grass, dew hugging each strand. Mud crept its way onto her Converse hi-top shoes. She didn't care, she took her time.

Wind whistled through the trees, sending more leaves down, committing themselves to the cycle of the ecosystem. Branches groaned as they dispelled their life. Bark peeled away from trunks. Roots battled for space, raising through the earth.

The flowers were beautiful – a bright decadent pink, standing out against the decay. The old bunch would need to be removed, fallen petals had left sickly stalks in their place. Stagnant water, mixed with dirt and grime, formed a thick layer of slime on top.

Everything needed to be cleaned. Adelina couldn't do it then, the place put her on edge. Stepping into its boundaries, wandering through rows of people that had passed, made her fearful of life and what happened afterward. Every stone signified a death, sometimes more than one, their bodies buried deep below, still in the boxes from the day they were lowered.

A black headstone, chipped from a falling branch. Only Adelina had visited recently, the last flowers were also hers. She wondered when the ground would settle. The mud still protruded, only reminding her of how the remaining parts of the woman she loved were buried deep below.

Creaking trees, flowers shifting. The grave beside her was full of ornaments. Pebbles boarded the plot. A beautiful white marble headstone. An inscription that brought tears to her eyes. Their family cared for them, missed them. They visited often; no dead flowers, no moss growing over the stone.

Prickling skin: it wasn't a good place to feel like she did. Tales of ghouls frightened her; they made her quake in the night as a child and even a teenager. Adelina withdrew from the grave, edging towards the nearest exit.

Wispy clouds turned shades of pink. The moon still high in the sky, casting light upon her. In a few hours, she would sit her final exam. Graduation, a real vocation within reach. No one cared for that. No one was proud of what she achieved. Nova would have been.

Squelching ground beneath her. Headlights passed by sporadically. An old woman stood against the gate's pillar, her dress billowing. Long grey hair swirling, moving freely in the wind. A recognition, like she knew the woman. In the dull light, she almost looked like Nova, as if she waited to meet her at the gates.

Rows of unmarked headstones, white rock weathered by time. No dates, no names, no bodies beneath. A symbol of those lost to the wars, to those whose bodies had never been recovered.

The woman turned. Bright blue eyes shone into her soul. It was her. The flowing clothes, the beauty mark upon her cheek. The stature, the wrinkles that graced her face. Pale skin, sunken lips, her mouth moved like she spoke.

Adelina stopped, petrified to move forwards. Nova, her grandmother, stood before her, but she'd died. It couldn't be her in front of her.

When anything strange happened in the past, she turned away, wanting to suppress her connection. Adelina didn't want such a thing to flow in her veins. Seeing things made her uncomfortable; it struck fear within her.

Stones screeched beneath her feet. She screwed her eyes shut, trying to banish the image from her mind. She took a step backward.

A piercing shriek, like the horn of a train. Singular, loud, whistling. Hot breath against her neck. The voice of a demon. Adelina looked towards her grandma.

A crack, glass shattering. Vision turning black. Cool liquid poured from her. Iron sat on her tongue. A vague tugging sensation as awareness faded.

'Your life is not going to be straightforward, Adelina; you're going to feel like you're going backwards. It's not a bad thing. To move onward, you have to go backward to achieve it.'

TWENTY-NINE

The house creaked, wind whistled around its side. Rain splashed upon the window, a tapping like someone was knocking from the other side. A roaring fire ejected another plume of smoke into the sky.

A pale, lifeless body covered in a ratty blanket. Eyes closed, lids almost transparent. Skin icy, colder than the night's air. Out of their world, trapped within her own. Flattening out her jacket, Etta let the wool fall around the girl, covering her in another layer.

'You were right to come get me,' Etta said to Frederick.

Pacing, her heels disturbed the air. Dust swarmed her, lifting from the old floorboards.

'Do I want to know why Ada never came back to my house?'

'This isn't the time to scold me.'

Etta would put the blame on him, like always. If Adelina hadn't spent the night with him, then she would have been in a different position.

'What happened to her?'

'I woke up with the front door banging, I didn't even know she was outside.'

Adelina's body appeared frail against the stairs; she couldn't hold on to anything as she slipped down. Gravity took its effect, and she couldn't do anything to stop it. At first, Frederick watched over her, concerned with her sudden ill appearance.

Skin piercing white like snow. He rushed over. She stung his hands, setting him ablaze like he touched hot coal, not a body. He lifted her carefully, taking her to the sofa. His coat hung loosely from her shoulders, far too big, swallowing her whole, yet it seemed to suit her.

'Did she say anything?'

'Nothing. It's like she had a fit.'

A single harsh breath caused Adelina to bolt upright. Without thinking, he knelt beside her. With her, he got lost far too easily. There was a concern within his gaze that said she meant something to him. There were other things in the world than a troublesome young woman, but everyone breaks their rules for someone.

The tea leaves would be right. They wouldn't change anything. Etta coughed, trying to gain their attention, pulling them away from each other.

'Make us some tea, then leave us alone to talk,' Etta said to Frederick.

With fresh tea in her hands, Etta sat opposite Adelina. Blankets bundled around her frame, the cuffs of his tatty jumper loose around her fingers. Cigarette smoke drifted down the staircase. Frederick wouldn't sleep, not now.

There, he would wait for what Etta would discover. Staring out at the street, he hoped his sister would repeat the conversation, that she wouldn't be like him and hold the information hostage.

'You can tell me anything,' Etta said. 'Why you were outside at past midnight would be a good place to start.'

'You're like me, you believe in the absurd, don't you?'

'Why?'

'I need you to trust me. What happened was completely irrational. I need to tell someone; I'm not sure I'll be able to move past it otherwise. I think I'll go mad if I don't…'

'Nothing surprises me,' Etta said, taking a sip of her drink. 'I've seen and heard it all. I know some things can only be understood by certain people.'

'I couldn't sleep. I debated going back to your house. After the cards, I should have been with you. I made a mistake. I was outside, contemplating what to do, when I saw Esmerelda, the one the Youngs call the black witch. You know who that is, don't you?'

'Of course, I told Freddie to stay away from her.'

'I don't think she was here for him, but rather for me. She spoke to me in riddles, it didn't make sense. Blood poured from her eyes like she was cursed. I followed her. I ran after her. I wanted answers, to all this, but I couldn't find her.

Before I knew it, I was back here, slamming the front door. I panicked; I couldn't remember how I got inside. The world went bizarre, like I was drunk. Then, this weird thing happened. That's when it gets unbelievable, even for me.'

'Go on, I believe you. If you told me that you saw the devil himself, horns glistening in the full moon, I'd trust you. The way your hands are trembling, how you're holding onto them, trying to stop them, I understand that you're telling your truth.'

'I remember how I got here. I don't want to accept it. It can't be real. This all can't be real.'

'I trust you. It's ok, you're safe with me. Tell me what you saw.'

'I must sound insane. I don't belong here, in this world.'

'You never have,' Etta said, smiling.

'No. Please, listen. I don't fit in because I'm not from here, from this time. When I woke in the Youngs' vardo, I thought I was dreaming or in a coma. That was weeks ago, and here I still am.'

'The knock to your head was quite nasty.'

'Etta, I think I'll make sense once I tell you. I didn't lose my memories. I remembered who I was within hours. I just didn't know what happened. I recalled my date of birth, nearly at the turn of the millennium. I'm from a hundred years in the future. That's why I'm different, why I speak weird and dress like no one else. I know nothing about here. All I remember is that there's been a war.'

Each breath became stuck in the back of her throat, even with Etta reaching for her hand, looking at her so intently as if she wasn't mad. The story was irrational, no normal person would understand.

Adelina forgot that Etta, the Clarks, they weren't rational

people by her modern definition. Etta, at least, believed in the paranormal. They were from travelling ancestry, they sinned daily, they owned their city and their gang. They didn't live by the law nor the holy bible, they lived for themselves. They decided what they wanted to believe.

'Go on, tell me what you remember, get it off your chest.'

What she remembered couldn't be real. Something logical must have happened, a psychological break, surely. Looking to the lifeline on her palm, she questioned the fork, how it split into two.

'After I saw Esmerelda, I had a vision. I was visiting my grandma's grave. As I left, I saw this figure, who resembled her. A part of me knew it was her, but I was petrified. I'm scared of ghosts, always have been. I froze. I wanted to get away. I took a step, but when I did…'

A sob escaped her. Clasping her hand across her mouth, she tried to keep in the wails. Frederick couldn't hear; she couldn't bear his questions.

'Someone was behind you,' Etta said, coming to sit beside her. 'They hurt you.'

Etta said it so she didn't have to. Adelina told herself that what she remembered happened to a different person. But she struggled to forget the sensation, the feeling upon her skin as she slipped away.

'I believe you.'

Adelina screwed her eyes shut, trying to stop the tears. Every time, her mind's eye didn't dissolve into darkness; instead, Nova appeared before her, screaming, panic written across her.

Etta turned Adelina's hand, examining her palm. Finger tracing across the line, slipping along one side of the fork.

'My grandma never understood that line. The last thing she said was that my life would not be straightforward. I thought she lost her mind as death took her away.'

Etta folded Adelina's palm into itself, knowing that nothing could be said to comfort her. Adelina was stuck forever; there would be no escape.

'I died, didn't I?' Adelina whispered, unable to understand why she was still seemingly alive. 'Why am I burdened with life when it should have been taken from me? I should be with my grandma, with the other resting souls, in a place I belong, not here.'

'The world is a mysterious place, as are the resting places of people who've passed. Your time wasn't up yet; your grandma understood that. I think she tried to stop it, but it didn't go to plan.'

There were other cases of magic, divination, and spirits; Etta believed wholeheartedly in the event. Nova tried to protect her granddaughter with unwavering love. Powerful, she cast magic. Yet Adelina didn't believe; she sobbed uncontrollably, not wanting the paranormal to be real.

'Something went wrong. I think somehow the graveyard–'

'There were war graves, from the World Wars.'

'When was that?'

'The first has just happened. I can't remember the dates; I was no good with history. Freddie fought in it... The Great War. I meant the Great War.'

The premise of Adelina falling back in time didn't scare Etta, it was just another odd thing that happened. But what she slipped up on, sent her heart sinking, bile rising.

The silence was not a virtue. While Adelina shook, Etta grew quiet, body stiffening. They'd barely recovered from the war, she couldn't let her brothers go away again, they wouldn't survive. Mark would be old enough soon, he couldn't go. Frederick, her brothers, had fought for the king and got nothing in return, as far as she was concerned.

'It's not for a while. Freddie, the boys, they won't go back.'

'Back, to France?' Etta asked.

'To... war?'

'Do I want to know?'

'I'm not sure,' Adelina said, staring at the tea, unable to look in Etta's direction.

'How long do we have, until the next time?'

'Late 1930s, 38 or 39.'

With time, hopefully it would filter from Etta's mind. What Adelina said in the dusty living room would be forgotten or remembered vaguely, like an odd dream she once had. Adelina wouldn't be able to do the same thing. What she learnt in school would never leave her. Born in 1996, nearly at the turn of the millennium. If time still worked the same, she could live until the 1980s, years before her birth, but always living through some form of war.

'Esmerelda, did she mention your past?'

'No. I remembered everything afterwards.'

The prospect of never returning home, to the world she understood, didn't strike as much fear in her as it should. There was a purpose to life in 1919, she gained a family, who she liked more than her own. With them, she never felt homesick, alone, or lost. Maybe her destiny was to be with them, she had always longed to be elsewhere.

'Lines are fate; tea leaves can change. That's what Esmerelda said.'

'The thing with personal futures, is that they can change easily; they often depend on the steps you take, as well as other people and their circumstances. You can take many different paths, but you can only choose one. A person's life is written in the stars but decided upon the ground.'

'The warnings are all about Freddie. I find myself thinking, what could be so bad, but then, do I really want to know? Either way, I don't think I could leave Holbeck. Not because of him, but because of you and Isla. For so long now, you've felt like family. If I am stuck here inevitably, I don't want to give that up.'

'You need to rest, get some sleep. I will say nothing to Freddie about this. Keep your past a secret, with everyone, even Isla, but especially him. He's a sceptic at times, he'd never believe it, and he'd only go back to questioning the real you, but the truth is safe with me.'

THIRTY

Low sun, dipping behind lines of terraced houses. Branches creaked, flowers shifted, grass rippled. Melting patches of frost glistened in the last beams of light. Gravel scuffed at Adelina's leather shoes. Tripping on a stone, she clattered alongside the gusts of wind.

In the opening of trees, the aging war memorial rose tall. Names etched into the weathered marble. Poppies and wreaths decayed underneath. Benches tainted with melting snow.

A rustle from behind her. A discarded newspaper, pages lifting in the breeze. The logo distinct, she'd seen it all her life. The black ink ran between the rows, the text barely recognisable. Only the headline was readable: 'search for missing student nurse called off.'

The font too large. It was all the paper said. Falling rain splattered around her, turning the words into blotches. Taking away the story, her life, all she had been.

Adelina felt nothing, no sadness nor despair. A dream, like she was trapped somewhere temporarily, she'd be able to go back someday.

Goosebumps rose on her skin at the sense of being watched. The inevitable.

Harder than the time before. A piercing scream. The cracking of her skull. Hands failing to break her fall.

Aware of everything. Damp ground soaking into the fibres of her clothes. A harsh northerly breeze that brought crisp burning air. Moisture upon her skin, fingertips in a puddle, her scalp creating its own. There was more, from the man behind her, lingering over her, but she couldn't let herself focus upon that.

Unable to move, all sense of being began to deplete. Not wanting to subject herself to the torture for any longer, she gave up, wanting to be at peace.

Eyes squashed closed, she didn't find darkness but a kaleidoscope of swirls.

The feeling of being watched. Bumps prickled her skin. The pulling of a hand against her hair. Body scraping backwards across the concrete. In the clutches of another man. Head smacked against a desk. His voice spluttering, speaking to her like an animal, telling her she would never get away again.

The scream from her dream sounded in reality. The dark morning greeted Adelina with nothing more than fear. Long shadows distorted what resided within the living room corners. Charlie stared at her, the man waited for her, Frederick came down the staircase watching over her. At first, she wanted to flinch away from him too.

Frederick's chest rose and fell dramatically, only reminding her of the day before. Them together, it seemed like fiction, a daydream, not even a distant memory. Eyes wild, his hair unkempt, he had not properly woken yet. Most of the outside world slept, and she was up for the second time during the night.

'A nightmare?'

'Something like that,' Adelina said, not wanting to think about her dream that mirrored her own memories.

'I have them all the time. It's natural, I suppose.'

'I don't usually get nightmares. I rarely dream.'

Chimes of the knocker-upper. Clattering instruments outside their window. A light chatter now and then. All in the darkness of the seemingly ever-lasting night.

Frederick turned, intending to go back to his room, to start his day the right way; a glass of liquor to take the edge off his mind, a cigarette to calm his nerves, and maybe cocaine to make him feel alive.

Scampering after him, the blankets fell from the sofa like she created a tsunami. His old ratty jumper still over the nightgown, cuffs dangling over her hands. Reaching out to him, intending to bring him back, just for a moment.

Living within his mind, he hadn't realised she moved. Her touch sent shockwaves up his arm, causing him to fall still. There were things he wanted to do, but he stopped and let her lead.

'I don't want to be alone. Not after last night.'

Her body felt small against his, like he was strong, and she was weak. Tugging the material over her fingers, she balled the wool into her palms, trying to seek comfort in something.

'You can't let the past rule the present,' he said, wandering to his room. 'But you don't have to be alone.'

That was all she needed.

In his room, she sat by the fire, letting the dwindling flames warm her bare legs. It was true what he said, a person would always be tied to something if they didn't move on; held down by the past, unable to expand into the present.

'How do you move on from the past?' She asked, wondering how the men could forget the trenches and all the death they'd seen.

'You try to leave the memories behind. You consume your mind with other things. Don't allow yourself to think about what happened.'

'You supress it.'

Frederick's method was wrong, any person in the modern day would understand the trauma, the memories, would only come back in other forms and they would be an issue forever if dealt with that way.

'You try to control your thoughts,' he said, pouring a glass of alcohol.

The modern day dealt with trauma differently: talking therapies, cognitive behavioural changes, pharmaceutical medications. Without the trauma, without the ways he chose to supress his memories, he wouldn't be the man people feared. For him, trauma did have power. For Adelina, she didn't know if it could, anger only raged within her, and it came out in small bursts without thinking about its effects.

'You medicate yourself, try to wash everything away.'

'Try it,' he said, pouring her a glass.

'It's whiskey, isn't it,' she said, rocking the drink from side to side, the liquid splashing. An old man's drink, one that reminded her of pensioners, not someone like him. 'I've never tried it. It's going to burn, isn't it?'

Hot liquid against her tongue, almost turning it furry. It tasted like paint stripper, like a layer of her throat peeled away. Swallowing the alcohol, she scrunched her face, nausea overwhelming her from the taste leftover. He couldn't keep his chuckle in any longer.

Sitting, the bed groaned. Covers skewed, blankets upon the floor. He'd rushed to her.

Striking a match to light his cigarette, smoke entered the room. He never offered her one, she never smoked, despite them all doing so. They were all addicted to things that calmed them, that put sense into them amid the pressures of their chaotic lives.

'And the cigarettes, I suppose they do the same?'

'Why don't you try?'

'Because can smoke really be good for you?'

'Anything can be bad, and everything deep down tends to be.'

'Especially if you have too much,' Adelina said, her mind getting lost between the two worlds, what she knew and what she was growing accustomed to.

'It calms me down. I can't do moderation, with anything, you should know that by now.'

'You like excess, even the negative emotions that come with it. It makes you feel alive, doesn't it?'

Adelina was always thinking, her mind churning up ways to stir him. Forever questioning, wanting to understand a person's thoughts intricately. He wondered if she tried to find people's weaknesses, so she wouldn't end up hurt.

'There's nothing wrong with excess,' he said. 'If you don't care about death.'

Unwillingly, Adelina had been given a second chance. She wasn't sure whether she should care about death or not. In her new time, she was just existing, drifting through the in-between, waiting for it to be snatched away entirely.

'You don't care, because of the war.'

'Yes, the war.'

1914 was a completely different world. Britain had been gripped by madness that erupted across Europe in the August. Men everywhere responded to the call to arms. Recruits of all ages flocked to enlist.

The Great War wasn't a peasant's war, nor was it a war of professional soldiers. Whole university classes, workplaces, towns, and villages went to war. The people they lived and worked with became the people they died with.

For some, they had to go. Conscription was law. Single men aged eighteen-forty were liable to be called up, unless they were widowed with children or ministers of religion.

The war was not a swift glorious one that most enlisted for. It didn't end by Christmas. It took four years.

Frederick shouldn't have been alive; throughout the war he stared death down. Somehow, he managed to come home. Everything else became extra, because at times he didn't feel alive. Sometimes, in the depths of night, he longed for death, waiting to welcome him like an old friend.

When learning about history, she never thought about the soldiers, how they had to cope with the consequences for decades afterwards. Now, Frederick was in front of her, his mind still occupied by the enemy a year on. At times he seemed to be trapped there still, even though he said to leave the memories behind.

'Last night, when I saw Esmerelda, she called me sinful one,' Adelina said, taking a seat beside him, the mattress squeaking. 'It's the first time I've been called that.'

'You don't live by the book.'

Frederick sipped his drink. He referred to the day prior, to what they'd done, to how it was clear she'd done it before.

Adelina was never innocent nor naïve.

'I don't believe in the bible,' she said, tucking her legs up onto the bed. 'We're living in different times. Rules are weaker, right?'

'Weaker for those who don't believe, you mean.'

'Freddie, if God is omnipotent and benevolent, then surely, if I do nothing evil, then he should allow me into heaven. Is he not the opposite if he sends me to hell? Shouldn't God forgive me for not seeing how he isn't omniscient? All around us people are in need, their prayers go unanswered by him.'

Frederick laughed; he'd never heard such words before. Despite understanding her, somewhat believing her, he couldn't help but be taken aback, even with his lack of faith.

'Well, Ada,' he said, pouring them another drink. 'May you be in heaven a full half hour before the devil knows your dead.'

Adelina's stomach sank at the old Irish toast. The cool liquor burnt her tongue. A tear drew from her eye, like the words were a reflection of what happened before. That she could be dead, waiting for the devil to claim her.

THIRTY-ONE

The offices buzzed. Lydia transferred cash into the back room, securing notes away from prying hands. Isla shouted at the kids, putting them back in their place. Adelina sorted betting slips into piles.

George and Paul bounced in, Frederick stalked behind. Another day in the Clark offices, one of glory and fighting. Another day as winners. Slowly, they climbed up in the world, with fishhooks sewn into the lapels of their coats.

Smoke shrouded the person Frederick longed to see. With a gentle breeze, the cloud faded, unveiling the details of her face. Fingers holding onto a cigarette, the end coated in lipstick. A rouge colour adorned her lips, like she was going to a ball, not working.

George swooned over Isla, knocking papers as he sat on her desk. He didn't care for the mess; he hadn't seen such a decadent shade of lipstick since France. Only toffs in their mansions could afford such luxury after the war.

Lydia wore the same colour too. Frederick wondered how the women had come to possess such makeup and why they chose to wear the outlandish shade in the offices, of all places.

That morning, the women ditched work. They became sick and tired of doing the same tasks and getting no thanks for their effort. They bunked off. They went to town with the money the brothers owed them.

The act reminded Adelina of school, when she used to skive from lessons to go into town with her friends. Adrenaline soared at doing something mischievous again. With the knock to her head, she had forgotten how enthralling her rebellious teenage lifestyle had been.

Isla dragged Adelina towards a department store. Niamh had mentioned a new makeup stand the other day and Isla wanted to see what all the fuss was about. People parted, gawking at the three giggling women, judging them immediately. They could spot their kind from a mile off; something about their hair, their clothes, the cooped-up laughter, like they hadn't been outside in days.

The new range of beauty products caused quite a stir amongst the customers. Older women chuntered about how it would demean a person's reputation, scoffing as others stopped to browse. Young women found the brand daring, they liked the idea of catching people's attention. It would go with the change of fashion, with their bobs, dropped waist dresses, and shorter hemlines.

Isla eagerly purchased a lipstick to share between them. As she applied the stain to herself in the store's mirror, Lydia sampled the fragrances. What appeared so simple to Adelina was all new and exciting for Isla and Lydia.

They acted like teenagers; they caused havoc, trying on the most expensive clothes to not buy them. They doused themselves in perfume samples. They laughed at the glares from snooty wealthy women. Isla insisted they would have money like that, one day.

'Then, I'll come back in here, with pound notes piled up, waving my money in their faces,' Isla said, believing they would eventually accept her into their circle. Adelina wasn't so sure, and the women's scowls were starting to affect her confidence.

'They're only mad they're not having as much fun as us,' Lydia said, noting the change in Adelina. 'They'll never accept us; there's no getting out of what we've been born into. That's the way of life, but it can't stop us from being happy.'

Isla kissed her reflection, leaving a bright mark as security approached. The store's management, the more well-to-do customers kicked up a fuss. They weren't their kind, they didn't belong.

The Clarks didn't rule all the city yet. They were kings of the poorest parts. Adelina ran after Isla and Lydia as they darted from the store.

Not thinking about the consequences, living in the moment, Isla turned wild. As they exited, she knocked into displays, sending them falling. A fine piece of jewellery, ready to be put into a counter, was taken. Lydia smashed a bottle of perfume at an old woman's feet. Adelina sprinted away, not wanting to go to jail.

In the safety of their own land, they leaned against a building, cackling. Isla opened her hand, the bracelet glistening in the midday sun. To steal and cause a kafuffle was wrong, Adelina understood that, but she couldn't help but love the buzz, the surge of her heart racing.

Ladies upon his mind, it was the last thing Frederick wanted. David's funeral still needed to be planned. The murderer was still at large. There were the races too, and his ascent to the top.

To settle his nerves, Frederick grabbed a bottle of alcohol from his drinks trolley. When the office door opened, he almost snapped. He wanted to scream, shut everyone out. He needed time alone to deal with the ever-growing issues in his life. The urge to shout grew stronger upon seeing her.

Ida's eyes were like a dagger to his soul. It felt like he had no secrets with her, like she knew everything about him, because at times he'd given himself up to her.

As always, she appeared perfect – blonde flawlessly styled hair, pale blemish-free skin, baby pink lips that once called his name. Anger seeped out of her; she was never pleased to see him anymore.

'Did you forget about me?' Ida asked, her face flushing as Frederick squinted, questioning why she was there. His oblivious, uncaring reaction hurt her even more.

'Did you forget about last night? You promised,' Ida said.

Frederick set down the bottle, their plans suddenly returning to him.

The day prior, around mid-afternoon, Frederick discovered David had never made a will. After meeting with an old family friend, some adjustments were made, and the Clarks came into possession of The Clarendon.

At dusk, Frederick found his pub free from police, the front doors banging in the breeze. About to change the locks, he found Ida inside, weeping over the remnants, the staining, of David.

Loss only reminded Ida of war, of losing family. In a moment of weakness, she broke down, telling him how she was struggling to cope. Traumatised by David's death, she found herself overthinking everything, from him to Charlie's threat.

Ida was petrified that Frederick would end up like Violet and David and that she would follow the same fate. They had agreed to go out together, a few hours later, to take her mind away from death. But last night, other things had consumed Frederick's mind instead.

'I've got work to do,' he said. 'Two people are dead, do I need to remind you?'

'Talk to me about them. Tell me how you feel. I could help you. We could help each other.'

'Ida,' he said monotonously. 'How could you help me.'

Taking a sharp inhale, she tried to make her mouth settle into a line. There was no need for him to act like that, she'd done nothing wrong.

Paying no attention to her, he looked to his desk. A letter that needed his signature amongst other notes. The paper was heavily crumpled, lines ran throughout it, blood dotted upon it. He sighed.

'I'll talk to you later, Ida.'

The night prior, Ida had waited for hours at their usual meeting spot, down by the canals. It was his favourite place to meet; no one ever disrupted them there. The mist steadily rolled in, and Ida remained, hoping he would come, even as the orange glow of the gas lanterns became lost against the grey.

Everything she had said at the Clarendon was true, but she

also needed to tell him something paramount, something that would change everything. They needed to be by themselves, away from the offices and everything that distracted him. What she needed to tell him couldn't be said in front of anyone else.

Too lost in her own world, Adelina forgot to check if the room was occupied. Obsessed with work, she hadn't realised Frederick and Ida had entered the building.

'I'm sorry,' Adelina stuttered as she nearly crashed into Ida. 'I didn't see either of you come in.'

Sheepishly, Adelina placed the paper on his desk, pointing to where he needed to sign. Turning back, her dress blew in the gust she created. A new sweet perfume drifted towards him. The girls had bunked off again. That explained the lipstick and the lustrous scent. A call to McCormick would be needed to find out what trouble they'd caused.

Frederick's gaze followed Adelina as if Ida wasn't present. The look made Ida's stomach sink – Adelina ruined everything.

When Ida first met him, she never thought she would have to fight for his attention. Before her, she thought they'd been in love. In retrospect, that was funny; Frederick didn't seem like the type of man that could have such soft and fervent emotions.

Ida couldn't keep her frustration in any longer. Adelina was the reason why she endured so much pain. Snapping, Ida took out everything she ever experienced on her because she was to blame for her downfall.

'How many times do I have to tell you, I don't want to see you, ever. Please, can you leave us alone or are you incapable of separating yourself from him for a moment?'

Guilt swarmed Adelina. She was disgusted with what she'd done. It wasn't her to cave to a man, to let go of her morals. To do such a thing was unforgivable. Though she couldn't back down to Ida. Not only were the Clarks her protection, but Etta knew her darkest secret.

'I'm returning to my desk. I work here, Ida; you should expect me to be here.'

'I don't know who you think you're talking to. You have no

business being in these offices, you're not family. I've known Freddie for longer, for God's sake. You've swanned in here, a stranger, looking and acting like a whore. Look at you, with your cat piss perfume and tart-stained lips. You're nothing but cheap.'

Ida wanted to be in Adelina's position. Long ago, she'd grown sick of the Clarendon, of men hitting on her and saying the crudest things. At times, she longed to go back to her old life, but she held out, hoping that Frederick would offer her a role in his company.

'I'm not a whore, Ida,' Adelina said, before addressing Frederick. *'If I was, I'd be fucking expensive. Sort her out, or I will.'*

In the main room, she found Lydia alone, waiting for her to emerge. With reddening cheeks, Adelina rolled her eyes, intending to play it off. Yet Ida's shrill voice leaked through the door.

'All because of you,' Lydia said.

'I never did anything; Ida took an instant disliking to me.'

'That's Ida.'

'Don't let her make you feel bad,' Lydia said as Ida and Frederick's shouts washed over them. 'She's trying to keep a hold of a man that can never be tied down.'

'That's Freddie,' Adelina muttered, her head spinning as she thought back to the error she'd made.

Wanting to escape her mind, she took some documents to the filing system. It didn't work. With sanity slipping, she thought of all the reasons why she shouldn't have given in to him. Everything her modern education told her not to do, she'd done.

'Frederick can break a heart and snap it in two with ease,' Lydia said.

With the documents securely placed away, Adelina rested against the wall. The cooling sensation only weakened her boiling blood for a moment. Dread seeped in, knowing there wouldn't be help – no clinics or unjudgmental doctors. Nothing legal or safe as a precaution. Fucking hell, she thought she was going to collapse.

'I'll take it my warnings have came too late,' Lydia said,

looking up from her typewriter.

'Evidently.'

Adelina looked up at the ceiling, existential panic setting in. The paint flaked above her, damp seeped across the plaster, looking like it could fall at any moment.

'Lemon juice,' Lydia said. 'I've seen that look before.'

'What?'

'A trick I was taught once. Squeeze a lemon and put the juice up. It might be too late now. In the future, use half a lemon and take it out after. You might struggle buying one, with it being the off-season. Normally, Betty has them. And bloody hell, Ada, don't just buy one, people will start gossiping then. Get some turnips or something else too.'

Frozen against the wall, only her eyes fluttered to Lydia and then to the files opposite. She couldn't believe it; Lydia spoke so lackadaisical about natural contraceptive methods. Adelina's heart raced, overthinking the medical side of inserting foreign objects inside herself. It was wrong, school taught her the opposite.

'I'm sorry,' Adelina said. 'I don't think I understand.'

'Oh,' Lydia said, face scrunching. 'You weren't a virgin, were you?'

They neglected to hear the office door creak open. Ida's smug face appeared, looking between them.

'Maybe you're not a whore, but you're a slut now,' Ida cackled. 'Getting tips about lemons from an ex-prostitute.'

Such comments didn't bother Lydia, she'd heard them all before. There was no changing who she once was. She'd learnt not to bite; it was more powerful to not let the insults affect her because, after all, that was what people wanted.

In Adelina's time, men would prey on girls in clubs, trying to lure them back to their beds. Men didn't have that option in 1919. They had dances, but they weren't the same. Men who wanted fun without a relationship lived throughout time, and they were most likely Lydia's previous clientele.

An entire history Adelina would never understand. Lydia's life had never been easy, and the Clarks, Frederick specifically, had saved her. The job that she acquired was never a choice it was a means to survive.

'Who was it then,' Ida said. 'That took–'

'Why would I tell you,' Adelina interrupted.

'Aw, are you too shy? Except you're not modest enough to ask for help from a moll.'

'I never asked for help,' Adelina said, only speaking because she was concerned with what he thought of her. 'You're so petty and manipulative, Ida. Do me a favour and piss off. I can't deal with your shit right now.'

'You shouldn't talk to me like that.'

'I can talk to you however I like; you don't control me. How are you going to stop me? Run to Freddie? Tell him to fire me? Learn to fight your own battles.'

Adelina returned to her desk, not willing to let another argument result in violence. Taking a leaf out of Lydia's book, she tried to remain detached. Eventually, it worked. Ida retreated, bidding a hasty goodbye to Frederick.

As Lydia packed her things, she couldn't stop laughing. Before departing, she dropped a piece of paper on Adelina's desk – a concoction that might help with her situation. With a wink, she left, knowing she'd helped a girl she despised a few weeks ago. But now, they seemed to be on the same side, at mercy of Frederick and the Clarks, and battling against Ida.

The piece of paper would be taken to the market. Afterward, Adelina would retreat to the safety of Etta's home. There, in privacy, she would decide if she could live to fight a bacterial infection over having an illegitimate child. In fact, it didn't seem like such a hard choice with that thought.

THIRTY-TWO

Fresh air hit Adelina like a slap to the chest, as if she fell backwards onto a hard surface, winding herself. The world became a blur as she spun, head tilted back, looking at the clear sky. She didn't care about the temperature or thick frost on the ground. For once, she was outside the polluted city.

Frederick remained in the car, observing her, noting how she, like Isla, became happier in the open space of the country. As Adelina turned, her skirt lifted, showing her heels and stockings, never caring if the material moved above her knees.

A match sparked within his hand. Once his cigarette was lit, he returned to her, finding a glare instead. Adelina's smile faded as did the gusts she created.

'Put that out, Freddie. We're finally in the fresh air, I don't want any smoke, at least for half an hour.'

Doing as told, he dashed the end out. He would hold off, only for her and the pure joy that was written across her.

On the road once more, she rolled the window all the way down. The air flowed into the car, the chill biting them.

'I've never seen you so happy,' he said, without giving a second thought to his words. He hadn't meant to speak them aloud, but he struggled to keep secrets with her.

'Where are we going? I thought you agreed to teach me how to shoot,' she said, not noticing his slip of character, too consumed with where they headed. 'Why are you taking me back here? I told you I never wanted to see them again.'

'I have to deal with business first. Something's come up.'

The sense of being free was ripped from her. The walls that dispersed with the country air were being knocked up around her again. Shrinking away from him, she nestled into the car door.

Adelina understood he was busy, that he still dealt with them, but she would rather he abandon her on the side of a road than continue down the lane with her.

The end of the road loomed before her. Back to where her story began.

'I'm not getting out, not here,' she said, the Young's field before her.

'Margaret might want to see you.'

'I told you what they did to me. You were there when they spoke to me like utter shit. You should've left me up there when I got out the car. I don't want to see anyone, not even Margaret. Sometimes I wished they'd left me on the roadside. It would have been a virtue in a way; they would have saved me from all that's happened since.'

For once, Frederick realised how fragile she could be. Since the altercation with Lydia, he perceived her as tough, someone who would fight back. Adelina always appeared strong, but she was before him, trembling before she even saw the Youngs.

The car stopped. The gates to the field were open, waiting for him to drive on. Instead, Frederick turned to her, gripping at her hands. Pulling her attention to him, he became softer than she'd ever known.

'What they did to you, they won't ever do again. They won't speak a bad word about you. I won't let them.'

'I've told you before, I wouldn't let them. I don't need you or anyone else.'

Adelina spoke without thinking. Since meeting him, she'd been obsessed with having him to protect her. Yet, there she was, adamant she could do it herself. And with everything she remembered and experienced, she believed she could do anything. She would fight two grown men because she refused to let another bad thing happen to her.

'I need to finalise the deal today. You don't have to get out.'

'I didn't realise they were still here, I thought you would have sent them packing, with you suspecting them for the murders.'

Frederick chuckled. The Youngs weren't smart enough to deceive him. The plans they created to take him down were well known. They were relaying information to Charlie, but none of that mattered anymore, because he was half-dead in hospital.

'Who committed those acts wasn't the Youngs,' Frederick said. 'I know that for a fact.'

'Then why did you name them in the meeting that day? You told the others they could be capable of murder, but you'd already cleared them. Why would you do that?'

'Etta's son, Mark, is coming to collect the horse today. Then, I only need to find the true culprit and snatch Charlie's last patch of land, and we'll be sitting pretty. At least for a while.'

'What horse?' Adelina questioned, her brows knitting together in confusion as the car rolled forward again. 'You're going to let them stay?'

'The Young's horse. It's payment for staying here.'

'Why do you need a horse? You've got a car.'

Frederick laughed, his eyes crinkling as he drove.

'Why would you want them to stay, after all they've said and done?'

Another question of Adelina's that went unanswered.

They pulled alongside a barn. Piles of horse manure and mounds of hay filled the air with a familiar scent, reminiscent of her childhood.

Growing up, her cousins had horses. All her mother's side of the family owned them. As a child, she begged her parents for a pony, always receiving the same excuse – they were too poor. In the modern day, mostly the rich had horses because almost everyone owned a car.

Intrigued, Adelina found herself following Frederick inside the stable. She imagined John and Thomas to be inside, waiting for her. But it was only him, speaking gently to a dark horse.

Frederick appeared calm, kind, like he wasn't all bad. To her, he rarely came across as evil, despite how so many people treated him. Beside him, Adelina petted the horse, the grease of its coat moving across her fingers. Tenderly, she brushed the side of him as he nuzzled into her.

'I think he likes you,' Frederick said, lighting a cigarette. And, for the first time, he offered her one.

'I'm far too content for that. I don't need a distraction.'

'You can go for a ride, before Mark gets here, if you want. I'll deal with business whilst you're away.'

'I've barely ridden horses; it was mainly ponies when I was younger. I grew up in an industrial town, after all.'

'There's plenty of horses in cities. What are you on about?'

Kicking at stray pieces of hay with her heels, Adelina tried to wash harsh memories away. They itched at her, working their way up her insides once more. An urge to tell him her past, to make him understand, but she had to be careful.

Sighing, she gestured for a cigarette. With her past creeping back, she wasn't elated anymore.

'My mum would disobey my father. He thought horses were dirty, a waste of time and money. While he was at work, mum would take us to the farm, not caring if we were meant to be in school or even asleep.

Her side of the family had horses. We borrowed them all the time. We mucked them out, took them for a ride. Me and my sister didn't have a clue, really. I was only ten, Leonora was two years younger. No one taught us how to ride. Mum was too busy. She was…'

The summer breeze brought a relief to the warm air. The heatwave was well underway, the temperature gauge only ever increasing. The farm being near the sea was perfection. The sea air lifted at their clothes, making them more comfortable.

Leonora wore her riding boots, her hard hat had been worn for hours, sending her hair slick with sweat. Despite anything, she would ride, it was her favourite thing to do. It was the only thing Adelina and her looked forward to. Their father was an evil man, for not letting them come to the farm. But their little minds couldn't comprehend that it might not have been because of the horses.

Leonora saddled up a Shetland pony, full of character and will. The heat only made her coat greasier, sweating from the added warmth of the saddle. Adelina's mother hadn't told her to not take the horses out, that they weren't used to such drastic weather.

Adelina led out an Irish cob, its coat immaculate despite the heat. She always cared for the horses, cleaning them over and over. When she was there, they were at their happiest and prettiest. It was on those days they'd been attended to adequately.

The two girls were independent. They dragged themselves up. Their father too busy with work, trying to make a wage so they could afford to live. Meanwhile their mother didn't seem to do anything but sit in front of the television. She would never leave the house unless it was to go to the farm.

Like most children, they didn't realise their upbringing was so different from most. It was only as a teenager did Adelina connect the dots. Some mothers sat over their children day in and day out, watching their every move. Adelina and Leonora always played by themselves, in the field and the muck heap. No one watched over them.

As they left, Adelina caught sight of her mother in the hay stable, bottle in hand. There were other shadows moving, like someone else was with her. Waving happily, Adelina tried to catch her mother's attention, hoping she would be proud. Her mother ignored her. Adelina made excuses for her; she hadn't seen her.

They rode the horses further than ever before. Across the fields surrounding the farm, up to the bridleway of the nearby woods. They explored the land, just them. They didn't speak to each other, only to their horses, telling them they were doing good.

Bringing the horses into full gallop, the children relished in the shade of the trees and the cool breeze. The horses became irritated by the weight, by the saddles that burnt their skin. They were frustrated with the uneducated riders, wanting them to gallop forever.

A rumble in the distance. Machinery from a nearby farm. The horses bolted through the woods to places unknown. A series of bangs echoed, giving the impression they neared the noise itself. Unbeknownst to the girls, a silo was being knocked down, sending shatters into the sky.

The fiery Shetland pony spooked, kicking and running as fast as its body would allow. Leonora hung onto the reins, trying to steady herself. Adelina attempted to retain control of her cob. Neither noticed the dip in the path, the creek that cut in beside it. With one wrong hoof, the pony stumbled. They fell to the creek bed, sprinkling water running over their heads.

Screeching. Wailing. Adelina frantically dismounted, her feet tangling in the process. Falling to the mud, pain seared through her body, but she couldn't lay still. Stumbling to Leonora, she saw the pony's mangled leg beneath it, harsh screams emitted into the woodland. Leonora whimpered, her neck twisted unnaturally away from her body.

'My horse bolted. I don't blame him. I ran to the nearest farm I knew of. The family there sent for help, and I returned with the farmer to Leonora.'

The old man stood over them. Adelina whispered to Leonora that everything would be fine, that help was on its way. But the man knew it wouldn't be ok. He couldn't bear the sounds from the pony; it only upset the girls more, he thought.

With some words, telling Adelina to look away, he brought the handgun from his pocket and took its life away. Despite bracing herself, Adelina jumped; even in her young mind, she understood the farmer's intentions.

In the ensuing silence, the man muttered questions to Leonora. Could she feel her toes? Could she see anything at all? It gave Adelina the chance to look, to see the Shetland pony, blood oozing from its body, joining the trickling stream.

'I don't want to ride, not by myself. It's like a metaphor for how I've been alone ever since.'

'I would ride with you, but I'm not sure you'd want me as

company.'

'It's not only that. I'm not scared of falling or hurting myself. I never want to hear the noise that pony made again, like a banshee, like death is coming.'

'You can't ever get used to that noise. In the war, the generals thought our morale would be boosted by the presence of horses. They didn't work. I could never get used to seeing a horse collapse from exhaustion as it tried to free itself from the mud. In the war, losing a horse was worse than losing a man because ultimately, we were replaceable and horses weren't. Your sister, was she–'

'Leonora died in the creek. I wasn't fast enough; she needed help within minutes.'

Adelina thought of herself as different than the Clarks. The men experienced the war, women took their place at home, ensuring there was something to return to. She couldn't comprehend either experience, to her it was distant stories. But she didn't realise how her own trauma made her like them.

Frederick led a horse from the stables. An Irish Cob. Welling up from behind her smile, she greeted the horse like she was reacquainted with an old friend.

'Time to correct the past, make a better memory instead.'

The feeling bundling in Frederick's stomach worried him. Everything they did together felt like the first time, like they had never experienced something on such a scale. She was starting to open herself up, telling him about her childhood, her regrets, and her fears. The horse ride seemed like something more, like the stars of the universe were aligning just for them.

The light dimmed. Pink clouds turned darker, ready to unleash snow. For what felt like hours, Adelina waited for Frederick. Not wanting to see the Youngs, she remained in the car, the winter night gripping at her. Shivering uncontrollably, she pulled her scarf and coat ever tighter until he returned.

'Maybe you should go down there,' Frederick said once he returned. 'I think Margaret's in labour, she's screaming bloody murder.'

'That's not a good idea. If anything went wrong, then the blame would only be put on me. Besides, we need to go, it looks like it's going to snow, and we can't get stuck out here, with David's funeral in the morning.'

Without questioning her decision, Frederick started the engine. There would be no window on the way home. It would be them and the dark lurking world.

If something bad happened to Margaret, Adelina would only blame herself. The decision was self-preservation, but it wasn't like her to be selfish. Frederick couldn't help but feel the same way, like he would regret not begging Adelina to see to Margaret. There was something the matter, he could tell, but it wasn't his place to enquire.

'Did you want to learn to shoot because of Charlie or was it because of the Youngs?' Frederick asked. The thought had been bothering him for a while. He wasn't done talking, but she was waiting, ready to interject.

'If anyone attempts something similar to what Charlie did, I want to be able to use a gun, so I can end him or anyone else that tries. That includes Thomas and John because they threatened me with the same thing Charlie tried.'

Frederick continually glanced to her, the words hanging in the air. Fumbling inside her pockets, she looked for a cigarette. A stupid reaction. Still, she couldn't help herself, there was a growing need for them.

'It won't happen again,' he said.

Charlie nearly ruined everything for Adelina. After that night, Frederick vowed to shield her at all costs because ultimately, he had led her into a dangerous position. He felt like a failure, even when his plans had gone well, because, for the first time, he thought about the repercussions of his actions on other people.

'I won't ever let it happen,' she said, trying to sound confident, sure of her herself, but her voice came out weak. 'I hope you intend to do the worst thing to Charlie, to get that patch of land from him.'

'You don't hope, I will. I'll do more as well. I'm going to take over Chester, his last source of income. When I'm done, Charlie will be penniless.'

'I thought maybe the horse was for Chester, but Mark told me it was for a dowry. For a girl you've never met. I guess, I'm asking why you've done that.'

'I accepted the Youngs' pitiful offer because of what my dad used to say: keep your friends close but your enemies closer.'

'It's all a show with you, isn't it?'

'No. It's not.'

'I'm wrong?' Adelina asked, her eyebrows raising.

'I was hoping with them staying, Peter would come back, or at least visit.'

'So, you could get revenge?'

'I wasn't sure if you knew what happened, with Peter.'

'Isla talks, a lot.'

'I need to take care of Peter. Even if it's the last thing I do. You understand that all too well, don't you?'

'I'm not sure of how far I'd go if I saw Charlie again. What I did, what I so desperately wanted to do, scared me for a little while. I'm not sure I want to feel like that ever again.'

'You won't have to feel like that. You'll never meet him again. I promise.'

'I don't understand why, but I feel safe with you. Despite all the violence that surrounds you, that is inflicted upon the people you encounter, I feel protected by you.'

Adelina caught him off guard; he didn't know how to respond. It felt like she poured her heart out to him, and she deserved something in return.

It wasn't like that for her. Adelina wanted to tell the truth. That Frederick could be the devil sometimes, a man that describes himself as no angel, but despite everything, she thinks he is one to her; her guardian angel, always beside her, to protect her.

THIRTY-THREE

The storm hit the city like a bomb. Thick snow blanketed the buildings. Mist shrouded the air. Everything grey, from the sky to the street. The new flakes would turn the road white again, for the horses and carriages, the motor vehicles had turned the snow into black sludge.

Etta's living room was far too small for the abundance of people that swarmed the space. The Clark family, dressed all in black, waited for the horse-drawn carriage. Lydia waited too, holding onto a cup of tea, feeling like she didn't belong. Ida was there as well, in the centre of the room, eyes drifting across the family.

'Why is she here,' Dorothy muttered to Isla, only receiving a slap on the head from her mother in response.

'Manners,' Etta said through gritted teeth. It wasn't the time for arguments, though even she thought the same as Dorothy. Surely, Ida had invited herself. She certainly hadn't been on Frederick's mind recently.

The stairs groaned under Adelina's weight. The noise barely audible over the chatter and screeching of George and Isla's children. They ran in circles, disobeying their parents, hiding beneath women's skirts. Every now and then they received a kick from a disgruntled family member.

From a market stall in town, Adelina had purchased a new outfit, no longer wanting to wear hand-me-down clothes that didn't fit her. There was nothing else to spend her wages on; Etta wouldn't accept board, and she wasn't sure if there was anything worth saving for.

The dress glided over her body, masked by the woollen

coat. Sick of the current fashion trends, Adelina wore her hair differently. Light strands framed her face, a chunky braid tied with the scrunchie she kept.

Frederick eagerly waited for her. As soon as he entered Etta's home, he wanted to see her.

Finally, she looked to him; he had been the least of her concerns when she tried to place everyone she knew in the room.

Silence encased them. Others fluttered around them. Reaching the last step, she grew still, knowing she needed to say something to him.

'*I'm sorry for your loss.*'

Frederick reached out to her. To the other mourners, it was a simple embrace on a sorrow day. For him, it was different. Leaning into her, his hand gripping onto her, he whispered in her ear.

As quickly as they touched, he departed. Frederick didn't feel regret, he continued to make the right decisions. Etta's eyes were upon him. She wanted to shake her head, but her stomach sank instead.

Adelina's body set alight. Despite him moving far into the room, she could still feel his hot breath against her, a tingle where his hand touched her. While her body was sent into overdrive, her rational mind told her to be calm, to not become caught up in him in his words.

For minutes, his voice spun around her; she couldn't help but be overwhelmed. Never had he paid her a compliment like it. The first time she'd heard him utter the words to anyone. Frederick had said, '*you look beautiful.*'

And for a moment, Adelina thought he meant her. That she in herself looked beautiful. When he held her, she forgot about what he said in the past, about her similarity to Effie. It was only a compliment because she reminded him of her, surely. He never saw her as her own person.

Ida witnessed it all. Adelina's cheeks flushed afterwards. In a trance, she thought about what he said to her. Ida's blood pressure soared.

Hooves knocking against the cobbles drew the front door open. Within an instant, the heat escaped. The weather took away the warmth he'd created.

The immediate family left first. Each step was made with precision, the road more akin to an ice rink. Feet delicately placed, heels sliding beneath them.

'What did he say to you?' Ida asked Adelina as they stepped outside.

'We exchanged an old funeral greeting.'

'You blushed.'

'I misspoke, and he corrected me on my grammar.'

The best fib Adelina could create, she couldn't admit the truth to Ida. It was a lie, Ida understood that, but she would win in other ways. Gliding past Adelina, she came to Frederick's side. It was all a show, to anger her, knowing she would have to fall behind and watch. Frederick would be the one to stop Ida falling, while Adelina had no one.

With Charlie, David, the Youngs, and Adelina, taking up so much of his time after the races, Frederick hadn't had the opportunity to properly speak to Ida. Whilst she wanted to speak to him about something important that would change everything, he wished to do the same. No longer did he want to settle for what he was used to; he wanted freedom instead. In the coming days, he'd break it to Ida. Of course, he couldn't do it on the day of David's funereal – Etta would only kill him for making a scene.

Adelina tried to avoid the ice, standing on mounds of snow and black sludge instead. Her stockings and the hemline of her skirt became sopping with the constant brushing of snow. The other women held upon their men: Ida with Frederick, Isla with George, Etta and Dorothy linked arms with Paul. Lydia and Adelina remained at the back, fending for themselves.

None of them wanted to trip, not in front of the crowds that lined the streets. Men tipped their hats. Women stopped with their children to pay their respects. They prayed as they watched. The city said farewell to a man they'd known so well.

The church brought a sigh of relief, they could move with grace upon the stone floor. Adelina was still uncomfortable, her shoes wet, slowly infiltrating her skin with damp.

Lydia and Adelina took a seat in the second pew, Frederick and Ida in front of them, their bodies distant from one another. They'd grown disinterested in each other. They all sat in silence until Etta spoke the traditional saying, '*I now leave you to God.*' Those who understood repeated the words.

Frederick, being Frederick, muttered underneath his breath, just loud enough for Adelina to hear. Even with the pew separating them and Ida by his side, his mind was still firmly upon her.

In return, Adelina bowed her head, trying to not let anyone see the smile that formed. He reminded her of how they acted alone, of conversations they'd shared. She was ahead of their time, not understood by the people surrounding her. But so was he, for those simple words made her believe that he thought she was good, that she was right in what she'd said that one fateful morning.

'*Says the girl who has no God but will go to heaven.*'

The Clarendon was different without David as landlord. The same barmaids, the same punters cluttered the bar. The glasses, the pints, the liquor – they hadn't changed but the ambience had. A weight loaded upon every person. A nightmare lingered in the back of their minds, slowly creeping forwards, becoming reality. They drowned their sorrows in alcohol, trying to move past the tension and unease, but fear consumed them.

It was vastly different to Violet's wake. Adelina walked to the pub side by side with the Clarks. No one, not even her, questioned whether she was invited to their table. As the men gathered the alcohol, she took a seat beside Etta.

Unlike before, James didn't lurk at the bar nor glance in Adelina's direction. Lydia stood beside him, waiting for the drink he'd purchased her. Once she received her gin, they huddled together on their own table.

Not in the mood for arguments, Frederick sat beside Ida, separating himself from Adelina. The table melted into different patterns, Adelina's eyes were glued to the wooden top as if the meaning of life was written upon it. All because Frederick had glanced towards her, causing a wave of emotions to wash over her.

They thought they were clever, that they weren't being observed when they glanced at one another. Etta knew better. They played an open game of footsie; it only became more evident as the others grew intoxicated around them.

'Lydia told me you needed some help,' Etta said, leaning into Adelina. 'It only confirmed what I thought. I should have told you that night, what to do. I thought you would have known, being a nurse.'

Etta spoke lightly, so no one else could hear. The words affected Adelina like she'd been scolded. She'd been told many things about the 20th century, like if how a woman was caught with a man, they would be forced to marry. The stories were nothing but exaggerated truths. People gave in to one another, into the need that burned inside of them.

Adelina was complicated, and Etta wanted to look out for her, but she didn't know where to begin with educating her. Etta thought that in a hundred years' time there would be no wars. The vision of the future she saw was skyscrapers on every street and roads in the sky. Those in the present are always starkly wrong about the future; they often overestimate the power of human want.

'Let's hope the outcome of you and Freddie isn't the addition I read in your tea leaves.'

With the pulsating horror of what Etta insinuated, Adelina drew her eyes away from the table.

'Don't be afraid,' Etta said. 'Hopefully the lemon juice will have worked.'

'Does it really work?'

'Lydia wasn't joking when she said you're innocent. It works sometimes.'

'I'm only innocent to your world. Things are different where I'm from. I was brought up freer than any other generation. That doesn't mean I don't regret what I did. I hate myself for it. With him, I get lost. And he only views me as someone else anyways.'

'I think you'll tell me that again,' Etta said, pouring them another drink. 'Don't live your present angry at the actions of the past. You put too much pressure on yourself to be good. Look around you, at who you're sat with.'

The alcohol burned Adelina's tongue, she barely registered it within her mind, too preoccupied with feelings, with thoughts about Etta and their conversation, and how she only ever pushed her further towards Frederick in the end.

With the copious amounts of gin seeping into her veins, the world spun. Vision blurring at the edges, like she looked through a lens into another world. Her gums tingled, reminding her of him, how he could make her feel.

'Why can't we be like men?' Etta asked, a mischievous look growing across her, one that was reserved solely for intoxicated flirtatious states. A performance commenced. Etta's walk was sultry; the epitome of seduction as she neared a man at the bar. He was infatuated with her, like she was a film star.

Etta was right; Adelina would speak to her about Frederick again, she had fallen for him. A mere touch of his fingertips was enough to set her mind wandering. Etta didn't give her comfort. The inevitable in front of her and the dreaded outcome of her actions petrified her. Adelina had no reason to believe they would provide for her; Frederick could abandon her. Etta once said to Dorothy that Harry may never come back, because that's what men do best, and women allow their sons to do that.

Lydia had disappeared. Two empty drinks were left at the table she shared with James. Isla and George pawed at each other, laughing. Dorothy slumped forward, too drunk to move, because she started to believe her family – Harry would never come back. She loved him, and she thought he adored her too.

She couldn't wipe the feeling that Frederick had something to do with his disappearance.

Dorothy would never go to the backstreet clinic her mother wanted to take her to. Regardless, she had tried it all so far: hot baths with brandy, falling down the stairs. She'd heard of the torture of an abortion. Elsie, her school friend, had one. She was never the same again.

Weeks after visiting Susannah, Frederick found Elsie's lifeless body floating in the canal. The death was ruled an accident, a trip on the way home in the dark. They weren't privy to the true reason. Elsie was unable to cope with the pain Susannah left her with.

Ida glanced at Dorothy, recognising the frightened look on her face, how her life had already started to fade. Shifting in her seat, Ida's hand reached out towards a glass.

'We need to talk,' Ida whispered to Frederick. 'Alone.'

'There hasn't been time.'

For the umpteenth time, Paul ordered more alcohol. They needed fresh bottles, more buckets of beer. They'd drunk so much but he didn't feel better yet.

'Can you come outside with me,' Ida said, taking a hold of Frederick's hand, trying to drag him away. 'I need to talk to you. Now.'

'Why not here?'

Ida sighed, her grip loosening. Scanning the room, she found everyone in their own worlds. George and Isla obsessed with each other. Etta dancing with a man. Paul swigging alcohol at the bar. Dorothy nodding off in her seat. Lydia making her way back inside, hair askew. Adelina staring at the table, glass in hand.

'I don't want anyone else to know,' Ida said. 'You wouldn't want to hear it here.'

'Hear what?' Frederick asked, pulling his hand from her and reaching for his drink instead.

'You'll get mad.'

'When am I not?'

'It'll change everything, I need you to know, before–'

'There's a man at the warehouse,' Tom stuttered as he burst into the pub. His rapid breaths echoed against dimming conversations. 'I've never seen him before. He's asking for you, Freddie.'

THIRTY-FOUR

The alcohol made the run to the office jubilant. Isla, Lydia, and Adelina giggled as they tripped over cobbles, surging with adrenaline, finally a part of the brothers' actions. They should have feared it, but instead, they skipped into the unknown.

Not everyone galloped to the offices. Dorothy skulked home, falling against walls as she left the pub. Etta remained behind, captivated by the man she danced with. Ida was glued to the chair, the words she meticulously put together still on the tip of her tongue.

The office swayed gently, like Adelina was on a pleasure boat in summer. Alongside Lydia and Isla, she pressed her ear up against the wall, trying to hear the conversation in Frederick's room. They had been left out – they were women, and they weren't blood.

The smartly dressed men inside seemed richer than the Clarks and even Charlie. Their cars new, the best model. They were groomed immaculately, not a single hair astray, dressed in tailored three-piece suits with gold pocket watches. The way they held themselves, they seemed better than them.

The women hadn't caught their names. They'd been too busy catching their ragged breaths. The floor seemed to move beneath them, the wall slipping away as they pressed against it.

They listened to no avail, only a deep murmur of Frederick's voice occasionally breaking through. Their breaths stifled. They held onto the bricks, clinging to the adrenaline that had been building.

Frederick's voice grew louder, cutting through the wall, speaking in their language.

'There's a mole?' Adelina asked.

Isla nudged Adelina, eyes narrowing. She'd drowned out Frederick's voice. Hopelessly, Isla tried to tune back in to the noise that seeped out towards her – weak mumbles of English, no context for his statement.

They gave up on their attempt to be spies. They shifted away from the bricks, scuffing the floor with their shoes.

'Freddie's screwed over the whole world,' Lydia said. 'Now we have a mole. I bet they're the murderer.'

Isla stumbled towards her desk, taking a purple vial from inside her dress. Fumbling with the top, she dashed out a line onto her desk.

'It has to be the same person,' Isla said. 'Who else would kill Violet and David.'

'What do we know?' Adelina said, swigging from a discarded bottle of alcohol. 'Does Freddie tell us anything?'

'We're always in the dark,' Isla groaned, her body slamming against a pillar, tossing the vial to Lydia.

'Look at little miss perfect,' Lydia laughed. 'Finally realising what Freddie is like.'

'It only took a night in his room,' Isla joked, knocking the heels off her aching feet.

'Christ, does everyone know?' Adelina asked, her cheeks flushing ever brighter.

'It's written all over you, when you're with him. God knows what Ida thinks.'

Isla offered her hand to Adelina, wanting her to join in with an intoxicated dance. Their grip was loose upon one another, hands like ice from the storm outside. Isla pulled her into a spin, heels clicking as she struggled to regain her balance. The laughter, their joyful movements, reverberated around the building.

'*Can you be quiet?*' Frederick grunted from his doorway.

Isla dropped her hands. Their elated faces sank upon hearing the tone of his voice.

'You'll have to forgive them,' Frederick said to the men. 'They don't speak much English.'

Isla and Lydia exchanged a glance. Adelina, in her drunk state, swayed, wanting to understand why he was so enraged. Their dazed and perplexed faces only added to his plan.

'I'll send them out of our way,' Frederick continued. *'Isla, take Lydia back to your house, wait there. Ada, go back to the pub. There's an office out the back with a phone. Wait for me to call.'*

As quietly as their feet would allow, they moved from the offices. They were under strict orders, and they didn't want to fail him.

'Why do I have to go alone?'

'You said it yourself, Freddie never tells anyone his plans,' Lydia said.

Frederick poured the men yet another glass of liquor, seizing the chance to think about the situation. He tried to hold his nerve against them, yet the walls felt like they were closing in.

'Some pretty girls you've got there,' Elias Charlton said, puffing on a cigarette.

The younger man, Elias' son Edward, smirked. George's knuckles turned white, his hands forming fists. No one would comment on Isla or look at her in that manner. Women had nothing to do with their conversation.

'One is yours,' Elias said, pointing to George.

'Yeah, she is. Now, do you want to stop talking about women and get down to why you're here?'

'Edward doesn't have a wife. If we can agree on business, we can decide on women too. It'll create an unbreakable bond, one we could both benefit from.'

'They aren't for sale. I'm not going to offer them up for some plan you've curated,' Frederick said. 'The women aren't apart of this meeting. Like George said, let's talk about why you're here.'

'I own all the racecourses north of the Ouse, and you're denying a deal with me? Why don't you reconsider? What about the pretty one, with the long-braided hair?'

'What don't you understand? They aren't a part of this.'

Frederick tried to keep his composure. Elias was merely

testing his patience, trying to find his weakness.

'I could give you licences at my racecourses for one woman. Surely, she isn't worth more than that to you.'

'Ada is one of us,' George spat. 'She's not marrying one of you.'

Elias cleared his throat. So far, his plan had not worked, though he'd been assured it would. No matter what happened, by the end of the week, Frederick Clark was going to owe him everything.

'Like I said, a little bird told me that once you're done with Charlie Black, you're going to expand north. I can't be having that.'

'I don't recall ever saying that,' Frederick said.

'I know you have an issue with Charlie. The difference between you and him is that he's more connected. Charlie has contacts in London, partners that his family works with. You're only small in comparison. You only have one betting licence south of here, right? Most of your money comes from poxy robberies and racketeering. I – we – can help with that.'

'What makes you think we want your help?'

'I wasn't finished. There's a spy close to your family, I know who he is and where he's from.'

'Go on then,' Frederick said, taking a drag of his cigarette, trying to portray nonchalance towards the man he was starting to fear. 'Enlighten me.'

'The spy is working for Stefano Mancini.'

'Stefano from Clerkenwell?' Paul questioned, his face curling as he turned to his brother.

'The Mancinis despise Charlie,' George muttered back. 'They shouldn't be sniffing around us.'

'Stefano's man isn't the brightest spark. He got wind of a rumour about you both meeting at the Clarendon. He thinks you're working alongside him. Stefano's concerned that together you'll push south.'

'And?' Frederick said.

'Who do you think has been killing your acquaintances?'

'Stefano Mancini was behind Violet's death?' Paul said, his

eyebrows crinkling.

'You should be worried with the Italians taking an interest in your business.'

'We've dealt with people before; we're dealing with Charlie,' Frederick said, nonchalantly.

'Oh, I know you are,' Elias chuckled. 'I'm going to give you a piece of advice: take on the Italians as soon as you can, before they're aware that you know about their spy.'

'We're not going to London,' George said, shaking his head. 'I've heard stories about down there. We've always agreed to stay out of their business. I'm not losing my life fighting a battle that means nothing to me.'

'Yeah,' Paul said. 'We'll just show them we're not working with Charlie. Then, they'll be uninterested in us. Why an earth would they care about us then?'

'That's not how this world works,' Elias sneered. 'Christ, do you know nothing?'

'If we knew nothing, would we really have got this far? After all, the Italians are interested in us, so that says we've made it,' Frederick said, placing a glass to his lips, emptying it of liquid.

'You're worried about the Mancinis. Rightly so, they're a big organisation. Like your brother said, the stories about them are well known. But, if you side with me, if we work together, taking on the south will be nothing. We take it. We split it. We keep everything else separate. Easy.'

'That's not my decision to make, I'm sure you know that. Besides, why should I trust you?' Frederick said. 'See, I'm not the only one who keeps tabs on people. Elias Charlton of Newcastle, an Englishman–'

'Are we going to state the obvious, just for egos?'

'Obvious?' Frederick laughed. 'You married a Catholic Irish woman against her family's wishes. Caused you some problems at first, didn't it? People tell me that one glance from her can make you do anything, that she can make you place a bullet inside your own head.

Esther and you have been busy. Four sons, two daughters.

Three of your sons are still in France, they never returned. Edward is the only one left. A bit young, isn't he, to be following you around doing business? I'll congratulate you a month prematurely on your eighteenth birthday. Lucky you, missing out on the war.

I never got given your two daughters' names. They'd assumed it wouldn't be important. The thing is, I know you, Elias. Let me see if I can get them right...'

'Enough. Have your family meeting. But consider this an ultimatum. You side with me and take on the Mancinis, or you've got a war coming from the north. Remember, I'm bigger than you. I'll take over your city with ease, end both you and Charlie, then I'll move on to London, with all the men I gather here. I'm sure you've learnt by now that I always get my way.'

Frederick's disciples stood before him, waiting for him to start. George and Paul muttered between themselves. Isla and Lydia sat on their desks, slowly sobering up. Etta preened herself back into order. Dorothy sat in Adelina's chair, swaying side to side, not really caring to be a part of the meeting.

'It's been a long day, but this can't wait. It isn't about business, it's about war,' Frederick said.

From the hallway, the sound of clipping heels carried toward them. Adelina's breath was raised and erratic. Stomping across the cobbles, she let her breath expel as hard as needed. Inside the building, she tried to be light on her feet, supressing her breaths. Unable to bring herself under control, she felt like she was going to explode.

No one understood her lateness. They hadn't been told of her mission. Adelina came to Frederick's side, whispering news that only he could hear. A hand ran through his hair, his eyes dull, like he was crumbling before her. The others still saw him as capable, but they hadn't heard his voice on the end of the phone.

'Tonight, the Charltons of Newcastle paid us a visit. They know of my plans for after we're finished with Charlie. We've been infiltrated by two spies, one is a Mancini the other is a

Charlton. We're lucky the whole world doesn't know our secrets.

I fear we have no choice; we're going to need to take sides to pull through this mess. They're both bigger than us. They could kill us in an instant. We need to choose because we can't fight them both.'

'Can't we tell the Mancinis that we're not working with Charlie?' Paul said, unable to stand still. Itching to get the meeting over with.

'They won't take our word over one of their own,' Etta said. 'Think about it Paul, why would they believe us?'

'By going to them, we'll be taking our advantage away as well. They don't know we know about their spy,' George added, his eyes darting between Paul and Isla. Paul's face contorted in a grimace of pain, sweat beading on his forehead. Isla's hands were jittery, she shoved them deep into her pockets, away from Frederick's gaze.

'I vote to side with the Charltons then,' Isla said. 'If I'm allowed to vote on this. And I should be, I am–'

'Do we really have a choice, with which side to take?' George said to Frederick. 'If the Mancinis won't believe us, then we're stuck, right?'

'I'd put money on it being the Mancini spy who's been causing all our issues,' Etta said, striking a match for her cigarette. 'I can feel it.'

'Elias says he'll tell us who the spy is if we side with him,' George explained to Etta, aware she'd missed the details while obsessing over some man at the pub. 'Then, we can deal with him however we want.'

'We have to side with the Charltons,' Paul grumbled, interjecting into the conversation with a dark determination. 'I need to deal with whoever murdered Violet. I've been dreaming of the torture for weeks. It's all that's been getting me through–'

'What's the point in this?' Lydia asked, cutting Paul off, who continued to mutter about axes and blades. 'We've never really had an option, have we, Freddie?

'Once we get through this, we can still come out on top,'

Frederick said, looking away from Lydia and her questioning stare. 'Choosing a side doesn't have to be forever.'

'You would know all about that, wouldn't you?' Isla said, shaking her head, a smile creeping over her lips despite the bitterness in her eyes. 'That's what you did with Charlie at the races, and look at all that's happened since.'

'We can outsmart the Charltons,' Frederick said, his voice loud, rising above any other sighs or mutters. 'We're a closer-knit family. Elias wants to take Mancinis' racecourses. If we do that...'

'We'll receive legitimate money, something to build upon,' Etta said, finally understanding Frederick's vision. She marvelled at how she hadn't seen it before, how it all started to make perfect sense.

'We can do both, good and bad, like we always have,' Frederick clarified, his eyes not tearing from Etta, the only one who seemed to really understand his thoughts.

'You're saying we can be greater than the Charltons someday?' George asked, unable to see the same future as his siblings.

'If we work together now, we can own them later,' Frederick said definitively, almost like it would be easy for his plans to succeed, like the brothers' lives wouldn't be on the line.

'I told you to stay away from Charlie. That things would only get messy, and here we are.' Lydia said, slipping off the desk, ready to leave. She couldn't share the same outlook as Frederick and Etta; they were too positive at times, ignoring the changes and danger that Charlie had brought into their lives.

'There is no proof we'll make it to the other side,' Isla said, siding more with Lydia than anyone else. She thought of the mortality of it all, how easy death is served in their world.

'It's too late to say things like that now. We're in it,' Frederick said, his eyes settling on George and Paul, hoping that their faces had changed, that they would begin nodding like Etta had.

'So, we're all in agreement. The Charltons for now,' Etta said, her voice wavering slightly as she looked toward the other women present. 'Then we'll...'

'What do you have to do around here to get a simple life,' Isla muttered to Lydia. 'I want away from the city and this evil. To side with the devil doesn't feel right.'

'You're wrong,' George said, gently taking Isla's hand. As he spoke, he looked between Isla and Frederick. Finally, he understood where his siblings were coming from. 'Working with the Charltons can get us what we want.'

'Peace and quiet, Isla?' Etta guffawed, her laughter bitter, unable to let Isla's comments slide. 'Us Clarks are incapable of getting that.'

'Working with the Charltons, taking over racecourses and expanding south could make us richer than our wildest dreams. If all goes well, our children will never struggle like we did,' George said, addressing Isla's concerns, feeling her hand tremble slightly in his. While he was for the idea, he couldn't let Etta speak to his wife like she had. Isla's dream was also his, and hand in hand, he told his family what he truly wanted. 'And Etta, I do want peace and quiet. To eventually get out of these streets, to find somewhere with cleaner air. Hell, I'd even get an old vardo and go on the road. It's not just Isla's dream, it's mine too. It calls out for us.'

'This kind of life, there's no getting away from. It's with us forever,' Etta said bluntly, dashing out her cigarette. 'You just haven't realised that yet.'

Slowly, the room emptied. Paul left via the back door, intending on searching through the barrels that had been dropped off for a little pick-me-up. Lydia chuntered about Etta's harsh stance. Isla held George's hand tightly, making him promise they would achieve their dream one day. Etta grabbed Dorothy's side and led her out.

In the end, only Frederick and Adelina remained. Like her, he hadn't moved from where he gave his speech. Burdened by his own words, he scolded himself, believing he could've been stronger in his deliverance. He longed to be somebody, to be the man he wished his father had been.

Sleeves rolled up to his elbows. Eyes dim, barely standing out in the dark room. Hair flopped in front of his face, and he didn't preen it back into order. Defeated already.

'I think you need to remember the saying, *he who willingly gives you one finger will also give you the whole hand,*' Adelina said quietly, her eyes searching Frederick's face for any sign of agreement or rejection. 'From what I understand, the Charltons need help to move south. They want to work with you after observing you. This isn't a truce like with Charlie, but something else entirely.'

Too dingy to be sure, but she thought she saw a light smile form. That she, in the darkest of times, gave him hope. With that, Adelina left Frederick to be in peace.

Etta's house seemed like a different place. Elias had pushed everyone over the edge. The tension had been building since Adelina arrived, and now everything was collapsing beneath them. All Adelina wanted was her cards, for Etta to read her tea.

At one with her thoughts. At the bottom of the stairs, she kicked off the shoes she despised. Tired of wearing heels every day, she missed trainers, central heating, soft furnishings – not family or friends.

In 1919, there weren't rules and regulations. No fear of impending doom. Global warming didn't exist, nor did fears of nuclear war, of Russia or China invading the West. The world was simple, no social media or artificial intelligence. A war with the Charltons seemed like nothing when she'd grown up with the twin towers falling and all the hell that followed.

Mind crowded with fleeting thoughts, she climbed the stairs. There was no hearing nor seeing anything different. She paid no attention to her surroundings. When a hand brushed against her arm, she nearly screamed.

But it belonged to him.

Frederick rushed after her. Standing on the step lower, he allowed her to be almost his height, for her to look deep into his eyes. Flecks of golden brown hidden amongst the green. Wonder laid within them. And, for the first time, she couldn't see sadness or distress. There wasn't confusion or apprehension.

There appeared to be happier things laid within his eyes, like hope and trust. As though, somehow, she managed to switch a light within him. Frederick would never be the same as before the war, business was different, but Adelina allowed him to conduct it within the best atmosphere.

'It's true what you said, I didn't think of it like that.'

'You should have. The saying applies directly to this,' Adelina whispered, wanting to say more, but she stood on the staircase inside Etta's home.

'I trust you the most, and I don't trust easily.'

'I hope you don't. You had two spies; you should be guarded. Imagine what could have happened.'

'If it weren't for you,' Frederick said, placing a hand behind her neck. 'I would know. I wouldn't need to imagine.'

Adelina began to say something, but he abruptly cut her off with a gentle kiss. One far more tender than before. His move shocked her; all they knew before was passion, and the kiss he gave her was ever so different.

'Ida is the Charlton's spy, I'm almost certain,' he said. 'In a way, you distracted me from her. It was the best outcome.'

Adelina didn't believe him; Ida didn't appear capable. A woman within the time wouldn't dare put herself in such danger. Adelina had yet to learn that anything could be possible.

'What are you going to do?'

'I was going to consult you. After all, you gave me the best advice five minutes ago.'

'I can't give you advice, when you're looking at me like that.'

'Like what?'

'Like you're going to break my heart someday.'

A doting look, like they were becoming something more. The hall became so quiet they could hear the buzzing within their own ears, as they fought for something to focus upon. The house didn't creak, the wind didn't howl. The whole world waited on them.

'You're no angel,' Adelina whispered, hoping Frederick

wouldn't be able to decipher her, that he would brush off her words like she never spoke them.

'Neither are you.'

'I don't break people's hearts, I don't–'

'Does it matter?'

Frederick didn't give her a chance to reply. Kissing her once more, so delicately and sweet, like he would never be capable of hurting her. But he could, she knew that. If they continued, if they...

'My heart matters.'

'Why now?' Frederick said, his face so close that when he spoke his lips brushed against her.

'It matters because you're looking at me differently. You kissed me like you never have before. I'm not her, Freddie, the girl you loved before the war.'

'I know. Effie, she... In some ways, you're nothing like her.'

'But you see me as her when you kiss me, don't you? I'm different. I'm not a ghost of your past girlfriend.'

'All this time and you've been thinking that? You're wrong. Effie would have run away from all this. With her, I wanted to be good, to be someone else instead of myself. You don't ever tell me not to do something. You help no matter what. What you said back there, what you said in my room that time – that made me fall for you, not someone that I used to know.'

THIRTY-FIVE

The second time was easier. Adelina moved from underneath his bedsheets, head pounding with hungover thoughts. No longer riddled with guilt, not with Frederick's doubts about Ida. Now, she craved for him to be all hers, all because of the way he looked at her, how he kissed her like never before.

With that, her stomach sank. Frederick wasn't hers; she shouldn't have been thinking such things. God, she was so angry at herself. It didn't matter what he said about Ida or Effie, he had a reputation, and she failed to recognise it when it mattered the most. All she should ever have wanted was his protection, not his love.

Searching for her slip, she glanced at his body next to her, passed out from the copious amounts of alcohol. Away from the bed, she trailed her hand across the chest of drawers, dust coating her fingertips in a grey matt.

There were places free of dirt, objects that had been undisturbed for a while had vanished. The bedside table, the mantel piece, the windowsills. Knocking items, examining clutter, moving picture frames, she searched for any sign of Ida. Nothing. He'd removed her from his home, prior to the night's revelations.

The fire was a mere dwindle. Adelina stared at the orange fragments that remained, knowing she would need to take Lydia's concoction all over again. With that, her skin prickled.

It wasn't her wandering mind that caused the goosebumps, but the feeling of being watched. On the edge of the mist, she stood, the woman Adelina hated to see. Esmerelda glared at her, knowing she spent the night in sin.

Adelina couldn't help herself; she needed to speak to her. Plucking Frederick's coat from the floor, from the place he discarded it earlier, she shoved it on. The material masked her body, the silk lining trailing against the ground.

Adelina ran. Pounding down the stairs, one hand on the banister, the other gripping onto his revolver. The front door sprang open, swaying in the wind. She was still there, waiting. Taking a step out into the bleak air, Adelina didn't care for the frost biting her bare toes.

A blast rang through the night. Finally at war, like she could learn how Frederick felt. The discharge clung to the air, echoing. Adelina didn't understand how she ever mistook the sound of a car backfiring for the noise of death before.

Sprawled on the floor. Heart pounding. Hands itching to hold onto the metal. Believing the gun had been fired at her, she waited for searing pain, for a wet leaking sensation to overcome her. Nothing.

Fight or flight. Crawling forwards, she peeked past the houses and to the road. A figure, their gun raised in her direction. A still body, on the cusp of the mist, in front of Esmerelda.

The world slower than ever. Breaths airy and rapid, jumping around her as if she were a jigsaw.

Sliding against the black ice of the doorway, she lurched forwards towards the figure who began to run. Frederick's gun in her hands, aimed to them, but she didn't fire. Instead, she glanced at the body. A man, dressed sharply, his face resting in the snow.

Everything was unclear. In the dark, dreary street, she didn't recognise either. Then she realised, a hero wouldn't run. With that conclusion, her finger twitched towards the trigger, willing to shoot down the enemy.

Only clothed on his bottom half, Frederick sprinted to her. Footsteps hitting the road before she managed to turn to him. The assailant was unrecognisable to her, but he knew instantly.

'Lower it. Now. You'll never hit them.'

The world came alive. Creaking stairs echoed in her ears, even as Frederick stood beside her, looking to the body. White snow enveloped in blood. Everything tainted. Crimson ran, staining each small piece of frost.

Holding the gun, she continued to aim, pointing the barrel down the empty street. Frederick seized the weapon, almost too easily. With empty hands, he waited for Adelina to get to work, to come to the aid of the man.

Motionless, there was too much blood. An artery had burst upon the bullet's impact. He bled out before Frederick woke. Even in the modern day, he wouldn't have survived.

Paul stumbled toward them, gripping his gun, his hand pulsating, adrenaline surging through his intoxicated body. Adelina continued to stare into the shadows, waiting for Esmerelda to reappear, to speak. It was Paul who realised who laid upon the ground, as he crouched beside the man.

'The art freak.'

They expected the victim to be somebody else, a gang member, one of their own. The man upon the floor, turning the street into a river of red, was James.

Frederick left, moving inside, leaving Adelina alone, barely dressed, to stare at the body of a man she thought was good. Paul remained, gawking at James, captivated by the way his body expelled the blood that once pumped through his veins, how it slipped silently across the snow. A scene from France, from the harshest times of his life. There, he'd seen a similar image far too often; a body with a gunshot, steadily draining its fluids into the darkness of the night.

Dressed, Frederick pounded back to the street, keys jingling in his hand. Seeing Paul, he sighed. He was going to be different from that night. He would slip back into bad ways, ones he'd been trying to claw his way out of. The image would never leave Adelina's mind either, but Frederick didn't realise that.

'Clear out, Paul. Let the coppers do their work.'
'No, we'll tidy this up, we'll take him to the docks, can't have…'
'No. They'll be on their way. I've got to get out of here.'
James was dead, and Adelina didn't understand why he, of all

people, was. Paul became more concerned with the police, and how they'd arrive to a body in front of Frederick's house. The details would be on record forever, something that could tarnish them, be used against them. He didn't understand; they usually covered things up. They would tell Sergeant McCormick not to come.

'Go home, I'll explain in the morning,' Frederick said, guiding his brother away, telling him that everything was going to be ok, no need to worry. No need to binge on drugs, kill himself with alcohol.

Frederick turned back, intending to go to his car, but Adelina was still outside, frozen, her skin a sickly grey. The shock set in. Another lifeless body. Another murdered person before her.

The way the blood appeared on the snow bothered her the most. The warmth of his fluid melted patches away. James laid in diluted pools of his own being. The streaming water a soft pink like rose petals, and gravity only drew it closer towards her toes.

'Go inside,' Frederick said, taking her rigid body into his. Instinctively, he brought his lips down onto her icy forehead. 'Go to my room, relight the fire, wait for me to come back.'

The feeling of being alone never hit her harder. She moved only to sit upon his bed, waiting for him to return, to take her into his arms once more, to look at her the way he did on the stairs.

Adelina should have wanted the sanctuary of five Barnabas Road and the time she grew up in. Instead, she wanted him because she felt like she belonged beside him, regardless of the world she found herself living in. She wouldn't have even cared if there was a way back home when she had him coming back for her.

THIRTY-SIX

Deep snow, pure white. Only light tracks beaten into the pavement from those who still resided in the half-derelict crumbling houses. No one owned a car. No horses came by. People left, they didn't come in. The streets' residents were poorer than Frederick could ever imagine because his childhood, his struggles, were locked away.

Wet seeped into his clothes, shoes slipping across the icy doorway. With one loud bang, she answered. Despite the early morning hour, she still wore her day dress, the one he'd last seen her in. Hair pinned to perfection like usual.

'Are you going to tell me the truth,' Frederick said, entering the familiar hallway. 'Who are you, really?'

God, she'd done a good job; he'd fallen for all of it. The flat's furnishings, the small little trinkets, it seemed so realistic. Even then, knowing the truth, it appeared like a long-term abode, that she wouldn't move anywhere else. It would be such a hassle to pack it all up, to take it back to where she belonged.

Photographs of her brothers in their war uniform beside her picture of the King. The carpet lifted in places, curling up at the corners. The wallpaper loose and saggy. Damp riddled the air. A decrepit sofa concealed the abundance of stains upon the floor for two or so metres.

A roaring fire. Steam spiralling from a teapot. Two cups, saucers, and spoons ready. His body flushed with fury. She caused his downfall. She made him lose control. Because of her, everything was slipping away from him.

'You know who I am, you're not stupid. I'm sure you've figured it out. How could you not?'

'I want to hear it from you. Tell me who you are. You were going to earlier, weren't you?'

'What's the point?' Ida asked, prodding the fire, glancing between the flames and the reflection of him in the mirror. 'It'll only make you furious.'

'Quite the actress. I only put it together recently, even with all the police at the racecourse, with you acting so odd. I want you to know that when he came to my offices, he fell apart.'

'My father would never fall apart,' Ida said flatly, the distance between them greater than ever.

'You didn't see the look upon his face. Why weren't you there?'

'I think you've got a bad perception of people. You once called me weak. Am I still that to you?'

Taking a gun from the waistband of her skirt, she threw it towards him, letting it slam onto the floor. The only weapon she had, but it didn't matter because Frederick would never kill a woman in cold blood. He only came to her to ask questions; he couldn't hack the fact a woman had played him.

'I said those things because I never trusted you. Turns out I was right all along.'

'That's not true. You trusted me until Ada came. Without her, we could've been king and queen, royalty.'

'Don't mention her, she's got nothing to do with this. I didn't trust you because you were always prying. I caught you in my room, raking through my things. Your excuses were the worst. The way you acted, I knew something was off. Have you ever known hardship?'

'This has everything to do with her. *Adelina* waltzed into your world one day and never left your mind since. You changed the way your business works for her, you do realise that?'

'I've told you, she's a nurse. We need her.'

Ida scoffed, throwing the fire iron down, letting it singe the carpet.

'Why do you care about her? She's done nothing to you.'

'Adelina ruined our original plan. Everything was going fine, and then you took her to the races. She nearly killed Charlie

Black for Christ's sake.'

'Admit the truth, Ida, that not all of this has been a façade. You're jealous of her, aren't you?'

'Fine. Have it your way. Of course, I fell for you, but I know you fell for me too. In the beginning, we had something together, and you never cared what your family said. They never liked me, but you still found time for me. Then Adelina came along. I heard everything from Tom and your brothers because you never spoke about her. That said everything I needed to know.

Then, I saw you together, how you looked at her. It's different than the way you glance at me or any other girl. I wanted to be with you more because you always seemed to be around her, looking at her like…'

When Ida spoke about him, she appeared soft and delicate. She was in love, but her heart was breaking, crumbling into a thousand pieces. A failure, she'd let herself fall for the man she was trying to crush. Elias would be disappointed; he would lock her away forever, to never be trusted again.

'Adelina was no one. You still don't know who she is or where she came from. We tried to find out about her, like you tried to find out about me. You found my records eventually, didn't you? But Freddie, we never found hers. Adelina doesn't exist, anywhere. She's lying to you. She could be anyone, and you…'

Ida's voice grew lower. Frustration, sorrow, complete agony leaked from her. All emotions tumbled within her because Adelina had ruined what she had with Frederick.

'You cast me aside for her. All you do is break hearts and tear people apart. No one lasts underneath your grip. I was falling in love with you, Freddie. Then you fell for her instead.'

'You fell for me? You were giving me up to your father. Did you think I would continue whatever we had once I'd learnt you betrayed me? You thought we'd live happily ever after? You've got to be kidding me.'

'You don't know the power of the heart then.'

'I don't, that's why I didn't fall for your games.'

Frederick dropped his cigarette, extinguishing it with his

foot. The fire nibbled at the carpet, scorching the cotton. As her character that she lived for months came to an end, she appeared weaker than ever.

'Don't forget me, and what I did for you,' Ida said, her voice strong. Though her eyes, they were starting to fill. 'I helped you after the war. I made you forget Effie. I thought that we'd–'

'You didn't make me forget Effie. You didn't help. God, you never came close to her.'

Frederick only said it to insult her. Deep down, he truly didn't feel such a way. At least, that's what Ida prayed.

'There's going to be a war, Freddie. James was a spy, sent by Stefano Mancini. He was stupid; he thought you were working with Charlie. The meeting in the Clarendon didn't go unnoticed.'

Like him, she started to say things to hurt him, in a vague attempt that he would understand how she felt.

'The night of Violet's funeral, when you were all over Adelina, James followed me. I spoke with him as he walked me home. Together, we figured each other out. We used to meet up, to discuss you. I was playing all of you. You need to watch your family, Adelina, and Lydia too because they were practically giving you up to James.'

Once Ida started, she couldn't stop. All the anguish from the weeks in turmoil flooded to the surface.

'I believe my dad gave you an ultimatum. I bet you thought you had two choices: my family or the Mancinis. Well, I chose for you. I secured your future, with my family. You're never going to escape us or me.

You're always going to have to side with my family because there's no other option, not now. Not with James dead in front of your home and the police making reports. Don't worry, I'm sure if you play your cards right, Sergeant McCormick will write up the account and forget it ever existed. Well, that's if my father tells him to.

And don't forget, Freddie, that everyone has a big mouth down here. The Mancinis will easily find out what happened to James and where he lost his life. A target will be on your back. My family will help you survive.'

A nonchalant man stood before her. Stony, expressionless. He was capable of emotion; she'd seen it briefly, down by the canals and when alone in his house. Ida wanted that back because he was pulling her apart.

'Think about it, Freddie. Charlie wanted you dead a long time ago. His family wants revenge, his allies have lost a lot of money because of you, so they want payback. The Italians will want you dead. Their allies – Matthew McKibben, Harry King, Hoxton, Limehouse – they will all be against you once they find out. They'll want revenge for James' death. You need us. You need *me*.'

In the dim light, she swore there was a hint of emotion etching over him. His mind turning, thinking about her. Finally, Ida got what she wanted.

Frederick turned away; there was nothing to say to her.

Ida should've killed him there and then because he had no plan, no way to tackle the various people that opposed him. London was different; their battles made newspaper headlines, they were brutal compared to him.

Frederick didn't know what he was being thrown into.

Even without Ida's gaze locked upon him, he couldn't breathe. Battling home, he tried to keep his composure for as long as possible.

Ida flopped onto the sofa. She won. She beat him. That was the only thing that stopped her from sobbing.

Frederick had sapped every ounce of happiness out of her, and with a few words she managed to break him down, making him feel pain the way he made her feel. He was Elias' for the taking. Her family could do anything they wanted with the Clarks.

At the heart of it, the victory meant nothing. She never got to say what was so important. The final chance was over. Anger got the better of her, and she made herself into an enemy. He would never know her emotions, all that had happened. She lost the opportunity to make him understand her.

They would try to forget the other existed, burying all

previous occasions of them laid bare together. Frederick mastered the art of shutting out his life experiences, it would be easy for him. Ida would find it far more difficult because she knew everything, and, in a way, he knew nothing.

A scummy, half-broken kitchen met him. With the police removing James' body, he couldn't use the front entrance to his home. Sneaking around, in the place he slept, called back distant memories of evading the police, of escaping bigger and stronger men.

Of course, the Sergeant would think he pulled the trigger. There would only ever be circumstantial evidence against him. Anyone else, and they would sentence them regardless. Not with Frederick Clark. The Sergeant wouldn't dare bring him before a judge, it would end in chaos. The case would be recorded and left to sit without clues forever. At least, he hoped that would be what happened.

The whole world was turning against Frederick. It made him uneasy, for his name to be recorded alongside something so serious. The gravity of the situation made his chest ever tighter, ribs crushing his lungs. Struggling to breathe against himself, he tried to think of a way out.

He failed. Instead, he slipped back to Ida, thinking of how she played him, how she didn't care for him anymore. Frederick fucked over the daughter of a bloody king. She ensured a miserable existence underneath her father's thumb as revenge for a broken heart.

Siding with the Charltons seemed like a death sentence. With Elias, he would have no autonomy. Closing his eyes, he could see the rope hanging, waiting for him. He could no longer keep it in.

Frederick screamed a series of profanities at the top of his lungs. He lost touch with reality, not knowing how to cope anymore.

The floor creaked beneath him as he paced. A series of flashes in his brain, outcomes he wanted but wasn't convinced he would achieve. There were too many people to think about.

Relationships and inner workings he couldn't comprehend. It was too much for him to handle. He couldn't continue.

'Freddie?'

Against the dreary living room, he could just make out Adelina's frame. Fragile against the looming space. After everything, the last thing on his mind had been her, and how he told her to wait upstairs for his return.

People didn't stay for him. Most changed their minds, or got tired of waiting, not believing in him anymore. With her, she put all her trust in him, like she would never leave despite anything.

With a step forward, the silk nightdress caught in the streetlight, illuminating her. He imagined her to be petrified by his choice words, though she came across as more inquisitive than anything else.

Frederick froze, not knowing what to do. He'd never appeared so vulnerable to someone, not even in the war. Slowly, she came to him, not frightened by his presence or what he thought. In that moment, she wanted to help him, to ensure he was ok.

Adelina took his hand into hers, rubbing her fingers across him gently. She longed to ask questions, though she kept them at bay. It wasn't her bedside manner, but her perception of him that made her unworried. Frederick could battle anything; he would achieve anything he wanted in the end.

With him on the sofa, she poured him a drink, her hands shaking. Not because of nerves, but because of an apprehension towards feelings bundling within her.

Frederick's damp hair, from the blizzard that raged outside, hung in front of his face, dripping onto his shirt. He made no attempt to move it, he let it hang there, even when he took a sip of alcohol or when he lit his cigarette. His body didn't feel like it belonged to him. He could only perceive his mind, all the thoughts cramming inside of him.

'Ida said something funny,' Frederick said finally. 'That all I do is break people's hearts and tear people apart.'

Adelina questioned whether she needed to respond. Taking an inhale on her own cigarette, she looked outside. Within the snow that gripped at the police as they tried to work, she could see a figure amongst the night.

'If all I do is hurt people, then why do I feel so broken?'

He never intended for it to be a question; he didn't want an answer. Frederick was simply talking, in the company of a woman he could speak to. It was hard, but she made it easy. Adelina didn't think too much about the power of his words, like what he said wouldn't define him forever. But that's because she didn't want a single event to rule her for eternity either.

The police vanished against the snow that pummelled them. All sense of the world white against the dark grey back drop of the night. Through the misted window, growing ever translucent with the snow, it felt like she stared into a different world. Not her own anymore.

The figure came closer, ratty hair hanging around her slumped shoulders. Dark eyes welling up with something crimson that she didn't want to acknowledge.

'When I saw you, after that gunshot, I...' Frederick began to say.

Adelina pulled her eyes away from Esmerelda. In a high-pitched shriek, she spoke. Voice echoing through the building, but only Adelina heard. Every cell captivated, pulling her towards the window, but, somehow, her own need to stay with Frederick, to hear his words, sent the black witch's voice into a lull.

'I felt something, for the first time since the war. Something I thought I was incapable of feeling anymore.'

Through his wet dangling hair, he looked to her. For the first time, he wore his heart upon his sleeve. Something more frightening than that was coming for him, and despite that, Adelina consumed him.

'I don't care what the black witch said, what cards were dealt, I want you,' he said, the words catching in the back of his throat.

The most real he'd been in years. Men returned to that, and he never got it back. She dragged him out, though she allowed him to stay on the path he wanted. Everyone else sought to change him, whilst she allowed him to do whatever he wanted.

'I want you too,' Adelina whispered, trying harder than ever to avoid the window, to stop the noise that was becoming shrill.

'Everything is going to change, there's going to be a war, but I want you to stay with me.'

Her heart pounded like the beat of a drum as Esmerelda sung. Her fate was sealing, but she didn't have the power to stop herself. There wasn't fear, only anticipation.

'Promise me, you'll stay with me,' Frederick said. 'I'll need your help.'

There was no hesitation. The words tumbled from her mouth before she even gave them a second thought. Adelina could never say no, not to him. Despite the warnings she'd been given, the cards, the tea leaves, the black witch, they were all redundant because she'd found the man that was written into her hands. The one she was destined to fall in love with. Nothing could change that.

'I promise.'

Printed in Great Britain
by Amazon